L. 9

D0853325

THE
MAGNIFICENT
SIBERIAN

ALSO BY LOUIS CHARBONNEAU
White Harvest
Stalk
The Ice
No Place on Earth
Night of Violence
Nor All Your Tears
Corpus Earthling
The Sentinel Stars
Psychedelic–40
Way Out
Down to Earth
The Sensitives
Down from the Mountain
And Hope to Die
Barrier World
Embryo
From a Dark Place
The Lair
Intruder
The Brea File
Trail

AS CARTER TRAVIS YOUNG
The Wild Breed
Shadow of a Gun
The Savage Plain
The Bitter Iron
Long Boots, Hard Boots
Why Did They Kill Charley?
Winchester Quarantine
The Pocket Hunters
Winter of the Coup
The Captive
Blaine's Law
Guns of Darkness
Red Grass
Winter Drift
The Smoking Hills

THE MAGNIFICENT SIBERIAN

A NOVEL BY

Louis Charbonneau

DONALD I. FINE, INC.
New York

Copyright © 1995 by Louis Charbonneau

All rights reserved, including the right of reproduction in whole or in part in
any
form. Published in the United States of America by Donald I. Fine, Inc. and
in
Canada by General Publishing Company Limited.

Library of Congress Catalogue Card Number: 94-68090
ISBN: 1-55611-422-2

Manufactured in the United States of America

10 9 8 7 6 5 4 3 2 1

Designed by Irving Perkins Associates, Inc.

This novel is a work of fiction. Names, characters, places and incidents are
either the product of the author's imagination or are used fictitiously. Any
resemblance to actual events, locales, organizations or persons, living
or dead, is entirely coincidental and beyond the intent of either the
author or publisher.

For Diane, Again and Always with Love

PART ONE

THE TAIGA

1

CHRIS HARMON HEARD the shot.

He beckoned urgently to Alexander Grovkin, who was driving the Jeep. It was a battered, vintage World War II American Jeep, Grovkin's pride and joy. It jerked to a halt with a screech of brakes. The Jeep's brakes always screeched—an announcement, Grovkin would grumble affectionately, to any nearby poachers that Grovkin was here. He saw this as a way to make things more even. The Russian game warden's hatred for poachers, and his heavy-handed treatment of those actually unlucky enough to come within his reach, were legend in the bars from Terney to Vladivostok.

Dust billowed around the two men as they listened. At another gesture Grovkin killed the engine. They waited in the silence. Their noisy arrival in the Jeep had silenced anything in their vicinity, but the stillness they listened to was different, more comprehensive. The echoing slam of a rifle shot had brought instant suspense to the taiga.

Listen to the sound of falling dust, Harmon thought. It had been a long dry summer and early fall. There was a forecast of rain before the end of the week, and Chris welcomed the prospect, even though it would make many of the roads in the preserve nearly impassable. For *them,* too, he thought grimly.

"Poachers," he said.

"We cannot be sure—"

"Oh hell, Alex, who's out here target shooting?"

Grovkin shrugged, his blue eyes glaring fiercely toward the surrounding hills.

Alexander Semyonovich Grovkin was one of a handful of

wardens, earning the equivalent of about twenty dollars a month, charged with patrolling the Sikhote-Alin Biosphere National Preserve in Russia's Far East Primorskiy province. The preserve was one of three that together spanned the eight-hundred-mile length of the Primorskiy. Their dense forests, where hunting had been forbidden since 1947, offered the last remaining protected habitat of the Siberian tiger. The Sikhote-Alin preserve itself covered some 1,314 square miles of mountain and forest defined on the west by the Amur River and on the east by the Sea of Japan, with the Sikhote-Alin range forming its spine.

The protected area was closed to all but a handful of scientists like Chris Harmon, who was part of a joint Russian-American research team investigating the tigers surviving in the preserve. Usually working alone in his Jeep, Alex Grovkin was responsible for covering sixty thousand hectares, where individual poachers and organized gangs operated in brazen defiance of government laws. Grovkin considered himself lucky. Of the two dozen guards on the staff of the preserve, more than half patrolled on foot, armed only with outmoded Simonov rifles once carried by Red Army soldiers in the Great Patriotic War. They offered a feeble line of defense against poachers in Toyotas, Ford Broncos and Range Rovers, armed with modern high-powered rifles and assault weapons.

In Far East Russia, nearly six thousand miles from Moscow, a degree of independence from the central government had prevailed even under harsh Communist rule. Now, with the nation in political turmoil, with no one in charge, the president and the elected Parliament at odds, the KGB divided and its power broken, the atmosphere of a free-fire zone prevailed. Food was available in the shops of the cities, goods of all kinds were plentiful where they had once been merely promises, but prices were out of reach. Factories were idle or at half-production. Many people were out of work or poorly paid in relation to runaway inflation. Anything that put meat on a hungry family's table was fair game—protected species or not.

But the Siberian tiger was different. It was no ordinary

game. It was a valuable commodity. A tiger's meat and bones, sold on the black market and destined for eager buyers in Taiwan and mainland China, would bring $3,000 and up. A whole skin in fine condition would sell for five times as much. A bowl of tiger penis soup, valued as an aphrodisiac, sold in an upscale Taiwan restaurant for more than $300. The tongue was a delicacy. The teeth were said to cure sores; the nose, hung on the roof of one's house, induced the birth of boys. Virtually every part was coveted for use in medicines or elixirs. The bones, powdered for use in medicines, cured everything from ulcers to burns and fevers. Choice bones like the forelimb went for $500 a pound. The claws were a talisman. Even the whiskers would ease the pain of toothache.

Predictably, Siberian tiger hunters were not clumsy amateurs. Such poachers had been squeezed out—or frightened off. Hunters invading the preserve, especially the mafia gangs moving to control the market, were cunning and dangerous, well armed and well equipped. And better paid than the guards who were supposed to catch them, as Grovkin frequently complained.

Chris Harmon had a map open across his lap, so old and worn that it was beginning to separate along the folds. He checked the coordinates against the compass mounted on the Jeep's dashboard. "Oh, Christ!" he muttered.

"What is it, my friend?"

"There's a tiger up there."

They stared at each other. Grovkin looked back along the road to the west, then ahead. "That's Sector Five," he said.

"I know. That Range Rover we saw was heading this way. It didn't turn back. Take us in there."

"I can't do that, you know rules."

"For Christ's sake, Alex, are you telling me poachers can go into Sector Five and set up a tiger shoot and we can't go after them?"

"They don't follow rules," Grovkin shrugged. "Directive is clear—"

"Forget the directive!" Chris snapped. "Come on, Alex, this is me you're talking to—Chris."

"Directive is very explicit," Grovkin said, scowling. "No one is to enter Sector Five for any reason, not even guards. Don't ask me why. It's politics, maybe. Everything is politics."

"Don't tell me you're willing to let those bastards take another tiger while we sit here arguing!"

"No, I will not tell you such a thing. But it is my job we're talking about. What do you think, I can just go into Vladi and get another job, maybe at bank? Or—what is it you Americans say—I will become brain surgeon?"

"I'll take the responsibility," Harmon said.

"Tell that to Yavlinsky." The director of the preserve, Grovkin's boss, was a by-the-rules *apparatchik*.

"This is ridiculous! Damn it, Alex, if you won't break a stupid rule, get out and let me drive this thing. You can say I tricked you, took off when you were pissing in the woods."

"I can't do that." The Russian stared lovingly at the Jeep. "I can't give you keys."

"She's not a lover, you clown, she's just an old Jeep!"

"All the same," Grovkin said stubbornly. He sighed. "I think this is not good idea."

"We don't have any time to waste." Chris Harmon sat back, relieved at the guard's capitulation. "If they've shot a tiger, they'll be working fast. They know we saw them earlier. Let's go, Alex."

"You're sure there's a tiger? You did not bring radio today."

"I wasn't expecting to do any tracking. But one of our tagged tigers is in this area. A female, the one we called Risa. Her territory was a little west of here, but she's been moving lately."

Grovkin shoved the gearshift into first. The Jeep jumped back onto the road, wheels spinning. Once he had committed himself, the Russian didn't hesitate. He was a good if reckless driver, trusting his intimate knowledge of the road and his vehicle. Chris Harmon spent much of the time airborne between slams against the seat bottom and the side door. He hung onto the panic bar set into the door frame, leaning away from the stinging dust cloud that blew past the open side of the Jeep and the occasional lash of an overhanging branch.

* * *

Two men in a Range Rover had pulled off the service road that wound along the southeastern flank of the Sikhote-Alin preserve a half-hour earlier. The driver drove the vehicle behind dense brush about a hundred yards from the road. Painted a dark red and coated with dust, the four-wheeler all but disappeared in the fall hues of gold and red surrounding it.

"At least let us pretend to hide," the passenger said as he climbed out of the vehicle. He wore a thin, mocking smile.

"Do you think the patrol spotted us earlier?" the driver asked. He was the stockier and more muscular of the two men, but his tone and manner were deferential.

"They're following. I've seen their dust, which means they could see ours."

"Will they come into this sector? I mean, it's—"

"That depends on how eager they are," the lean, dark figure snapped impatiently.

He set off without another word, setting a brisk pace. The terrain was hard walking, deep valleys leading to thickly wooded, rounded hills that in turn stepped toward the rugged Sikhote-Alin range. In the clearings and on the open slopes, the golden grasses were chin high. Brush was often thick and virtually impenetrable. The tall grass and brush, even more than the shadowed forests, made Leonid Brunovsky uneasy.

Of the two men, Brunovsky seemed more out of place in this wilderness. With his short, thick legs and heavily muscled body, the product of endless hours working with his weight machines, he was built more for power than distance. His close-cut hair was blond, his eyes a watery blue, his skin pale except for the telltale reddish blotches of the heavy drinker. He carried his rifle awkwardly, using it to ward off the brush that snatched at his clothing or the tree branches that flicked toward his face. He was also overdressed. Early in the day the air had been chill, and he had dressed for it. He had removed his corduroy jacket as the afternoon warmed, but when they left the truck he had been reluctant to leave the jacket behind. He was sweating profusely and laboring to breathe well before the first climb ended on a ridge with a long view of forested hills folding upon each other under the bright, nearly cloudless sky.

When Brunovsky paused on the ridge to stare out over the hills and catch his breath, Sergei Lemenov spoke sharply. "Do you wish to make a formal announcement that Brunovsky is here?"

Brunovsky realized belatedly that Lemenov had paused before reaching the top of the promontory. Before showing himself against the skyline. His heavy cheeks flushing a dark red, the color of the Range Rover, Brunovsky stammered, "I— I thought—that is, you wanted them to follow . . ."

"To follow, yes. To find us, no."

Without looking back, Lemenov marched down a grassy slope and plunged into the forest. My God, he doesn't even carry his rifle ready, Brunovsky thought, stumbling after him, feeling a quiver of protest in his thighs. Lemenov had his rifle on a sling over his shoulder, while he gave more attention to the hand-held radio antenna he carried. What will he do if we meet something in the forest? Brunovsky grumbled to himself. Does he expect me to do the shooting if we meet a bear? Or, God forbid, a tiger?

At the edge of the wood he glanced around, peering nervously into the tall grass that covered the slope behind him. Then he hurried after his companion.

Brunovsky was not privy to the details of Lemenov's real mission. He had been ordered to drive the former KGB agent into the preserve, and he knew that Lemenov carried a high-powered rifle. Brunovsky could put two and two together readily enough. One came secretly to the Primorskiy forest, avoiding the patrols and bringing a big-game hunting rifle, for only one purpose. Early that morning Lemenov had spotted another illegal vehicle like their own, almost certainly carrying poachers. It had retreated hastily in the opposite direction.

But Lemenov was no ordinary poacher. Brunovsky thought he knew a real hunter when he met one. Sergei Gregorevich Lemenov was a dangerous man. He even looked the part. He was of average height and thinner than most, but his body was all corded muscle, not with the bulging pectorals and biceps of a weight lifter but with the fluid tension of a trained, superbly conditioned athlete. He drifted through the wilderness with the effortless ease of an animal. At the end of the last climb he hadn't even been breathing hard. All of this earned Brunovsky's respect, but it was the eyes that quickened a nameless fear. The gray, pitiless eyes that seemed to look right through you, exposing the slightest pretense, the aristocratic face with its unforgiving mouth, and the way Lemenov's sharply cut nostrils flared a little when he talked of hunting and killing . . .

Suddenly the man in the lead raised his arm. He halted at the edge of a clearing. Brunovsky caught a glimpse of a river in the distance, flashing over rocks, twisting down the mountain and darting across an open valley before it dove out of sight behind the brow of an intervening hill.

"What is it?"

"Shut up!"

Lemenov had fitted his earphones over his head, and the hand antenna was fully extended. He listened intently. His expression, with its tight, bloodless lips and cold gray eyes narrowed, made Brunovsky think of a dhole, one of the breed of fierce red dogs that roamed the taiga in packs, a danger even to a full-grown tiger. Watching Lemenov, Brunovsky thought of one of those lean, handsome predators with blood dripping from its jaws . . .

Lemenov smiled his tight, cold smile. "We have found our tiger."

Brunovsky's stab of excitement was laced with fear. "You are certain?"

"It is one of the banded ones. The signal is faint, but he—or she—is not far away."

"How far away can you pick up the signal with that antenna?"

"Two miles, perhaps. No more than that, and that would be on level ground without interference. In these wooded hills, we're lucky to pick up any signal at all. Which means that it can't be much more than a mile away. Beyond that next range of hills, I think." Lemenov spoke quietly, but Brunovsky heard the tension in his voice. "Come—hurry! We must get another reading from a different position. That will give us a fix on where the tiger is."

Lemenov hurried off, striking north, thrashing through thick brush, too impatient to search for the easiest path. Brunovsky followed behind, warding off branches. Is that what he's after, then? Brunovsky wondered. A trophy for his wall? A tiger penis souvenir, or a beautiful tiger skin to place in front of his fireplace where he makes love to his woman? Is that why he was called the Collector?

There was more to it than that. Brunovsky's powerful patron, Boris Provalev, chairman of the District Council and a deputy to the People's Parliament in Moscow, would not have ordered Brunovsky to accompany Lemenov on a simple poaching mission, even for a $15,000 tiger skin.

Ten minutes later, reaching another rise, Lemenov paused for a second reading of the faint signal audible through his earphones. The two areas where he had picked up the signals established the base points of a triangle. Lemenov stared eastward toward the apex of that triangle.

"Over there," he said. "We can use the forest to cover our approach. The tiger is near the river." He smiled. "Like us, comrade, it is also hunting."

Then, to Brunovsky's astonishment, Lemenov shoved the antenna into a sheath attached to his belt, unslung the long-barreled rifle from his shoulder and, in motions too swift to separate, released the safety, chambered a bullet, raised the rifle to his shoulder and fired at the sky.

The hunter smiled at Brunovsky's consternation. "Don't look so surprised, Leonid Andreyevich. We wouldn't want our loyal patrol to miss the climax of our little performance, would we? Come, comrade . . . it isn't every day you get a chance to see a Siberian tiger outside of a zoo . . . in the forest where it has as good a chance at you as you have at it!"

2

THE TIGER LAY stretched out in the tall grass a short distance from the tree line. Against the background of dry September grass, as gold as ripe wheat, her pale coat with its brown striping provided a nearly perfect camouflage. Having eaten well the night before, she was not really hungry, and she had not set out this afternoon to hunt, but her reaction to the glimpse of a small *sika* tiptoeing down the slope toward the mountain stream, no more than fifty paces away, was instinctive. Game was becoming scarce in the taiga. With the coming winter it would be scarcer still, and she had three mouths to feed.

Her usual prey was larger, like the Siberian wapiti, a species of elk, but the *sika,* a close relative of the North American spotted deer, was a favorite delicacy—when it could be caught. To come upon a single unwary deer was a chance that could not be ignored.

She began to creep stealthily through the grass, skirting brush that might have betrayed her presence. Her powerful muscles rippled beneath the handsome coat, which was thicker than that of most tigers. She was a magnificent Siberian, the largest tiger species in the world, one of fewer than three hundred left in the wild. Stretched out low to the ground, she measured nine feet from head to the base of her tail, which was another two feet in length. She weighed just over five hundred pounds. Her noiseless movements through the grass were followed by other, more audible rustlings, as three similar but smaller shapes followed her, each mimicking her stalking posture, belly to the ground.

Now forty yards away, the small deer approached the stream. The tiger flattened, instantly still. Her cubs, one male and two females, hugged the ground in imitation. Like their mother, they were now aware of the creature approaching the bank of the river. The *sika* lifted its head nervously, looking about with its large ears erect, listening. But there was no sound from the wilderness to warn it of danger. After a few moments the deer bent its graceful neck to drink again. The tiger's tail lashed slowly. Three other tails worked in unison. She shifted her weight, getting her hind legs under her body in position to launch her charge. Once more the deer lifted its head, water dripping from its soft mouth, black eyes huge. It danced a little way along the bank, skittish, still looking around. Overhead a hawk rode a thermal, skating a long smooth stroke down the flank of the mountain. The morning sun was hot and bright over the Pacific to the east, but here on the mountain the air was cool, cooler still in the shade of the forest the tiger had left just a short while ago. She felt the sun warm on her back. Her keen eyes, sensitive to the slightest movement, watched the deer for the moment when it was most relaxed, most unaware.

The cubs, growing restless, lost their concentration. In the instant before the tiger charged, one of her female cubs slapped the male with an ungainly paw. The male spat back in mock ferocity. The tiger burst out of her grass cover, but in the stillness of the morning the hiss of a tiger cub was a distinctive sound, as clear to the *sika* as a bugle call. The deer broke, bounding across the river in one leap and fleeing up the far bank.

The tiger's charge was awesome in its blend of speed and grace and power. Almost from the moment of hurling herself out of her crouch she was at full speed, a muscular projectile flying at over sixty miles an hour. But the little deer on its stick legs was faster. She flew away from the river in long, agile bounds. The tiger's chance for success had been a narrow window, limited to the first seconds of attack, and she had lost the vital element of surprise that might have enabled her to reach the deer before it was in full flight. She gave a frustrated roar as she charged after the elusive prey, vaulting the stream in one jump that landed her on the patch of grass where the deer had stood an instant earlier.

Briefly the tiger bounded after the frightened *sika,* but she knew that the chase was fruitless. After a moment she turned back. Concern for her cubs quickly resurfaced. They were less than four months old, not yet weaned, and could never be left alone away from their den for more than a brief period. The mountain and the forest were home for other predators.

The cubs romped toward her as she returned. She gave no thought to the failure of her attack; that too was a lesson for her young. They were actually too immature to accompany her on the hunt, and their presence owed more to the fact that she was moving their den than to a planned hunting exercise. That would come when they were a month or two older.

She led her brood back to the cool shade of the forest, her preferred habitat. At an elevation of about four thousand feet she moved through an ancient stand of spruce, fir and pine, following an animal trail almost as old as the taiga itself. She walked with an unconscious spring to her gait, her weight up on her pads and toes. Keeping to the trees, she followed the course of the stream as it wound down the mountain, keeping it in sight through occasional glimpses of flashing water. She was searching for a new den. Once the cubs were settled there, she could think of hunting in earnest. The water was not only essential for her; it was also the primary lure for all of the animals of the mountain.

The particular part of the forest through which she moved was new to her, but only in its specific details. Nothing in the area was strange, for this was her territory, a range covering up to twenty-five miles or more in any direction. Once, she had lived comfortably in a smaller territory, but with game decreasing she, like other Siberian tigers, had been compelled to extend her range, even at the risk of encroaching upon the territory of other tigers. Only the fact that she was a female lessened the risk of attack for herself. That would not protect her cubs from a male tiger jealous of his domain.

With shadows falling long across the mountain, she padded

through the forest above the river, moving at ease, relaxed and unafraid.

Unaware of the faint signal, a *tsh-tsh* almost like a kiss, emanating from the collar around her neck, a lightweight plastic band so familiar that she had forgotten its existence.

It was Grovkin who spotted where a vehicle had recently left the road. Brakes squealed. The clutch banged noisily in reverse. The two men stared at twin tracks where the grass and brush had been beaten down. Today, Chris Harmon thought. In twenty-four hours the wilderness would have rebounded, obliterating any sign of intrusion.

"Look," Grovkin said.

Less than a hundred yards away, through a screen of brush, a shaft of sunlight reflected off the rectangular rear window of a Range Rover. Flecks of rusty red paint escaped the natural camouflage.

Grovkin climbed out of the Jeep. He did not examine the vehicle hidden in the brush but the terrain leading away from it. He was an expert tracker, and within minutes he was back. The tracks of two men crossed the flat valley bottom from the spot where the Range Rover had been hidden and headed north of the service road into the hills. Ironically, their tracks passed within a few feet of a wooden sign by the side of the road. *"BRAKUNYER—VRUG PRERODA,"* the sign read, over the stylized outline of a furtive figure carrying a rifle. "THE POACHER—NATURE'S ENEMY."

"They were here within last couple hour," Grovkin announced. "We could wait for them. They must come back this way."

"No," Chris said quickly. "We only heard one shot. That doesn't mean they hit anything. They could still be hunting."

"Is possible," the Russian admitted reluctantly. The idea of lying in wait and surprising the poachers appealed to him.

"You know that fire road that goes up to Cherchi Point?" Chris asked.

"I know it."

"We can take that and get up behind them. At least get closer before we have to walk into the bush."

Grovkin didn't argue. He wound the Jeep back up to speed immediately. He concentrated on the bouncing vehicle and the wheel that kept threatening to twist out of his grip. Chris looked at the Russian's hands, broad and square and scarred. Chris grinned into the wind. There were no hands he would have trusted more to ride a bucking Jeep into the Primorskiy.

He had met the Russian guard shortly after his arrival at Terney, headquarters for the director and staff of the Sikhote-Alin Biosphere National Preserve. Grovkin had learned English from American soldiers while he was stationed with the Red Army of Occupation in Germany, and he had been assigned to the joint research team as a combination game warden and translator. Though Chris spoke a rudimentary Russian and understood more than he could speak, Grovkin used English with Chris whenever possible. It was the first time, he would point out, that he had been able to use his acquired English since he was in the army, and he had to take advantage of the opportunity as much as possible.

"There it is!" Chris shouted into the wind. He pointed toward a narrow track that wound away from the main service road toward the mountains. It was hardly a trail at all, no more than a suggestion of twin ruts where a vehicle had thrashed its way through the untouched wilderness.

Controlling a sliding skid as he left the road, Grovkin slowed of necessity. Long grass and brush whipped at the Jeep as it plunged forward, bouncing and jerking over uneven terrain. Harmon peered ahead at the higher surrounding hills. Sounds could be deceptive in the wilderness, both as to distance and direction, and he was only guessing that the shot he had heard had come from the area of a ridge to the north and a little west of the firebreak. If he was right, they might surprise the poachers. If he was wrong, he would have given the illegal hunters the leeway they needed to finish their dirty work and get away.

"Why did they walk so far?" Alex Grovkin speculated after a few minutes. "They could have taken Rover partway into hills."

"Too much noise," Chris guessed. "Especially—" He brought himself up short.

"What is it?"

"If they *knew* a tiger was up there."

Grovkin considered the possibility soberly. "Not many poachers will go into forest on foot after a tiger," he said finally.

Chris was surprised by the comment. But Grovkin was right. What did that mean? What kind of hunters were these? And if they were prepared to go into the taiga on foot, how had they known where to hunt? Most poachers skulked around the preserve in their four-wheelers, hunting by sight, often at night when many of the forest animals were on the prowl. They used powerful searchlights mounted on their vehicles to penetrate the darkness and freeze their prey. Was it possible that sophisticated poachers might be using radio telemetry to track the tagged tigers in the preserve, turning the Biosphere research team's work against them? The thought was chilling.

The Jeep crested a low hill and veered along the fringe of a deep stand of spruce and pine. Grovkin slowed, then stopped as the land dropped away to their left toward a river bottom.

"Maybe this is far enough," Chris said.

Grovkin stared at him.

"If these hunters are professionals of whatever kind, maybe we shouldn't let them know we're coming."

Grovkin said nothing. He was thinking it was a little late for secrecy. The growl of the Jeep climbing into the hills could have been heard from a mile off.

They made no attempt to hide the vehicle. Grovkin carried only his rifle and a canteen of water on his hip. He was not surprised when Chris Harmon looped the strap of his camera over his shoulder. The American seldom went anywhere without his camera. "What will you do, my friend? Take poacher's picture and scare him to death?"

"Maybe," Chris grinned. "They don't like having their pictures pinned up on the wall."

The truth was that he felt naked in the field without his camera. It was a natural appendage, as essential as sun-

glasses, and as crucial to his field work as firsthand observations. Sometimes more so. The Nikon 8008 with its 70–210
millimeter lens, capable of producing razor-sharp images
even at full zoom, could leap across physical barriers to peer
intimately into secrets of animal behavior inaccessible to the
observer behind the lens.

"Maybe you will take picture of tiger, too," Grovkin said
softly.

Chris felt a quivering in his gut, a scared eagerness like a
teenager embarking on his first date. "Let's go find out," he
said.

3

TWENTY MINUTES LATER Chris Harmon lay in a narrow depression carved by runoff behind a hollow log. He could smell the dampness of the earth beneath the rotting log, and the sharp scent of pine needles. The depression was not quite big enough for his length. It was the story of his life in the field, he thought. He seemed invariably to be trying to fit his six feet two inches into a five-foot-ten opening. He had his camera mounted on a stubby, swiveling tripod, its six-inch legs firmly planted on top of the log. There was only a thin screen of brush to his left, nothing in front, but Chris was no longer worried about concealment. At this point he *wanted* the poachers to know their actions might be seen.

Alexander Grovkin squatted on his haunches beside him, surveying the scene through binoculars. They had climbed through dense forest to a promontory looking down on the river valley to their left. Beyond the river was more of the taiga, tall fir and pine trees spreading over the hills in an unbroken panorama. Chris imagined the forest continuing out of sight beyond these hills, beyond the Sikhote-Alin peaks to the west, marching across Siberia for thousands of miles, the greatest forest on earth.

There was no sign of the poachers. Chris was guessing they had used open terrain beyond the river for easier climbing and were now somewhere in the forest, waiting. From this height he could see the ribbon of service road far below them and to the south. He was convinced the poachers hadn't slipped past them and fled.

Waiting for what, then? Did that mean the first shot—nearly forty-five minutes ago—had missed?

Grovkin broke a prolonged silence. "I remember her. Risa."

It was impossible to forget a Siberian tiger you had met up close in the wild. Risa was larger than most females, as imposing as most male Siberians. Chris had put her age at five years. She had taken a heavy dose of tranquilizer, and she had slept for nearly three hours. Paws as large as a man's head. Bold stripes framing her massive head, and a distinctive pattern of markings above her eyes, three stripes descending like the tines of a fork to a cross. The facial markings of all tigers were as unique as fingerprints. Chris would recognize Risa in a moment, anywhere. He had been in awe every moment he was with her.

"It was in spring, March, soon after you came from America. Still plenty of snow on ground, and we found her in Russian way, following tracks in snow. You were afraid she would die from anesthetic. Is it not so?"

"I was worried."

"I remember when she woke up and tried to stand, all wobbly. I saw you smile. That was when I knew you were okay, even though you were American."

"Thanks," Chris said dryly. "I love you, too, Alexander Semyonovich."

"What got you into this business? You grow up with dog, maybe?"

"Sure." Chris was silent a moment, a smile of reminiscence touching his lips. "My favorite was Kipling—Kip for short. He was part Samoyed and part whatever. Pure white and full of hell, only half a Samy's size but he didn't believe it. Gave the mailman fits."

His love of a dog was not the reason, of course, for his becoming a biologist, or for spending most of the past two years working with the joint Russian-American research project in the Sikhote-Alin Biosphere National Preserve. It wasn't entirely unrelated, but the answers to human behavior were infinitely more complex than for most species. What was he doing here, scrunched into a space too small for him, in the middle of a vast wilderness that, until a few short years ago, had been closed to the entire Western world for more than half a century? No short answer, is there, Nancy?

Maybe he was there, as the joke went, because a naive nineteen-year-old decided this was what he wanted to do with his life, having absolutely no real notion of what was in store. Maybe it was because, wanting to impress a pretty coed in biology class, he had actually studied hard and surprised himself by becoming fascinated with the marvelous mysteries of animal behavior. Maybe it was because Dr. Mellett's passion for his subject in that same class had proved infectious. It took root in Chris's imagination, leading him from one class to another, one mystery to another.

Suddenly Chris remembered another dog, and an incident he had tried to block out of his mind. He was a teenager, going home late from high school basketball practice one winter night in Boston. He had just got off the bus. It was already dark, the street shiny wet from an intermittent drizzle. The bus pulled away. Chris heard a squeal of tires and looked up just in time to see a large dog darting across the street. A car swerved sharply, skidding on the wet pavement. There was a thump, a yelp of pain. The car hesitated, then quickly gained speed as it sped down the road. Heart drumming, his stomach queasy, Chris stood momentarily frozen, staring at a lump on the ground by the far side of the road.

A door burst open. Light spilled across the sidewalk from the interior of a bar on the corner. Chris heard music and some raucous shouting within the bar. Three men converged on the dog lying in the street. One of them shouted. Another man emerged from the bar. The dog was whimpering.

"Hey! We gotta do something."

"Put him out of his misery."

"Sam? Sam? You got that bat?"

One of the men grabbed the dog by the hind legs and hauled his body onto the sidewalk. The dog screamed. Chris wanted to yell at them. *Don't move him!* But the words choked in his throat. A sense of horror gripped him, as if he knew what was coming.

There was more commotion in front of the bar, the men milling around. Chris waited for a car to pass, tires squishing on the wet road. He started across the street, running now.

Then he saw the bat in one man's hands, raised above his

head. It lashed down. The solid thud seemed to jolt through Chris's whole body. It stopped him in his tracks. Another car swerved to avoid him, the driver yelling angrily as he flashed by. Chris ran forward, shouting, "No, don't!"

Another solid thud. The bat lifting and slamming down. A burly man blocking his way at the curb, peering down at him. "What's the matter, kid?"

"Stop it!"

"Hey, you want him to suffer? Get lost!"

"Get him out of here!"

Another thud, then silence. The men standing around on the sidewalk, moving restlessly. Chris staring at them, his eyes avoiding the shape on the sidewalk. The dog lay motionless, no longer whimpering. Tears streamed down the boy's face. He should have done something! Why hadn't he acted? How did they know the dog had to die?

Chris Harmon shook himself. My God, even after fifteen years that memory shook him up. The questions remained unanswered. Was it necessary? Could he have done anything for the dog? A million small tragedies every day, in every corner of the earth, why did that one incident stick out of his memory like a shard of broken glass?

He had never told Nancy about the dog, though they must have talked about everything else in their lives during the four years they were together. He could imagine the reaction.

"There you go again. My God, Chris, you're not responsible for the whole world."

"Maybe I could have done something."

"No, you couldn't, and anyway that was a long time ago. What is this, one of your Catholic things? Whipping yourself over and over, as if that will make it right?"

"No, it's not one of my Catholic things."

"Well, it's stupid blaming yourself."

Not that Nancy was unfeeling. She would have cried if she had seen the accident, but she would have put it behind her quickly. She was, Chris thought, more practical than he was. Had her act together.

She couldn't believe it when he told her about the joint project with some Russian biologists in Far East Russia. How he and some friends with the Global Wildlife Federation had been working to bring off the project for over a year. How the federation and a big oil company had come up with grants funding the effort, and the Russians had finally agreed.

"How come you never said anything? Where is this place?"

"It's north of Vladivostok."

"Great, that tells me everything."

Chris, laughing: "It's at the edge of Siberia. That part of Russia adjoins both China and North Korea. The coastline faces the Sea of Japan, so it's right opposite the northern islands of Japan."

"That's the other side of the world!"

Later, when the talking became more serious, more edgy, Nancy was to say, "What can you possibly learn over there about the Siberian tiger that isn't already known?"

"The Russians have had them all to themselves for the last half century. Now that's over. They're opening the gates over there, and this isn't something I can pass up. Corny as it sounds, this really is a once-in-a-lifetime opportunity. You know how I feel about this."

Chris had explored his dark vision for her many times. How the human race was spreading like a tide over the entire surface of the globe, obliterating whole environments, destroying scores of species every day. How, in a few short years in biological terms, there would be only domestic animals left to share the planet with humans, cats and dogs as household companions, cows and pigs and chickens preserved as a food source. How, in the time remaining, there was a race to learn as much as possible about species that would soon have vanished from their natural habitats, if not from the face of the earth.

"Why does it have to be you?"

"I've studied the big cats. I'm known in the field. And I have one qualification very few American biologists can match. I speak a little Russian."

Chris's grandfather on his mother's side had emigrated from Georgia. Chris remembered him as a small, wiry man with a huge brush mustache who, at family gatherings, drank enormous quantities of Russian vodka and American beer. In his cups he would sing boisterous Russian folk songs and tell dirty jokes in Russian that, as a teenager, Chris had been eager to learn.

"Next thing you'll be telling me you're doing this because of your grandfather."

"No," Chris said. "I'm going because it's what I do. I know we can accomplish some things the Russians can't do on their own over there. We have equipment they haven't been able to afford. Some of their science is right up with ours, even ahead of us. Hell, they were pioneers in studying animal behavior. We're all students of Pavlov. But not anymore. The Communist regimes, to give them their due, stopped the killing of endangered animals in their preserves way back in the forties. It was worth your life to shoot a Siberian tiger during Stalin's reign. But funding behavioral research in the Primorskiy wasn't high on Stalin's agenda, or Andropov's or Khrushchev's or Brezhnev's. Like us, the Soviet leaders were too busy building bigger and better bombs."

"You're going because you want to, Chris, not because you have to. My God, you're talking about two years!"

"I know," Chris said softly.

"You were keeping it as a surprise?"

"I'm sorry, Nan. I didn't want to talk about it because I didn't really think it was ever going to happen."

She tilted her head, as if to study him better. Her long blond hair fell loosely about her shoulders. Long lovely neck, perfect oval face, clear blue eyes, a wide mouth perpetually lifting at both corners, as if getting a jump on laughter. That's Nancy . . .

The smile was wry. "I guess this means you're not making a commitment."

"It doesn't mean that at all!"

"You could've fooled me. Two years." She shook her head, hair swirling like a model's in a television hair commercial. "A lot can change in two years apart."

"I know. But not the basic things."

She raised an eyebrow. She had perfect control of her eyebrows, left or right, and could use them with comic effect. "It isn't as if you're just going to prison where you had no choice, and where I could come and visit you, maybe even wangle some conjugal rights. You'll be on the other side of the world."

"You're making me feel like a prick."

"Good. That's how I want you to feel." She fell silent. He felt miserable, kicking himself for not trusting her with his hopes about the tiger research project from the beginning. "Are there any temporary nunneries, you think? Two-year tryout deals?"

"Nan—"

"Don't say it." She stared at him for a long time, as if she wanted to fix his image in her memory. At the end her eyes filled with tears. "This is a lark for you, but not for me. I'm not sure I can be here when you get back."

"Then I won't go."

"Yes, you will. You *have* to go. It's what you do, right? I can't take that from you and keep you. It's just that . . . we don't really know what the price is, do we?"

Four years together, he thought. For at least two of those years he had been away from home on fieldwork of one kind or another. Add to that the conventions, committee meetings, endless late nights at the university laboratory . . . how much time had they really had together? The cliché about *being there for me* came to mind. He hadn't been there for her. His biologist's belief in the interconnectedness of all living things on earth underscored the irony. Always seeking links in the marvelous chain of life on earth, he had lost his fundamental connection with his partner, the woman with whom he had paired and bonded.

Great, Chris thought as he squinted past the log, using his camera lens to pull a distant pine tree into his lap. *Stroll down memory lane with me. A laugh a minute.* Small wonder Nancy hadn't found reason enough to wait.

The "Dear Chris" letter had come in February. Dated January 3, so it had taken a month to cross the Pacific Ocean and find him in Terney. *"Dear Chris, I'm more sorry than I can tell you to have to write this letter . . ."* What the hell had he expected? There were no two-year, in-and-out convents. Life didn't stand still for anyone, and Nancy was both too attractive and too vibrant to be left on the sidelines for long.

A week after Christmas. Nancy had always hated being alone on holidays, especially Christmas . . .

Chris shook himself, peered through the camera's lens. A cluster of needles and a fat brown pinecone jumped into view. A break there at the edge of the forest, he noted, might be an animal trail.

"You know what my problem is, Alex?" he murmured.

"I have not been giving this much thought lately."

"I think too much like a biologist."

"I can see where that would be a problem."

"No, I'm serious."

"So am I."

Chris grinned in spite of himself.

"Pay attention, Mr. Biologist!" Grovkin's mocking tone of voice changed abruptly. "Over there!"

"Where?"

"To the right . . . coming out of taiga."

Chris Harmon followed Grovkin's gaze. He felt breathless, as if he had been struck in the chest. A tiger paused at the edge of the forest, surveying the scene below like a monarch on a balcony looking down on her subjects.

4

Tsh! Tsh!

SERGEI LEMENOV LISTENED to the soft signal in his earphones, so faint that it was inaudible to Leonid Brunovsky, crouched nearby. Lemenov felt the muscular tightening that brought an almost sexual tension to such moments as this. It was as if in the presence of imminent death he was most alive, his body taut and ready, every sense alert, every nerve end acutely sensitive, his concentration absolute. He had stalked and tracked down his quarry. That was the hardest, and most intriguing, part of the game, for it pitted his skill and cunning against that of his target. No matter that it was not a man he hunted this time, but a tiger.

The tiger, after all, was incidental to his real purpose.

Lemenov felt no qualms about shooting a Siberian tiger. Killing was his business, and he brought a total professionalism to the task. There was no room for sentiment.

In the past, in the glory days of the Soviet empire, Sergei Lemenov had been a specialist in *mokrie dela,* or "wet affairs," with the *Komitet Gosurdarstvennoe Bezopasnosti,* the Committee for State Security—the dreaded KGB. He had been a youthful protégé of Yuri Andropov, head of the KGB from 1967 to 1982 and briefly the first Soviet secret police chief to rise to leadership of the entire Union of Soviet Socialist Republics. By the time of his patron's death in 1984, Lemenov was established in Department V, the secret Executive Action Department of the First Chief Directorate, the directorate responsible for all foreign operations. The secret division, or *taini otdel,* trained, developed and deployed assassins for assignment outside of the Soviet Union's borders. The training took place in a massive, ugly Stalin-era building with thick doors and slit windows as discreet as narrowed eyes, located on the corner of Metrostroevskaya Street and Turnaninski Pereulok in Moscow. It was Lemenov's home for sixteen months.

In the years that followed, Lemenov was sent to carry out covert lethal missions in South Africa, Egypt, the Middle East, France and Great Britain. Two of those assignments had required killing at close quarters, once with a knife, the other time using a poisoned needle concealed in the tip of an umbrella. But Lemenov's particular skill, discovered early by his instructors at the spy school, was as a marksman. He had been trained in the use of more esoteric weapons—gases, drugs, poisons, guns concealed in pens or cigarette packs— but he was unrivaled in the service as a sniper. He could place three shots within a circle the size of an American nickel at 300 yards. He had once killed a target with a single shot at nearly twice that distance. The bullet had blown away the target's head; no one knew if Lemenov had actually attempted the head shot or not, but the remarkable kill added to his reputation.

It was an unorthodox mission closer to home, however, in a small village named Podtyograd in the eastern Ukraine about fifty miles south of Kramatorsk, that cemented his reputation and gave him his nickname: the Collector.

Through an informant, the village had come to the attention of the deputy director of the *sluzhba,* a division of the Second Chief Directorate of the KGB with an office in Kramatorsk. The *sluzhba* was responsible for the investigation of "economic crimes," including black marketeering and the theft of state properties. For years there had been rumors about the activities of a local collective-farm director who was widely known to be an avid collector of paintings, books and artifacts. His name was Pavel Chulyinski. He was a Communist Party member with powerful friends in the Party and in the KGB itself, and a brother who was a highly placed prosecutor. It was suspected that Chulyinski had amassed a hoard of icons, rare books and paintings. Some of the spoils had been taken long ago from old czarist estates and hidden by farmers from whom Chulyinski bought them for a song. But most of the collection, according to the rumors, had been stolen from the state—from libraries, museums or torn-down churches—by corrupt workers or officials only too willing to sell them. Because of his powerful friends, however, Chulyinski could not be accused without proof. The gossip of jealous villagers was not enough. The deputy director of the *sluzhba* saw the desirability of reaching out for an agent unknown to the local KGB. He asked a friend in the First Chief Directorate for the loan of an agent to carry out a covert operation that could, if anything went wrong, be blamed on outsiders.

Sergei Lemenov was chosen.

Whether in a crowded city or a small village, Lemenov was skilled at remaining invisible. Pavel Chulyinski lived on a one-acre farm outside the village in a house that was, while larger than most, outwardly plain and unexceptional. Lemenov scouted the village, the farm and its surroundings for four days.

In spite of the suspected treasure trove he had hoarded—or perhaps because of it—Chulyinski was a recluse. He dressed and lived modestly, displaying no signs of affluence. A widower, he lived alone except for an elderly servant couple who had been with him for more than forty years but did not stay overnight on the estate. The couple lived in a small cottage at the edge of the village. They had never had access to several rooms of the house, Lemenov learned, rooms that were always locked. Village gossip speculated that Pavel Chulyinski kept his illegal hoard in these locked rooms. At night he was alone in the house with his treasure . . . if it actually existed. Everyone in Podtyograd knew that the farm director was a collector, but no one really knew what he had kept for himself or sold off at a profit on the black market. It remained a mystery.

On the fifth night Sergei Lemenov broke into the house. Chulyinski kept a shotgun beside his bed, but Lemenov easily overpowered and disarmed him. A quick search of the house, including the locked rooms, produced only a number of musty and dirt-coated books, a small wooden box containing some old coins, and several ordinary paintings displayed on the walls of the bedroom and living area. The locked rooms, Lemenov guessed, had been a ruse designed to confuse thieves by diverting attention away from the real location of the old man's treasure.

Lemenov, whose training included techniques ranging from subtle interrogation to unsubtle torture, set to work patiently to question the hoarder. The old man was a fanatic, his collection the passion of his life. He did not break easily. Lemenov had to work through most of the night. The seclusion the old man had sought now became his cross; there was no one to hear his screams. Lemenov used an exquisitely sharp knife with skill and care. When the truth finally emerged it poured out like blood and water from a blister, a babble of pride and hate, vanity and terror.

Lemenov tore up the floorboards of the bedroom. Beneath them he found stairs leading down to a secret, brick-walled storeroom twice the size of the room above. It was jammed with piles and crates of rare, centuries-old books and manuscripts, gold- and silver-framed icons, rare coins and valuable paintings purloined from churches and museums in the Soviet Union, Poland and Germany.

When the elderly servants came to the house in the morning, Lemenov sent them away. He did not open the door. He was a doctor, he told them. Comrade Chulyinski was ill. They would not be needed that day.

That night several trucks were heard rumbling through the countryside near Podtyograd. Residents assumed they were military vehicles, and no one dared question them. The following day, when the servants were unable to rouse Chulyinski, local militiamen were called out from the village. The house was found looted. Chulyinski's body lay on the blood-drenched sheets of his bed. The secret storage room beneath the bedroom held only some piles of old books and manuscripts—the least valuable, it was concluded, of Chulyinski's secret trove.

Parts of the old man were missing—three fingers, one ear, the left nipple from his breast, the knob of his penis, strips of skin neatly peeled from his thighs and under his arms. Like his treasure, the severed parts were never found. The story whispered through the village was that the old man's murderer had taken them with him. He too was a collector.

The crime was blamed on gypsies traveling through the community, or a Chechen thug. The truth was never suspected.

Within a very small circle of people privy to the actions of Department V, Sergei Lemenov's code name was born. The hoard he had uncovered disappeared into the labyrinth of the KGB, except for a single gold icon and a rare gold-embossed medieval manuscript he kept for himself. The human artifacts, shriveled bits and pieces of human tissue, amused him briefly, but he soon found them smelly and ugly, trash to be discarded in the nearest dump.

In the aftermath of *perestroika* and the breakup of the Soviet Union, after a series of purges and reorganizations, the KGB was broken into two new agencies—the Foreign Intelligence Service (SVRR) charged with intelligence operations outside Russia, and the Federal Counterintelligence Service (SVR), which conducted internal investigations and intelligence. In a harsh order abolishing the old KGB and condemning its excesses, President Boris Yeltsin divided its work between the two new services and also ordered a recertification process for all employees of the SVR and SVRR.

Some agents could not stand such scrutiny. All trace of Sergei Lemenov, the Collector, vanished from the files of Department V.

"They're over there," Leonid Brunovsky said. "Off to the right. They must have left their Jeep below the lower ridge."

"I know," Lemenov said.

"I don't understand why you *wanted* them to follow us."

"You don't have to understand." *All in good time. Leonid Andreyevich,* he thought. The shooting of a tiger was but the first act in a drama that would shake the new Republic of Russia to its foundations.

The Collector smiled his thin cold smile, the one that gave Leonid Brunovsky the shivers. How ironic that he would receive the code name by which he was known to select employers from a single isolated incident unrelated to his primary skills. Reborn as a free-lance entrepreneur, he remained what he had always been since his mentor, Yuri Andropov, had recruited him for the secret Department V: a hunter of men, a superb marksman, a sniper of uncommon skill. An assassin.

He lay prone on the ground, his legs spread out behind him for stability. He was in a classic shooting position, with his left hand holding his rifle's forepiece directly under the long barrel, his right arm resting out at an angle with the tip of his forefinger gently touching the trigger. It was a comfortable position that he could maintain for a considerable period of time; it was also the steadiest position for a long-range shot.

The *tsh! tsh!* told him where the tiger was, and that she was moving toward him. His target was in the far wood beyond the river that ran below his position. The dark trunk of a pine tree at the edge of that forest was, according to his laser range finder, exactly 1,530 feet away. Five hundred and ten yards.

His rifle was a bolt action, but the venerable design was in this case thoroughly modern. The bolt action and unusually thick-walled barrel were Swiss-made of stainless steel. The custom stock had been adapted from a Kalashnikov single-fire sniper's rifle. The telescopic sight, a 3-12x Pentax variable scope, would cause an object sighted at 500 yards to appear to be less than 50 yards away at the top end magnification. The silver gloss of the polished aluminum scope matched the sheen of the stainless-steel action and barrel. It was a beautiful rifle, but for the Collector its true virtues were its accuracy and reliability. The rifle held four cartridges, but he had never had to use more than two. One was generally enough. Even at 500 yards he could select which eye of the tiger he chose to hit.

He lay near the edge of the forest west of the river and above it. The trees around him provided cover without impeding his forward view. The downward slope on this side of the river was steeper than on the other side, which meant that he would have to allow for a drop of about sixty feet—more if he could not get a clear shot before the tiger reached the river-bank. The wind was from the northwest at less than five miles per hour. He calculated a two-inch drift at this distance with the powerful 250 grain, .357 Magnum cartridge.

"Can you still hear him?" Leonid Brunovsky asked anxiously. The waiting was getting to him.

"Be quiet," Lemenov snapped.

He took deep, slow breaths, willing himself to relax. The visceral tension he felt before a kill was pleasurable but it also impeded precise motor function and magnified the tiny bumping that occurred as each heartbeat sent blood through the muscles. He checked his sight alignment again. He had had to choose his prone position carefully to avoid having low ground cover, a branch or even a blade of grass, between himself and his expected target. His line of sight was clear.

Tsh! Tsh!

He waited. Heard Brunovsky's gasp of excitement. Moved his scope very slowly to the right, in small increments, and watched the head and shoulders of a tiger swim into view, threading through the tall grass near the edge of the distant forest.

5

CHRIS HARMON PUT his eye to the Nikon's lens, rotating the camera on the swivel base until he found the tiger, then zooming in. The image grew, filling the lens. "It's her! Risa!"

"She is not hurt," Grovkin said. "She is fine!"

Chris stared at the tiger fixed in his lens. What he felt was more than wonder. It was elation. He had seen this tiger close up, spent over two hours with her, sketching her markings, taking photos, weighing her, examining her skin, her eyes, her teeth. He had removed an incisor, using it later to establish her age at about five years. Sponged her with water to lower her temperature, which tended to rise under the drug's influence. Fit the collar with its tiny, lithium battery-powered radio transmitter around her neck. *This* tiger, but she had been sedated then. Beautiful, but with all of her power and grace suspended. Now she was herself, in all her strength and beauty and uniqueness.

As a scientist, life's infinite variety delighted Chris Harmon. Most species were variants, and it was the variants that made life truly interesting—and not only for the biologist. But Risa held a different fascination. She was more like an original, her species unchanged for thousands of years. Through her Chris peered down the channel of centuries at a different earth. Much of the taiga was exactly as it had been before man's first rude attempts at communal structures were built out of mud and grass. And in that forest primeval creatures exactly like this Siberian tiger had walked unchallenged, and stalked their prey, and slept full-bellied in the sun.

"Maybe the poachers were after something else," Grovkin suggested. "Like ibex we saw this morning."

"I don't think so." Chris had had the Nikon fitted with an automatic shutter release. When he pressed a button the camera began to click steadily, taking picture after picture a few seconds apart.

"Look, she is going down to river."

Slowly the tiger emerged from the shadows of the trees into the late afternoon sunlight. The sun was above a flat-topped mountain to the west, brushing the tips of the trees that covered the mesa, and the tiger cast a long shadow across the grassy slope. For a moment she disappeared behind some brush. Then she came into the open again.

Chris held his breath, as if he might freeze the moment.

Something about the tiger caught Chris's attention. Something different. The long back swayed more than he remembered. Her belly almost touched the ground.

"Oh my God!" he breathed. "She hasn't been moving much this summer. Now we know why. Look how swollen she is. She's full of milk! She has nursing cubs!"

At that moment a smaller striped head appeared behind the tiger, poking out of the thick grass. A smaller tiger body bounded into view, followed seconds later by another. Chris was grinning. How many did she have? Two in sight. Were there others? Three or four months old, by the look of them.

Without warning the idyllic picture shattered. The tiger leaped into the air, her long body twisting as if she were being jerked upward on a powerful leash.

"Yob tvoyu mat!" Sergei Lemenov swore.

The moment had been perfect, everything calculated down to the most minute detail. He knew his weapon as a lover knew the precise touch that would make his woman quiver, and his fingertip caressed the trigger. He felt the hard recoil against cheek and shoulder, but it was horror that jolted him, the horror of a perfectionist who knew that he had failed.

In that unmeasurable fragment of time between the sending of the message from his brain to his finger, and the whisper touch on the trigger, the tiger had moved in an un-predictable way, turning her head as one of her cubs pounced on another in play.

In the fraction of a second before Chris realized the tiger had been hit, he heard the delayed crash of a high-powered rifle shot echoing through the hills.

Chris jumped to his feet. He started to shout, cursing. The tiger had fallen back to earth. She crawled away, disappearing behind a tangle of brush at the edge of the forest. One of the cubs jumped around in the grass, bewildered.

"Bastards are in those woods beyond the river!" Grovkin roared. "I saw flash of light off glass. They're looking right at us!"

"She's alive! I just saw her move. She's trying to get to those trees."

Grovkin's words registered a few seconds late. On impulse Chris swung the camera lens on its pod toward the woods Grovkin had indicated. Rage clouded his own vision, but the camera's shutter was still clicking automatically. How much film left? He hadn't been counting. He saw no puff of smoke, no splash of color or glint of reflecting glass, nothing but a dense march of trees. Old growth, tall and straight, the shadows deep at this time of day. The hunter, safe in the cover of the woods, had shot to kill at long range. Five hundred yards at least, Chris judged. No ordinary marksman would attempt such a shot.

Anger engulfed him, so deep and harsh that it brought tears to his eyes. He could hear Grovkin swearing in Russian.

The Nikon's shutter stopped clicking.

"We will catch them!" Grovkin growled. "We can get back to their Rover before they come."

His words broke Chris's paralysis of rage. "No, we have to get to Risa! She might not be dead."

"She is back in woods." Grovkin stared at Chris. "Poachers will not go into forest after wounded tiger. Neither can we."

"The hell we can't! We can't leave her—"

"I have only this old rifle. You have nothing. We can't go after tiger. If she is alive, she is very dangerous."

Chris Harmon heard the stubborn truth in the Russian's words. It cut through his anger and raw grief. It's like that dog all those years ago, he thought bitterly. And once again he was helpless to do anything.

"Besides, she's in Sector Five," Grovkin continued. "We have already done too much. How can I explain this?"

"We can bring in the damned poachers! At least we can do that much."

"Maybe." For the first time Grovkin sounded doubtful. "If we hurry, and we're lucky."

"And I'm coming back," Chris vowed, a promise more to himself than to the Russian guard. "Risa may survive. And there are her cubs. They can't be more than a few months old. What if she doesn't live, or can't hunt for them? They won't have a chance to survive without her. We can't abandon them . . . we have to try to find them."

"Take it easy, my friend."

"There is no easy, not in this."

Chris glared across the river valley toward the far woods. *I'll find you, you bastard,* he promised.

Then what? Make sure he's socked with a five thousand ruble fine—less than five dollars at the going rate of exchange?

6

TEN MINUTES LATER Chris Harmon and Alexander Grovkin reached the Jeep. Grovkin started the engine and quickly reversed, spinning the wheels as he swung the vehicle around and started back down the mountain, crashing through the tall grass and brush, their way made slightly easier by the path they had cut on the way up. The Jeep hit a bump and was airborne. It slammed back to earth with a tooth-loosening jolt, bouncing and rattling as if it were about to fly apart.

Far faster, it seemed, than the time consumed on their way into the wilderness, they reached the rudimentary firebreak that climbed toward Cherchi Point. Grovkin swung around a small grove of spruce onto a long slope. Above and behind them the forest blended into a solid wall of green, but the grassy slope was open except for scattered trees and thickets of brush.

Confined inside the wall of noise made by the Jeep in its descent, neither man heard the sound of a shot. The right side of the windshield seemed to disintegrate before their eyes like magic. The safety glass held together, but where there had been a clean expanse there was suddenly an intricate jigsaw puzzle made up of a thousand tiny pieces. Grovkin swerved instinctively. Another bullet whacked the body of the Jeep.

Grovkin slowed, braked hard. As the vehicle jerked to a stop in a cocoon of dust, the Russian dove from his seat to the ground.

Chris Harmon sat motionless in his seat, stunned.

A few seconds passed before another shot reverberated through the hills. The Jeep's right front tire popped, the sound oddly small, like a child's party balloon exploding.

From behind the hood of the Jeep Grovkin broke off his string of oaths to roar at Chris. "Get down! You want to get shot?"

Still Chris didn't move. It wasn't bravado or courage. He had his first intuitive understanding of the man with the high-powered rifle.

"He doesn't want to kill us," Chris said.

"He is doing good job pretending. How the hell do you know that?"

"He's a very good marksman. Where is he now, Alex? Do you have any idea?"

"Somewhere on that mountain. He hit windshield at angle, and he hit front tire on right side. He has to be in those trees, not so far from where he was when he shot tiger."

"He's on foot. We're moving too quickly for his liking. Those were warning shots, Alex."

Grovkin slowly climbed to his feet. He slapped dust from his pants and shirt. "More than warnings. Look at windshield. And tire is ruined."

"He's telling us not to get too close," Chris said. "How far away are those trees?"

"Five, maybe six hundred kilometers."

"Can you shoot that far with that relic of yours?"

"No way, my friend. I might hit something at three hundred, if it was big enough and slow enough. Besides, we can't even see them."

"The shooter knows that. Which means he knows exactly what he's doing."

"If he is so good, how come tiger is still alive?"

Chris thought back to that awful moment when he knew the tiger had been shot. "She turned to look over her shoulder just before she was hit. Probably heard one of the cubs behind her. She must have moved at the instant the poacher fired. Otherwise he wouldn't have only wounded her. I know him, Alex. At least I know that much about him."

Very cool, Chris thought. Businesslike. No wasted bullets

when he couldn't get another clear shot at his prey, no un-
necessary killing of game wardens who stumbled onto the
scene.

Grovkin glared across the no-man's-land between them and
the poachers. The two rises were separated by the mountain
stream that, in its descent, carved a deepening gorge between
the hills. The far hill had a flatter top, completely crowned
with forest, and above the river valley the woods were thick
most of the way down to the main service road. The poachers
would not have to reveal themselves throughout their descent.

"At least they didn't get what they came for," the Russian
guard said.

Harmon thought of the poachers' actions that day. When
their Range Rover was spotted earlier in the afternoon they
had easily outdistanced the game warden's Jeep but they
hadn't fled from the preserve. In fact, there seemed to be
something calculated in their deliberate penetration into Sector Five even after their vehicle had been seen. Chris had no
doubt at all that the poachers were as well informed as the
preserve's own staff about the recent edict setting that sector
off limits.

"They knew we were there when they shot Risa," he muttered. "Knew and didn't care . . ."

"But they go away empty-handed," Grovkin said. "No tiger
skin. No meat, no bones. They have nothing for all their trouble. Even if she is dead, there is no profit."

"They may come back."

"Is possible."

"They weren't worried about witnesses to the shooting.
They just don't want us to get too close to them."

Grovkin offered a noncommittal grunt, not seeing where
such speculation led. He squatted to examine the shredded
front tire, then walked around the Jeep to the tool chest.
"There is something I have been meaning to ask, Christopher, my friend."

"What's that?"

"How good are you at changing tire?"

* * *

It was nearly full dark when they crossed the southern boundary of the Sikhote-Alin preserve. The darkness flowed out of the mountains on either side as if pursuing them down the long river valley toward the coast and the village of Terney.

They rode in silence. Both men were weary and unsettled over the day's events, which had left them frustrated. By the time the Jeep's ruined tire had been changed and they returned to the service road, the poachers in their Range Rover had disappeared. Grovkin had raced along the road away from Sector Five until dusk and his cooling temper told him the quest was futile, not to mention foolhardy. Even if he had caught up to the poachers, their four-wheeler, like their weaponry, was a half-century newer and much more powerful than anything Grovkin or Chris Harmon had at his disposal.

The darkness flowed around them. A thin cloud cover lidded the valley, and the night became a wall on all sides, pierced only by the Jeep's headlights, as if it were burrowing through a long tunnel. Harmon welcomed the cooling night air, its bite making him wonder if it signaled a weather change.

He was not sure what made him turn around. Had he actually had a peripheral glimpse of flickering light before turning? He wasn't sure.

The road behind them was dark. Even the looming bulk of the mountains was lost to the night. He started to turn his head away. Then, far behind the Jeep, a line of trees bordering the long empty road lit up briefly as if a torch were being played over them.

Chris stared at the returning blackness until his eyes watered. He blinked, looked again. Blinked. Almost missed the second glimpse of light. Two headlights suddenly bobbed into view over a rise in the road. The twin beams joined, reaching out along the long, straight, empty road.

"Slow down, Alex."

Grovkin glanced quickly into the rearview mirror. He scowled, puzzled. The headlights had briefly disappeared but in a moment they were back, keeping pace with the Jeep. A safe distance back, Chris thought. Perhaps two miles.

Grovkin slowed the Jeep's rush through the wall of darkness. For a few seconds the following headlights began to close the gap between them. Then their pace adjusted, falling back once more.

"They're hanging back," Chris murmured.

"What the hell for?"

"I don't know. They're not scared of us, obviously. They know we can't match their firepower."

It seemed to make little sense. The poachers didn't want a direct confrontation. They could have had that back in Sector Five, and with little doubt of the outcome. So why were they following Grovkin's Jeep? What were they up to?

"I don't like it," Grovkin said. "They play games with us."

"The question is why."

The night offered no answer.

"They have seen us," Leonid Brunovsky said. They had followed the Jeep without lights for some distance until Brunovsky ran off the edge of the road in the darkness, then Lemenov told him to turn on his headlights.

"They will know we're following!"

"Better they should know than have you kill us both."

Brunovsky adjusted the Range Rover's speed to maintain the distance between it and the Jeep ahead, which had slowed down.

"I don't understand, Sergei Gregorevich. You wished to have the *Amirikanits* take pictures of tiger. Now you talk of getting these photographs from him."

"Not *those* photographs—the ones he took of us."

"But he could not see us in the taiga. It was too far . . . the trees—"

"Can you give Comrade Chairman Provalev your assurances that your face will not be in one of those pictures? I can assure you, Leonid Andreyevich, that he would not want a link to be established between our actions and him. You are that link."

"But you're not. Why are possible photos of you so important?"

Lemenov was silent for a moment, watching the road ahead. It was possible that Leonid Andreyevich was right, of course, and the photographs taken by the American would reveal nothing clearly in the forest. But could he take that risk?

"A good reason," Lemenov murmured. "I do not exist."

Five miles from the outskirts of the small town of Terney, the first tiny yellow windows appeared with their promise of warmth and comfort, the reassuring disorder of human voices and laughter. The headlights behind the Jeep vanished as abruptly as they had appeared. It was almost possible to believe they had never been there.

But the poachers had wanted to know who had been watching them, Chris Harmon thought. Who they were and where they were going.

Why?

The brakes screeched wildly. Grovkin threw the Jeep into a skid. It shuddered to a stop at the edge of a ditch.

From the middle of the road a black-and-white cow stared at them with placid indifference, in no hurry to move. Her eyes reflected the Jeep's headlights, white, as if she were blind.

7

CHRIS HARMON WOKE suddenly in the middle of the night, sweating under a pile of wool blankets, one of which was itching his neck. The room was pitch black. He lay tense, wondering what had awakened him? The itch? A cramp in his calf?

Someone was in his room.

Off in the night a dog barked. Chris could feel the chill in his room. If it weren't so dark he suspected he would be able to see his breath. The hotel—the only one the village of Terney had to offer—did not have central heating. Chris relied on blankets and a charcoal-fed samovar to provide warmth when it became really cold. Charcoal was precious, and use of the heater at any temperature above freezing brought a frown of disapproval to the frugal eyes of the hotel's manager, Irena Godinova. At night no electric lights were left burning in the hotel. The only night light was a wall sconce in the lobby holding a cup with a wick burning in a pool of oil.

"Who's there?"

Chris regretted the foolishness of the question even as he spoke aloud. Was an intruder going to identify himself?

Maybe it was his imagination. Was that the whisper of soft breathing, or the sigh of the wind outside his window? Why would anyone break into his room? There were no locks on any of the doors in the hotel. What traveler would stop there who had anything worth stealing?

His camera, he thought. But he had left it in the cubicle of an office set aside for the research team in the building used as headquarters for the staff of the Sikhote-Alin Biosphere National Preserve. Gregory Krasikov, Chris's Russian counterpart on the research team, had a heavy steel file cabinet in the office which he kept locked. On Krasikov's advice Chris habitually locked his camera in the cabinet overnight.

He had done that tonight after removing the finished roll of film. He had brought the film back to the hotel with him. What had he done with it?

Still in his pants pocket, Chris remembered. He had been exhausted on arriving at Terney at the end of the long day, and the mandatory glass of vodka with Alex Grovkin had finished him off. Back in the hotel, Chris had stumbled out of his clothes, dropping them carelessly on the chair beside the bed. Within arm's reach right now. Lying on his side, he was staring directly at the chair two feet away, even though he could barely make out its outline.

Underneath the mound of blankets, Chris began to coil his body, ready to throw off the covers and jump to his feet. A tick of sound stopped him. He waited. It was not his imagination. He could *feel* another presence in the room. He didn't have to see the intruder, or hear his carefully controlled breathing.

Click!

This time Chris recognized the sound of the door latch closing. He threw off the blankets and rushed toward the door. Caught his toe on the torn patch of linoleum beside the bed, stumbled and rammed his foot into a bedpost. Stifling a gasp of pain and damning his clumsiness, he hobbled toward the door. Groped for the knob and jerked the door open.

The hallway was as dark as his room. He heard footsteps on the stairs at the end of the hall. By the time Chris reached the top of the stairway, still limping from what he was convinced must be a broken toe, the steps had faded across the narrow lobby below. He heard the outer door close.

Wide awake now from the rush of adrenaline, he returned to his room. He fumbled for the wall switch inside the door. The feeble forty-watt overhead bulb revealed the disorderly heap of blankets on the sagging mattress, the ancient iron bedstead, the peeling wallpaper, the ragged tear in the linoleum that had caused him to trip in the darkness. His suitcase, undisturbed, stood on the floor beside the old wooden armoire with its cracked panel where it had been resting since his last trip to Vladivostok six months ago. Nothing unusual. No evidence of intrusion. He would have to check more thoroughly in the morning, but Chris had the feeling the thief had escaped empty-handed.

Perhaps he hadn't had time enough to find what he came for, Chris thought. The discovery of a thief in the hotel did not surprise him. The boldness did. Anyone after items of value—the concept of value in Terney differed greatly from what it might have been in America—such as cotton socks, soap, shaving gear, even his cheap portable radio, was more likely to have come while Chris was away from his room, as he so often was. As often as possible, he thought wryly, peering around the gloomy room. The Hilton, it wasn't. It did not even approach the level of Motel 6 amenities taken for granted across America.

He turned off the light, went to the window and drew aside the stiff, heavy curtains. The hotel was a two-story building, and Chris's upstairs room overlooked the rear yard. By day a view of the two outdoor privies that serviced the hotel, but on this overcast night Chris could not make out their sentinel shapes at the back of the yard.

He returned to his bed, crawled under the covers. His breathing had slowed to normal, but he was far from sleep. He thought again of the film in his pants pocket, debated waiting till morning, then sat up and groped for the clothing on the chair. Fumbling in the right-hand pocket, he felt the outline of the plastic cylinder into which he had dropped the film the night before.

He wasn't even sure why it had occurred to him that someone might want to steal the film. Maybe it was the way that Range Rover had trailed them all the way back to Terney . . .

He thought of Risa leaping skyward. He had activated the shutter before he heard the shot. Had his camera caught the crucial moment of violence and terror, the tiger's wounded leap? For the first time Chris realized that his film might have captured more than proof of a crime. It might have recorded a dramatic image of man's destructiveness that could be used effectively in the fight to save the Siberian tiger from extinction.

Early the next morning Chris went out into the yard, wearing only his pants and a sweatshirt, his feet bare in his moccasins. Frost crusted the bare ground and he shivered with cold. Before coming to Terney he hadn't used an outdoor privy since childhood visits to his maternal grandfather's farm in New Hampshire. Cold there in autumn, too. The mountains of New England were not unlike those of the Sikhote-Alin range, rounded rather than snowy peaks, covered in the same kind of hardwood forests. Had those remote hills also reminded the old man of his native Georgia?

One of the two privies was occupied. Harmon had been in the other only a moment when the proprietress of the hotel jerked the wooden door open, letting in a blast of the colder morning air, and plunked herself down on the end hole. Chris wondered if a three-holer was considered upscale in Terney. The privies were communal and unisex, as Chris had discovered early on. Irena Godinova showed no embarrassment over Chris's presence. A peasant woman in a black dress, built like a blocking guard in the National Football League, with skin as brown and seamed as a walnut, she nodded at Chris and gave a heavy sigh, leaning forward as if in prayer.

"*Dobraya utra, babushka*," Chris greeted her. "It's cold today."

Irena Godinova grunted.

"It looks like our"—Chris groped unsuccessfully for a Russian word equivalent—"our Indian summer is over."

"Indian summer?"

"It's what in America we call the false summer that comes late in autumn."

"Ah! Yes, yes, Indian summer." She nodded to herself, as if pleased with the name.

"I don't wish to complain, *babushka*," Chris went on, "but have you had any trouble with thieves lately in the hotel?"

"Thieves?" she repeated, as if the concept were as foreign to her as Indian summer.

"I think there was someone in my room last night."

"You must be mistaken. We do not have thieves in my hotel. What are you saying? Have we not treated you well?"

"No, no, I'm not saying that at all." Chris regretted getting her excited. After an initial period of strangeness, the woman had warmed to his efforts to speak Russian and to the novelty of having an important American staying at her hotel. For the past twenty months she had acted almost like a surrogate mother toward him. "I'm sure it was someone from the outside. He ran out of the lobby when I chased him."

"You chased him?" Chris realized she was taking his question as a personal accusation.

"He ran out. I'm not complaining, *babushka* . . . it's not important, really. I don't think anything was taken."

Chris rose and zipped up, anxious now to escape the consequences of his clumsy questioning. He was stepping outside when Godinova said, "I hear you have pictures of tiger."

Startled, Chris turned back. "When did you hear that?"

She shrugged. "It is just talk in village. You saw tiger?"

"Yes, we did."

"I saw one once. I was a little girl. They used to come closer in those days. Sometimes they would be in the woods outside of the village. We were not supposed to play there."

"Near the village?" Chris asked, interested. "They used to be that close?"

Irena Godinova nodded, a softness altering her normally stolid expression. "It was very beautiful."

"So was this one," Chris said quietly. Then he added, "Someone shot it."

He closed the door on the woman's wounded eyes.

Terney was a village of about five thousand people. The few streets were wide, like the villages of Colonial America, lined on either side with weathered wooden cottages and a few shops. There was only one hotel, one general store that displayed a few articles of last year's Moscow fashions in the window, a supplier of herbal remedies, a bakery, a meat and fish market whose window was more often than not empty, an auto repair shop whose yard was filled with the relics of rusting Soviet cars, stripped of their tires and radios and upholstery. The main street was paved, though the macadam was riddled with deep potholes casually filled with sand. Cows, pigs and chickens wandered across the street or browsed among the buildings.

The administrative offices allotted to the staff of the Sikhote-Alin preserve were in a low wooden building two blocks from the hotel, next to the Communist Party headquarters building, which still served as the town's meeting hall. The nearest building on the other side of the Party hall was the militia headquarters for the district.

A small corner office had been set aside for the joint Russian-American scientific research team, which at one time had numbered four men. Two American scientists had left for home at the end of summer, leaving Chris Harmon and Gregory Krasikov to complete the project, which was funded only through the end of the year.

Walking down the street in the early morning, Chris was grateful for his quilted nylon jacket. The air was raw, heavy with the promise of rain. It might even be cold enough for snow, he thought. He greeted several men he passed, receiving nods and brief greetings in return. Two men in a pickup truck stared at him without acknowledgement as he went by. There was a scattering of cars along the street, Toyotas and Hyundais, a Zhiguli, an ancient Lada with rust eating through the fenders, and Grovkin's Jeep parked outside the preserve headquarters building. No red Range Rover around, Chris thought. Was it parked somewhere in that wonder of wonders, a real garage?

He realized what had been puzzling him as he walked along the street. He was a curiosity, of course, the only American currently within a hundred miles, but after more than eighteen months he was no longer a source of excitement. This morning, however, Chris sensed a fresh interest. And it was not necessarily friendly.

Grovkin, he thought. He had left the Russian drinking at the small corner bar that functioned as the village's social club. Alex must have told anyone who would listen about the shooting of the tiger in the preserve.

That explained the unfriendly scrutiny, Chris thought. Poaching might be officially forbidden, and Terney might house the headquarters of the Sikhote-Alin Biosphere National Preserve, but the village was populated with hunters. At this time and place, that meant poachers. Far from being regarded as criminals, successful poachers were accorded the respect due heroes. They earned money, which in Russia's new era of capitalist enterprise was the recognized proof of success. They also defied the government and officialdom in general, which was another reason for admiration.

Chris remembered the shock of his first arrival in the area. The pilot of the small aircraft that had flown him from Vladivostok to Plastun, the closest airport to Terney, had become quite friendly. Confiding in his passenger, he had let Chris know that he was personally able to supply bear gallbladders in any quantity if the American was interested. Price was negotiable. Chris was still reacting to this suggestion when the driver of the bus taking him from Plastun to Terney inquired as to his interest in a musk deer penis and glands, the latter a very effective restorative. Similar entrepreneurs could be found anywhere in Terney. The rarity, in fact, was someone like Grovkin, who hated poachers, or Chris himself, who had devoted his life to the study of wild animals that were now so indiscriminately threatened.

Larger questions of the survival of species, such as the Siberian tiger or the black bear or the Amur goral goat, were not subjects for thought or debate in Terney. Many children in the area were hungry. Most of the potatoes grown in the flat fields south of the village were shipped to other parts of Siberia. Anyway, one could not live forever on potatoes. Meat of any kind was a treasure. Who would question the hunter who put meat on his family's table?

Grovkin was waiting for Chris in the office. He had brewed tea in the electric samovar, and Chris gratefully accepted a chipped mug of hot tea. It was infinitely better than the bitter coffee he had had with a stale bun at the hotel.

"You slept well, my friend?"

"Someone broke into my room during the night."

"No kidding! While you slept?"

Chris nodded.

"Was it a woman? You can tell me, my friend."

Grovkin had become increasingly concerned over Chris's celibate life. He himself, though unmarried, had two or three girl friends in the village and he had confided to Chris that friendly companionship was not unavailable. One of his young woman friends, Anna, was particularly intrigued because she had never been with an American and was curious about them. It would not cost Chris any of his dollars, Grovkin assured him. Minor gifts would be gratefully accepted. Lingerie, perhaps. Chocolate biscuits. A tin of smoked sturgeon. Chris had declined. *So far,* he thought.

"It was a man. He escaped down the stairs before I could catch him."

"What did he take? By God, we'll find the son of a bitch. What did he get?"

"Nothing, as far as I can tell. There's nothing missing."

"Not a very good thief, then. Probably it was a boy."

"I don't think so. I think I woke up before he could get what he was after."

"What could that be?"

Chris hesitated. "I understand you were talking about the tiger we saw yesterday. Did anyone seem particularly interested?"

"Everyone is interested in tiger stories." Grovkin refilled his mug with tea. "It was not secret."

"I'm just trying to figure out if there's any connection between the thief and the film I shot."

"Is possible. Are you thinking of truck that followed us?"

"Have you seen that Range Rover anywhere in town?"

"No, I look."

"Have you ever seen it before?"

Grovkin shook his head. "I ask about it. No one knows anything about red Range Rover. The poachers are not from Terney."

"That's interesting. Where is Yavlinsky, by the way?" Chris glanced curiously around the sparsely furnished office he shared with his fellow biologist Krasikov, then through the open door into Yavlinsky's larger office. That room had begun to appear less spartan lately. It boasted a relatively new electronic typewriter, a red leather upholstered chair behind the desk, a modern lamp, an icon in a wall niche—all acquired since Chris last took notice.

Grovkin smiled without amusement. "He is trying out his new car. He will be late."

"Yavlinsky has a new car?"

"A very fine new car. It is a Toyota with four doors. The color is green, like emerald. It is called Camry."

Harmon was silent, sipping his tea. He wondered how the director of the preserve, a bureaucrat far from Moscow and not very high on the scale of things in the new Russia, could afford a new Toyota Camry sedan.

8

CHRIS HARMON AND Alexander Grovkin sat in uncomfortable wooden chairs facing the preserve director's desk. Both men admired the sleek modern lamp on the desk ("Italian," the Russian boasted). They had already admired the emerald green Toyota sedan parked outside.

Vladimir Yavlinsky did not speak English, and Grovkin served as an interpreter whenever Chris Harmon met with the director. Chris had been disappointed when the man who had held the position during the prolonged negotiations over the joint research project was transferred on the eve of the American scientists' arrival in Far East Russia. Where his predecessor had been a biologist with impressive credentials, who had worked with the renowned Aleksei Volkov at the Institute of Evolutionary Morphology and Animal Ecology in Moscow, a division of the Soviet Academy of Science, Yavlinsky was a career *apparatchik* with little knowledge of or special interest in the animals of the preserve and the future of their habitat. ("He is administrator," Grovkin sneered.) More to the point, perhaps, he remained a member of the Communist Party. He always wore the same dark suit to work, festooned with the red lapel button identifying a member of the Party. His skin was pallid, his pinched features accented by unruly black eyebrows. He was a pale city dweller in a village of sun-weathered peasants. With a new chair, a new lamp, a new Camry, Chris thought.

"*Eta n'ilza,*" Yavlinsky said firmly when Alex Grovkin had translated Chris's request. "It is not possible."

"But we know the tiger was wounded," Chris protested.

"We can't leave her like that, or abandon her cubs if her wound is mortal. All I need, Director, is a small rescue party, two or three armed men—Grovkin has volunteered to be one of them. Once we locate the tiger, tracking with the radio transmitter in her collar, I assure you the operation will be brief. No more than a few days."

"We cannot spare the men for such a mission."

"But that's what we're here for," Chris argued, trying not to lose his temper. He had dealt with enough bureaucrats, academic and otherwise, to know better.

"That is not for you to decide."

"You don't understand. Those cubs are only three or four months old." Grovkin's hasty translation was like an echo. "They aren't mature enough to hunt for themselves or to defend themselves."

"Nature is cruel," the director said.

"Oh my God!"

Those words, with their incredulous tone, did not require translation. "You tell me I don't understand," Yavlinsky said. "I know perfectly well all I need to know about Siberian tigers, Dr. Harmon. They are *my* responsibility, not yours. But I also have other obligations. Is it not true that this tiger you supposedly saw shot was in Sector Five?"

"Yes. And there's no question about her being hit."

Yavlinsky waved off the protest. He produced a pack of Marlboros from the left-hand drawer of the desk, shook out a cigarette and lit it with a disposable Japanese lighter. He did not offer either of the men facing him a cigarette. "You are also aware, as I am certain Comrade Grovkin has told you, that Sector Five has been specifically designated off limits to all personnel."

"But not to poachers?"

"Being offensive will not advance your cause, Dr. Harmon." Yavlinsky pursed his lips to release a stream of smoke. Chris wondered where he had got the American cigarettes. From a sailor on his last trip to Vladivostok? Or from the same source that supplied Italian lamps and Japanese cars? "I see no need for further discussion."

"Look . . . I'm sorry. It's just that this is very important. I came to your country at the invitation of your government to study your Siberian tigers. You must understand how concerned I am when I witnessed the shooting of one of the tigers we have been studying. I'm a scientist, Director. Let me do the job I came here to do."

"Why were you in Sector Five, Doctor?"

"We were following the poachers. We'd seen them earlier, and then we heard a shot. It came from Sector Five. We had no choice but to go in after the poachers."

"On the contrary, you had the choice of obeying the specific directive I issued against such action. Comrade Grovkin will have his error called to the attention of his superiors and will be appropriately disciplined. You, on the other hand, are a visitor here, not subject to such penalties. I think we can agree, however, that your work here in the Primorskiy has come to an end."

Chris stared at him. He glanced at Grovkin, who squirmed in his hard wooden chair. Chris recognized that he was getting a glimpse into the inflexible Soviet bureaucracy as it had existed under the absolute and tyrannical power of the Communist Party and its officials in the repressive decades before Gorbachev and his reforms so dramatically altered the shape and future of the Soviet Empire. Conditions had changed in Russia and the other former Soviet republics, but *apparatchiks* like Yavlinsky had not changed, and many of them were still in the government, even still occupying the same roles. They had been stripped of much of their authority to express their potential for cruelty or vindictiveness—Yavlinsky would probably not dare to have Chris arrested and clapped in jail—but they were not powerless.

"My work has been funded through the end of the year," Chris pointed out. Grovkin appeared unhappy at having to translate the words. "Along with that of my Russian colleague, Gregory Krasikov."

"Comrade Krasikov has been ordered to report to Kedrovaya Pad Preserve," Yavlinsky replied with a small smile.

Chris was stunned. Another protected preserve in the district southwest of Vladivostok, Kedrovaya Pad was now the southernmost reach of the Siberian tiger's range that had once extended into China, Mongolia and Korea, and west into Siberia almost as far as Lake Baikal.

"Why wasn't I told?"

"It was not necessary that you be informed. The decision was not yours."

"But we were coordinating our findings, working together—"

"That will no longer be possible."

Chris stood so abruptly that his chair skittered across the floor. Yavlinsky flinched, rearing back in his new red leather chair. "My authority to work in the Sikhote-Alin preserve comes from the Russian Federation's Board for Nature Preserve Management, under the Ministry of Environmental Protection and Natural Resources. I believe they are also your superiors, Director."

Yavlinsky was unfazed. "You are, of course, free to appeal to the board. I can assure you it will do you no good."

"Don't be too sure! The Ministry of Environmental Protection is not so indifferent to American aid—or to our help in preserving Russia's ecosystems."

"We do not need your American handouts! Russia is for Russians. We will achieve our own goals without the help of you Americans, without you or your Jews or those who would betray our history."

Chilled, Chris recognized the xenophobic ultranationalism of such demagogues as the politician Vladimir Zhirinovsky, who were exploiting the new Russia's problems through appeals to old prejudices and to nostalgia for the past glories of the feared Soviet Empire.

"I'm going to Vladivostok," Chris said. "We'll see who's betraying the new Russia."

Yavlinsky was cool. "I am in charge of the Sikhote-Alin preserve, Doctor. But you will find that the prohibition against entering Sector Five comes from authority in our government higher than the Board for Nature Preserve Management . . . higher than the Ministry of Environmental Protection and Natural Resources."

"Why? Just tell me *why*. What's in Sector Five that you don't want anyone to see? What's going on?"

When Grovkin had finished translating, Yavlinsky seemed to debate with himself whether or not to reply. Finally he said, "An announcement will be made shortly in Vladivostok. You might as well know. An agreement has been reached between the Republic of Russia and the Republic of South Korea and the Sunsai Corporation of that country regarding a thirty-year logging contract to begin in the Primorskiy. Sector Five is the first area chosen for development."

"Development! My God, are you talking about clear-cutting in the heart of the tigers' habitat?"

"We have our priorities, Doctor. They are not necessarily the same as yours."

"When?"

"A delegation from Sunsai and the Korean government is arriving this week in Vladivostok to meet with Russian officials to conclude the agreement."

"A thirty-year logging contract? You'll destroy any chance the tigers have to survive!"

There was no need to translate the outrage in Chris's words. Sunsai was a major Korean corporation with divisions in auto manufacturing, electronics and publications. It did nothing in a small way. Its intrusion into the Sikhote-Alin Biosphere Preserve's ancient forests would be devastating.

"Russia is trying to survive!" Yavlinsky told him. "You live in a fantasy where everything in nature is perfect but we Russians must live in the real world. The Russian people are desperate. It is necessary to take difficult, even painful steps. We are a great and rich country, but it is time for us to become what we have been in our past, a Russia for Russians. Some sacrifices will have to be accepted."

"Like the sacrifices in the Gulag?"

Yavlinsky was on his feet. "Your work is finished here, Doctor! You will no longer be provided assistance or transportation into the preserve. If you attempt to enter Sector Five on your own, you will be arrested!"

Before Grovkin had finished translating, Chris was moving out of the office. He threw his reply over his shoulder. "I have evidence to show them in Vladivostok. We'll see if slaughtering the last tigers in Siberia is the policy of the new Russian republic!"

"Do you think Russian people care about animals when people are starving?" The shout that pursued Chris Harmon was Yavlinsky's, but the translating voice was that of his friend Alex Grovkin. It sounded like the voice of Russia. "You are a damn fool, Doctor. You will find out in Vladivostok!"

Storm clouds piled high above the mountains west of Terney, but Chris Harmon was unaware of them at first. He had calmed down enough by the time he got to the street to perceive that he had handled the confrontation with Vladimir Yavlinsky just about as badly as he could. The Russian was a small-minded, self-important bureaucrat, but instead of playing to his ego he had tried to make him seem unimportant.

Politics, he thought. As Grovkin said, everything was politics. But even if he had handled Yavlinsky more diplomatically—never his long suit—would it have made any difference? The proposed agreement with the Koreans was a major initiative—it had to reach high into the Russian government. Chris realized that his only hope was that Yavlinsky was overstating the case or exceeding his authority. The joint Russian-American project in the preserve had been approved in Moscow Central and down through the bureaucracy. There were dedicated conservationists in the Ministry of Environmental Protection and serving on the Board for Nature Preserve Management. *Someone* in authority could be persuaded at least to allow the rescue of a single tiger and her cubs. How could *that* impact the proposed contract with the Koreans?

They might not want to confront the situation, Chris thought. Yavlinsky was not the only Russian official with a sense of desperation. And at this crucial time, no one would want to play up the poaching problem or the environmental impact of clear-cutting in the preserve.

He at least had to try, Chris thought. He became aware of the damp cold cutting through his jacket and of the black clouds behind him filling half the sky. Would he be able to charter a flight from Plastun to Vladivostok? It was still early —he thought a bus left for Plastun at noon. There was no time to waste. Every hour the wounded tiger was abandoned decreased her chance to survive and put her cubs at greater risk. If he could catch a plane—if the weather didn't ground him—he could be in Vladivostok before nightfall.

He was not without resources. The Global Wildlife Federation had an office in Vladivostok, and Chris had a good friend there. He had also met officials from the Ministry of Environmental Protection on his arrival. He would make the simplest case to start with, deal with the logging catastrophe later. Get the ministry's officials to overrule Yavlinsky and allow him to enter Sector Five with a small rescue party. If the Russians and Koreans were concerned about negative press, would they want a poaching disaster on the eve of their conference? He hoped not.

In his anger his thoughts tumbled over each other. Check the bus schedule—hire a car if necessary to get to Plastun. Grab a few things from his room, his passport, the film . . .

The film.

Chris stopped in his tracks in front of the hotel. Was there more to Vladimir Yavlinsky's actions than he had revealed? What if the poachers had not simply happened into Sector Five? What if they had tracked Risa by tapping into her radio signal? What if someone had given them the radio frequencies? What if they were not ordinary poachers at all but commissioned hunters?

The questions led to a possible conclusion that left Chris shivering, and not with cold. That nothing was to interfere with the proposed logging activity. *That Sector Five was being cleared of animal presence.*

Deep in the forest the tiger lay on her side in the den she had found the previous afternoon. It was in an area of old growth and the woods were thick, filtering the morning sun. The forest floor was cool. The den remained lost in shadows.

Her cubs nursed at her swollen teats. Once she gave a deep

cough, a spasm of complaint, but the instinct to feed her young was stronger than her distress.

During the night she had licked steadily at her wound, which was high on her left shoulder, luckily within reach of her tongue. The bleeding had stopped, but not the pain. Flesh had been laid open, muscles torn, a fragment of bone in her shoulder shattered by the passage of the bullet. The wound was not lethal but it had left her front left leg useless. She was also weak from loss of blood and hungry. She had not eaten in thirty-six hours.

She could walk on three legs but she could not hunt.

Her cubs were not yet weaned. They were uncomprehending and voracious, ignoring her growls. Without food her milk would soon begin to dry up. Just under four months old, the young cats had already made clumsy attempts to imitate her skill in stalking and chasing down prey, but they were still ungainly, inexperienced, neither quick enough nor strong enough to bring down anything other than unwary rodents or other small animals.

Without her they would soon starve.

From far off in the taiga the snarls of a ravening pack of red dogs erupted. A male tiger's answering roar shook the air. The forest trembled, and the cubs stirred uneasily.

The wounded tiger could no longer protect them.

It seemed only a matter of time.

PART TWO
VLADIVOSTOK

9

CHRIS HARMON HATED flying. He was one of those travelers who gripped the arms of his seat, white-knuckled, during the most routine takeoff in a jumbo jet. He hated even more going up in a small aircraft, more directly subject to the whims of weather and the weaknesses of those to whom he was entrusting his life. He knew his fear was irrational and he had overcome it sufficiently to do the considerable flying that his work demanded. But he rarely managed to relax while in the air.

The flight out of Plastun had to be one of the worst of his life. The plane, a Russian aircraft with a single high wing and propeller, was a relic. It resembled the *Spirit of St. Louis* in which Charles Lindbergh made the first solo nonstop flight across the Atlantic Ocean into the imagination of the world. The pilot, who recognized Chris from earlier trips, was the same genial entrepreneur who more than a year ago had offered him a supply of bear gallbladders at a price. The airstrip, which had visible potholes, was being swept by sheets of rain as the small plane rumbled down the runway, hesitated as if reluctant to release its grip on reality and slowly lifted into the air. To make matters worse, if that were possible, the pilot turned immediately eastward. Most of the flight to Vladivostok would be over the Sea of Japan. If the plane went down it would be into those cold gray waters.

The rain had begun during Chris's bus ride over the mountain from Terney to Plastun, where he had telephoned ahead to book a charter flight—bribing the pilot with a fee double his normal rate because of the ominous weather.

Chris knew that taking off in the face of those black storm clouds in a dubious small aircraft was near-suicidal. Peering through the rain-streaked side window at the green forest slipping away beneath him, he recalled the advice of a scientist friend who knew about his fear and was also an amateur pilot. "The big commercial airliners almost never go down, Chris. You're safer than you are on the ground. Small planes are different. They're mostly safe enough if the pilot knows what he's doing, maintains his aircraft and doesn't do anything really stupid—like taking off in bad weather. Almost all small plane crashes are from some kind of pilot error, starting with deliberately flying into trouble."

No choice this time, Chris told himself, leaning back in the seat and closing his eyes. Less than an hour to touchdown. He could handle it . . .

A gust of wind and a fist of rain caused the small plane to lift abruptly, then sink like a runaway elevator, leaving Chris's stomach behind. His eyes opened but there was nothing to see. They were inside the rain cloud.

Harrowing minutes passed, groping blindly through the thick blanket while the rain pelted the thin fuselage and hammered against the windows. Then, suddenly, they flew out of the cloud. The rain was behind them. More clouds all around, but blue sky above and off to the west. Chris sank back in his seat again, thinking of a line from a television commercial: *You're stupid, Chris, but you're lucky.* God let you get away with this one.

No choice. He was not going to abandon Risa and her cubs without making every effort to help them, but he couldn't do it alone. However willing he was to challenge Yavlinsky's edict, without transportation he couldn't go into the preserve on his own, even if a solo rescue attempt were feasible. He had to go over Yavlinsky's head, and flying as quickly as possible to Vladivostok was the only course open to him. At least there he could appeal to the preserve director's superiors in the bureau, try to bring as much pressure to bear as possible. A spooky plane ride was just part of the price.

Eyes closed, ears sensitive to the occasional hitch he heard in the drone of the aircraft's engine, hands locked on the arms of his seat, Chris forced himself to think of something else. Anything. Alex Grovkin. The Russian had caught him in his room just before he left Terney. "I am sorry, my friend." Grovkin's expression was sad, his eyes filled with that uniquely Russian melancholy.

"It's okay, Alexander Semyonovich. You need to keep your job. I don't think you're ready to take up brain surgery."

"That is true. I will learn what I can for you here, but . . ." Alex shrugged. He was a man, after all, who had been born while Stalin was still alive, drawing up his lists of the soon-to-be-dead. He had grown to adulthood under Khrushchev, Andropov, Brezhnev. *Demokratizatsiya* was still a novelty to him as it was to most of his countrymen, a marvel like a magician's trick. The bureaucracy was reality.

"Yavlinsky is making deals with the poachers?"

"There are such rumors. One never knows for certain."

"What do *you* know for sure, Alex?" Chris sensed that his friend knew more than he was saying.

"I know only that at his parties Yavlinsky serves caviar from the Caspian Sea and smoked salmon, that there are pastries to make the mouth water just to look at them. And all can be washed down with real Russian Kubanskaya vodka, which I have not seen in five years. Of course, I am not invited to his parties."

"Not to mention Toyota Camrys."

"And Italian desk lamps. Did you know that bulb in his lamp is made by GE? It is not Russian bulb that burns out in first week."

"Poaching in the Primorskiy is a profitable business if the bribes can be so large."

Grovkin shrugged. That went without saying.

"How many poachers are caught?"

"We do what we can . . . some of us. Those who are caught are fined, that is all. Or they disappear quickly, and pay no penalty." Grovkin smiled. "None are sent to the Gulag. That is only American propaganda."

"I wonder if higher officials on the Board for Nature Preserve Management know about Yavlinsky's new Toyota?"

Grovkin's smile broadened, the blue eyes snapping with anticipation. "It would be good to tell them of his sudden good fortune, I think."

"I agree." Chris felt a real affection for the burly game warden in his worn jacket and his thin leather boots. "Is there anything I can get for you in Vladi? Some Marlboros? New shoes?"

"Snickers," Grovkin said eagerly. His grin over mentioning the American candy bar turned shamefaced as he drew a folded sheet of paper from a pocket of his jacket. "I also have a short list, if you have time . . ."

Chris felt a change in the angle of the aircraft's flight as it began the long descent toward Vladivostok. Its path crossed over a finger of mountains that spilled down toward the rugged coastline. It would be landing in minutes. Takeoffs and landings were the worst times. To distract himself Chris fished Alex's list from his pocket and glanced down the scribbled column of items on the paper that had been torn from a small notepad. Halfway down the list, just after cigarettes and vodka, were three familiar items: *lingerie, chocolate biscuits, a tin of smoked sturgeon.* Chris had to smile in spite of his fear.

It was dusk and the city seemed to be wreathed in smoke. Smog or fog? Chris wondered. At this hour, in this fading light, more than ever Vladivostok resembled San Francisco, a dramatic series of steep crowded hills tumbling toward Golden Horn Bay. The impression faded a little as the aircraft flew lower. The Russian port city's setting was as dramatic as that of San Francisco, but this was a darker place, and the bay was crowded with merchant ships and a large portion of the Russian Pacific Fleet—huge battleships and aircraft carriers, cruisers, frigates and icebreakers. The latter, in active use, were better maintained than the other ships. With funds and manpower sharply reduced, the rest of Russia's Pacific Fleet was rusting in the bay.

Until a short time ago Vladivostok had been accessible even to Russian citizens only with a special permit. The harbor had been closed to Soviet citizens and outsiders alike, since it was not only the home of the Soviet Union's surface Pacific Fleet but also the base for the Soviet nuclear submarines that patrolled the Pacific and Arctic oceans. Now, though the submarine pens were still secured, both the city and the main harbor were wide open. Tour groups had begun to arrive by sea and air. For fifty dollars any curious visitor could take a tour of the bay in an open boat, passing under the very shadows of the hulking ships at anchor, shooting pictures at random, and with a guide to point out anything the visitor might miss . . .

Chris felt the impact as the plane's wheels touched down on the runway at Vladivostok Airport. His death grip on the arms of his seat slackened. He blew out a long breath, his cheeks puffing out. Live to tell another day, he thought.

"Taksi!"

A vintage Lada jumped forward and stopped in front of Chris Harmon. It was a faded black with a sheen of rust on the roof, and its upholstery was taped together here and there with gray duct tape. The driver was a small wiry man with a curly gray beard, a big nose and a black visored cap. Because the interior light did not work Chris could not see the driver's eyes clearly.

"Kuda vew hatitya papahst?"

"Ulitsa Naberezhnay 10," Chris said. "Hotel Vladivostok."

"Da." Without hesitation the Lada shot away from the curb into the flow of traffic. Chris heard a horn and a shout. The driver glanced over his shoulder. *"Vwe Amirikanits?"*

"Da."

"You are wondering how I know?" the driver asked cheerfully in English.

"A little."

"You speak Russian like an American. All Americans speak Russian like Americans."

"Your English is very good." Chris was constantly surprised by the number of ordinary Russians who spoke English well, from an obscure game warden like Alexander Grovkin to a charter pilot-poacher based in Plastun to a grizzled cabdriver in Vladivostok.

"It is a simple language, English, compared to Russian. The

Russian language is like Russian people, devious and many-layered, is it not so?"

Chris laughed. "You don't speak either language like a taxi driver."

The bearded man shrugged, talking over his shoulder as he drove. He drove as aggressively as any New York cabbie, constantly switching lanes, gunning for an opening as he cut in and out of the steady stream of traffic speeding along the wide boulevard toward the heart of the city. His name was Mikhail Vsevolodovich Fyodorov, and he was an electrical engineer with a degree from the University of Minsk. He was Byelorussian. Like most of his people, he had fought with the Red Army against the Nazi invaders. Byelorussia was the gateway between western Europe and Moscow, the road would-be conquerors had followed from Napoleon Bonaparte to Adolf Hitler. One of every four people in his republic had died in the battles with the German army, Fyodorov said, including all of his family.

"Why aren't you working as an engineer?" Chris asked.

"There is not enough work for an electrical engineer in Russia."

"With all the rebuilding, I would think—"

"There is no money to pay us." The driver shrugged, expertly changing lanes and cutting off a Volga truck that blasted him with its horn. "So I am taxi driver, and I fix wiring in hotels and restaurants where tourists go and there is money to pay me."

The traffic was surprisingly heavy—Polish Fiats, German Trabants, Russian-manufactured Moskvitches and Zhigulis, and a glut of Toyotas, Nissans and Hyundais. Few American cars, Chris noted. The volume of traffic seemed to suggest greater prosperity than one felt in other major Russian cities, but otherwise the approach to the city was unpromising. It was now dark, and the city with its steep crowded hills and its glimpses of the crowded bay off to the right once again suggested San Francisco. But that illusion could not survive the dark streets with their broken streetlights, the grimy, dirt-encrusted buildings with peeling paint so old the colors were indistinguishable, the broken sidewalks and potholes, or the march of ubiquitous Soviet apartment buildings clumped across the hills like a child's building blocks, as featureless and soulless as a generation of high-rise office buildings in some American cities.

On his arrival from the States nearly two years ago Chris had spent little time in Vladivostok. His impression then of the city of a million people, despite its spectacular setting, had been of a grim, unwelcoming place, dominated by the presence of Russia's Pacific Fleet in the harbor. The eyes of its citizens had been wary as they hurried along the street or stood numbly in long shuffling lines. For his part, Chris had been too anxious to explore the province's protected preserves —so long closed to the Western world—to play tourist. Later, his occasional overnight forays to the city had been driven by immediate needs for supplies, formal contacts with Russia's Ministry of Environmental Protection and Natural Resources, and informal ones with the Global Wildlife Federation and Britain's Tiger Trust, both of which had offices there. Each time Chris had returned to Terney as quickly as possible.

"*Bozke!*" Fyodorov cursed.

"What's wrong?" Out of the corner of his eye Chris saw a flashing red light behind them. A police car drew alongside and waved the Lada over.

The angry exchange in Russian was too rapid for Chris to follow. It ended with Fyodorov handing the traffic policeman a fistful of rubles. The official car then pulled away and the taxi driver lurched back into the stream of traffic with an angry clashing of gears.

"What was that about?"

"Money! They're as bad as the mafia with their payoffs. You know what we call our traffic police? Milkmen! They milk us of our money."

"What did he stop you for?"

"Nothing! This is Russia, even if Moscow is six thousand miles away. They do not need a reason to pull you over, except that they must do the shopping for tomorrow's dinner.

It's the poor taking from the poor. Not like in America, eh? There it is the rich who take from the poor."

Chris had to laugh. "That's Russian propaganda."

"Maybe so."

"Is that an everyday part of doing business? I mean, do the police all take bribes?"

The driver shrugged, as if the question were irrelevant. "The police must also eat. And the militia, they have their hands full with the mafia."

Harmon had been struck before by Russians' matter-of-fact acceptance of official corruption. Seventy years of Communist Party rule had left a legacy of cynicism that would not easily be changed.

"Are things very bad here?"

"What is bad? This is Russia. There is not enough work. The people feel they can do nothing, they have no faith in their leaders. They see no future, they can only live day to day." The driver shrugged. He floored the accelerator to beat a changing traffic light, heedless of his recent payoff for an imaginary violation. "But there is food in Vladi, if you have a little money and coupons. You can find cigarettes and vodka and American bluejeans. We have artists, too, and good music. It is not such a bad place. Of course, it used to be more lively. We still have sailors but not so many as before. Our ships rust down there in the harbor."

On impulse Chris said, "In America, if I wanted to find something in a city I didn't know, I'd ask a taxi driver."

The Russian's eyes studied Chris in the rearview mirror. "A driver must know his city well."

Chris leaned forward, arms resting on the back of the front seat. "I'm not looking for a woman, but you mentioned the mafia gangs. I take it they control the black markets here in Vladi?"

Fyodorov laughed. "Who told you such a thing?"

"If I wanted to go to such a market, could you take me there? Not tonight—I have other things to do. Tomorrow?"

The dark eyes continued to study Chris in the mirror. "It's possible."

"How can I get hold of you?"

The driver scribbled a number on the back of a small business card and handed it over his shoulder while he drove one-handed into the center of the city. "Leave a message," he said. "Say that you have some wiring you want fixed."

The Hotel Vladivostok was one of the ornate, turn-of-the-century buildings that gave the heart of Vladivostok an air of faded grandeur. The brick walls and turrets badly needed cleaning, but the outside woodwork—elaborate window arches, frets and cornices—was freshly painted, perhaps in hopeful anticipation of an influx of Western tourists. Inside, the lobby was grand in size with gilded columns and vaulted ceilings, but the carpeting was threadbare and there were cracks in the exposed marble floors and counters. Chris's room turned out to be high-ceilinged and spacious with over-sized, heavy furnishings, a telephone, a small black-and-white television set and a private tiled bath large enough to contain a billiard table. He threw his overnight bag on the bed and stared out of the tall window at a view of steep hills and a corner of the bay. One dark cruiser tilted slightly, as if it were sinking into the black waters. He placed telephone calls to the Ministry of Environmental Protection and the Global Wildlife Federation. Both offices were closed for the night.

Restless, Chris left his room and the hotel. In strange cities where his work had taken him around the globe he always found walking the streets the best way to get his bearings and a feel for the city. At this early evening hour a surprising number of people strolled along the sidewalks or darted across the streets with a careless disregard of traffic. The variety of faces painted a mural of the former Soviet peoples. Fair-skinned Ukrainians looking like transplanted Poles. Russians with their broad Slavic features, high cheekbones and oval faces. Darker-skinned, sloe-eyed Armenians. Kirgiz, Tatars and Uzbeks, slant-eyed Kazakhs and Buryats. There were Western European faces, too, even a few that might have been American, as well as troops of Japanese, Chinese and Koreans. The city was as much a melting pot as New York or Los Angeles, Chris thought. The perception seemed to offer an exciting promise at odds with the gloomy picture Chris had got from the taxi driver.

At an intersection Chris paused and noted the young men in black jackets leaning against walls, watching the passing traffic or staring at pedestrians. Men like them had hung around the hotel's parking lot or lounged in heated cars, smoking cigarettes and apparently doing nothing but killing time. "Mafia," the taxi driver had muttered to Chris when he dropped him off in front of the hotel. "You don't have to look for them, they will find you. But they won't bother you if you don't give them a reason."

Passing a busy restaurant that resembled a McDonald's, called Magic Burger, Chris caught the tempting aroma of grilled meat. He was suddenly hungry, realizing that he hadn't eaten since morning, and then only a roll with his coffee. Ignoring the American-style hamburger place, he passed a small cafe with a half-dozen tables, white tablecloths, candles in jars. He stepped inside. Only a few diners sat at isolated tables but the atmosphere was warm, the smell of cabbage soup overpowering. Chris ate soup and a small, meatless cheese-and-potato pie. Comfort food in any country.

When he went back outside he felt full-bellied and warm. The city seemed more upbeat, the lights on the hills brighter, less like distant stars glittering in a great black void.

Near the hotel he turned around twice, sensing that he was being watched, but he saw nothing out of the ordinary. At the entrance he looked back once more. A blocky figure in a gray suit, square blunt Slavic face, dark felt hat, turned away to study a window display. He didn't look like someone who would be interested in ladies' handbags, Chris thought. He was certain he had seen the man before, once on the street and again when he emerged from the restaurant.

He walked into the spacious lobby, shrugging off the feeling as borrowed Russian paranoia. Who would be following him along Naberezhnaya on his first night in Vladivostok?

Who even knew he was there?

*   *   *

Leonid Brunovsky reported to his principal by phone. It rang for a long time before it was answered, the voice brusque. "What is it?"

"I am sorry to disturb you, Comrade Chairman, but you wished me to report—"

"Yes, yes, get on with it."

Brunovsky wondered if Boris Provalev was alone or with one of his young companions, perhaps the pretty young woman who read the evening news on the local television station.

"The American has returned to his hotel for the night."

"Alone?"

"Yes. He spoke to no one while he was out. He had dinner, that is all, and walked."

"I want to know everything he does. Where is . . . the Collector?" Lemenov did not want his name used even in private conversations. "Is he with you?"

"No." Brunovsky refrained from saying that Sergei Lemenov would not be found trailing along the street after an insignificant American scientist or standing outside in the shadows while the subject ate hot soup in a restaurant. "He arrives in Vladivostok on the morning flight."

"Nothing is to be done about the American without my specific approval, is that clear?" The chairman's tone was heavy with the weight of one forever burdened by the actions of fools who could not follow orders.

"It is perfectly clear, Comrade Chairman."

"For your sake, I hope so, Leonid Andreyevich. If anything happens, call me."

In his room Chris switched on the little black-and-white television set. A news broadcast was in progress, anchored by a pretty young woman. Chris could follow only fragments of the rapid Russian words but the pictures hardly needed them. A clash between Russia and Ukrainia over warships in the Black Sea. Food strikes in Kazakhstan. Bloody ethnic clashes in Armenia. Civil war in Azerbaijan. Angry demonstrations in front of the Russian White House in Moscow. A railroad strike at Sverdlovsk in the Urals, and a shoot-out between mafia gangsters and militiamen at Omak in Siberia. Locally, protests at the shutting down of a chemical plant here in Vladivostok.

It was a portrait of a society in chaos, but Chris wondered if the total picture was accurate. You might draw the same impression of the United States from some American television where the tabloid mentality had virtually taken over the news, exaggerating trivial events, manufacturing crises, portraying a land drowning in crime, corruption and violence.

You live in a fantasy, Vladimir Yavlinsky had accused him. *Do you think Russian people care about animals when people are starving? You are a fool!*

Maybe so, Chris thought, but people had to find an accommodation with the rest of nature. It wasn't us versus them . . . it was us *and* them.

He stared out again at the dark hills and the blocks of prefabricated apartments with their blank faces, housing their thousands of unknown lives. At the moment he shared the emptiness of someone no one waits for at nightfall, no one worries whether he will come safely home.

10

KENNETH LANGERT WAS an animal activist in charge of the Far East office of the Global Wildlife Federation. In the past he had worked as a field investigator for CITES, the Convention on International Trade in Endangered Species, and for the cat specialist group at IUCN, the International Union for the Conservation of Nature, based in Geneva. Chris Harmon had first come to know him as a classmate and touch-football rival at Boston College. Both had gone on to graduate studies in biology, Langert at Harvard, Chris at the University of Michigan. Ken's family was Old Money, Chris had heard at college, but you would never have known it. Later, his family connections had groomed Langert for a fast climb up the corporate ladder with McKesson's drug research division, but he chucked it after three years. "I'm too lazy to be a vice-president," was all he would say of the experience. They had gone their separate ways but met again ten years later when both were investigating the work of India's Tiger Crisis Committee in the early 1990s. Sharing a mutual concern for the survival of the big cats, they had stayed in touch.

The GWF office in Vladivostok, which consisted entirely of Langert and two clerical assistants, was on the corner of Aleutskaya and Svetlanskaya Streets, the city's main boulevard, across from the stately facade of the GUM department store—built early in the century by German traders, Langert said. Langert seemed hardly to have changed since his college days. He still wore his wavy black hair shoulder length, dressed in denim shirts and jeans and affected a jaded demeanor, with lazy eyes and a perpetually ironic lift at one corner of his mouth. The appearance of indolence was deceptive.

"Let's go out and get some coffee," Langert suggested after they exchanged warm greetings. "My secretary hasn't got the hang of brewing decent coffee yet. She's a Yakut, and anything without whale blubber is a mystery to her. Are you hungry?"

"I just had breakfast."

"Well, I didn't."

They walked along busy Svetlanskaya toward the Central Square. The sky was as gray as smoke, the wind cold and blustering, whipping the beech trees in front of GUM's and scattering leaves along the sidewalks. The threat of more rain persisted. Ahead of them Chris recognized the anachronistic Bolshevik monument dedicated to the Fighters for Soviet Power in the Far East—1917–1922. It was one of the few revolutionary monuments still visible in the city. Such legacies of Communist rule were being torn down all across the former Soviet republics, just as the streets were being renamed. Svetlanskaya had formerly been Lenin Street; Aleutskaya had been 25th of October Street. The years bracketed on the monument in the Central Square were significant. During the revolution Vladivostok had been a czarist holdout. After the first bloody clashes in St. Petersburg it had taken over five years of fighting before the Bolsheviks were able to take control of this strategic outpost in the Far East. Those years of civil war and the harsh reprisals that followed had never been forgotten.

Change was in the air. Street traffic was busy. Smartly dressed young women in short skirts and leather jackets walked briskly along the sidewalks. They would not have been out of place in Paris or London, Chris thought. A flock of Japanese tourists, armed with cameras, followed a tour guide toward the square. Colorful kiosks stood at every corner, jammed with goods—including the ubiquitous Marlboros and Snickers candy bars. Chris made a mental note to stop later to pick up some of the items on Alex Grovkin's shopping list. There were also street vendors, some of them with only a few household items to sell, a doll or articles of apparel. Such *tolkuchki,* or "push markets," had become a commonplace in major Russian cities since selling goods on the street had been declared legal by President Yeltsin's government.

One image was more disturbing. Some of the same breed of young men in black leather jackets Chris had seen near the hotel the night before hung around the Central Square this morning, chain-smoking cigarettes and turning their flat-eyed stares at vendors and pedestrians with the same predatory appraisal. "Mafia?" Chris murmured, recalling his taxi driver's description.

"They're all over Russia," Langert confirmed in a low aside. "Chechen mafia—they're the dark, beetle-browed ones built like gorillas . . . Ukrainian mafia, even Chinese gangs. We have them all in Vladi, though I understand Moscow is worse. The biggest difference here is the Asians. Chinese and Korean prostitutes flock here the way would-be movie starlets used to head for Hollywood."

"The mafia gangs control prostitution?"

"Drugs, prostitution, the black markets, you name it. The Chinese gangs control drugs and prostitution because they have the pipeline to the sources in China and Southeast Asia. The Chechens are heavily into the black markets and extortion."

"Extortion?"

"Protection rackets. You want to stay in business, you don't want a stink bomb in your restaurant or your waiter's legs broken, you pay for protection."

"Like the old days on the New York waterfront."

"Not so old."

Chris shook his head. "I never heard of the Chechens before the last couple of years."

"They're one of the Soviet Union's sins come home to roost. Stalin, when he wasn't shipping any suspected opposition to the gulags, had other ways of getting rid of real or imagined troublemakers. He accused the Kalmuks and the Crimean Tatars of collaborating with the Nazis, and they were exiled from the Crimea to Central Asia. The whole population of the state of Checheno-Ingush—that's Chechnyes now—was deported en masse to Siberia. The Chechens weren't even given time or the opportunity to take their personal possessions. After they were gone, Stalin used the same trumped-up charge of Nazi collaboration to seize their lands and goods. Now, since the collapse of the Soviet Union, the Chechens have drifted back from exile. They hate all Russians, and it's like they're exacting vengeance for what Stalin did to them by turning loose crime and corruption. That's also why they fought so damned hard in Chechnya when Boris Yeltsin tried to put down their rebellion this past year."

"Vladivostok is a long way for them to reach out."

"They go where the money is. Vladi is going to be a major trading center for all the Pacific Rim, Chris. Korea, Japan, China, Taiwan . . . they're all on our doorstep."

Langert led them to a small cafe with its own bakery. The smell of fresh-baked bread and rolls revived Chris's appetite. There was a line for bread to take out, but they found a small table inside the cafe in a corner. A couple of the leather jackets stared at them from a nearby table. They were burly men with broad, flat-featured faces and blank eyes. Chris wondered if they were Chechens. They probably spotted him and Ken Langert as Americans in an instant, he thought.

The coffee was strong, black and slightly bitter. The roll Langert ordered for him was still warm, crusty on the outside, soft and delicious inside.

Langert studied Chris. "You heard from Nancy?" he asked.

"No. Not since . . . a little after Christmas."

"You okay?"

"I'll survive. Anyway, it's not like she didn't warn me."

"People like you and me, running around the world after lost causes, we should never get married. Maybe when we finally go home and buy the La-Z-Boy recliner and put our feet up, but not before."

Chris stared at his coffee cup. Was Ken's description accurate? Chaser of lost causes? The leather jackets left the cafe after staring at the two Americans for some ten minutes. Outside, the leaves continued to skitter along Svetlanskaya Street. Hurrying pedestrians held their coat collars tight around their necks and bent their heads into the wind. Some of the street peddlers were packing up their meager offerings and shuffling away. To change the subject, and also because he felt less constrained now that he was no longer under that glowering mafia scrutiny, Chris brought the conversation back to the criminal gangs. He recalled a story in *Pravda* claiming that organized mobs had grown so powerful they could threaten the government itself. "It's like they sprang up overnight," he observed.

"Well, so did the Russian democracy and the free-market economy. They used to say there was no crime in the Soviet Union, unlike decadent America. The KGB took care of that. Soviet socialism was supposedly the perfect society. The truth was the state's brutality was accepted as the norm, and the corruption that riddled the system was kept out of sight. It was official, you might say. It was only freelance crime that was crushed. Well, all that's changed. Now the old republics are beginning to discover one of the less attractive fruits of a free economy: big-city crime. Organized crime." Having finished his roll, Langert lit a cigarette without hesitation. No Smoking sections had not yet found their way to Russia. "It's bad enough here for you to be careful. The streets are okay in the daytime, and the main thoroughfares are safe enough at night if you use common sense. Just don't make yourself a target."

"What about the black markets?"

"The day markets are more or less open. No one pretends they're not there. They're a lot like flea markets in London or Paris. That's where you can find cigarettes and imported liquors, bluejeans, American music tapes, foodstuffs that aren't available in the stores, lightbulbs, toasters, everyday things. I can take you to one of them if you want."

"If I wanted medical supplies, is that where I'd go?"

"Now you're talking about the night markets. They're out of the way, they're a hundred percent mafia-run and they're bad news. Stay away from them, Chris. If you need something let me know and I'll find someone to get it for you."

"I've always wanted to go to a mafia flea market." Chris grinned. "What else would I find there?"

Langert shrugged. "Besides medicines? Illegal drugs of all kinds. Big ticket items like stolen cars, some of them with new engine numbers, television sets, VCRs. Weapons—including military weapons. There are rumors the army itself is in the business. There are also money dealers who'll trade you pounds, marks or dollars for your rubles."

"They're bankers, too?"

"That's right. And the markets deal only in cash, which means you have to go with your pockets full. If you went you'd be doing just what I warned you about, making yourself a target. Forget it, Chris."

"Is that also where a buyer would find some bear gallbladders, or tiger meat and bones?"

Langert nodded. "Poachers' paradise. Promise me you'll leave those markets alone. We need you doing what you're good at, Chris . . . which isn't taking on Chechen thugs. Which brings us to what brought you to Vladi this trip. Is this just a social call or is something special on your mind?

"Something's happened on the preserve."

"I guessed as much. I figured you might like to get out of the office somewhere we could talk. Your phone message sounded urgent and you've got that crusading look in your eye."

Chris described the shooting incident in the Sikhote-Alin preserve, his attempt to raise a rescue effort for the wounded tiger and her cubs, and Yavlinsky's refusal, citing the negotiations with the South Koreans over logging in part of the preserve. "Maybe you can fill me in on this Korean deal, Ken. You know about it? Opening up the preserve to logging?"

"We know." Langert's tone was bitter. "All the wildlife agencies are upset. We're fighting it but we're not being heard, at least not here where it matters right now."

"Yavlinsky said something about a delegation from Sunsai coming here this week."

"Tomorrow. Your timing was always good, Chris. South Korean government officials and representatives from Sunsai fly in tomorrow, and some officials of Russia's trade bureau are supposed to arrive in Vladivostok on Friday. Maybe one of the Sunsai people will want to swing an ax at the first tree, sort of like breaking a champagne bottle to launch a ship."

"Is there any way to stop it?"

Langert studied him. "You have to remember, Chris, this country's in a bad way economically. Their leaders are desperate to bring in revenue. They're making deals for Siberian gold and oil, selling off some of the country's prime resources. To many of them the taiga is just another resource. And Japan and Korea will buy all the logs they can talk the Russians into selling."

"They don't have to do it in a protected tiger preserve!"

"You know that and I know that but we're talking politics here. We're talking about a very shaky government and a people so frustrated they're starting to talk about the good old days under the Communist dictators. Memories are short, Chris, especially when you're hungry."

"We're also talking about the extinction of a whole species. Do you have up-to-date figures on how many tigers were killed in the Primorskiy in the last year?"

"In the whole province?" Langert slowly uncoiled his long legs, dropping his languid air. "Between eighty and a hundred."

"And we started the year with less than three hundred."

"That's right. Outside of zoos, that's the entire world population of Siberian tigers."

Neither man had to be reminded of the significance of the numbers. Experts had estimated that if the entire Siberian tiger population in the taiga dropped below one hundred and twenty its extinction was inevitable. Nothing would save it. And that doomsday figure was drawing close. Runaway poaching and shrinking the tigers' habitat went hand in hand. The Siberian tiger now had eight hundred miles of evergreen forest to roam from one end of the Primorskiy province to the other, but as its territory shrank and the forest became more crowded, the threat to the remaining population increased proportionately. Logging in the protected preserves meant more people moving in, new roads being built that would provide easier-than-ever access for poachers to get in and out. And with winter coming on, the deep snows would make it easy for poachers to track tigers in the forest . . .

"Who's behind it? Selling off part of the Sikhote-Alin preserve, I mean?"

"A better question might be what Russian politician could be against it right now. The word I hear is that one of the rising local stars may be pushing the right buttons, a guy named Boris Provalev."

"Who is he?"

"He's a deputy chairman of that extremist Vladimir Zhirinovsky's party, the LDPR. Got elected to Parliament as a so-called Liberal Democrat for this district in the last elections when Zhirinovsky scared the hell out of the reformers by grabbing twenty-five percent of the vote." Langert sniffed as if smelling something bad. "Provalev's like Zhirinovsky, he's neither liberal nor democratic—but he is effective. He tunes in to what people want to hear. A hard-line Communist yesterday, a radical nationalist today. And he's ambitious. Some people say he doesn't plan on staying long in Zhirinovsky's shadow. Here in the Primorskiy province, he's the real power."

"You wouldn't expect someone like that to be eager to give away Russia's resources, or to cozy up to South Korea."

"No, but who would have believed they'd all be calling themselves capitalists?"

"Any way of getting to him? If he's an ultranationalist, how about appealing to national pride in the Siberian tiger?"

"Forget it, Chris. You're talking about a mind as open to persuasion as Stalin's. He's an opportunist, of course, but that's what this logging contract is. Opportunity knocking."

Chris was silent. What was left of his coffee was cold. He felt cold inside. "I'm seeing someone over at the Ministry of Environmental Protection. I was surprised—they've always been open and supportive but today I had trouble even getting an appointment. I made some noise about the president's special interest in ecological matters."

"Who are you seeing?"

"His name is Nikolai Likhachiev. Know him?"

Langert sighed. "We're not drinking buddies but I've met him. Unfortunately he's one of Boris Provalev's new appointees—I told you he's starting to call the shots here in the Far East. Likhachiev's a career *apparatchik,* and that's your problem. Likhachiev will say the right things but he's not going to stick his neck out. There's a lot of pressure over this Korean contract. You have the South Koreans flying in here with all kinds of hoopla, Provalev himself preening for the picture taking and the TV bites, someone from Moscow coming to give the government's stamp of approval . . . there's too much momentum building to stop it now."

"Maybe all that buildup is an attack point. They wouldn't want to look bad with the whole world watching,"

"Just how do you plan on pulling that off, old buddy?"

"Suppose I could give you a photo no one could ignore . . . one you could feature in that *Global Alert* bulletin you put out . . . one you could offer to the other wildlife groups and maybe even sell to newspapers and magazines around the world."

"Elvis is in the Primorskiy?"

"I'm not kidding. What about a photo of that Siberian tiger leaping into the air when she was hit?"

Langert's lazy eyes hardened. "I'd like to see it."

"I don't know exactly what I have yet, only that I had my shutter clicking when it happened. I left the film at a photo shop on my way over this morning. I should have a set of pictures for you later this afternoon. I'll either send them over or bring them myself. Are you going to be in your office?"

"I'll stay until I get those pictures. I'll alert some of the other wildlife agencies. I'm not saying we can stop a runaway train with a photograph, but we can make some politicians squirm. That's always a worthwhile goal."

11

THE MINISTRY OF Environmental Protection and Natural Resources shared offices with other government agencies in a gloomy building on Vorotsky Prospect facing an empty square. The center of the square was new cement, and Chris Harmon wondered if a revolutionary monument had recently been leveled and paved over. Inside the building were the cavernous spaces of a Communist-style official structure but also clear evidence of a shrinking budget. The corridors were poorly lit, the walls badly in need of paint. There was no central heating. A number of offices were empty, and the *apparatchiks* Chris saw at their littered desks or tapping listlessly on manual typewriters appeared as cheerless as their surroundings.

Chris was met by a short buxom woman in her thirties with a round, pretty face, yellow braids and a sweet, shy smile. Her skin was an unblemished pink. She led him down a long dim corridor. Nikolai Likhachiev's office was at the end of the corridor on the left. It was in a corner of the building, with a ten-foot ceiling and space enough, Chris thought at first glance, for a bowling alley. Its front windows overlooked the square. The director, noting Chris's glance at the window, said something in Russian. The young woman translated. "It was a statue of Joseph Stalin," she said. "The square was called Stalinagrav."

"Now there is a better view."

Likhachiev chuckled, not waiting for the translation. He waved Chris toward a chair with worn upholstery that faced a massive oak desk, the most impressive thing in the office.

In the huge room, the spare furnishings looked as if they might have been items forgotten when a previous occupant moved out. In addition to the desk there was only the director's swivel chair, Chris's chair, two wooden file cabinets in one corner, a long table piled with stacks of environmental magazines and pamphlets, and a smaller table behind the desk holding an ancient Royal typewriter. It had its own small posture chair. The blond woman pulled it closer to Likhachiev's desk, facing both him and Chris, sitting primly with her knees together.

"You have met Ludmilla Ivanova Proskurina. I speak little English, so I talk in Russian. She will translate. Is okay? We do not want misunderstand."

"Fine."

Likhachiev was a compact man in his forties, made to seem smaller by the size of his desk and his office. His pale bureaucrat's complexion contrasted sharply with Chris's weathered tan. He had a politician's smile that did not touch his eyes.

Ludmilla Proskurina translated his words almost as soon as they left his mouth. "It is good to meet you, Dr. Harmon. I know of your work with our people in the preserve. What can I do for you? I am sorry I could not see you earlier, but this is a very busy time."

"Because of the conference with the South Koreans?"

The director stiffened, placed the tips of short fingers together in a delicate gesture. He had very small hands. "I am not prepared to discuss that proposed agreement, Doctor. It is beyond the province of this department. If that is the purpose of your visit—"

Chris interrupted the translator. "It is and it isn't. I've come to you for your help, Comrade Director. I was a witness to an attack on a Siberian tiger in the Sikhote-Alin Biosphere National Preserve two days ago. She was a mother with several cubs. She was shot at long range by a poacher."

"Appalling! You are right to protest."

"The point is, she was still alive. The poachers didn't risk going into the taiga after her. I proposed to the man in charge of your office in Terney to lead a rescue party. Even if the

tiger can't be rescued her cubs might still be saved. He refused—"

Likhachiev's small, busy hands waved off Chris's proposal
even before Ludmilla Proskurina finished translating. "No,
no, impossible. Your intentions are admirable, Dr. Harmon,
but what you suggest is out of the question."

"Why? It's been done before—some cubs were saved a couple of years ago after a similar incident. They were sent to
American zoos."

"Not all of them survived, as I recall. Anyway, this situation is quite different."

"How?"

"They are in a forbidden zone."

Chris was not really surprised. Likhachiev had said nothing about hearing from Vladimir Yavlinsky, but there was no
other way he could know where the tiger had been shot. The
director of the Sikhote-Alin preserve had wasted no time
warning his superiors. "Comrade Director, what I'm propos-
ing would not interfere in any way with whatever is planned
for Sector Five in the preserve. As I told Comrade Yavlinsky,
we could be in and out in a day or two. If the tiger is dead,
there will only be the matter of catching her cubs with nets.
Difficult, perhaps, but with a small rescue party it can be
done quickly."

"And if the tiger is not dead?"

"She could be tranquilized and treated—if necessary, even
transported to Terney for treatment."

Leave the Koreans and the logging contract out of it, Chris
had told himself on the way over from the Global Wildlife
Federation's office. Limit your request to a carefully defined
rescue effort. The bureau couldn't ignore the fate of a family
of tigers in the Primorskiy forest without making a mockery
of its function. Politics would only cloud the issue.

The Russian got up from behind his desk and walked over
to the front windows, appearing to ponder Chris's words. After a moment he turned abruptly. "We do not condone poaching, Dr. Harmon, as you know well. But I have received instructions from my own superiors in Moscow. Sector Five is
not to be entered for any reason."

"But surely this is an exception, no one could have anticipated—"

"Please do not put me in a difficult position." Ludmilla Proskurina looked flustered as she translated. "What is your American expression? My hands are tied."

Chris choked off saying what he felt. Becoming angry would only hurt his cause. Bureaucrats were alike the world over, jealous of their turf, however small, easily ruffled when their authority was questioned. In Russia this was even more true than usual. Whatever could be done—if anything—had to be accomplished through channels. This small fussy man with his soft pale hands that had never felt the massive weight of a Siberian tiger's head had the power to stop Chris in his tracks. Had he ever even seen a tiger? Chris could not risk asking the question.

Chris said, "You could appeal to your people in Moscow, Comrade Director. Explain the situation. They know the work we've been doing in the preserve. They've supported our research. They will listen to you."

Likhachiev appeared to adjust the heavy damask draperies framing the front windows. They didn't need adjusting, but Chris caught a faint whiff of dust when they were disturbed. The Russian returned to his chair behind the desk.

"I will be frank with you, Dr. Harmon. A conference affecting Sector Five is taking place in Vladivostok this week. That conference is the reason what you propose is impossible."

"I don't see why my rescue effort would interfere with the agreement between your people and the South Koreans. They don't even have to know about it."

Likhachiev glanced around the empty room as if someone might be listening. He leaned forward, lowering his voice. Russians, Chris had learned, were by nature secretive. Or maybe that was simply another characteristic of a people accustomed to three generations of strong-arm rule. "I will tell you this in confidence, Doctor. There is a matter of the utmost security involved. It has not yet been announced, but we are not talking of minor Korean officials or factory representatives coming to sign this important agreement. The chairman of the Primorskiy district council, who is also deputy to the

Russian Parliament from Vladivostok, has arranged this meeting. One might almost say, he has orchestrated it."

"Boris Provalev?"

Surprised, Likhachiev said, "You are aware of the chairman's work?"

"I've heard of him," Chris said dryly.

"What you may not have heard," the Russian said carefully, giving his anxious translator time to absorb his words, "is that the representative of the Sunsai Corporation who is to attend the conference, Chang Pyon, is that corporation's highest-ranking officer. And the South Korean government will be represented by none other than Kim Su, that country's prime minister himself. It is an historic occasion. It is Su's first trip to Russian soil. Chairman Provalev will also be joined by important officials of our government from Moscow. You must understand that nothing can be permitted to jeopardize the conference or impede the proposed agreement."

Chris heard a slight tremor in Ludmilla Proskurina's voice as she spoke. Her features were composed—cheeks a little pinker than before?—and her eyes averted. The director noticed nothing, or if he heard the quaver attributed it to his assistant's nervousness. Did she have thoughts of her own? Chris wondered. Working in a bureau ostensibly dedicated to the protection and preservation of endangered habitat, was she shocked by the words she had to translate? There was no way to tell.

"You can't approve of that agreement!" Chris said, as if giving voice to the woman's imagined protest.

"It is not for me to approve or disapprove. I am sorry, Dr. Harmon, but Comrade Yavlinsky was quite correct in denying your request. I must concur in that decision."

"Comrade Yavlinsky is too concerned with his crates of good vodka and his new Toyota sedan to worry about the actions of poachers or the fate of tigers. I expected more from his superiors."

Likhachiev flushed. "I will not listen to such unsupported charges—"

"If you'll just ask your people in Moscow—"

"I will forward your request to my superiors." Likhachiev

stood up, fingertips braced on the top of his desk. His body language spoke more clearly than his words. The interview was over.

"Spasibo," Chris said shortly. Thanks for nothing.

12

He walked for an indeterminate time, hardly aware of his surroundings. The cold wind blew off the hills and scoured the canyon streets, matching his mood. The gray sky made the city with its dirt-encrusted buildings seem grimmer. There were fewer street vendors than before. After a time a fine drizzle began to fall and the day's chill seeped under his old London Fog raincoat. Finding himself in unfamiliar streets, Chris thought of hailing a taxi but none appeared. Just like New York taxis when it rains, he thought. He had been climbing, and glimpses of the bay below helped him to orient himself. He turned along a cobblestoned side street leading back toward Svetlanskaya Street and the Central Square.

Chris understood he had been given a bureaucratic brush-off. He doubted that Likhachiev intended to relay his message to Moscow, and even if he did, nothing would be done. The conference, he thought. Provincial council chairman Provalev had invested too much of his political capital in it. The coming of the South Koreans was taking on more significant proportions the more Chris heard about it.

The politicians and the government's beleaguered economists didn't want him or anyone else near Sector Five, Chris thought. Or tigers running loose. Well, he wasn't through. The more important the conference became, the more he had to hope that those behind it wouldn't want a dose of negative press.

He glanced at his watch. Two-thirty. His film had been promised for five o'clock. He hoped he wasn't counting too heavily on what his camera had recorded. Two and a half hours to wait . . .

He had been only semi-aware of the growl of a motorcycle behind him but had paid it no attention. He heard the hiss of its tires on the wet cobblestones. Suddenly he realized that the bike had been keeping pace with him. He started to turn, and the motorcycle accelerated toward him. He thought of Ken Langert's warning about straying away from busy streets, making himself a target. There was no one else on this narrow side street, as if everyone had suddenly taken cover . . .

The cycle, a black Suzuki, drew up by the curb next to him and the rider was quickly on the sidewalk. Chris took a step back, bracing himself. The biker turned toward him. He was slim, shorter than Chris, good shoulders but hardly a threatening figure. He swept off his shiny black helmet, shook his head. His blond hair was nearly shoulder length—

Not *his! Hers!*

Chris was assaulted by clear no-nonsense blue eyes. *"Gospodin* Harmon? I am sorry if I startled you."

"Who are you? I wasn't expecting . . ." Chris stammered. "How do you know who I am?"

"I have look for you. I thought you would have return to your hotel."

She was clearly Russian, no mistaking those Slavic cheekbones. Her English, in spite of the occasional missing verb endings, was fluent and almost without accent. Had they all learned English in Russian schools, preparing for the New World Order that never came? Slender figure encased in Guess jeans, black boots, a turtleneck sweater under a quilted blue jacket. Cheeks burnished to a lively color from the cold wind. The color was her own, Chris thought. She wore no makeup other than the shine of moisture from the rain.

"How could you be looking for me?" he said after a moment.

"I am a journalist. I write for *Izvestia.*"

"Izvestia?" Chris's skepticism was audible. "Here in Vladivostok?"

The woman smiled. It softened her features and made her,

for the first time, pretty. Under thirty, Chris judged, athletic enough to have caused him to step back when she got off her bike. "It is perhaps an exaggeration. For *Izvestia* I am what you call in America a . . . stringer? I am also freelance journalist. I have publish articles in *Rabotnitsa* and *Krestyanka* and many other Russian magazines. I think you have need for me."

"I'm afraid I don't understand." Belatedly, Chris was beginning to feel foolish over his momentary anxiety when the motorcycle slid alongside of him. Since when do slender pretty women on bikes make you jump out of your skin? he asked himself. Is that a sign of age?

"It is not so difficult." The journalist glanced along the street, which dropped steeply toward Svetlanskaya. Chris thought he recognized the thin spires on the cornices atop the three-story GUM department store in the distance. He wasn't lost, after all.

"I have friend who works in Ministry of Environmental Protection. Ludmilla Ivanova Proskurina is dedicated ecologist like you, Doctor. I believe you have met her?"

"She did the translating when I met the director."

"Comrade Likhachiev." The woman's mouth curled at one corner. It was, Chris thought, a very expressive mouth. Its softness, however, was not reflected in those blue eyes. They had examined Chris from head to toe, summing him up, not too impressed, he suspected. This was a young woman who apparently knew her own mind. There was nothing of Ludmilla Proskurina's shyness about her. "Russia has many such men. They are Party hacks, you understand?"

"It's an American expression," Chris said. "But you mean Communist Party, right?"

"Of course. Times have changed in my country but such men do not go away."

"What did your friend at the ministry tell you? I still don't know why you're following me."

"It is simple. I am looking for good story. You have story you would like to have told. Is it not so?"

Chris felt a nudge of excitement. He had been thinking only of somehow using the photographs he had taken in the taiga,

hoping that Ken Langert might be able to exploit them in his
Global Alert bulletins. Like most environmental publications,
however, Langert's messages were seen and heard mostly by
the already converted. A popular journalist, especially one
with potential access to Russia's leading newspapers and
magazines, was something else.

"I believe we can be useful to each other."

"Where can we talk?" Chris said.

"I've lost them," Leonid Brunovsky said.

"Try the next street—to the right."

"She deliberately tried to avoid us! You saw that for yourself, Sergei Gregorevich."

"Perhaps," the Collector said. "Perhaps she simply changed
her mind."

Brunovsky slammed the heel of his palm against the steering wheel in frustration.

"Be careful, Comrade . . . you will break the wheel. You
don't know your strength."

Brunovsky flushed. He didn't like being needled about his
weight-lifting and strength regime.

"Don't take offense, Leonid Andreyevich," Sergei Lemenov
said, amused. "Strength has its place. We may yet have good
use for yours."

Brunovsky downshifted, driving slowly. The Fiat had a
noisy transmission but its short, firm manual shift was comfortably familiar to the Russian driver. The little car was,
after all, the grandfather of the Russian Zhiguli, so everything about it was familiar. It even had lousy windshield wipers that smeared the glass without cleaning it. Russian cars
either had poor wipers or none at all since they were frequently stolen if you didn't remember to remove them at
night.

In a high-speed pursuit on an expressway the rented car
would have been ineffective, but it was ideal for the steep
hills and the warren of streets in this city. It was not as quick
and nimble as the woman's motorcycle, however, even with a
passenger clinging to the seat behind the cyclist. The woman

had made several quick turns, leaving the wide boulevards for narrow side streets, then, as if on impulse, doubling back on her route. By the time Brunovsky had duplicated her maneuvers without giving away the fact that he was tailing the bike, it had disappeared.

After a moment the Collector said, "Where did you and your comrades find all this weight-lifting equipment? I would not think such equipment would be easy to obtain these days, not even for our professional Olympic athletes."

"We didn't buy it or steal it," Brunovsky said proudly. "We built it."

For once Lemenov showed real surprise. "You built it? Out of what?"

Brunovsky grinned. "Out of a Russian tank. You would be surprised what materials can be found when you dismantle a tank . . . bars and steel beams, wheels and bearings, chains for your lifts, heavy-duty springs for resistance, even gas-powered lifters, braces, pulleys and all manner of parts to use as weights. It doesn't matter, Sergei Gregorevich, what is the shape of a weight, or whether it used to be part of a tank's track or a wheel housing, only how much it weighs."

"You astonish me."

Brunovsky was inordinately pleased. Compliments of any kind from the Collector were as rare as winter roses.

"Take us down toward the waterfront," Lemenov said. "She was working down that way, I think."

Brunovsky thought the likelihood of coming across the motorcycle again was remote but he said nothing. Count your blessings, he told himself. He had expected Sergei Lemenov to explode when the motorcycle eluded them. Instead Lemenov seemed merely thoughtful.

The Collector was curious about the woman. She had picked up the American not long after he left the Ministry of Environmental Protection and had followed him for a time before he became aware of her. Lemenov had been surprised when the American climbed onto the back of the bike. It seemed out of character. He was a scientist, a specialist in animal behavior with particular interest in the big cats, according to the file Lemenov had been given on him. Part of a

Russian-American joint research project in the Primorskiy. A serious amateur photographer and an ideal witness to the drama the Collector had staged . . . except that he had become a little too enterprising with his camera. That, too, had been a surprise. Lemenov did not appreciate that . . . there was no room in his line of work for surprises.

Who was the woman? Trim figure. One did not often see middle-aged Russian matrons on Suzuki motorcycles—young, then. Aware of being followed and clever enough to throw off her tail. What was her interest in Christopher Harmon?

After fifteen minutes Sergei Lemenov concluded that they would not be lucky enough to discover where the motorcycle and its two riders had gone. Could the woman simply have taken the American back to his hotel . . . or hers?

They drove slowly past the Seaman's Social Club, a hangout for sailors attached to the Russian Pacific Fleet and for merchant seamen visiting the port. A pair of sailors emerged. They stood quarreling near the entrance, both drunk. The Collector flipped his hand in a forward gesture. "Take me back to that camera shop. I'll wait there across the street. He is certain to be returning there for his photos."

"You're not going to—"

"Everything has been arranged. You need not concern yourself. I want you to find out who and what the woman is. You have the license number of her motorcycle. That should enable you to get the information. Meet me later at my hotel."

It was still raining when Brunovsky pulled up across the street from the camera shop and studio. They could see the proprietor inside. "You'll get wet, Sergei Gregorevich," Brunovsky said as the Collector opened the car door to step out.

Lemenov rewarded him with an ironic smile. "I won't shrink, Leonid Andreyevich."

The Seaman's Social Club had a long wooden bar, a small dance floor with tables placed around its oval, and more tables along the walls on three sides of the spacious room. It was large enough to accommodate the crew of a cruiser with tables to spare, Chris Harmon thought, but on this dreary, rainy afternoon it was almost deserted. A half-dozen seamen sat on stools scattered along the bar, and small groups were at three tables smoking and drinking. Chris and the Russian journalist faced each other across a small oak table layered with the accumulated smells and stains from years of spilled beer and vodka.

"Will you have something to drink, Miss . . . ?"

"Vodka is good when it is so chill . . . chilly. It warms the stomach."

Chris glanced around the room after giving the order. He was surprised that the journalist had chosen a seaman's bar, but this young woman was full of surprises. She had had him climb onto her motorcycle behind her, and during the short frantic ride she had taken several quick turns along side streets, skidding on the wet paving, then had darted along an alley and slid the bike neatly between huge trash containers.

"I did not wish us to be seen by . . . the wrong people," she said. "Sailors are more used to Americans. They think nothing of seeing us here."

"I think they're interested in you."

She had taken off her blue jacket. The knit gray turtleneck sweater defined her breasts and narrow waist. She was slim for a Russian woman. Did the sailors find her too skinny? he wondered. Not to judge by their glances this way. Chris might not have been there for all they cared . . .

"I don't know what to call you," he said.

"I am Yelina Vassilyeva Mashikova."

"That's a mouthful."

"I am called Lina. You have seen my name, perhaps, *Gospodin* Harmon? In one of our journals?"

"I'm afraid not. You don't have to call me *Gospodin* Harmon, by the way. Chris will do."

"Is that for Christopher?"

"Yes. How does one become a stringer for *Izvestia* way out here in the Far East? Do you come from here?"

Lina Mashikova explained that she had been born and raised in St. Petersburg—until recently called Leningrad but now returned to its proud origins. She had studied at the university there. She had wanted to become a poet but was not good enough. She had soon moved to Moscow, where there was more opportunity for a journalist.

"I'm surprised you didn't become a television anchor."

"An anchor? Oh, yes . . . a news announcer. Why do you say that?"

"Russian TV and American TV are alike . . . they favor pretty women as anchors. Problem is, you're actually a journalist."

"That is a problem?"

"In America it could be. Sometimes."

She was right about the vodka. Wet and chilled after his brief motorcycle ride, Chris felt the liquor burn all the way down to his stomach, where it left a puddle of warmth. It also eased the knot of anger left from his clash with the bureaucrat at the Ministry of Environmental Protection.

He felt the steady blue eyes watching him. No reaction to being called pretty. She was all business.

"So . . . you are a long way from home, Yelina Vassilyeva. How did you come to Vladivostok?"

"It was a story assignment . . . Christopher. One cannot always choose where to go."

"But you stayed?"

"For now. However, I am not the story." She smiled as if to soften the rebuke. He thought the blue eyes warmed slightly. "You are my story."

"Are you married?"

"I am . . . widow."

"I'm sorry, I didn't . . ."

"It is all right, you could not know. But we have other things to talk about, yes?" She took a good swallow of vodka and looked at him directly once more.

"Of course. How much did your friend Ludmilla Ivanova tell you?"

"She spoke of a tiger being shot by poachers. There was some talk about you having pictures of this. And you wish to rescue this tiger, yes?"

"Yes to both questions. I do have pictures, and I do want to take a rescue party into the preserve."

"What if she is dead?"

"If she is—and I'm not ready to accept that yet—her cubs are still alive. They won't be if I don't get in there soon."

"They cannot feed themselves?"

"They're too young."

She was silent a moment, as if weighing her government's official indifference to the fate of creatures who, however unique and beautiful they might be, were not a priority in a country facing chaos.

"But they are in restricted area, is it not so?"

"You're a journalist, Lina. Maybe you should ask yourself why that area is restricted. What is so important that we must abandon the animals we're supposed to be trying to save? What's in Sector Five that we're not supposed to see?"

"The director has explain that to you . . . important work is coming to the Primorskiy. If the contract is signed between the two countries, many people will be coming to the preserve where this logging is to begin. There must be no danger to them. You do not find this reasonable?"

"No," Chris said flatly. "There's more danger leaving a wounded cat in the wild. She's been attacked by humans. It doesn't matter that she didn't see the attacker, she knows they were there. She might have left humans alone before. She won't now, and for damned good reason."

"You feel this very strong . . ."

"Yes. Very strong."

"You think you have pictures? Of tiger being shot?"

"Yes . . . at least I hope so. I'll know in another hour or so. I'm having the film developed." He hesitated, uncertain whether to mention that he also hoped to have other photographs, those he had taken after swiveling the camera toward the marksman in the woods.

"I would like to see them. If they are good maybe I can see that they are publish."

"You could do that?"

"I can try. I must see them first."

Chris, who was not at all reluctant to see Lina Mashikova again, had an inspiration. "There's something else you might help me with. You must know what goes on in this city, any good journalist would. I'd like to go to one of the illegal black markets."

"The night markets?"

"Where I could see for myself what the poachers are selling."

"I am not sure . . ."

"You take me there and show me around and I'll bring along the photographs."

She surprised him by smiling suddenly. "It is still rain, Christopher. You enjoy your motorcycle ride so much?"

"Well . . ." The thought of a night ride on the bike along wet streets was not exactly appealing. "We can take a taxi. I have a friend who will take us. Is it a deal?"

"It is deal."

"How about meeting me for dinner? We can go to the market afterward." When she hesitated, Chris said, "I'm a stranger in town. You can choose a good restaurant."

She smiled. There remained something distancing in her eyes, but Chris felt that they had warmed a little.

"You stay at Hotel Vladivostock, yes?"

"Yes."

"I will meet you there at seven o'clock."

13

THIRTY MINUTES LATER, in another part of the city, Yelina Mashikova stood under a broad but thinly leafed maple tree in a small park. The tree offered little shelter from the drizzle. Wind and rain had caused most of the trees in the park to shed their leaves. *"Bare ruined choirs,"* she murmured to herself, *"where late the sweet birds sang."* Shakespeare must have visited Russia, she thought, must have watched winter come in St. Petersburg or Moscow. How else could he have described it so perfectly? No wonder so many scholars were reluctant to believe he had written all he did, doubting that one man could be so universal.

She watched the old man hunched inside his greatcoat in a store entry across the way. He had insisted that she delay. Still practicing his tradecraft, an anachronism in a world that had left him behind.

She thought of the American. He had reason to be watchful. Someone *had* been following him, though she was quite sure she had lost the tail before they went to the Seaman's Social Club. Who was so interested in Christopher Harmon? Was it his photographs?

An earnest man, she thought, passionate about his work, with that strange naivete about the world that Americans seemed to possess. Attractive, but . . .

The figure in the doorway glanced her way but she doubted that he could see her in the mist and shadows of the park. Anatoly Isaevich Bukanin was not really old. Mid-fifties, certainly not yet sixty, but he looked and acted like an old man. She remembered his vanity. He used to travel regularly outside the Soviet Union—he was KGB, after all—and he bought English tailored suits, Italian shirts, good Czechoslovakian shoes. His hair was thick and wavy, handsome even when it turned silvery gray. He was a fleshy man then, the result of good food and drink, and there was vanity even in the way he filled out his skin, in the full cheeks with their faint whiff of cologne. Now his clothes looked baggy—he had evidently lost weight. They also looked Russian, which meant serviceable rather than well-tailored. His hair was too long under the hat pulled straight to his ears—he needed a haircut. She wouldn't have been surprised if he had holes in the soles of his shoes.

Bukanin lit a cigarette from the burning stub of the one he was just finishing. He coughed. The coughing, which lasted for some time, interrupted the lighting of the second cigarette but did not deter him. Why was it that Russians continued to smoke so much when everyone knew it was bad for you? She was as guilty as Bukanin. Watching him light up made her long for a cigarette but she was not yet ready to reveal her presence.

What was it Tolstoy said? "To inhale on an empty stomach is a quintessentially Russian habit." Tolstoy, who knew everything there was to know about Russians. In that respect little had changed since his time. Which was to say, everything had changed but Russians were still Russians.

Conspirators, she thought.

The meanness of the day had cleared the streets and she was convinced that neither she nor Bukanin was being observed. She wondered at the former KGB agent's caution. How long had it been since anyone cared what he did, or what he knew?

She crossed the street, heedless of the fine cold drizzle. Bukanin drew himself up as she approached him. She saw pleasure bring his gray face alive. "Yelina! It's good to see you. I was beginning to think you had forgotten—"

She laughed. "I was just doing what you told me. Anyway, you can't believe I would forget, Anatoly. I was delayed. I had an interview for a story."

He embraced her in a clumsy bear hug. His greatcoat was

damp from the rain and smelled like wet wool. She had known him in Moscow, in that other life that seemed like a fairytale of long ago when Yuri was young and eager, excited about his career and their future. Anatoly Bukanin was a friend of Yuri's father. She suspected that it was Bukanin's influence through the KGB that had won Yuri his appointment to the *spetznaz,* the elite special forces unit he had so proudly gone off to Afghanistan with.

Bukanin took her to a nearby cafe that faced the park. There were outdoor tables, deserted because of the weather. They sat inside. Bukanin apparently had an arrangement with the waiter because he brought them tumblers of vodka while they were waiting for the hot tea they had ordered. You have to stop drinking so much during the day, Lina Mashikova thought. She offered Bukanin a Marlboro from her pack, which again caused his face to brighten. Seeing his eyes follow the pack to her pocket, she handed it to him.

"No, no, Yelinita, I couldn't—"

"You will offend me if you don't take them, Anatoly Isaevich."

He deeply inhaled the American tobacco. If the Americans had only known, Lina thought with irony, they could have conquered the world with their cigarettes and pantyhose. It had taken longer with their ideas.

"You look well, my dear."

"So do you, Anatoly."

He coughed. Waiting until the spasm had passed, he said, "You tell an old man beautiful lies. I am not sure if that is a kindness or a kind of torture."

"Come now, it can't be as bad as all that."

"Can't it?" She saw the slackness of his once plump cheeks. He was definitely thinner, adding to the bagginess of his Russian suit. Had he sold the English tailored suits? Were things really going that badly for him?

"I have read some of your stories, Yelinita. You are a good journalist. Yuri would be proud."

She said nothing. That was one trouble with seeing Bukanin. The reminders of Yuri never stopped.

"What did you want to see me about?" she asked.

"Is not wanting to see you enough? But I also have a story for you. It could be very important for you."

"I'm always interested in a good story."

Bukanin leaned forward over the table, as if afraid someone might hear them. The cafe was empty except for the waiter, who was reading a magazine with a brown paper cover. Pornography? she wondered. She dismissed him.

"I have a copy of the plans for the defense of the nuclear submarine station." He sat back, waiting for her reaction.

She was both startled and dismayed. What was he thinking of?

"Don't you see, Yelina Vassilyeva? Everything is opening up now, it's *perestroika* with a vengeance. We have tourists inspecting our ships in the harbor, American generals visiting our missile sites."

"But who would I sell such a story to? You are mad, Anatoly!"

"Everyone is doing it!" Bukanin said. "It is free enterprise. The Red Army is selling weapons to whoever will buy them. You could buy a Russian T-34 tank on the black market if you wished. There are no real secrets anymore, but the American newspapers and magazines covet them all the same. They will pay well for such a story even if the CIA will not."

"And I would pay you for the information, Uncle."

"But of course."

She had no doubt that Bukanin had the plans he was offering to sell. He was one of those older KGB agents, an official of the second rank, who had been caught in one of the post-Gorbachev purges. Or had he? One never knew for certain with the old secret police. To have been dismissed from the service was a classic cover role. Some of Bukanin's colleagues, she was sure, had gone underground, waiting for a coup to restore the good old days of repression. *(You are thinking like a reformer,* Lina thought.) Others were surely still serving with the reformed intelligence agencies.

She shook her head. What Bukanin was offering her would have meant instant death a few short years ago. Even to listen to the proposal would have irretrievably compromised her.

"I'm afraid it is not something I can use, Anatoly Isaevich, but I will see if there might be interest elsewhere in such a story. That is all I can do."

"That is all I can ask, Yelinita."

Bukanin's disappointment was transparent. What once had been vain, a little arrogant, was now a face that mirrored anxiety and desperation. What did old spies do when the Cold War ended? They became entrepreneurs, selling secrets wherever there was a market, even to their former enemies . . .

"I will try, Anatoly. But in the meantime perhaps you can help me with another story, the one I told you I was working on. Do you still belong to the Communist Party?"

Bukanin hesitated, as if revealing anything about himself was still troublesome for one who had devoted his career to the secret life. "Yes . . ."

"And you have many friends in the Party?"

"Yes, but what of it? No one cares—"

"It is the conference with the South Koreans that interests me, Anatoly. You know there is to be a meeting here in Vladi?"

"It is not a secret."

"You have just told me, nothing is a secret anymore. But this agreement interests me. It will make a good story. Even *Izvestia* is interested. What I need to know is whether there is more to it than appears on the surface. Who is for it and against it? What about the Communists? And why are the hardline nationalists like Provalev and Zhirinovsky, who say they hate foreigners, not opposed to such an agreement?"

"I don't know . . ."

"Have you met Boris Provalev? He was a Party member before he became involved with Zhirinovsky and his Liberal Democrats."

"I have met him, which is not to say that I know him," Bukanin said. "He has a big mouth but he is very clever."

"He is for the restoration of the Soviet Union—"

"He is for Boris Provalev," the ex-KGB man said.

"Then why has he promoted this agreement? The North Koreans have been Russia's friends, the South Koreans our enemy. Didn't Zhirinovsky say that if the South Koreans and the North went to war, and a single hair on one of our Russian advisers to the North was lost, as president he would drop a bomb on South Korea and take a million lives in return for each Russian hair?"

"Madness! He said the same about Estonia. Have we Russians changed so much that we make such men our heroes? We used to value courtesy and politeness. Now our streets are infested with bullies. Bullying and bluster are signs of weakness. Only the strong can be generous. What are we now?"

"I'd like to know," Lina Mashikova said quietly, "why has Provalev engineered this conference?"

Bukanin shrugged. "It's economics. Where there is no character, no faith, look for who is making money."

"Is that it? That's what I want to be sure of. If you can use your old sources to learn something of this, then I can pay you."

Bukanin looked skeptical. Or was there something else in the watery eyes that shifted away from hers? Was there also uneasiness? What did Bukanin already know?

"I . . . I'm sorry, Yelina Vassilyeva, I cannot pay for our vodka . . ."

"That is all right, I can pay. I can also give you something in advance for the information I'm looking for."

"I may learn nothing . . ."

"I'll take that chance. This can be a very important story for me, Uncle. Perhaps important enough to buy me a ticket back to Moscow."

He looked surprised. "I often wondered why you came here."

"I couldn't bear it in Moscow," she said after a moment. "I would see Yuri on every street corner."

"I will see what I can find out."

Before Bukanin left she gave him ten thousand rubles. He remained in the cafe after she stepped out into the dreary rain. Looking back from across the street, she saw him light a Marlboro from the pack she had given him and signal the waiter for another vodka.

So this is free enterprise, Russian-style, Lina thought.

She had hidden her Suzuki behind an apartment house two blocks away. Even though she had chain-locked the bike to a metal post, she was relieved, and surprised, to see that it was still there.

14

CHRIS HARMON ARRIVED at the camera shop a few minutes before five o'clock. The proprietor, whose name was Dimitri Zhdanov, was also a photographer—family portraits and passport photos—and he did his own developing in a darkroom in back of the store. He seemed excited to see Chris and eagerly brought out the packet of color photographs. There were thirty-six pictures on the roll of film and Chris had ordered two sets of each.

Chris had put the shutter on autodrive when the tiger first appeared out of the forest. Thumbing slowly through the prints, he felt adrenaline pumping into his blood, his heartbeat accelerating as if he were back in the taiga. The first suggestion that something was wrong came in the twelfth shot of the sequence. The following shots, as if in slow motion, showed the tiger turning her head, lurching upward on her hind legs and leaving the ground.

The sixteenth photograph was like a blow to the chest. It showed the tiger stretched out in her leap of agony, clawing toward the sky. It was one of those chance photographs in which everything was perfect—the background, the composition, the play of light and shadow, the striking colors. The image was both beautiful and terrifying.

Chris stared at it for a long time. Zhdanov from behind the counter asked in Russian, "Is it not all right? Is something wrong?"

"No . . . that is . . . you did very well." He turned picture number sixteen toward the photographer. "Can you make me an enlargement of this one? *Uvlichyenia?*"

"Is no problem. The tiger . . . she is dead?"

"I don't know."

"I have never seen such a picture. It is . . . very sad, I think."

"Very."

Chris had to force himself to go through the rest of the pictures. They recorded the tiger's fall to the ground, her attempt to drag herself into the cover of the tall grass and the woods, the bewildered actions of the cubs as they milled around her. Number twenty-five was blurred—Chris had been moving the camera, turning its lens toward the forest from which the shot had come. The next one was also slightly blurred. The last ten shots seemed to picture nothing but a thick stand of evergreen forest. The slope leading down to the river was there, and the river itself was a thread across the bottom of each frame.

Chris peered closely at the batch of ten photographs. After a moment's study he picked out specks of paleness, like white spots on the film. Disappointed, he shuffled through the range of pictures of the forest. Looking up to find Zhdanov watching him, he said, "Do you have a magnifying glass?" He spoke in English, not knowing the Russian words. The proprietor did not understand. Chris pantomimed, holding a magnifying glass up close and peering at one of the photos. Zhdanov nodded, stooped behind the counter, rummaged in a drawer and came up with a three-inch, five-power glass.

Chris felt a tightness around his chest as he peered through the magnifier. What had been meaningless specks were now discernible as human faces. Two of them: one man lying on the ground—the marksman—the other rising to his feet from a kneeling position, staring straight toward the camera lens.

They knew we were there and didn't give a damn, Chris thought. Why so openly brazen? What's missing here?

With the magnifying glass Chris studied each of the ten photos taken while the Nikon was aimed at the forest from which the shot had been fired. The poachers became more clearly discernible as he familiarized himself with their position among the trees. The marksman had placed himself for a clear shot across the river toward the woods from which Risa had emerged.

He knew she was there. The bastard was listening to her.

Chris's suspicion that Vladimir Yavlinsky or someone else on the preserve's staff had sold information to the poachers was reinforced. The marksman must have tuned in the radio frequency used for the faint signal emitted by the transmitter in Risa's collar. How else could he have known exactly where the tiger was and how to position himself so perfectly?

"You are sure nothing is wrong?"

Chris realized his rage must be showing. "I need blowups of some of these photographs. How soon can I get them?"

"It will take time."

"As soon as possible. I don't care what it costs."

Dimitri Zhdanov smiled. "Ah . . . *Amirikanits* . . . you are always so much in a hurry . . . always money is nothing. Russians are different. We are not in so much hurry, and to us money is everything."

"It's very important. I would like the second set of pictures sent to someone . . ." He wrote down the address of the Global Wildlife Federation's office. "He is waiting for them now. Do you have a delivery service you can call?"

"I have very good delivery service . . . my son Georgi Dimitrivich. He will take pictures at once."

"Good. And I'll need the blowups of these pictures as soon as I can get them . . ."

He went through the stack of photos from the beginning, selecting the best shots of the tiger and of the poachers in the forest.

When the American emerged from the camera shop, Sergei Lemenov's first thought was that he was taller than Sergei had thought. He had good shoulders and moved well. Still, he should present no problem. The only concern was that he might be lucky enough to spot a taxi immediately, but that did not happen. As soon as Chris Harmon began to walk away the Collector put his right hand up to the fur hat he was wearing. Two men lounging against a wall beyond the camera shop immediately started along the sidewalk after the American. As they came close to him, a flock of Japanese tourists spilled out of a store directly in front of them. The American ducked around them and walked on.

Sergei Lemenov followed. He was a man in no apparent hurry.

Chris was excited about the packet of photos in the side pocket of his jacket. The pictures of the tiger, especially that striking image at the peak of her twisting leap, were all that he could have hoped for and more. Ken Langert was certain to be pleased when he received his set of prints. But how much good would they do? Already forty-eight hours had passed since the shooting. How soon would Langert be able to use the photographic record of the atrocity? Would other wildlife and conservation groups jump in? Would the Russian journalist be able to help? And would the pressure the photos might generate be enough to persuade officials at the Ministry of Environmental Protection to listen to Chris's request?

With the Koreans due to arrive in only twenty-four hours, was it already too late?

It was still raining lightly, and the rain combined with the thick black clouds to bring a premature darkness to the streets of the city. The old brick and granite buildings, dark with the accumulated dirt and pollution from decades of neglect, turned black in the rain, soaking up light. The cars on the streets all had their headlights on, reflecting off the black shine of the wet macadam, making it even harder to see. Pedestrians hurried along the sidewalks under umbrellas or with newspapers over their heads. Only a group of Japanese tourists seemed in no hurry to get out of the rain, and Chris had to go into the street to get around them.

Near broad Svetlanskaya Street a few homeless derelicts huddled in the doorways of empty shops or in passages between buildings. On the steps of a pedestrian underpass beneath the boulevard, sheltered a little from the rain and the cold wind, an old woman wearing a shapeless hat and thick clothing held out a plastic bag with a few coins at the bottom.

Chris wondered if she was really old or simply looked it because of the dark circles under her eyes and the exhaustion in her face. He dug in his pocket for what coins he had and added some paper rubles.

Hurrying through the underpass, Chris heard footsteps behind him coming down the steps, then quickening along the dark tunnel. He had a sense that those behind him were almost running to catch up, but then he reached the steps on the far side of the underpass and went up onto the busy sidewalk. Glancing back, he saw two men in dark raincoats as they got to the top of the stairs.

Three more blocks to his hotel. He was going to be thoroughly soaked by the time he got there. The bottoms of his pants legs beneath his coat were clinging to his skin. His hair was plastered to his scalp; he hadn't thought to bring either a hat or an umbrella to Vladivostok. His shoes were wet, too, and he hadn't brought another pair. Maybe he should pick up another pair from one of those street kiosks.

As he walked his thoughts returned to the photographs. The Koreans were scheduled to arrive tomorrow afternoon. If Ken Langert could get one of his *Global Alert* bulletins on the street, if his and other groups protested noisily and if Lina Mashikova could interest one of the larger newspapers or magazines . . . well, at least the timing was good. Ministry officials and those promoting the conference with the Koreans just might panic a little, at least enough to authorize his rescue effort.

Another forty-eight hours at the earliest before he could hope to get back to Terney.

How much time did the tiger cubs have?

He recognized a side street on his right that cut through to Ulitsa Naberezhnay. It would bring him out near his hotel. He would save more than a block walking in the rain.

Chris swung into the narrow street. The rain-dark buildings closed in on either side, and the narrow street, stone-paved, was as dark as night. He gave no thought to the fact that it was nearly empty. A woman ahead of him peered over her shoulder, and her steps quickened as she neared the far end of the street.

Behind him a footstep slid on the wet stones. Glancing back over his shoulder, Chris smiled wryly at the thought of the woman made nervous by the sound of *his* steps. All that talk about mafia gangs, he thought, and the disturbing image of young men in their black leather jackets hanging around on street corners and in parking lots, looking for trouble. The two men behind him were not leather-jacket types, they wore long black raincoats.

They had been behind him in the underpass, he thought. Hurrying to catch up . . .

Chris started walking faster. He was halfway along the narrow street, completely deserted now except for himself and the two men behind him. Their steps kept pace with his, hurrying—

No, running.

He looked back once more. The two men were closing in on him, their black raincoats flying out like capes.

Chris ran. The sidewalk just ahead was blocked by trash cans. He veered into the street. His shoes slipped on the uneven stones. An ankle twisted with a stab of pain and he nearly went down. Saved himself with one hand touching the ground. One of the men grabbed at him and he ducked away. He ran free again. Mafia thugs? In raincoats? Why were they after him? Money? Thank God he had left his credit cards in his room.

A hand caught his sleeve, hauling him back. He twisted around and hit out at the nearest man. He missed and realized it had been a mistake, it allowed the second attacker to reach him.

One of the men grabbed his arm. Chris felt a blow to the side of his face, stunning him. My God, the attacker had something in his fist—steel balls? His legs wobbled like a straw man's. The second man, shorter, jerked Chris's raincoat down from his shoulders, tying up both of his arms. The man with the steel weights in his right fist stepped in.

Arms tangled in his coat, Chris had no chance to defend himself. A blow to his chest seemed to stop his breathing. Another hammered his jaw. He tasted blood where a tooth was mashed against his lower lip.

He kicked out at the man with the steel fist and by pure luck connected with the man's shin. *"Yob tvoyu mat!"*

Suddenly Chris had one arm free of its sleeve. He twisted, felt the resistance slip away as his coat came loose in the hands of the second man. The fist came at him but Chris stepped inside the blow and counterpunched. Solid impact on flesh and bone. The man staggered back.

Chris ran past him, down the dark canyon toward Ulitsa Naberezhnay. His breath was raw in his throat. They came after him, but he had gotten a short lead after he surprised them and slipped out of his coat. Five steps ahead . . . four . . . those blows had taken something out of him . . .

Someone appeared at the mouth of the canyon. He was pointing. Chris heard a shout. As he stumbled forward a car skidded to a stop just beyond the opening. Doors opened and brown uniforms spilled out.

Behind Chris the footsteps broke off, retreated. A whistle blew, shrill in that narrow street. Militiamen pounded over the stone paving in their heavy boots. One of them glanced at Chris, hesitated, then ran past him. The two men in the black raincoats dissolved into the shadows far down the street.

Neither Chris nor the militia had seen a third man in a fur hat who scooped up Chris's raincoat where it had fallen onto the paving stones and stepped through the back entrance of a shop with the coat. Out of sight, he dug quickly into the side pockets. His hands came out empty. In a gesture of angry frustration he threw the coat onto the ground outside the entry.

The Collector walked quickly through the shop, smiling at the openmouthed stares of a woman behind a counter and a customer buying fish for her evening supper.

15

A HALF-HOUR LATER Chris Harmon had managed to get himself back to his hotel. It was nearly six o'clock. He didn't know how he was going to be ready to meet Yelina Mashikova for dinner at seven. Or be able to eat dinner. His jaw was swollen, a front tooth wobbled when his tongue pushed at it.

He had recovered his raincoat from the street where his attackers had discarded it, but it was a mess. Maybe he could sponge some of the dirt off and get it halfway dry before going out again.

He patted the side pocket of his jacket. The packet of photographs were safe. The militiaman who had talked to him had been sympathetic but brusque. He should be more careful where he walked. There were thugs who looked on foreign tourists as targets of opportunity. The American was fortunate that the presence of militia had been increased in the city for reasons of security, anticipating the arrival of important principals from another country. The militia patrol had been alerted by a pedestrian who had witnessed the attack on Chris from the end of the street. Otherwise the incident might have been much more serious. Well, it was serious enough for him, Chris thought, touching the loose tooth with the tip of his tongue.

The plump gray-haired *babushka* who served as the maid and general *provodnik* for the fourth floor of the hotel recognized him as he stepped out of the creaky old elevator. She smiled, showing a gap between two front teeth. Chris managed an answering smile. *"Dobri v'yecher, babushka.* Good evening."

114

His room, number 432, was only a short distance along the corridor. The door was slightly ajar and Chris glanced back at the *provodnik*. She was at another door, fumbling with a huge key ring. Still smiling, Chris entered his room with a sigh of relief.

A shoulder slammed into the door, closing it behind him. Strong hands shoved him back into the room. He caught a glimpse of a black raincoat, then a second figure stepped in front—the taller of his street attackers. The steel-weighted fist clubbed the side of his head.

Time stopped. He was on the floor, holding onto the rug. He could feel the rough nap against his cheek. Hands dug into his pockets—the photos . . . He was helpless, but a corner of his mind knew what was happening, knew that it was the photos the attackers had been after all the way.

Someone screamed, the sound lanced into his head. Something spilled onto the floor, like cards flying from the hands of a skilled dealer. One of the cards landed in front of his face. He stared at it. Not a card. A photograph of a tiger stretched out like a ballerina at the height of her leap . . .

The questioning of an alleged robbery victim in room 432 at the Hotel Vladivostok took place at 1820 hours. The interrogation was conducted by police investigator Ladislav Yochenkov.

—You are able to answer questions?

—I think so.

—Your passport gives your name as Christopher David Harmon. Is that correct?

—Yes.

—You are an American tourist?

—Not exactly. I'm an American but I was invited to the Primorskiy territory by the Russian government as part of a research project in the Sikhote-Alin Biosphere National Preserve. I've been here almost two years.

—I see. And your business in Vladivostok?

—To see representatives of the Ministry of Environmental Protection and Natural Resources. I was there earlier today.

—So . . . you returned to your hotel room at approximately 1800 hours. You were alone?

—Yes.

—What happened then?

—I noticed the door was not closed.

—This did not concern you?

—I had just seen the maid down the corridor when I got off the elevator. I assumed she had been to my room and left the door ajar.

—Then what happened?

—There were two men waiting for me—the same two men who attacked me on the street less than an hour ago, I'm sure of it. They both wore black raincoats.

The interrogator did not bother to say that this was hardly a useful description. Vladivostok on a rainy day was a sea of black raincoats.

—You saw them clearly?

—It happened too fast. One of them shoved me in the back. I was off balance. Then the other one hit me, knocked me down. He had these steel balls in his hand . . .

—It is a common mafia weapon. Can you further describe these men? Did they wear hats?

—One of them had a knitted cap. The other—the one who hit me—no hat.

—What was the color of his hair?

—Black, I think. Dark, anyway.

—Were they tall? Short? Thin or heavy? Young or old?

—One was shorter. The other was . . . not as tall as I am but heavier. They were both well-built, young.

—Why do you say that? Young?

—The way they moved, both here in the room and in the street.

—Were they Russian? Did either man speak?

—One of them gave the other an order? I didn't catch

the word exactly but it was Russian. Beyond that, they didn't say anything. It happened very fast. There wasn't much time for anything. I was knocked down and I heard a scream—that's when one man gave the other an order. It was the maid screaming . . .

—She heard a commotion from your room. Fortunately for you, she came to see what it was. She opened the door, saw what was happening and screamed. They ran past her, knocked her down. That is all she has been able to tell us.

—Too scared, I guess.

—Can you think of any reason these thieves might have attacked you in the street and again in your room?

—I don't know. They grabbed those photos from my pocket but they dropped them when they ran out.

—Are any of the photographs missing?

—I don't know. I haven't had a chance to go through them.

—But your wallet is missing.

—Yes. It had some money in it—not much. I left my credit cards here at the hotel along with my passport.

—You know that under the law you must carry your passport with you at all times?

—Yes, I know . . . I just happened to leave it with my cards.

—Do you have other funds, *Gospodin* Harmon, other than what was stolen?

—Yes. And I can use the credit cards for emergency funds.

—Ah, yes . . . credit cards. What a wonderful thing, to be able to command funds at any time, any place in the world. Of course, it is also necessary to have funds in a bank somewhere, against which this credit is drawn. Now then . . . do you need medical attention, *Gospodin* Harmon?

—I don't think so. No . . . I'll be fine. I might have to see a dentist.

—And to your knowledge nothing else has been taken from your room.

—No.

—You are fortunate. I believe you are correct in suggesting that you interrupted the thieves before they could decide what to steal. And the maid's intervention caused them to panic and run. I regret to say that street thugs exist in our city, although it is not here like in America. And hotel thieves are common. This is no more true in Vladivostok than in other cities but it is something we deplore.

—You think these were just common thieves?

—Can you suggest another explanation, *Gospodin* Harmon?

—No.

After the police investigator left, along with the hotel manager, who also deplored the activities of thieves in his hotel, Chris moved restlessly about the room, checking his one piece of luggage, the dresser and the bathroom. He had left most of his clothing in his bag, not bothering to unpack for what he hoped would be a brief stay. Nothing was missing.

He went back to the spill of photographs on the bed, most of which he had retrieved from the floor. Of course, they took the wallet as a last-minute cover. It was the photos they wanted. But if so, why had they left them behind?

He shuffled the pictures, arranging them in the proper sequence as he remembered it. Through the first twenty-five shots he was fairly certain of the order. None was missing. The next two were the blurred photos taken while the camera was being swiveled around. Of the last group, shot while the lens was directed toward the forest where the poachers had hidden to wait for the tiger, six were missing.

The six pictures with faces in the woods, Chris thought . . . the photographs that might have identified the poachers.

16

BORIS PROVALEV WAS a man who projected energy and power. As a politician, it was his good fortune that this impression was transmitted on the television screen as forcefully as it was in person.

He was not a big man, an average five feet ten inches tall and weighing a hundred eighty-five pounds, but he had a burly chest and a large, handsome head that made him seem bigger on the small screen. His manner was cool and sharp. The energy was in his commanding voice, in his wiry gray hair, which looked as if it had been curled by an electrical charge, and in his eyes. They were a dark brown, and when he stared into the camera lens they seemed to catch all the available light. They blazed out at the viewer.

Provalev smiled paternally at Anna Zilya Valeyeva, the twenty-seven-year-old woman who moderated *Moya Pozit-siya,* a weekly television program featuring interviews allowing important public figures to present "My Position." Anna had spent the previous night with him, and she flushed a little under his burning gaze. Provalev made love roughly and her breasts and thighs still felt bruised. Nonetheless, though she had experienced a confusing mixture of pain and pleasure during his lovemaking, his stare caused her nipples to harden. Glancing away from him toward the red light over the camera focused on her, she licked her lips. Anna was a very pretty young woman, elegant in a pale blue silk blouse. Her hair was black, cut fashionably in a short bob that framed an oval face with striking hazel eyes and a wide, full mouth. Her nervous habit of licking her sensual lips was one that endeared her to her viewers.

"Why is it important that Russia should reach this rapprochement with the South Koreans at this point in time, Chairman Provalev?"

"Why is it important to run up your sail when the wind blows? Opportunities pass quickly. The wind dies. The present government has allowed such moments to pass us by. Now we must seize the helm, catch the wind and set our course. It is time for Russia to take leadership in the East. Our proposed new agreement with the South Korean government and the Sunsai Corporation is part of that initiative."

"But aren't there some environmentalists who argue that extensive logging in the Primorskiy Kray forest is bad for Russia and bad for the environment?"

"You can't chop down a forest without making some splinters," Provalev said, invoking an old Russian proverb that sounded more relevant than it really was. "Are jobs bad for Russia? Is the sale of Russian raw materials bad for Russia? Is the creation of Russian products bad for Russia? Is the opening of a broad-new market in Asia bad for Russia?" His strong voice rose in righteous wrath. "Who are these people who criticize us? They are not true Russians."

"Some of them are leading—"

"Russia must once again become the country of all Russians! Billions of dollars have been spent to fight the Liberal Democratic Party of Russia, but they cannot stop us. The Japanese would buy the Kuril Islands from us with money. The Americans would make us their satellite with money. The sycophants within Russia would fall on their knees before our enemies if there was money on the ground for them to stuff in their pockets. But the soul of Russia cannot be bought!"

Provalev had the politician's trick of turning any question into an excuse for a speech that often had only a tangential relationship to the question. Anna Valeyeva appeared perplexed. She offered Provalev a quick bright smile and said, "You have been called an extreme nationalist—"

"I have been called many things, Anna Zilya." The young woman was a very popular television personality, and

Provalev's deliberate use of her patronymic established for viewers a relationship between them that went beyond professional courtesy. "They call us fascists. They are frightened of us, frightened of the people who hear us, and they try to frighten others with their words. But the truth will not be hidden."

"Yes . . . I see. Then you believe your Korean initiative is a positive step for Mother Russia."

"Our Motherland is a ship foundering in a storm, in darkness and despair," Provalev said, launching into another of his standard speeches without missing a beat. "How have we let these so-called democratic leaders of ours come to power who kowtow to foreign patrons, leaders who seek their blessings not from the Russian people but from abroad, leaders who do not love their own country? Under such men Russian greatness has disappeared. What does the poet say? We are a proud beggar with an atomic bomb. Well, Russians are not beggars! And under the dynamic new leadership of our great Party Chairman Zhirinovsky, we will reclaim our rightful place in the world. Once again our country will be wide and powerful and proud." The last words, lifted almost verbatim from a popular patriotic song, were uttered with a passion that made his voice shake.

"Thank you, Chairman Provalev," Anna Valeyeva said. She turned toward the camera. "You have been listening to *Moya Pozitsiya,* news and interviews with Russia's newsmakers . . ."

As the program ended, Boris Provalev leaned forward and patted Anna Valeyeva on the knee. His hand was square, short-fingered, the nails chewed short, a hand as blunt as the man. It lingered a moment on the smooth curve of her knee. She sat transfixed, as if mesmerized by the energy radiating from him to her knee and points beyond. Then the great man caught a glimpse of Leonid Brunovsky peering anxiously through a studio window. His manner changed, the hand withdrew. "Very nice, my dear. You were charming as always."

"Thank you, Comrade Chairman." Her cheeks were flushed

again, her nipples hard under the silk blouse. "Will I see you—?"

"I will call you."

"What is it?" Provalev asked brusquely.

"He's here."

Provalev's composure slipped. He glanced at the figures hurrying along the corridor or waiting at the nearby elevators to leave the television studios. "Here? Is he mad?"

"Not . . . not in the studio," Brunovsky stammered hastily. "I mean . . . he is waiting across the way." The chairman's aide hesitated, looking around them as if to assure himself that no one was listening. "Where the new construction is under way . . . in the east end of the building."

Provalev stared at him a moment, then chuckled. Like many other churches in Vladivostok and throughout the Soviet Union, the city's ancient Russian Orthodox church had been dynamited and paved over by the Red Army after it occupied the city. A giant statue of Lenin had replaced the medieval church on the site, across from which new television broadcast studios had been constructed in the 1960s. In the euphoric first days of *demokratizatsia,* Lenin's statue had been demolished, and where it had stood construction had now begun for a new cathedral that would be called St. Innocent. The Collector's choice of a meeting place was, under the circumstances, amusing.

Brushing off well-wishers, Boris Provalev left the building by a side entrance and walked up to the nearest corner with Brunovsky. The rain had stopped but the night air was damp and cold. As they walked Provalev examined the construction site across the way. The walls of the main nave were up, open to the heavens. Flying buttresses reached outward toward their supports, silhouetted against gray, fast-moving clouds. There were warning lights at the entrance to the long nave, where the narthex or lobby of the cathedral would be, but the interior was as black as a mine.

Satisfied, Provalev and Brunovsky crossed the street and continued past the front of the unfinished cathedral until they were out of sight of the busy television building across the way. The far side of the cathedral site faced an anonymous, bulky government building, all but one of its streetside offices in darkness. The street lamps, one of which was shattered, threw only a feeble light toward the broken shadows of the construction site.

Provalev and his aide picked their way past mounds of construction materials toward the open face of the structure, slipped past the low red warning lights and stepped into the shadows of the interior. Walls and columns rose upward into the darkness. The two men paused, listening. No one had followed them. From the long empty nave that stretched out before them there was only silence.

"Wait here," Provalev said quietly.

"Perhaps I should go first—"

"I do not need a nursemaid, Leonid Andreyevich. He works for me."

He works for himself, Brunovsky thought, but he remained silent.

Provalev walked slowly down the dark tunnel between the high stone walls, marveling as he often had over the powerful impulse that caused so many people to spend their lives and fortunes erecting such great houses of worship for something that was no more than a blind hope, a yearning for meaning instead of irrelevance. Smells of wet wood and cement and earth surrounded him. Once he stumbled over a thick plank. He did not encounter God, nor did he expect to.

Near the end of the nave was the scaffolding for an extension in a semicircular or polygonal shape. Provalev paused there, frowning with impatience. The silence was thick around him.

Then, softly, a single word: "Here."

Provalev jumped. Angered by his nervousness, he started toward the sound of the voice. He stumbled again over something hard. Cursing, he fumbled in his pocket for his cigarette lighter.

"No light."

"I can't see where I'm going—"

"You can see well enough."

Provalev flushed. He was not used to such arrogance in others. He had spoken to the Collector only three times, twice on the phone. The only other occasion on which they had met had also been, at Sergei Lemenov's direction, in darkness. Provalev had never seen his face. Only Brunovsky knew what he looked like. For the first time Provalev wondered if that was a very comfortable situation for his aide . . .

"What is your report?" Provalev asked, seeking to regain his customary dominant role.

"Leonid Andreyevich has informed you of the situation in the Sikhote-Alin preserve. The shooting went as planned."

"Did it? I was told that the tiger was not killed." The implied rebuke was another assertion of dominance.

After a moment's silence the Collector said, "The animal's death is not important to the mission. However, the photographs that you hoped to have taken of the tiger are exceptional."

"You've seen them?"

"Yes. They—especially one of them—will have a powerful impact if they are published."

"Has the American sought out his friends?"

"He has reacted exactly as you predicted, Comrade Chairman."

Was there a hint of irony in the Collector's tone? Provalev was annoyed that he could not see the man's face. He didn't like Sergei Lemenov, but then, one did not choose an assassin for his charms. Only his skill and efficiency mattered. Leonid Brunovsky had been with the Collector in the Primorskiy, and he had come away impressed—even awed.

"It must happen quickly, while the Koreans are still anxious to sign the agreement."

"In that respect the wounding of the tiger becomes an advantage. Also the presence of young cubs, which we did not know about. The American is desperate to attempt to rescue them. He can't delay. He will try to use his photographs as soon as possible. We might expect to see one of those Global Wildlife Federation panic sheets appear within twenty-four hours."

"Then . . . if the photos are as good as you claim . . ."
The reaction on the part of environmentalists would be outrage, Provalev thought. He could exploit that with the Korean prime minister, who had been sensitized to such out-
cries by the Americans and others. He would be open to
suggestions . . .

"As you say, Comrade Chairman."

"You've done well, Comrade."

"Perhaps."

More than the qualifying word, there was something in the
Collector's tone that alerted Boris Provalev. Was he simply
indifferent to the eventual outcome of his assignment? No, it
was more than that. He did not share Provalev's optimism.
He was holding something back.

"What is it you haven't told me?" Provalev asked sharply.

"There are other photographs."

"What do you mean?"

"The American was using a camera with an extremely
sharp telephoto lens. When the tiger was shot he did not simply stare in horror as one might expect. He was alert enough
to swing the camera toward the woods where the shot had
come from. In other words, toward Leonid Andreyevich and
me."

"But Brunovsky described the scene to me. You were deep
in the taiga, hundreds of yards away—"

Sergei Lemenov, until that moment a bodiless voice in the
darkness, stepped close enough for Provalev to see the vapor
of his breath but not his face. The chairman flinched. Then
the Collector pressed something into Provalev's hand.

"These are the photos. They show two men in the forest.
Their faces are only specks in these snapshots, but they are
there."

"But if they're too small to be identified—"

"They can be enlarged and enhanced. In the wrong hands
. . . they could be dangerous."

Provalev was silent a moment, wishing he could use his
cigarette lighter at least to get a glimpse of the photographs.
What would the Collector do if he defied his wishes about

striking a light? Provalev realized that he was not willing to find out.

"You are afraid that someone might identify your face."

"You forget, Comrade Chairman . . . Leonid Andreyevich's face is also in those pictures. And his presence with me in the forest at that moment is an arrow of truth aimed directly at Boris Provalev."

Provalev was jolted. Presented with the existence of these unexpected photos, he hadn't thought through their implications. Lemenov was right, they were dangerous—not only to the Collector but to Provalev himself. His role in this affair must remain invisible until it was too late for anyone to do anything about it.

"How did you get these pictures?"

The Collector explained the attacks on the American, the failed attempt on the street and a later one in his hotel room, by two hired thugs. "They left behind most of the photographs, those showing the wounding of the tiger. They also stole the American's wallet to make it appear to be an ordinary theft."

"Why didn't you do it yourself?" Provalev challenged him. "Why did you leave it to hirelings?"

There was a stillness. Provalev knew the Collector was staring at him from the darkness.

"I am not a street thug, nor a hotel thief."

You didn't want to be seen, Provalev thought. But—with a political animal's instinct—he knew better than to test Lemenov further. He said, "If he's got the tiger photos, he may not care about the others."

"We can't rely on that." The Collector paused. "I can't."

"Nothing must happen to the American prematurely," Provalev said quickly. "If a connection were made—even if he had an unexpected accident—it might frighten the Koreans. I need to get them out of their shell, not risk possibly aborting the entire operation. It will be enough if these other pictures are destroyed, including all copies, if any, and the negatives. Use Brunovsky, use anyone you need. Take whatever steps are necessary."

Sergei Lemenov did not bother to reply. The silence lengthened, and it was a long moment before Boris Provalev realized that he was alone in the darkness.

He didn't make a sound, Provalev thought, and shivered.

17

"WHAT HAPPENED TO you?"

"I ran into some thugs."

"You look as if you ran into a Russian tank in the dark." Lina Mashikova studied Chris Harmon curiously, but did not immediately press him for an explanation.

The Russian journalist appeared at ease in the lobby of the hotel. She would not have been outclassed in the lobby of the Ritz, Chris thought. She wore a fur hat, a long black leather coat and matching leather boots. Altogether dressier than her biker garb but still practical for a raw, drizzly night, part of which would be spent tramping around an open-air market over ground that was certain to be sloppy from the rains.

When they left the hotel it was not raining but the air was raw, the brisk wind cold enough for Chris's face to feel stiff before they had walked half a block. Black clouds scudded overhead, with patches of starry skies visible like rents in a fabric.

"Where's your motorcycle?"

"It's not safe to park it in the street, so I had a friend drive me to the hotel." She paused. "I believe we are taking your friend's taxi, yes?"

"I left a message for him, but he hasn't called back. If he gets the message and comes, he'll pick us up at the hotel at nine o'clock. Otherwise we'll have to try to get another taxi. Is that okay?"

She smiled up at him. "That gives us two hours to eat. That's about right for a Russian meal."

The restaurant she had chosen was called Novaratsky. It

was only a short walk from the hotel through streets emptied by the rain. Nevertheless, Chris kept a watchful eye out. Once he flinched when a gust of wind blew a twisting shadow out of an alley and sent it skittering across the street in front of them—part of an empty cardboard box. If the journalist noticed his reaction, she made no comment.

The restaurant was small enough to be intimate. The waiter recognized Lina Mashikova on sight and showed them to a corner table covered with a white cloth. In its center was a thin crystal vase with a small spray of fresh flowers, and a candle stuck with wax to a saucer.

Lina declined vodka with a smile. She ordered *kvas* for both of them. "It's a traditional Russian drink," she explained, "with only a little alcohol in it. We should have clear heads tonight, I think."

"It's just as well. I'm not sure how vodka would get along with all the aspirin I've taken."

"First I will order dinner . . . then you must tell me about your Russian thugs."

To eager nods of approval from the waiter, Lina ordered two bowls of *okroshka,* a cold soup with vegetables and *pirozhki,* black bread, and glazed *angulas,* a fish grilled simply with herbs and lemon. Chris studied her covertly. She was one of those women who became prettier the more you saw of them. Tonight she wore a different sweater, a pale gray mohair knit, over long black skirt. During the day she had been without makeup, but now tinted shadows enhanced her clear blue eyes, and her lips had been brushed with a pale rose lipstick. Across the table, by candlelight, she seemed both warmer and smaller than before, not so much the tough biker-journalist.

"Tell me more about yourself," Chris said over the bowl of soup.

"I have told you all. I am the journalist, remember?"

"I doubt you've told all," he grinned.

"You were going to tell me about these thugs who attacked you. How did this happen?"

Chris described the aborted attack on the street after he left the camera shop, and the confrontation soon afterward in his hotel room. "One of them slugged me. He had steel weights in his hand."

"You should have gone to hospital. You might have concussion."

Chris shrugged the possibility off. "All I have is a king-size headache."

"King-size?" She smiled. "We do not have kings in Russia."

"We have them in America, but they're called movie stars or pop rock stars."

"I think you are joking with me."

"He jests at stars who never felt a wound . . ."

To his surprise Lina laughed outright at the pun.

"You know Shakespeare?"

"I told you, I wished to become a poet. I wanted to be like Anna Akhmatova. She is from St. Petersburg like me. I saw her once when I was a girl, on the street. Do you know the wonderful lines, *You are free, I am free, / Tomorrow will be better than yesterday—*'?"

"I don't—"

"She wrote about herself and her lover, more than fifty years ago, but she might have been writing about Russia today."

"You can still be a poet," Chris said gently. "It's never too late."

"I think maybe it is." A shadow crossed her face, but she shook her head sharply, as if to banish it. "But I read poetry, including your Shakespeare. All Russians read some of his plays in school. He is like our Chekhov." She leaned across the table to peer more closely at Chris's face and abruptly changed the subject. "Your jaw is swollen. It will not be pretty. Are you sure you do not wish to see a doctor?"

"I'll be fine. It wasn't exactly pretty before, anyway."

"I think it was." The comment seemed to take both of them by surprise. After a moment's startled silence Lina said, "What did they take, these thugs?"

"They took my wallet . . . and photographs."

"The photographs you tell me about this afternoon? The pictures of tiger being shot?"

"They only took a few. I brought the rest with me."

"Can I see them?"

He watched her while she went through the photographs one by one, her expression intent and serious. She did not speak, but he saw her eyes widen and her lips part when she came to the picture of the tiger reaching for the sky. She continued through the rest of the photos before returning to that one.

"May I have copy of this one?"

"Yes. You can keep that. I'm having more prints made."

"It's very good. I am certain it can be published." She stared at it again for another moment before looking up. "What pictures did these men steal?"

"That's the odd part. You'd expect them to just grab the whole packet and run, if that's what they were after, but the best shots, those of the tiger, they tossed back, like fish you've caught that are too small."

"They looked at all of the photographs?"

"They must have. I was out of it for a while after being hit . . . I was on the floor . . . but they must have picked over the whole set of photos in order to find what they wanted."

Recounting what happened, Chris was struck more forcibly than before by his earlier conviction that the attackers were specifically searching for pictures that might identify the marksman and his companion.

"What was on these pictures—the ones that were stolen?"

"Nothing—that is, nothing you can see clearly. The marksman—the man who shot the tiger—and the man with him, they're both visible there in the woods, but you can't see them well enough to identify them. Even with a blowup of those shots, I doubt if there will be anything other than blurred faces."

"Maybe that's what they had to find out," she murmured.

"That's my guess, too. The poachers were afraid of what the photographs might reveal, so they hired a couple of mafia thugs to steal them. I doubt they have to worry now."

"The negatives . . . they were also taken?"

"No, thank God, they're still at the camera shop. I ordered some enlargements along with another set of prints."

She remained thoughtful while their soup bowls were

taken away, to be replaced quickly by white china plates with *angulas* and what Lina identified as Uzbek pilaf. When they were alone again she said, "It is interesting . . . that only those few pictures were taken. Also that these men knew where you were staying."

"I suppose they followed me."

"They were in your room ahead of you," she pointed out.

"Well . . ." Chris was momentarily taken aback. "I guess I was followed from Terney. Even if I wasn't followed, it wouldn't be hard to figure out where I might be staying in Vladivostok. I suppose it tells me the shooter took great pains to be certain he couldn't be identified."

"It also tells you that they wished you to have the pictures of wounded tiger. Who would want this?"

"I don't know."

That part of it had been a puzzle from the beginning. If the poachers had deliberately lured Chris and Alex into following them into Sector Five, as Chris believed, what could possibly be the motive? Chris's devotion to his camera was well known in Terney, and the situation as it unfolded in the preserve that day virtually guaranteed that he would get photographs of the Siberian tiger being shot. Why?

"Could someone be trying to sabotage Korean agreement?" Lina wondered aloud.

"Who? Environmentalists and ecologists are against it, of course, but they wouldn't dramatize their opposition by shooting an endangered species."

"We will have to think about this."

Both fell silent. The Russian woman gave serious attention to her dinner. After the first bite of the delicately glazed fish, Chris did the same. His thoughts drifted from the tragedy in the taiga to the young woman across the table from him, her features softened by candlelight. By what stroke of luck had she been on hand to learn from her friend Ludmilla of Chris's visit to the Ministry? She was going to great lengths for a story . . . not that he was about to complain.

For dessert there was hot tea, small round crackers called *sooshki,* and *sulguni,* a popular Georgian goat cheese. Chris congratulated Lina on the delicious meal. "Especially the black bread and the cheese," he added. "Just give me a loaf of that bread with the cheese and I'd be content."

"Aren't you forgetting the wine?"

By then the journalist seemed more relaxed, and the talk turned to other things. Chris asked her about the political climate in the province. "I'm trying to understand why there's so much pressure to sign this agreement with the Koreans now, and why our research project is being frozen out. They're not only easing me out of the Sikhote-Alin preserve, my Russian colleague, Gregory Krasikov, has also been transferred."

"It is said that all politics in Russia is intrigue."

"The politician whose name keeps coming up is Boris Provalev. Tell me about him."

"He is political leader in the Primorskiy province. There has been a . . . what you call a vacuum. Nobody was in charge, nobody knew what to do. Everyone was confused over all that was happening with government in Moscow and across Russia. You heard the same questions everywhere. What is going on in our country? What is happening here? What is to be done? Who is to blame? And suddenly this man appeared with confident answers. That was Comrade Provalev."

"Where did he come from? What's his background?"

"It tells you little, I think. Many of our leaders have been from peasant families—Gorbachev and Yeltsin among them. Boris Provalev's father was a laborer. As a young man the son worked in a textile plant in Vologda, in northern Russia. He didn't even serve in the army. He has one leg shorter than the other, though nobody talks about it anymore. He was a member of the Komsomol, you know it?"

"The Communist Youth Organization."

"*Da.* Then in his twenties he joined Communist Party. If you wanted to be someone in Soviet Union, if you were ambitious, it was necessary to be a member of the Party."

"Were you? A member, I mean?"

"No . . . but I was not so ambitious." She hesitated. "Yuri was."

"Your husband?"

"Yes. He was proud of the Party then. Yuri was . . . an idealist. He was also a patriot who loved his country."

Chris wondered about the emotion that shaped her words and tone, and what they left unsaid. Remembering that flash of pain in her eyes when she had first said that she was a widow, he decided his questions about her personal life could wait.

"So how did Provalev get from the textile plant in the north to become chairman of the Primorskiy District Council and a member of Parliament?"

Lina shrugged. "How does any *apparatchik* get ahead? During the Brezhnev years, he learned to play the game. He found the right patrons and he rose through the ranks of the Party. He discovered that he was a good politician. He knew how to say the right things to the right people, and he was a good speaker at meetings, people listened to him. Also he looked good on television, which is important now in *demokratizatsia,* when people choose their leaders."

"The Kennedy factor."

"Yes? He looked fine on television, your young president. I was not yet born when he died, but I remember pictures of him on television, of his funeral and . . ."

And his widow, Chris thought. "Go on . . . I didn't mean to interrupt."

"When Gorbachev's *perestroika* came along, and astounded everyone, including Mikhail Sergeyevich himself, by opening up the floodgates, Boris Provalev was ready, waiting for his moment. He had come to the Far East with the blessing of his patrons, and he never forgot which side he favored. Do you remember another of your presidents, Eisenhower, in a speech talking about your military-industrial complex?"

"Yes, of course."

"I read that speech. It was printed in *Komsomolskaya Pravda,* and all Soviet people read it."

"If you weren't born when Kennedy died, you weren't alive when Eisenhower gave that speech, either."

Lina smiled. "We read it in school. It was where we learned about America and capitalism. What they did not teach us was that we also had our own military-industrial complex in

Soviet Union. The bosses who ran the state military plants became Provalev's patrons. They were all violently opposed to radical democratic reforms. They didn't want to kill the goose that laid golden eggs. Because of them, Provalev became important."

"He's obviously not a reformer."

"No, he speaks for his patrons. For them and for the hardliners in the army who feel betrayed, and for all the *nomenklatura* of the Communist Party who have lost out to the reformers in the government. But now, more and more, he speaks also for people who are afraid, people who do not understand what is happening to their country."

Chris spread cheese on the last of his crackers, contemplated it soberly for a moment as he thought over what Lina Mashikova had told him, and popped the cracker whole into his mouth. After washing it down with tea, he mused aloud, "So Provalev is still working for his patrons when he cuts a deal with the South Koreans over logging in the Primorskiy . . . and opens up new markets."

"This would seem to be true."

"You have some questions about it?"

"Perhaps. I am still interested in your photographs, Christopher. How would they affect this conference?"

"My guess is, Provalev and his patrons wouldn't want these pictures to see the light of day. They don't want an environmental flap just before the signing."

"What is this flap?"

"Protests, demonstrations . . . too much attention. That's why I'm hoping they'll give me a little leverage."

"Leverage? Oh yes, I think I understand . . ."

"Something I can use to pry some concessions out of them . . . like letting me back into Sector Five."

The journalist was silent for a moment, her thoughts turned inward. Chris found himself staring at her soft mouth, at the line of her throat, at the shape of her small breasts under the sweater. He felt a stirring, a response he hadn't had for more than two years, most of that time spent in the wilderness. Alex Grovkin would be pleased, he thought.

"I think it is time," Lina said.

"Hm? What?"

Her eyes met his with characteristic directness. "For us to meet your taxi driver . . . yes?"

18

MIKHAIL FYODOROV WAS delighted with Chris Harmon's choice of companion for the evening. "I can see that you did not need my help!" he shouted boisterously.

"What did he mean about help?" Lina whispered as they settled into the back seat of the Lada taxi, which was barely wide enough for two to fit comfortably.

"To find a woman for myself in Vladivostok."

"Oh."

She glanced out the window. He couldn't tell if she was avoiding his gaze from embarrassment or amusement.

The taxi careened through the city with Fyodorov's customary dash. There was not as much traffic as usual, and in less than twenty minutes they were speeding through the suburbs of the city, past an industrial area where the smell of chemicals lingered in the heavy air. A few minutes later the driver swung off the highway and began to climb into the hills. They left behind rows of darker, turn-of-the-century buildings despoiled with graffiti—*Yeltsin is a traitor!* one of them read—and passed through ranks of anonymous apartment blocks.

Five minutes after leaving the main highway they came upon their destination without warning. Fyodorov swung around a corner and braked abruptly. Ahead of them a broad table opened out. Chris saw the heavy bulk of tiered concrete stadium seats bracketing an open field. Traffic approaching the area was funneled by road barriers toward a single entrance at one end of the field. The Lada was caught in the congestion as cars crawled toward the bottleneck. Beyond it the darkness soaked up what little illumination came from a bewildering variety of lights sprinkled over an area larger than a football field.

"What is this place?"

"It was our soccer stadium," the driver said.

Men carrying flashlights waved the Lada through the entrance toward a parking area off to the right. Suddenly the taxi scooted forward, cut past two lanes of parked vehicles, circled quickly and wedged itself into an opening facing the exit. "Sometimes one might wish to leave in a hurry," Fyodorov explained cheerfully.

While Chris and Lina were climbing out of the back seat, the bearded little driver disappeared at the front of the car. When he stood up and came back around the taxi he said, "I will leave the headlights on. If you wish to leave quickly, look for the wink."

"The wink? What do you mean?"

Fyodorov's teeth gleamed through his beard. Chris stepped to the front of the taxi. The driver had covered the top half of the left headlight with black tape.

"Do you think that's necessary?"

"It is best to be prepared."

Lina took Chris's arm as they started toward the soccer field over ground turned spongy by foot traffic. "I can see why you preferred to call your own taxi driver," she said.

"I'd say he was being overly cautious."

As they approached the market area, a mist curled around them and drifted across the field, more fog than rain. It added to the surreal panorama. Like a swap meet or flea market anywhere, the former soccer field had been divided into long rows of stalls or spaces for individual vendors. Some were selling directly out of their automobiles, whose doors stood open to reveal interiors crammed with cans of food or boxes of crackers. Many sold out of the backs of trucks. Others had erected tents or canopies, or displayed their wares on tarpaulins thrown over the wet ground. Display tables had been improvised from sheets of plywood placed over large crates or empty boxes. Piles of items filled bins and baskets, or were simply heaped on tables or on the ground—designer jeans and other Western clothing, medicines, radios and television sets, Polish glassware, real Russian vodka and French champagne.

Most of the grass had been flattened or destroyed by the combination of shuffling feet and tire tracks in the rain-softened earth. All across the muddy field individual stalls or display fronts were illuminated by the headlights of the vehicles attached to them, or by their trouble flasher lights. Some vendors had highway flares spitting and fizzing at the borders of the stalls, or fires built in oil drums to provide both light and warmth. Others relied on flashlights or camp lanterns. One row of canopied stalls, more formal in its setup than most, had a string of lights along the front extending for some fifty feet. The steady pulse of a generator providing power for the lights was added to the scene, a beat soon lost in the muffled uproar of idling engines, spitting flares, shouts and calls—the hum of commerce. Another large, open area had searchlights trolling back and forth against the low, swift-moving clouds, highlighting what might have been a car lot, where shiny new sedans, pickup trucks and off-road vehicles glistened under the passing lights. Next to it was a half-acre of automotive parts of every description, the equivalent of a parts warehouse.

"It's like something out of Dante," Chris said. "One of the levels of Hell."

"I think it is not as bad as that."

Lina was still holding his arm, as if she had forgotten her hand was there, and Chris found himself enjoying the warmth of her arm in his, the unspoken intimacy. They walked slowly along the first aisle, staring at the displays. One vendor beckoned Chris toward a stack of VCRs protected from the mist and rain by a tarpaulin draped over two columns of empty boxes. From a neighboring display pictures of naked breasts and genitals advertised pornographic magazines, videos and artifacts.

One truck required buyers to climb some wooden steps and enter the covered interior. Sharp-eyed men with lank black hair, permanent scowls and black leather jackets watched as

Chris and Lina glanced toward some buyers huddled over a table inside the truck.

"Drugs," Lina said in a low voice. "Heroin, cocaine, marijuana or drugs manufactured in our university laboratories. Those men are Chechens."

In the next aisle they walked past a vehicle whose interior dome light revealed a banker counting out a stack of dollars in an exchange. Men with automatic weapons flanked the car. A short distance farther along the aisle Chris spotted the first of the poaching products he had steeled himself against—a handsome Amur leopard skin. Lina felt the immediate, angry tension in his arm. Her grip tightened, pulling him along.

"Why did you keep me moving?" he whispered harshly.

"Did you not see the men waiting in the back seat of the car? They are also mafia gangsters."

Still angry, Chris allowed himself to be urged along the next makeshift avenue of stalls and cars, past a truck heaped high with rugs; past an ambulance dispensing morphine, LSD, boxes of prescription drugs; past a refrigerated truck in which hung whole sides of fresh red beef and stacks of bacon rising to the ceiling. Chris calmed down as he walked. What did you expect? he warned himself. What did you come to see?

After a while Chris and Lina Mashikova became numbed by the spectacle of abundance. In a society flirting with starvation, they had come upon a field of gluttons. Voices called out to them insinuatingly as they passed. They learned to pick out the most eagerly sought goods from the orderly lines that formed in the darkness.

In the fourth of the avenues that stretched across the width of the field, near the center of the huge black market, Chris saw a basket of teeth. He stopped in his tracks, suddenly breathless. He approached the stall slowly. Two cars and a covered pickup formed the back of the display area, which was unevenly lit by the headlights of the truck at one end of the stall. Sheets of plastic held up by tent poles sheltered the displays, which occupied an area twenty feet wide.

Bears' teeth, Chris saw, as he came closer. Bear claws filled a second basket, shriveled gallbladders a third. Nearby, a smaller box was filled to the brim with tigers' teeth. Like a damned candy store! Chris fumed. Next came a pile of tusks dumped carelessly on the ground. Too small for elephant tusks, Chris thought. Walrus ivory.

Near the middle of the stall was a crate three feet square and three feet high. An Asian—Chinese or Manchurian—nodded eagerly at Chris and Lina.

Chris peered into the box. "Tiger bones," he said involuntarily.

"Yes, yes, tiger! We have many more. Next box, see? Best leg bones."

There were glass jars of powdered bone as well. More jars containing black intestines, lips, testicles. One locked case held curved dark pieces of bone and cartilage Chris recognized as tiger penises. Smells of blood and rotting meat and dried skins overwhelmed him. He stumbled on, confronting a long table crowded with colorfully packaged tiger products—wines and soups, balms, tinctures, powders and pills.

By this time Chris was tight with rage. A pile of tiger skins heaped on the ground shattered the last shred of self-control. "Where did you butchers get these?" he demanded. "How much do they cost?"

The Asian stared at him blankly. Another man in the stall, also Asian, drifted toward them. Squat and muscular, he carried a handgun in a holster.

"Yob tvoyu mat!" Chris shouted, resorting to the most popular Russian curse. "You're the ones who should be shot!"

"Christopher! I think you must stop—"

Chris saw the heads and skins on a table in the far left corner of the stall. Because the headlights of the truck on the right side did not reach this far, an automotive trouble light in a wire cage had been clipped to the edge of the table. There, as if posing for a photograph, a half-dozen tiger heads were grouped together, baring their teeth in frozen snarls. Their yellow eyes glittered in the garish light.

"You bastards! Don't you know what you're doing? Can't you see the insanity of it?"

Whether or not he understood the words, the vendor understood Chris's anger clearly enough. He began to shout back, waving his arms. The second Asian quickly joined him.

Drawn by the apparent dispute, other vendors and buyers approached the area curiously. A pair of burly, black-jacketed men who were prowling the aisle as a security watch turned toward the commotion.

Chris grabbed one of the large jars of powdered bone and threw it to the ground. On the soft earth the jar didn't break but the lid fell off. White powder spilled onto muddy grass.

The vendor screamed at him. From a nearby stall another seller ran toward them, carrying a lug wrench in one hand.

"Christopher! *Paspishiti!* Quickly—we must go!"

Chris tried to grab another of the jars. One of the vendors seized his coat, spinning him around. Angry cries shrilled in his face. He was shoved backward. From the corner of his eye he saw the security black jackets running toward him.

Suddenly the red haze of rage lifted. He recognized the stupidity of making a loud scene in what amounted to the middle of the enemy camp. There was a time and place to make noise —not here. He had come to the black market to see for himself the harsh reality of the danger faced by the Siberian tiger and many other threatened species—not to make himself and Lina new victims.

Someone clutched his arm. Another yelled at him, spraying spittle into his face. Jerking free, Chris shoved clear of a tangle of bodies. Suddenly the headlights on the truck at the end of the stall went out, plunging the immediate area into almost total darkness.

What had been a confused scene of shouting, pushing and shoving became a melee. Fingers clawed at Chris's eyes. Something hard struck him on his left shoulder with brutal force. His arm went numb.

He staggered backward. A dark figure lunged toward him, but the attacker tripped over one of the taut lines supporting the stall's tent poles and sprawled into a pile of boxes. The pile crashed around him.

Lina appeared beside Chris, her face thrust close to his. "This way—hurry!"

She led him past a table and around the end of the stall. A gap between cars provided an opening to the next aisle. Before they reached it two men in black jackets blocked their way.

Because Lina was ahead of Chris, in the darkness he could not see clearly what happened next. The first security guard tried to grab Lina with one hand. She moved very quickly, using footwork that Chris could not follow. He *thought* her knee might have rammed adroitly into the man's groin. The man's breath whooshed from his lungs. He knelt in the mud, his hands clasped in front of him.

The second guard, directly behind the first, was caught by surprise. Instead of retreating, Lina stepped toward him, slipped inside his clumsy grasp and struck him across the bridge of his nose with the heel of her right hand. He collapsed like a sack of grain. Blood from a broken nose spurted over his mouth and chin, onto his black leather jacket, over hands cupped before his face in disbelief.

Chris stared at a pathway suddenly clear before them.

"*Edyom-tya!*" Lina called in Russian. "Let's go!"

Angry shouts rose all around them. "*Stoy!*" "*Vot on!*" "Stop!" "There he is!"

But in the poor light and general confusion they were not seen. Quick-thinking and coolheaded, Lina Mashikova ran ahead of Chris. She led him across one aisle, weaved through a tangle of cars and reached yet another row of stalls. As far as possible she avoided headlights and open areas, frequently ducking behind the cover of straggling crowds. Each maneuver took them back toward the western entrance to the market and away from the hue-and-cry behind them.

They reached the end of the soccer field at the far corner of the market. Here a fire burned in an oil drum but there were no other lights nearby. A patch of dark turf divided the market area from that set aside as a parking strip. Lina glanced back over her shoulder. She paused while Chris caught up. He was out of breath from running and stress.

"We cannot wait—they are hunting for us."

"Let's find the taxi. Look for the wink."

They ran across the open ground toward the rows of parked vehicles. As they slipped and stumbled, Chris understood why this patch had been left empty. Low-lying, it had been turned into a soupy marsh by the rain. It sucked at Lina's boots and Chris's shoes, slowing them down.

"He parked up front!" Chris gasped.

He was struck by Fyodorov's prescience in maneuvering his taxi close to the exit. Had the driver understood Chris that well as a potential troublemaker? Was he so transparent? Or had Fyodorov simply recognized the potential for conflict when an ignorant outsider ventured into mafia territory?

"There it is!" Lina said tersely.

In the same instant Chris saw the hooded headlight. They ran toward it over a patchwork of mud and spongy turf. Far behind them, but not far enough for comfort, more shouts rose into the night. "*Stoy!*" Chris translated. "Stop!"

Fyodorov had been standing next to the Lada, smoking a cigarette. Whether he was alerted by the cries or saw them running across the open ground, the taxi driver immediately threw down his cigarette, jumped into the driver's seat and switched on the ignition. By the time Chris and Lina reached the taxi, its engine was already racing. As they piled through the doors, bulky figures in dark jackets off to their right veered away and ran to block the exit.

Fyodorov jammed the shift into first and the Lada jumped forward. It reached the exit a split second before the first of the leather jackets got there. The taxi shot through an opening between barriers and skidded across a patch of mud and for a moment the wheels spun without traction and a hand grabbed at the handle of the door beside Chris.

The front tires gripped macadam at the edge of the road. When the Lada shot forward, the man at the door tried to run with it. Its momentum hurled him off balance. He fell away and sprawled onto his face, arms flung out like a parachutist in free fall. Careening onto the road, the taxi quickly gained speed.

A split second later the bark of a single shot rent the darkness, like a door slammed in frustration.

Chris whirled, staring back through the small rear window. He saw figures silhouetted against the hazy outline of the market, fists raised in the air.

*   *   *

"You have good time?" Mikhail Fyodorov called cheerfully over his shoulder.

"Yeah, great."

"Where do you go now? Back to hotel?"

"Are we being followed?"

"They will not follow Fyodorov—not for long."

Chris glanced at Lina. The journalist seemed calm, and she had certainly kept her head far better than he had when the trouble started. Not simply kept her cool, Chris thought. What the hell had happened back there?

"Do you realize you took out two men in as many seconds? Where did you learn *that?*"

She was silent a moment, looking away from him out the window. "Yuri was in *spetznaz* . . . he was highly trained in self-defense. He knew I would be alone for a long time when he was sent to Afghanistan. He wanted me to be able to defend myself. He taught me."

"He did a hell of a job."

She did not answer. Who are you? Chris wondered. It was an unanswerable question, but he didn't care. He was just glad she was there.

"Where do you live?" he asked after a moment. They were speeding down from the hills past the familiar Stalin-era apartment blocks. "We can take you there. Is it far?"

She glanced toward the taxi driver, who was watching them in the rearview mirror. "To your hotel," she said.

19

THE BLACK ZHIGULI was parked on the street across from the entrance to the apartment building. It was an older brick building, dating back perhaps to the 1920s, with crumbling ornamental cornices over doors and windows. In spite of its weathered decorations, cracked paint and grimy brick walls, it retained an air of faded elegance.

The nearest streetlight, half a block away, had been shattered. The interior of the car was completely hidden. Even someone passing on the sidewalk a few feet away could not have seen the two men in the front seats clearly.

There were, in fact, a few stragglers on the street—a sailor who had drunk too much, walking with an odd slide-and-hop motion, as if the sidewalk rolled beneath his feet; an old woman with a string shopping bag shuffling at an arthritic pace along the sidewalk past the apartment building; a pair of youths strutting toward the corner. The latter stopped to amuse themselves by taunting the old woman. What was in the bag, *babushka?* Something good? They were both hungry, would she mind sharing? The old woman inched along, her head lowered. It was covered by a scarf that was knotted under her chin. She had thick legs, as straight as posts. Tiring of their game, or perhaps because it presented too small a challenge, the teenagers moved on jauntily.

They cast covert glances toward the Zhiguli as they came abreast of it. After conferring secretively, one of the youths crossed the street behind the black car while his companion walked ahead.

Quietly Leonid Brunovsky opened the driver's door and

stepped out onto the sidewalk. He turned to face the young man approaching the rear of the car. Brunovsky looked bulky in his greatcoat, as immovable as a sea wall.

The youth stopped, uncertain.

"Get out of here," Brunovsky said with quiet menace.

He watched until the youth had skittered back across the street to rejoin his companion. They walked on, trying to regain their cocky strut. At the corner they looked back long enough to gesture with their middle fingers. Brunovsky took a single step forward and the youths disappeared hastily around the corner.

Brunovsky settled back into his seat, quickly closing the door. It was cold enough inside to see his breath. He started the engine again. The heater fan growled into action with a rhythmic clatter.

"You're certain this is the building," the Collector said.

"I followed her here, Sergei Gregorevich. She went inside. I talked to the manager. The woman lives on the sixth floor. She is a journalist."

"She lives well enough for a journalist."

"It's an old building. The rooms are larger than most, but all the tenants complain. The rugs are worn, the halls are filled with the smell of cabbage, the plumbing is noisy. So the manager says. However, the woman is no trouble."

"Yelina Mashikova . . ." Lemenov tried out the name on his tongue. "Still, the rooms are large, and she has her apartment to herself, with not one room but two, you said."

"Maybe she has a friend, an important patron. She is pretty enough."

"Do you fancy her yourself, Leonid Andreyevich?"

"If her shoes were under my bed, I would not throw them out."

The way the Collector talked one might have concluded that he was without passion, Brunovsky thought. But Brunovsky had seen him in the taiga with a rifle in his hands, his hot eyes fixed on the prey he stalked . . .

For a time they sat in silence. Though Brunovsky badly wanted a cigarette, Sergei Lemenov did not permit anyone smoking in the car with him. *He doesn't smoke, he doesn't drink, he doesn't appear to need a woman. Is collecting his only vice?*

"It's getting late," Brunovsky said. The heater was beginning to smell and he cracked a window. "What did you want with this woman tonight, anyway?"

"I thought we might have a little talk. I would like to know why she became so suddenly interested in the American."

Brunovsky stirred uneasily.

"It will have to wait," the Collector said. "It's getting late. Tomorrow you will find out who she is, where she comes from, who she sees. And if she is a journalist as she claims, I want to know who she writes for. For tonight . . . we still have other business."

"Now?"

"We will see if the photographer is working late in his shop."

"Would you like a drink?" Chris Harmon asked. "I have a bottle of Russkaya vodka I was taking back to a friend in Terney, but I can buy another bottle."

"Yes, that would be nice. We are both . . . chilled."

She had removed her fur hat and the long coat. Standing at the hotel room's window, staring out at the dark hills, she hugged her arms as if she were cold. She appeared slim, almost frail in her sweater and long shirt. Chris thought about the ease with which she had disposed of two strong-arm men blocking their escape from the turmoil in the black market. How the hell did she do that? he asked himself, still trying to comprehend what he had seen. As casually as someone swatting a couple of flies, she had somehow dropped one man to his knees, where he struggled to find a way to breathe, and flattened another thug twice her size with a single blow.

"Yuri really taught you how to take care of yourself," he said, handing her vodka in a paper cup.

"Yes . . . he wanted me to be safe." She shrugged the subject off with a faint smile. "You should be more careful, Christopher. It is not always wise to show everything you feel before strangers."

"I know . . . I'm sorry I lost my head." He paused. "You were terrific."

"It is easier to keep your head when you are not so angry."

"Tell me about it." Chris offered a rueful smile. "I didn't really intend to go berserk. It was just . . . seeing all that carnage in one place, all those teeth and bones and other parts dumped into baskets or boxes, or piled on the ground. And when I saw those tiger skins and heads, their eyes glaring out at me . . ."

"You went berserk."

"Yeah." He swallowed enough vodka to burn his throat. He tracked it all the way along the journey through his intestinal tract to his stomach. "The bastards. They seem to have no understanding of what they're doing, no conscience about it at all. What does it matter that there are so few of these animals left? When they're gone the earth will be poorer for it, and we're all losers. But try getting that across and you're classified with those who parade up and down with placards saying the end of the world is nigh."

"The poachers are making money," Lina said. "That's all that matters to them. The sellers are making more than the poachers. And at the end of the line are people who crave those things, who collect them or make soup of them. They covet these rare things enough to pay any price. If you don't change *them,* you will always have the rest of the chain, the poachers and the sellers of animal parts and artifacts."

Chris stared at her, surprised to find that she was thinking the situation through more clearly and rationally than he was. But then the subject was a lifelong passion with him. For her it was an excuse for a story in a newspaper or magazine.

"That market was . . . like a corner of hell. Except that the concept of hell is based on a belief in good and evil, right and wrong, crime and punishment. That seems to be dead and buried."

"That is what Yuri said . . . when he came back from Afghanistan."

"What?" The change of direction startled him.

"That there is no morality left in Russia. That there is nothing to believe in anymore, so there is no good, no evil."

"Did he really believe that?" Chris asked slowly.

Lina turned away from the window with a shiver. "It destroyed him. In the end . . . he could not accept it. That's why he took his own life."

"My God . . . I didn't know."

Without thinking, Chris opened his arms to her. She slipped naturally into the fold, resting her head against his chest. He held her quietly, pale blond hair tickling his chin. He was filled with the marvel of holding a woman after all this time, feeling the compact, vibrant warmth of her.

After a few moments he said, "You don't have to leave. You can stay here tonight."

"I would like that." Her face tilted up, tears had smeared her makeup. To those Chechen thugs she had been like a small bomb exploding. Now she was a vulnerable woman, tired and sad. "Christopher, I am not yet ready . . . do you understand?"

"There's no hurry," he said.

"I did not mean to come here under false . . . pretending."

"Pretensions . . ."

"I say it wrong? I'm sorry—"

"You said it fine. Your command of English is remarkable. Everything about you is remarkable."

"Not so remarkable as you say, I think."

"More."

They undressed slowly, not as strangers but as if they were old lovers. He admired the narrow hips and enviably flat stomach, the long tanned legs, the shoulders and arms a lingering pale gold, as if she had spent time this summer in the sun. He wondered where she had taken her summer holiday. She seemed unself-conscious, as if she had forgotten he was there. Looking at her neck and shoulders, at the small breasts that tumbled out of a white cotton bra, Chris swallowed and turned away. He retreated to the bathroom.

When he emerged she was lying in bed wearing one of his white cotton T-shirts. "I hope you don't mind? I am like old girl friend, I rummage in your suitcase."

"I'm glad you feel that way."

In bed she moved close to him. He put an arm behind her shoulders and she tucked her head against his chest within the crook of his arm. "You're beautiful, you know that," he said.

"I am beautiful and you are handsome, even if it is only in our own eyes. Isn't that the way it's supposed to be?" After a moment, as if she had found some kind of release, she began to talk. "Yuri was also beautiful. He was beautiful and brave before he left. After he came home from the war he was never the same. It was not that he was wounded in his body, the real wound was in his head. I told you he was idealist. Now he believed in nothing."

"Why?"

"It was because of all the things he had seen in Afghanistan . . . all the things he had to do. He was in the *spetznaz*. They were elite soldiers, our finest, and he was very proud of being chosen to be one of them."

"Like our Special Forces."

"Yes. They were carefully screened and specially trained. Then they were sent off to fight that terrible war, where they were not fighting for the *Rodina* but in a country where they were not wanted, where the people hated them and tried to kill them."

Like Vietnam, Chris thought.

"They were sent into the villages, our elite soldiers, but there were no Afghan men there, only women and children and old people. But our generals said they must be punished. The Afghans must be made to fear us. So the women were raped by our elite soldiers, children were shot, old people . . .

"Yuri would have nightmares about the children. By then he had begun to question everything, not only that idiotic war but also the politicians in Moscow who had started the madness and wouldn't stop it, and the generals who gave the orders that elite soldiers must batter the brains of children and impregnate the enemy's women with Russian seed. He came to believe that our leaders wanted the war for themselves, not for Russia."

Her thigh, bare under the T-shirt, had been touching his, and it had become a small spot of moist heat. He tried not to think about it.

"You don't have to tell me this—"

"It is okay, I want to." After a pause she said, "Yuri told me that he had decided he would not go into any of the Afghan villages again to kill the innocent, even if he was ordered to, even if it meant that he would be shot for treason. He prayed at night that I would forgive him."

Chris tightened his arm around her shoulders, as if to shield her from the pain of unbearable memories. He waited as long as he could before asking the question. "What happened?"

"His unit was ordered into another village, and Yuri went with them. He said that he was a coward, that when it came to the moment of truth he was afraid to defy orders, even when he knew they were evil, knew that the mission was a meaningless exercise in brutality and vengeance. He promised himself that he wouldn't fire his rifle. Then, before the soldiers reached the village, they were fired on by rebels in the hills. A mortar shell fell near Yuri and he was wounded. He never had to choose."

"I think he already had."

"Yes, but he condemned himself. He blamed himself for obeying his orders that last time, even though he didn't have to carry them out. He could not forgive himself or our leaders, the generals and the politicians." Lina was crying softly now. "In Moscow Yuri defied the soldiers in the coup, when the hard-liners tried to overthrow Mikhail Gorbachev while he was in the Crimea."

"Yuri was one of those soldiers who joined the people in front of the White House in Moscow, defying the tanks?"

"Yes. When the coup failed he was happy. The people laughed and cried and stood together in the square singing. He said we had won, we had beaten the politicians and the generals. He should have been proud again, but . . . he was soon disillusioned. The same people remained in charge, he said. And he still had the nightmares."

"You were with him all this time?"

"After he was released from the hospital, yes, but . . ." She hesitated, as if searching for the strength to face the final revelation. "He was taking drugs. He had started taking them in Afghanistan. Now he could not stop. When he saw what the drugs were doing to him, what was happening with us, and all the fine dreams of freedom and democracy collapsing around us . . . he didn't want to live."

"Don't talk about it anymore," Chris said.

"At the end he was not himself, you understand? I had lost him long before that. He had lost himself."

"Let it go," Chris said. "Let it go . . ."

"Just hold me, Christopher . . . just hold me."

20

"THE SHOP IS dark," Leonid Brunovsky said, disappointment in his tone.

"There's a light in back. And even if there weren't, he could be working in his darkroom." The Collector reflected a moment. "Does he work alone? Is there a helper?"

"*Nyet.* He works alone."

"Good. We don't want any loose ends. Whatever he is doing for the American, and it would be an urgent order, it must end here in this shop with him."

The statement was made calmly, without emotion, as if Sergei Lemenov were discussing the weather or the quality of a house wine. Its matter-of-fact tone made the admonition more chilling.

The two men were again sitting in the rented black Zhiguli, this time across the street from Dimitri Zhdanov's camera shop. They could not stay there for long. The Zhiguli, if noticed by a militia patrol or even by some homeless person huddled in a doorway, could point in their direction. Lemenov directed Leonid Brunovsky to a side street two blocks away, where they left the Zhiguli unobtrusively parked in an alley next to an office building.

They walked back, heading directly into a cold, gusting wind that whisked leaves and bits of paper and other debris along the street. It was nearly midnight, the city dark under a leaden overcast sky. Between the infrequent streetlamps that remained unbroken there was almost total darkness. Once Brunovsky stumbled on the sidewalk, which was broken here and there, and uneven. The Collector, on the other hand, drifted through this city canyon as if he were in the taiga, his steps leaving no impression, making no sound.

At the end of the short street on which the camera shop fronted, Lemenov paused in a doorway. Brunovsky had heard nothing, but a few seconds later a Volga sedan drove slowly along Svetlanskaya Street, hesitating at the intersection before it continued on. Two men sitting in the front of the Volga wore the brown uniforms of the militia.

"They have increased the number of patrols," Lemenov said when the car had disappeared.

"You don't think—"

"It is a routine tightening of security." The Collector smiled in the darkness. "Perhaps before the night is over we can give them something extra to worry about. Did you bring your materials?"

"*Da.*" Brunovsky patted a small black leather satchel on the floor between the seats. It resembled a doctor's bag.

"I will draw his attention to the front entrance. He may refuse to open the door at this hour. If he opens it, I will take care of him at once. If he refuses, you must go in through the back door. I trust it will present no insurmountable problems?"

"I looked at it this afternoon. It has a flimsy lock, and the wooden door frame is old and warped. I can either slip the lock or pop the door with a crowbar. Either way will require only a few seconds."

"Wait until you hear my voice outside. Give me two minutes. If I don't come through to the back of the store to open the door, you will enter on your own."

"I understand."

"If it is necessary to use force, make certain he does not reach a telephone." Lemenov was not worried about an alarm system. No small Russian shopkeeper could afford such protection, even if there were anyone to answer the alarm.

While Brunovsky made his way to the alley behind the camera shop, Sergei Lemenov walked along the street toward the shop's front entrance, confirming along the way that the street was deserted, the recessed entries across the way empty. For a moment he paused directly opposite the shop.

Although the window display was not lighted, his eyes were accustomed enough to the darkness to make out the shapes of two old cameras on cardboard mounts, along with a portrait in a painted gold frame (a young girl, Lemenov remembered from his earlier inspection, offering the photographer a bright, artificial smile) and a sheet of holiday color photographs of sailboats running before the wind and surf crashing over rocks.

Satisfied, the Collector quickly crossed the street, located the string that pulled a bell inside the shop over the entry, and gave it a sharp tug. When there was no response, he rang the bell impatiently, conveying a sense of urgency. "Hello?" he called out, just loud enough for Brunovsky to hear him in the alley behind the shop. "Is anyone there?"

A curtain divided the sales area at the front of the shop from a small corridor leading to the back rooms. Lemenov saw the curtain move. An instant later light flooded the shop. Dimitri Zhdanov, shoulders rounded from a permanent hunch that came from thirty years bending over trays to peer at negatives and prints, shuffled over to the entrance and lifted a shade drawn over the door. "Closed," he called out.

Zhdanov turned away and started back across the shop. Lemenov banged on the door. "Open up, please! It is important."

The shop owner turned but did not return to the door. His mouth tightened into a stubborn line. They were all the same, these shopkeepers, the Collector thought, rigid and unimaginative, incapable of changing fixed patterns, full of self-importance in their small domains.

"We are closed!" Zhdanov repeated emphatically.

He retreated to the curtain at the back of the shop, glancing over his shoulder before switching off the light. When he parted the curtain, Brunovsky was standing there.

Light from the back of the shop silhouetted the two figures, showing Zhdanov jump and grow rigid with shock. Brunovsky clamped one hand on his shoulder. The shop owner tried to twist free. Brunovsky's hand clamped down. The strength in his grip forced Zhdanov to his knees.

Brunovsky glanced toward the front door. He cuffed the

shop owner lightly on the side of the head, and Zhdanov was bowled over like a Russian doll with a rounded bottom. Leonid Andreyevich really was quite strong, the Collector mused as he watched.

Seconds later the lock clicked on the entry door. It swung open far enough for Lemenov to slip quickly inside. Brunovsky immediately locked the door behind him.

"Take him in back," the Collector ordered.

While Brunovsky watched the bewildered and frightened photographer, Sergei Lemenov inspected a work table on which several stacks of finished prints were waiting to be sorted and packaged. None of them portrayed scenes in the taiga, much less a tiger being shot. After examining a box containing packets of photos arranged in alphabetical order, the Collector opened a narrow door next to which a red warning light glowed. It was the shop owner's darkroom.

Some of the photographs from the American scientist's roll of film were pinned to a line over the developing area. Others were being processed in a tray filled with fluid, including one 8×10-inch enlargement of the wounded tiger. Lemenov studied it for a moment, impressed. Neither the animal's beauty nor its anguish moved him—in fact, he was annoyed by the reminder that his shot had not killed the tiger outright—but the striking composition of the photograph was undeniable.

He gathered all of the prints from the American's film into one pile, fishing those from the developing tank with a pair of tongs that he found hanging on a hook next to the tray. He added the negatives to the pile.

Stepping out of the darkroom, the Collector found Brunovsky and the shop owner in what apparently functioned as a combination office and storeroom adjoining the darkroom. The space was small and cramped, with hardly any room to move around a desk and chair, file cabinets and stacks of storage boxes. In one corner there was a samovar for making tea that also provided a little warmth.

"Well, now, Comrade . . . Zhdanov, isn't it? This won't be hard. We simply wish you to answer a few questions."

"Go to hell!"

The Collector smiled. "I think you can be quite confident of that, Comrade, if indeed there is a hell. But by the time we know for certain it will be too late, won't it? In the meantime we make our own heaven or hell."

"Who are you to debate theology with me? I don't know you. What do you want? You're not Chekist. They don't mean anything anymore."

"Chekist? Did you hear that, Comrade?" Lemenov asked Brunovsky.

Brunovsky shared Lemenov's amusement. "He does not fear us anymore."

The Collector sighed. "That is a mistake, Comrade Zhdanov. One that Mother Russia will soon discover." He dropped the bantering tone abruptly. "I'm going to ask you a few questions. You have only to answer them and your present difficulties will be over."

"I will tell you nothing. I will pay you nothing! Get out of my shop!"

Lemenov nodded to Brunovsky, who pinned Zhdanov in his chair with one arm while with the other he jerked the photographer's left arm out to full extension and, almost casually, broke the little finger of his left hand by snapping it back. Zhdanov's body convulsed, straining upward, but Brunovsky held him easily. He waited through Zhdanov's scream before efficiently breaking the adjoining ring finger.

The Collector produced a knife with a wide thin blade from a concealed sheath strapped to his right leg. He tested the blade with his thumb as Zhdanov watched, wide-eyed. Lemenov showed him a hairline of blood across the ball of his thumb.

He spoke with a chilling calm. "Are these all of the American's photographs?"

Puzzled, Zhdanov stared at him. "The American?"

"Don't toy with me. He presented you with a roll of film for development. Some of those pictures were of a tiger in the forest. You have been very busy making prints from this film, including enlargements. Is that correct?"

"Yes, yes," Zhdanov said hastily. "They are in my darkroom. You have probably spoiled some of the prints barging in like that."

"I'm sure you would have no difficulty making others. You have all the negatives, do you not?"

Zhdanov nodded, his eyes on the knife. He held his throbbing left hand between his legs. My God, what is happening to me? he asked himself in terror. Who are these men? Why are these photographs important? If I tell them everything they want to know, will they leave me alone?

Looking into the Collector's eyes, Zhdanov knew the answer to the last question.

"Are there any other prints?"

Something flicked by in back of the photographer's eyes. Lemenov, who missed nothing, was sure of it.

"There is one other set—a complete set. The American took it with him when he came to the shop this afternoon."

"I see. And that is all? There are no others?"

"What others would there be?" Zhdanov answered, but he spoke too quickly. "When he saw the first set he ordered others, which I am in the process of developing and printing. You saw them for yourself. He has not been back. He won't be back until the morning."

Georgi Dimitrivich, Zhdanov thought, his terror escalating. He could face anything, even death, for himself, but not for his son. What if Georgi stopped by the shop, as he often did after he had been out with his friends, listening to loud American rock music or watching girls? These men—they *were* Chekists, he thought, they must be—would torture and kill the boy as they surely intended to do to Zhdanov himself.

Why? The question baffled him. There was nothing in those pictures worth killing for. Nothing!

"This is most unfortunate," the Collector said mildly. "You have decided not to tell me the truth."

"No, no, Comrade, I swear it! I have told you everything!"

Lemenov nodded at Brunovsky. "Hold his arms tightly, Leonid Andreyevich."

Brunovsky pressed the smaller man down in his chair and at the same time jerked his arms behind him. Zhdanov struggled, his efforts rocking the chair but doing nothing to disturb Brunovsky's iron grip.

Lemenov waved the blade slowly back and forth before

Zhdanov's eyes. He touched the tip of the blade to the shop owner's neck and drew it across, creating a thin red ribbon from ear to ear, so shallow that seconds passed before the blood actually appeared.

"We are going to be here for some time, however long is necessary for you to tell me all."

"But I've told you everything! I know nothing about these photos. Why would I lie? They mean nothing to me! The American means nothing to me!"

"I saw it in your eyes, Comrade. You're lying."

"No, I swear to God—"

"Then may God forgive you," Lemenov murmured.

The stroke of the knife was so swift, the blade so sharp, that at first Zhdanov felt nothing. Then the blood began to pour from his nose over his upper lip, he tasted it with his tongue, and he began to sob.

"Please . . . please, I know nothing—"

"Are there any other prints?"

"No!"

Fifteen minutes passed before the Collector was convinced that Dimitri Zhdanov was unable to tell him any more. It seemed reasonable to conclude that Zhdanov would not have been able to persist in lies for so long. Still, the nagging doubt persisted. There had been that flicker in the man's eyes . . .

"That's all, then," the Collector murmured.

Zhdanov could no longer speak. His head barely moved.

Lemenov turned the blade in his hand, seating it rigidly against the base of his palm, and in a single thrust drove it deep into Zhdanov's abdomen just under the rib cage. The knife scraped bone as Lemenov pulled it sharply across his victim's body. Zhdanov bucked upward from his chair, his mouth wide open in a soundless scream, then collapsed back onto the chair. When Brunovsky released his arms, he spilled sideways onto the floor.

The Collector bent forward and with a surgical stroke severed the photographer's left ear. "I have a reputation to maintain, Comrade," he said. It was as close as he ever came to joking.

Turning to Brunovsky, he said, "You are ready?"

"Yes."

"There must be nothing left behind."

From his doctor's bag Brunovsky produced a plastic-wrapped packet of material that resembled artist's clay and was about the size of a brick. The material was a plastic explosive called Semtex, of Czech origin and a favorite among Palestinian and IRA terrorists as well as Russian experts in sabotage and terror. It could be shaped as necessary to fit into a suitable crevice or container. In this instance Brunovsky did not bother concealing the explosive. He casually punctured the plastic lump with a pencil-shaped detonator, glanced at Lemenov, who nodded, and broke off the end of the detonator.

"It is timed for five minutes."

"Out, then."

They went out by the back door and walked down the alley. They had reached the end of the street when a loud *whump* shook the ground and broke nearby windows. A split second later there was a second, louder roar as chemicals in Zhdanov's darkroom exploded.

By the time Lemenov and Brunovsky reached the Zhiguli, parked two blocks away, garish red flames and black smoke were climbing into the sky behind them.

The thump awakened Chris Harmon, who had drifted into uneasy sleep. Lina slept beside him undisturbed. She lay on her side with her back fitted to his front—spooning, Nancy had called it. Chris eased slightly away from her, stifling a groan. *This isn't exactly what Alex had in mind for my sex life*, he thought.

An explosion of some kind? Not far away, either. That bump had rattled the windows and even jarred the bed.

He eased out of bed so as not to awaken Lina and padded on bare feet over to the window. With few lights showing in downtown buildings at this midnight hour the darkness was, if anything, more complete than it had been earlier. Chris had been standing there for several moments before, smelling smoke, he also made out a thick black cloud of it, black on black. Near the base of the cloud, at ground level, red fingers combed through the smoke.

Chris's first thought was that a local mafia gang was teaching a reluctant shopkeeper a lesson. Evidently the flames were contained, for they soon died away. Chris wished for a clearer night so he could have seen more.

Finally returning to bed, he was far from sleep. The reflection about Alex, and the warmth of the slender body close to his, led Chris's thoughts inevitably to Nancy. When he first came to the Primorskiy he used to talk to her at length, trying during long periods of waiting in the taiga or on sleepless nights to make sense of what had happened to them. After the post-holiday letter he had talked less.

He knew that the memory of this night was not one that he could ever share with Nan. Oddly enough, he thought she would have understood. She was sentimental, cried at almost any movie, at birthdays and weddings, at Olympic ceremonies when the American flag rose over the victory stand or any time she heard taps played. There was no way Yuri Mashikov's story would not have moved her.

Ironically, when he left for the Far East, Nancy was so angry there had been no tears. She seemed glad to see him go. Did the private grief come later? And why did that thought carry such a weight of depression?

It's just that we had our time, most of it good, and I've wondered since your letter who you're with now and if you're happy. To paraphrase the poet Donne, "Have we all old vices spent,/And now must find out others?" Does it seem strange that I'm quoting poetry to you? It's only because I'm lying in bed with a pretty Russian poet who could also make Chuck Norris blink in a karate duel. I have to tell you, Nan . . . I haven't spent all my old vices.

Chris shook his head ruefully.

Outside in the lonely darkness, sirens wailed, drawing closer as he listened.

When the rain stopped that night in the taiga, the tiger stirred restlessly. She was ravenous, not having eaten in more than forty-eight hours. She slunk out onto the forest floor from her den. She walked with her belly close to the ground and dragged her left front leg, but there was still power in her movements and only a slight lurch to her gait. Like most animals, she was adapting amazingly quickly to her handicap.

Her bewildered cubs milled around her in the darkness. The trees overhead dripped steadily, but the forest floor, protected by heavy undergrowth, was surprisingly dry.

It was not hunger that had awakened the tiger. It was the noise. A sharp crack of sound that reverberated through the taiga, a sound she associated directly with the painful blow that had crippled her left shoulder, a sound she linked with the odor of human flesh and the knowledge that man was her enemy.

As she prowled through the forest, another alien noise reached her. She stopped, listening. This rasp was also identified with her newly perceived enemy. She listened until the growl of an automotive engine faded away into the distance.

Resuming her foraging, she followed a path that took her in the direction of the original sound that had awakened her. As she drew closer, other scents reached her sensitive nostrils—strange smells of rubber, oil and gas, and another that was not strange but sent a ripple of reaction through her body: the smell of blood. It made her both more eager and more cautious.

She came upon a tree where a male tiger had recently left his mark, identifying his territory. She was encroaching—another reason for caution.

The smell of blood became stronger as she advanced slowly toward the edge of the forest. She could smell and hear water now, the river coursing over its rocky bed a short distance away. Slinking low to the ground, every sense alert, the tiger eased out of the fringe of the taiga into tall, golden grass. Invisible there, she lay flat on the ground. Her cubs, close behind, imitated her.

For a full minute the Siberian lay motionless. The grasses stirred around her in the wind. Behind her the wet leaves dripped with a soft patter like raindrops. The mountain stream at the bottom of the slope before her, high with runoff from the day's rain, thrashed noisily down the mountainside.

Instinct and the evidence of her senses combined to tell her that the human hunters were gone. The male tiger's scent was very strong but it was coupled with the equally powerful smell of blood.

After several minutes her hunger overcame her caution. She crept through the tall grass toward the river. On the lower part of the slope the grass was streaked and matted with blood. In addition to the huge footprints of the male tiger there were many other, older tracks of smaller animals leading to and from the river where they had come to drink. And there were also the footprints of the two-legged hunters, their human smell interlaced with that of the tiger and the pervasive smell of blood.

Instinct told the Siberian that death had come here. The male tiger was gone, carried away by the hunters. Nearby, left behind, was the freshly killed carcass of a large ibex, the body intact except for one shoulder where the male tiger had fed.

Caution abandoned, the Siberian fell on the fresh kill. Another instinct told her that it was time to begin the weaning of her young, and she tore off pieces of flesh and spat them onto the ground. Two of the cubs, the male and one female, fought over the first piece, ending in a tug of war until the rag of flesh began to tear apart. The third cub, unnoticed, chewed tentatively at a piece of her own.

The tiger fed voraciously. After a half-hour she left the carcass to go down to the river to drink. Though sluggish with food, there was renewed power and grace in her movements. After drinking, she returned to the dead animal to feed again. By this time the cubs were trying to tear pieces of flesh from the carcass on their own with indifferent success. The tiger left them to it.

She would stay with the carcass, guarding it and feeding off it, all through the coming day and into the next night, while renewed strength poured into her body.

21

BY MORNING THE storm clouds had moved out over the Sea of Japan as far as the Kuril Islands, leaving the skies above Vladivostok a clear, sparkling blue broken only by small white clouds like popcorn. Crisp cold winds driving off the hills blew the prevailing mix of industrial haze and sea mist out to sea, ushering in a brilliant autumn day.

The sharp-edged outlines of the city's skyline were hard against Chris Harmon's eyes as he gazed out of his hotel room window. The corner of the harbor that he could see from his window revealed an azure blue sea. Even the naval ships at anchor appeared more sea-ready in the brilliant sunshine. Only a single thin column of smoke marred the scene. It rose above the flat roofs of some three-story buildings a short distance away. As the stain cleared the shelter of the buildings it was quickly shredded and dispersed by the wind.

Chris turned away from the window. Lina Mashikova, having showered, was dressing in the bathroom. In contrast to the night before, she had seemed shy this morning, even a little distant. He guessed she had probably had second thoughts about spending the night in his room. It was just as well, he thought wryly. After a restless night, he didn't need more images of creamy thighs and rosy breasts dancing before his eyes.

They rode the creaky elevator in silence to the lobby. Mikhail Fyodorov, who seemed to have nominated himself as part of their team, was waiting outside the hotel in his Lada taxi. "It is beautiful day, yes?" he greeted them cheerfully. "A day like no other!"

"Nice of you to order it up," Chris said. "I'd like to make one stop on the way over to the Global Wildlife Federation offices. There's a camera shop just a few blocks from here—it's on our way."

Before Chris finished giving directions the taxi driver veered in toward the curb and braked sharply. He swung around in his seat. "This camera shop, it is Dimitri Zhdanov's shop?"

"That's right. How did you know? But I don't suppose there are many—"

"You did not hear explosion?"

Puzzled, Chris stared at him, alerted by something in Fyodorov's eyes. "I heard an explosion in the middle of the night." Chris glanced at Lina. "You slept right through it."

"Then you don't yet know . . . ?"

"Know what? For God's sake, what is it? What's happened?"

"Trouble follows you, my friend," the taxi driver said. "Comrade Zhdanov's shop was blown up and destroyed by fire. Police say it was chemicals in his darkroom where he was at work, but you never know." Fyodorov was watching Chris, noting the shocked rigidity in his body, as if he had stiffened against a blow. "One asks, why would anyone blow up a small camera shop? But these days you always wonder. Maybe Zhdanov refused to pay some mafia gangsters for protection? What do you think?"

"Dimitri Zhdanov was inside the shop?" Lina asked sharply.

"Was he hurt?" Chris asked.

"The owner was inside when it happened. That is why the police investigator believes it was accidental explosion. Investigator was interviewed on television this morning. Zhdanov did his own developing and printing in back of his shop. That is where fire started. He had no chance."

"Dead?" Chris whispered.

There was a moment of silence. A truck rumbled by, rocking the taxi. Chris felt as if the earth itself had shaken.

"What time did this happen?" Lina asked.

"It was middle of the night," Fyodorov answered. "I'm not

sure exactly. After midnight. I myself heard explosion, many miles away."

Lina looked at Chris. "Why would he be working so late?"

"For me," Chris answered slowly. "Because I asked him to make another set of prints, along with some enlargements. I promised to pay him extra."

"A terrible accident," the taxi driver said.

"Was it?" Chris found it difficult to accept the terrible suspicion that was taking root in his mind.

He felt Lina Mashikova's gaze, intent and probing. She was a journalist, after all, with a reporter's instinct for a story. *She knows,* he thought.

Not an accident.

"You cannot blame yourself for what happen," Fyodorov said. "You could not know."

Suddenly Chris thought of Zhdanov's son Georgi Dimitrivich. He was supposed to deliver the second set of prints to Ken Langert. Had he made the delivery? And had he also been in his father's shop when the explosion ripped through it?

"What is it, Christopher?"

"Was Zhdanov alone? Was anyone else there in his shop?"

"There was only one body found," Fyodorov said.

Chris finally met Lina's questioning stare. "Zhdanov had a son . . ." He turned toward the taxi driver. "Take us to the Global Wildlife office as fast as you can get there."

Any worries Chris had that his photographs might not have reached Ken Langert, or that they might not have produced sufficient outrage, were quickly allayed when he entered the Global Wildlife Federation's offices. The main office was jammed with people, all of them seemingly talking at once. Ken Langert weaved through the crowd to greet Chris, who introduced Lina as a journalist eager to tell his story and use one or more of his photographs.

"I have a *Global Alert* bulletin being printed now," Langert told them, excited by the prospect. "It'll be ready this afternoon . . . just in time to shove it in the Koreans' faces when they get here."

"When is that?" Chris asked.

"I hear they're flying in around one o'clock. I wouldn't try to go anywhere near the airport at that hour, by the way, the security is heavy and traffic is being rerouted on some streets."

Chris glanced around the room. "Who all is here?"

"I have reps from the Tiger Trust and CITES, and from TRAFFIC—that's the organization that monitors the wildlife trade for the World Wildlife Fund," he explained for Lina's benefit. "Ivan Petrovic is here, Chris, he's with the Siberian Tiger Project, one of the Russian groups that sponsored your own research project. And there are other conservationists and some other Russian reporters. I hoped to have someone from CNN radio and the BBC, but it seems they're out at the airport to see the Koreans arrive."

"The photos got here safely, I see," Chris observed, noting a large bulletin board on which a half-dozen photo enlargements had been pinned. "Thank God for that."

"Why, what's wrong? Why wouldn't they get here safely?"

Chris told Langert about the explosion and fire that had destroyed Dimitri Zhdanov's camera shop, killing the proprietor. "It was his son who brought you those photographs. Everything Zhdanov had was destroyed, including the negatives."

"Do you think there's a connection? I mean, between your photos and the explosion?" Langert said.

"I don't know."

Chris was having trouble dealing with the suspicion that, in leaving the film with Zhdanov and pressuring him to make copies overnight, he might inadvertently have made the shop owner a target.

"Maybe this thing is a lot bigger than we know," said Langert.

His normally languid attitude dropped, the Global Wildlife Federation's Far East representative made his way over to his desk and turned to face the room, holding his arms up. "People, listen up. Can we have some *quiet* here?" He waited for the hubbub to subside before waving toward Chris. "This here's Chris Harmon, the man of the hour. He's the one who took those photographs I've put up on the board. The picture on top is the one I've used for my bulletin. You'll all get copies as soon as I have them this afternoon."

Chris suffered through a barrage of exclamations and congratulations over his photographs. Lina had drifted off, and Chris saw her talking to one of the other Russian journalists. He felt a twinge of concern. Why did Langert have to invite other reporters? Lina had been onto this story first, she deserved the credit—

He caught himself up short. What was that all about? Was he *jealous,* for God's sake? This story needed every media outlet that could be found for it. It wasn't about exclusives or personalities.

"Can I have some of those photos?" one man called out.

"I've made multiple prints of the best shots, those that show the tiger being wounded. We're also putting together a complete press information kit."

Langert fielded questions. A field investigator for EIA, the Earth Island Institute, asked for the floor. "We need to get across that stopping the poaching isn't the answer. I mean, we have to stop it, but it's the *market* we have to put an end to. It's like with the Asiatic moon bear in China, most of you know how bears are being clapped in cages with a steel tap on the bear's stomach and a catheter going to its gallbladder to milk the bile. The bears are caged and milked like that as long as they live, which can mean years. All because some ancient folk remedies attribute nonexistent magical powers to the bear's bile, just as they do for rhino horn, deer musk and tiger bone."

"Cut to the chase, Alan," someone called out.

"All right, the point is, it's these damned Oriental folk medicines that are the problem. We won't stop the killing and the tortures until we stop the demand. China's the biggest culprit. We've got to force the Chinese government to ban those practices."

"If we can't get meaningful sanctions against China over

human rights violations," another man growled, "how in hell are we going to get them over animal rights?"

"I'll tell you one thing would get their attention," Ken Langert said, "and that's a full-scale, worldwide consumer boycott. Taiwan has already shown its sensitivity to that threat. China and Korea are equally vulnerable."

"China's leaders are more stubborn."

"Chris's photos will help. They're just the sort of thing that will hit consumers hard and make them stop and think."

"Tears are all well and good," the EIA investigator said, "and don't get me wrong, I'm all for trying to help Dr. Harmon with his rescue effort and to make the most of those photos. All I'm saying is, none of this will be meaningful in the long term if we don't address the root of the problem, and that's the demand."

The meeting dissolved into animated discussions of strategy centered around Chris's dramatic tiger photographs as well as a longer-range media campaign. Several of the conservationists sought Chris out, expressing their outrage over the shooting and concern over Chris's negative reception at the Russian Ministry of Environmental Protection and Natural Resources. "I don't know what's going on in that building," said Nils Cartright, who was with Britain's Tiger Trust. He spoke with a strong British accent that said Eton and Cambridge but he was refreshingly down-to-earth. "Those people used to be very sympathetic to our goals—shared them. Then almost overnight everything's changed. They can't spare us the time of day. Likhachiev—is he the chap you spoke with?"

"That's the guy."

"Right. He's an *apparatchik,* what we would call a career bureaucrat, does what he's told and no mind of his own, if you know what I mean. If he's given you the brush-off it means the brush is being wielded by someone much higher up than Comrade Likhachiev."

"They want us out of the preserve," Chris said.

"Does make you wonder a bit, doesn't it?"

Some time passed before Chris was able to break free. When he looked around the room for Lina Mashikova, she was nowhere to be seen.

Ken Langert appeared beside him. "Looking for your girl friend?"

"I don't see her—"

"She had to leave in a hurry. Saw you were tied up so she asked me to give you a message. Said she had to run, see her editor or something, and she'd call you later. Say, what's going on there, old buddy?"

"Nothing."

"Uh-huh. How well do you know her, Chris?"

"I only met her yesterday."

"I was talking to one of the other Russian reporters about her. Knew her by name and reputation but not much more. She's a loner, it seems. You know how the press corps is in the States? Same here. It's a tight fraternity. They all hang together."

"Maybe it's a mostly male fraternity and she's on the outside," Chris suggested. "What else is new?"

"Could be, I suppose. But what about those clothes? And the makeup?"

"What about them?"

"Have you taken a good look at the general run of Russian women lately, Chris? Most of 'em don't wear makeup. And they sure as hell aren't wearing designer clothes and thousand-dollar leather coats."

Chris took a moment to answer, allowing his resentment to cool. Langert meant well, even if he was out of line. "Lina came from Moscow and St. Petersburg. Those are sophisticated cities, Ken. Some of the women have even discovered lipstick and eye shadow."

"Take it easy, Chris, I'm not trying to make waves here. I'm just saying that most Russian women can't afford those clothes, and they can't even obtain the cosmetics. Neither can most freelance writers. It's not like your Lina is a television personality or a household name in journalism."

"What's your *point?* She's been trying to help."

Langert looked uncomfortable with what he wanted to say. "Okay, here it is. Did anyone else know about that camera shop besides you and Lina? I mean, about your negatives being there?"

The question jolted Chris, who rejected the implication out of hand. "That's ridiculous," he said coldly. "Lina was with me last evening—and all night."

Langert made a wry face. "There I go, egg on my face. Sorry, old buddy. I suppose I've been over here so long I'm starting to think like a Russian. Devious and conspiratorial, you know? Like an Oliver Stone."

"Sure."

"Don't think I'm not grateful for those pictures of yours. We all are. Thank God you thought to send over a set of prints from that shop yesterday. At least we can get these on the street and into the media. One of my guys thinks we can get some good television time tonight, tied in with the Koreans arriving on the scene."

"I'd like another set of those prints myself."

"Anything you want—they're your pictures."

"All I see out on display are the shots of the tiger. What about the others? Particularly the last pictures on the roll, after the tiger disappeared?"

"Well . . . I didn't make copies of those. I just have the original prints you sent over, and your friend asked for them. I thought you knew."

"Lina?"

"She said you wanted them," Langert explained. "I saw nothing wrong—there wasn't anything in those shots that we could use. No way to identify those poachers in the woods." He paused, suddenly uneasy. "You have your own set, right? I didn't think you needed copies of everything."

"I don't have those pictures," Chris said. "Mine were stolen from my hotel room."

"Oh boy," Langert said. "Then Ms. Mashikova has the only prints."

22

LEONID BRUNOVSKY, ALONE at the wheel of the Zhiguli sedan, followed the Lada taxi when it left the building housing the offices of the Global Wildlife Federation. Sergei Lemenov had instructed him to stay close to the woman this morning, not the American. He was to find out everything he could about the journalist and what she was up to.

It seemed a waste of time to Brunovsky, but Boris Provalev had confirmed Lemenov's order when Brunovsky reached him by phone. "I don't see the point," Brunovsky complained. "We don't have to worry now, we've destroyed all the photos that show us in the taiga. All that's left are the pictures the American has of the tiger, and they are the ones you wanted journalists to see."

"Do what he says, Leonid Andreyevich. Perhaps the Collector has an instinct in these matters that we don't have. I'm curious that I don't know much about this Mashikova woman. I make it my business to know such people if they're important."

"Maybe that only means she isn't important."

"Do it," Provalev said curtly. "You only have to tolerate Comrade Lemenov for another forty-eight hours or so. By then it will all be over."

Out of habit Brunovsky glanced at the clock in the Zhiguli. Like so many things in Russian-made automobiles, however, the clock didn't work. He looked at his watch. Almost noon. The Koreans were arriving at Vladivostok Airport in an hour, and Sergei Lemenov would be there to confirm their arrival. *He could have done it there and then,* Brunovsky thought. But the Collector had vetoed that possibility when it was first raised. Looking out for his own skin, Brunovsky thought.

Brunovsky's attention, diverted for only a few seconds while he checked the time, returned to the road before him.

The Lada had disappeared.

Mikhail Fyodorov was pleased with himself. "We've lost him, *babushka.*"

Lina Mashikova peered back through the narrow rear window of the taxi. "You are certain? What kind of car was it?"

"A black Zhiguli sedan."

"Could you see who was in it? Were there two men?"

"One man only, the driver, that's all. No stranger can follow Fyodorov in his own city if he does not wish it."

"How do you know he's a stranger?"

"He doesn't know our streets like a native. It was easy to lose him."

Lina continued to watch the street behind them, directing Fyodorov through several turns. When it was clear that no one was following them, she said. "Take me to the park, then."

She checked the time, then took out the prints from the manila envelope Chris's friend Langert had given her. She regretted that Langert hadn't made enlargements of these along with the other photos. There were a half-dozen pictures. They revealed the presence of two men in the forest, one of them a sniper. Their faces were indistinct, but as small as the images were they revealed recognizable physical characteristics. The sniper was as lean as a Saluki. The other man was powerfully built with a thick chest and biceps that appeared to strain his shirt. A faceless Saluki and bulldog, she thought. Would Anatoly Bukanin see anything familiar there?

Thinking about last night, Lina squirmed a little in her seat. She had kept her emotions in a box for so long, the lid shut tight. Last night she had lost control a little, lifting the lid . . .

Heat gathered in her neck and cheeks as she remembered

the feel of Chris Harmon's body fitted against hers, remembered the moment that he had felt the need to withdraw slightly from their close contact. *You shouldn't have started talking about Yuri,* she thought. *You should never have stayed the night.*

Lifting such a lid was dangerous. Sometimes it was impossible to close it again.

Anatoly Bukanin was waiting on a park bench, within sight of the small cafe that faced the entrance to the park. Lina had Fyodorov drop her off in front of the cafe, giving no indication that she recognized the man on the bench not far away. Not that she didn't trust the taxi driver but you never knew who else might be watching, and in any event her precaution would make Bukanin the conspirator happy.

"Do you wish me to wait, *babushka?*"

"No, that won't be necessary. I'll find my own way from here. I'm meeting someone . . . a friend."

"As you wish. Fyodorov is always ready to be of service."

She waited while the Lada followed the nearest road out of the park, turned a corner and vanished from sight. Then she went inside the cafe, ordered two coffees and studied Bukanin on his bench through the rain-spotted window. There seemed to be a little more life in the former KGB agent than he had shown the last time they met. At least he wasn't hunched over in that dispirited body language. Perhaps being given something to do, however inconsequential, had restored a little of his pride.

She carried the coffees in paper cups out of the cafe to the park bench, which was in the sun. Though the day was sunny and clear, it was quite cool in the shade and the sun was welcome. Bukanin smiled with genuine pleasure as she walked up to him.

"I've brought you coffee, Anatoly Isaevich. Two packets of sugar, no milk, did I remember right?"

"That is perfectly right, Yelinita. How could you possibly remember such a small thing?"

She laughed. "I remember once hearing you castigate your

aide when he brought you coffee with milk and not enough sugar. It made a profound impression on a young girl, hearing a KGB colonel angry at his lieutenant over milk and sugar."

Bukanin shook his head. "We were so arrogant then. We had much to learn." His gaze became distant as old memories chased away his amusement. "I saw you get out of your taxi. Where is your beautiful Japanese motorcycle? I hope it wasn't stolen."

"It's safe, don't worry."

"A fine machine like that, it would be a prize for any thief."

"Your worrying about me must mean you're feeling well, Anatoly Isaevich. Does that also mean you have something to tell me?"

"Have you had any success with selling my information about the nuclear submarine security plans?"

"Not yet. But what have you learned about the other matter? What do you hear about the Korean logging agreement? It is Boris Provalev's involvement that especially interests me."

"Comrade Provalev is ambitious."

Lina smiled. "That won't make much of a headline."

Bukanin sighed, sipped his coffee and watched some birds search the brown grass for nonexistent crumbs. "He is as dangerous as Stalin."

The blunt charge startled Lina. "What makes you say that?"

"Stalin is not dead in this country, he is very much alive. For one thing, he has so many loyal followers, many of them still in positions of power and influence, people who still revere Lenin and the whole Communist legacy. And the second reason is, Stalin was in power so long, he had such a firm grip on the people, that he created a dependence many of them will never lose. The younger people, they are different, they think differently. They embrace reform and are not so much afraid of change. But the older ones, those who grew up during Stalin's reign, are waiting for another messiah, another leader who will solve all their problems."

In spite of the warmth of the sun on the bench, Lina felt cold. "And Boris Provalev is such a man?"

"He makes those promises. Forget about the Gulag, he tells us. Forget about the millions who disappeared in the night, forget about the official corruption, forget about the greed of the *nomenklatura* with their dachas and limousines. Just remember that you had a job, you were safe from attack on the street by criminals, and you knew what tomorrow would bring, even if it was mean and you were hungry."

"It's strange to hear you talk this way, Anatoly Isaevich."

"Because I was KGB? Because I was a loyal member of the Party? That doesn't mean I was blind." Bukanin fumbled in his pocket for a packet of cigarettes, found it empty and crumpled the pack in one hand. "I don't suppose you have any more of those American cigarettes?"

"I brought you another pack of Marlboros." Lina produced the pack from her purse and handed it to him. "Go on . . . what else can you tell me about Provalev?"

She waited patiently while he tore open the end of the cigarette pack, tapped one out and lit it. He inhaled hungrily, coughed and said, "There are whispers. One never knows how much credence to give them. I told you he is ambitious. It is also said that he is not patient, that he may not be willing to wait for the people to give him what he wants through the new democratic process."

"A coup?"

Bukanin shrugged. "He would not be the first to try it." After a pause the old man added, "In Moscow the army still backs Yeltsin. But we are a long way from Moscow. In the Primorskiy . . . who is to say how the army would react?"

"But how does this Korean initiative further Provalev's ambition? It seems to make no sense."

"I don't know. But there is an old Russian saying . . . if something smells like shit, it is probably shit."

"If you've heard anything more specific, Anatoly Isaevich, tell me."

"There's nothing more I can tell you, Yelina Vassilyeva. Only that . . . Boris Provalev is a dangerous man. You must be careful. Perhaps this story you are seeking would not be good for you to find."

Watching him inhale, she resisted her own desire to smoke. She sensed an uneasiness behind his vague warning. She opened the manila envelope she had been holding and withdrew the half-dozen photos she had obtained from Chris's friend at the Global Wildlife Federation.

"I have some photographs I would like you to look at, Anatoly Isaevich. Look at them carefully. Tell me if you recognize either of these men."

He removed a pair of metal-rimmed glasses from his jacket pocket. "My reading glasses," he explained apologetically. "I can see little without them."

There was curiosity in his eyes as he began to study the pictures, shuffling through them slowly. Taken in close sequence, the photos were similar. Each was a view of the forest from which the poachers had shot the Siberian tiger while Chris Harmon's camera was photographing the scene through its telephoto lens. In each photo two men were clearly visible near the edge of the wood. In the last two shots, the bulldog had turned toward the distant camera lens, as if sensing that he was being watched.

Observing Bukanin closely, Lina thought he stiffened slightly. The hand holding the photos trembled almost imperceptibly. He sucked on his cigarette, covering the reaction, but she sensed a charge of tension in his body. His expression, however, did not change.

"What is it, Anatoly Isaevich? What do you see?"

"These faces . . . they are too small, too indistinct." He shrugged his shoulders and tapped the pictures together. "I could not say who they might be."

"Is there anything familiar about either of those men? Anything at all?"

"No . . . no, I am sorry."

He's lying, Lina thought. What is he afraid of?

Bukanin handed her the photographs. He continued to stare at them as she slipped them back into the envelope. At the last moment she hesitated, withdrew one of the pictures and studied it briefly before handing it back to him.

"Keep this one and look at it again. Promise me you will think about it, old friend. Perhaps something will occur to you."

"I will think about it, Yelinita." But his tone was heavy, offering no encouragement.

A cloud passed over the sun, shutting off the warmth and brightness. The park with its brown grass and thinning trees suddenly seemed dark and uninviting.

Lina pressed a fistful of rubles into his hand. "Do what you can for me, Anatoly Isaevich, that's all I can ask. I'll call you."

He had seen something in the photos, she was certain of it. He only needed a little time to find his courage.

23

THE COLLECTOR HAD made no attempt to position himself near the arriving Korean Air jetliner from which the visiting dignitaries were to alight. From inside the terminal, through a window wall on the second level that faced the airfield, he watched the portable steel steps being wheeled up to the aircraft and, as soon as the stairway was in place, a strip of red carpet being rolled out at its foot. The area had been cleared of everyone except a group of reporters, cordoned off by militia with their arms linked, television camera crews and the official welcoming party. The latter group, headed by Boris Provalev, included the mayor of Vladivostok and the acting territorial governor, both of whom were terrified of Provalev, and the interior minister, Oleg Kholkhov, just arrived from Moscow, a man in his sixties with a long gaunt face and baggy suit who had the appearance of someone wasting away. Forming up on either side of the red carpet strip to create a human corridor were at least a hundred uniformed militia. Sergei Lemenov had also observed plainclothes policemen inspecting the crowds inside the terminal, spot-checking luggage, briefcases, handbags and shopping bags.

The heavy security was exactly what he would have expected. It could be breached, of course—no security was absolutely airtight as long as its object remained in the open and others were in the vicinity. An assassin could act before he could be stopped, whether bursting out of the terminal with an assault weapon and opening fire before he could be cut down, smuggling himself or herself into close proximity to the target among the reporters, for example, or finding a clear line of fire at long range with a sniper's rifle. The mission, however, would be suicidal. Acceptable for a terrorist bent on martyrdom, or one of those pathetic losers like Lee Harvey Oswald, who had assassinated the young American President Kennedy, but not the Collector's type of operation. He had no desire to be a martyr to a cause. He worked for two things: money and pleasure.

Even his coming to the airport today had been a risk. A small one, which he had determined to be acceptable, but a risk nonetheless.

He had wanted to get a look at his targets. To watch them bow and preen with self-importance during their little speeches. To observe them being hustled from their ceremonial steps to the waiting armored limousine, surrounded by protective bodies. To know their relief, their feeling of safety.

Boredom caused Lemenov's attention to stray during the ritual reception. The Korean prime minister, Kim Su, was a small neat man in an impeccable light gray suit with matching well-groomed hair. He spoke into waiting microphones while television cameras recorded the historic event, the first time a South Korean prime minister had set foot on Russian soil. Kim Su did not speak Russian, Lemenov noted with contempt, and a translator quickly repeated his empty words. The other Korean dignitary, Chang Pyon, who was flanked by a pair of stone-faced bodyguards, was a chunky man of about sixty, also gray-haired, round face the color of berries. He was the chairman of the Sunsai Corporation. A businessman who did not waste time in polite speeches, Lemenov thought. Leave that to the politicians.

Like Boris Provalev. He dominated the scene, virtually ignoring the mayor and the acting territorial governor and the frail interior minister. Beaming at his visitors as if they were personal guests, Provalev faced the television cameras with practiced ease. He acknowledged the Koreans' bows, expressed his flattering welcome, and led them toward the waiting bulletproofed Chaika limousine. The Collector thought briefly of the future of a Russia dominated by such a man, but he quickly dismissed the speculation. He was not a philosopher or political scientist. For most Russians, their dreary lives would not change. Were they any better off now than under Stalin and Beria?

Lemenov had been in Vladivostok for his only direct meeting with Provalev at the time Alexander Solzhenitsyn had passed through the city on his return from his long exile in America. The writer had galvanized the Russian people in much the same way Boris Provalev did, but the chords that Solzhenitsyn struck were appeals to Russian character and history. Provalev was more like Zhirinovsky, Lemenov thought, whom Solzhenitsyn had dismissed as "a caricature of a Russian patriot."

The Collector's interest in observing the writer's triumphant arrival and tour of Vladivostok had been purely professional. He had been able to note the elaborate security measures, the armed motorcades, the use of plainclothes police officers to work the crowds of well-wishers and the deployment of hundreds of militia. His observations had been instructive. They had buttressed his instinctive decision not to make his strike here in Vladivostok, as Provalev had initially urged. His reasoned objections had led to Provalev's subtler plan.

Hopefully not too subtle, Lemenov thought. The Koreans could still torpedo the entire operation if they proved to be stubborn or suspicious.

He watched the motorcade as it left the airfield through special gates and reached the main highway, two long black limousines with heavily armed troop carriers escorting it front and rear, and a pair of militia on motorcycles riding point.

Before turning away, the Collector glanced up at the roof of a corner of the terminal visible from his window. One of the snipers rose into view, relaxing and stretching. Lemenov recognized the Dragunov SVD sniper rifle the soldier was carrying, a weapon the Collector admired and had used himself.

There would be no rooftop vantage points in the Sikhote-Alin preserve, he thought.

* * *

Heavy traffic delayed Sergei Lemenov's return to the center of the city, where he was met at his hotel by Leonid Brunovsky. The hotel, located just off Aleutskaya Street, was small, convenient and suitably anonymous for Lemenov's purposes. The room was spartan, with a tiny refrigerator and a hot plate in one corner. Brunovsky thought he could smell cabbage cooking somewhere in the building.

Boris Provalev's chief aide, and the only person trusted with knowledge of his link to the Collector, had managed to view most of the airport arrival ceremonies on television. Talking about it now, he was disgruntled. "I should have been there. That clown Andrei Petrikov—did you see him try to push his face in front of the cameras?"

Lemenov smiled. From the beginning Brunovsky had been uneasy over having a junior assistant take over some of his duties for Provalev while he, Brunovsky, was assigned to assist the Collector in every way possible. "Don't worry," Lemenov said. "When this is over you can have him shot."

"It is not good to joke about such matters, Sergei Gregorevich."

"I wasn't joking. Ah well, to more serious matters, then." As if to underscore his comment Lemenov retrieved a bottle of Posolskaya vodka from the little refrigerator and poured generous cups for himself and Brunovsky. As they talked, Brunovsky sat uneasily on the edge of the bed while the Collector remained on his feet, occasionally pacing in thought. "What can you tell me about this Lina Mashikova?"

Brunovsky's eyes would not meet Lemenov's. "I was unable to follow her."

"What do you mean, you were unable to follow?"

"As you instructed, I was careful not to stay too close to the taxi to avoid being seen, but the driver must have spotted me. He turned down one-way streets, doubled back and changed direction several times. He managed to use the heavy traffic and his knowledge of the streets to escape." Brunovsky paused, his heart pounding, surprisingly loud in his ears. He took a hefty gulp of vodka.

The Collector's calm was alarming. "So she does not wish to be followed," he said. "That is interesting. Were you able to learn anything about her background?"

"She is from St. Petersburg. She went to the university there and married a young army officer with family connections, Yuri Mashikov. He served with the *spetznaz* in Afghanistan and was wounded there. Apparently he returned from the war with liberal ideas, which his wife shared. He was not well, however. He was drinking, using drugs, and his health deteriorated. Two years ago he committed suicide."

"Go on."

"That's where it becomes interesting. Lina Mashikova worked as a reporter for the newspaper *Moscow Komsomolets,* but she was regarded as a beginner. She was not well known. Then there is no record of her activities for more than a year. Six months ago she arrived in Vladivostok. Her articles began to be published in some of the better newspapers and magazines, even *Izvestia.* Yet there have not been many publications. You know that we had a journalist friendly to Comrade Provalev attending the meeting this morning at the Global Wildlife Federation offices. His name is Vasily Gurechev. I've spoken with him about the meeting. He insists that Mashikova must have influential friends in the business. She publishes only enough to maintain the role of a freelance journalist. Gurechev believes she is a dilettante. Of course, he may be envious."

The Collector considered all this. "Did your informant have anything else?"

"The meeting went as we expected—even as we hoped. The tiger photographs will receive a great deal of publicity. The conservationist groups will all make use of them, and there is certain to be considerable furor. There is one problem . . ."

"Out with it!"

"We thought we had destroyed the only copies of the pictures that were at the end of the roll, which we stole from the American's room. There was another set. It was delivered from the camera shop to the director of the Global Wildlife Federation."

"When?"

"Yesterday evening . . . long before we went to the shop."

Rage flared in the Collector's eyes. Lemenov was remembering Dimitri Zhdanov's interrogation. "I knew Zhdanov lied," Lemenov said. "But how? How was he able to hold out to the end?"

"Because of his son," Brunovsky said.

"What do you mean?"

"He sent his son with the set of prints to the Global Wildlife office. It was his son he was trying to protect."

"God save us from family sentiment."

Brunovsky waited uneasily while Lemenov paced his narrow room. Finally he said, "We will attend to this woman later. First I want to know where she went when she left the American this morning and why she was so anxious not to be followed."

"But how can we—?"

"I will talk to this taxi driver. You wrote down his license number?"

"Yes, yes, I have it."

"Find out where he can be reached. Then you must see Comrade Provalev, who is anxious to discuss his plans with you. Stay close to him until you can learn of his progress with the Koreans. Then report to me. Everything now depends on Provalev's success in persuading the Koreans to do as he suggests."

"Where will you be?"

"That depends on the taxi driver."

24

WHEN THE MEETING in the Global Wildlife Federation's office broke up, Ken Langert said he had to run over to the printer's. "I'll be back as soon as I have the first copies of the *Global Alert Bulletin.* You gonna wait, Chris?"

"I'd like to see it, yes."

"Have some more coffee." Langert had warned Chris about his Yakut secretary's coffee. "Listen, old buddy, I'm sorry if I got out of line about your friend."

"There's something you should know there," Chris said, a little stiffly. "Those thugs who attacked me in the street and in my hotel room—they obviously saw me leave the camera shop with my set of prints. They knew what they were after."

"Yeah, I should've thought of that before I opened my big mouth. Hey, buddy . . . do you really think they could have blown up that camera shop with the guy inside?"

"I don't know. It's a hell of a coincidence."

"Who would be behind it? The poachers? I thought you were more or less convinced they *wanted* you there in the woods taking those pictures."

"I know. They let Alex Grovkin and me follow them."

"They might even have known who you were, Chris. You know, the demon photographer."

"It's possible, but if that's the case, why try to destroy the photographs if you want the world to see them?" Chris paused. "Not all of them," he corrected himself slowly. "When those men jumped me at the hotel they didn't steal any of the photos showing the tiger being shot. They took only those last shots on the roll."

"The ones showing the two guys that did the shooting. But

hell, Chris, the figures in those shots are too small to be identified. Their faces aren't much more than little white blobs."

"Maybe they weren't sure of that."

"Yeah." After a brief hesitation Langert said, "They're the same pictures your friend asked for this morning."

"Right."

Both men fell silent. Their attention momentarily turned toward the thirteen-inch color television set on a table in a corner of the office. Live coverage of the arrival of the South Koreans was under way. The diminutive South Korean prime minister made a brief speech in his own language, an interpreter rushing to catch up.

"Nice suit," Langert said. "I'm going, Chris—hang in there. We'll talk when I get back."

"Do you think my photos will make any difference?" Chris nodded toward the TV screen. "Or are we just being naive?"

"If I didn't think we could make a difference—that we have to try—I wouldn't be here."

Langert left quickly, leaving Chris with his questions. Lina Mashikova's face with its sad eyes and the heat of her slight supple body kept getting in the way. Some of Langert's questions about her weren't as easy to brush aside as the one about the explosion in the camera shop. Why *had* she taken off so abruptly without saying anything to him? What did she want with those prints of the two poachers in the forest? And if she was really interested in publishing a story using one or more of his tiger photos, as she had insisted all along, why hadn't she taken copies of *those* pictures?

When Chris thought about the woman who had slept in his arms the night before, his entire instinct was to dismiss Langert's skeptical concerns about her. There would be answers to all of the questions when Lina was ready to give them. Still, there was no getting around the fact that there was more to Lina Mashikova than the surface appearance of a flashy journalist with good connections. Witness the way she had taken charge of their flight from the black market, and the ease with which she had dealt with the two mafia types who blocked their way . . .

He stared at the television set, unseeing. The motorcade

was leaving the airport. Events had their own momentum, he thought. Was Langert's optimism over the impact of his photos simply the product of enthusiasm?

Langert's Yakut secretary, whose name was Ruth, approached him, her moon face creased in a shy smile. She brought him fresh coffee in a chipped white china mug. It was, as Langert had warned, almost undrinkable. Sipping the scalding hot brew, Chris suppressed a grimace and managed a smile. "Very good," he said. *"Spasibo."*

Beaming, the young woman retreated to her desk. She had an appealing buxom figure, something Chris was certain had not escaped Ken Langert's attention.

He took another sip as the secretary peered over at him shyly. It took all of his self-control to cover his shudder as he drank the coffee. Some sacrifices were worth the price.

At that moment, in the Pacific port on the waterfront, Yelina Mashikova rode her Suzuki motorcycle past a long aisle of merchants selling sausages and eggs, butter, fruits and fresh produce directly from truck-size freight containers. Off to her left the bay was a poster blue laced with whitecaps. She was surprised to see that one of the ships of the Russian fleet had been taken out of mothballs and moved out into the bay. It was the *Minsk,* an aircraft carrier-cruiser, the largest class of ship in the fleet. She could see the tiny figures of sailors scurrying along the huge deck.

Past the line of freight cars she paused, the motor of her Suzuki idling. The market was busy, but no one on foot could have followed her this far, and she saw no familiar vehicles. No black Zhiguli sedan, for instance. She revved the motorcycle's engine thoughtfully, wondering if coming here today had been a mistake. Well, she would soon find out.

Inland from the waterfront were the formidable buildings housing the headquarters of the Pacific Fleet Command, but these, stretching over several blocks, were not her destination. Instead she drove past lines of old brick warehouses, many of them apparently abandoned, before she came to a narrow cobblestoned street. She glanced back along the waterfront. No one had followed her.

She cruised slowly past a row of unimposing office buildings black with age. Turning left at the end of the narrow street, she reached an alley and again turned left. A moment later she slipped the motorcycle into a lane between two buildings and cut the engine. She walked the bike forward to the side door of a brick garage, opened the door and wheeled the Suzuki inside. After chaining the vehicle she stepped back outside, returning quickly on foot to the alley. It was empty.

The building that fronted the street was grimy brick, two stories high. The tall corniced windows were closed to the view of the bay by heavy draperies. Lina went directly to the back entrance. Pausing there, she glanced up and spotted the overhead surveillance camera that monitored the entry. She waited long enough to be identified before opening the door and stepping into a wide hallway.

"Identification!" a young, uniformed militiaman demanded.

Lina presented her identification card, which bore her picture in color. The soldier looked carefully from the card to her face, then handed it back to her and came to attention. "Does the lieutenant know the room?"

"I know it," Lina murmured as she swept past him.

The office she sought was at the front of the building, one of those that, because of the dark curtains, was denied the spectacular waterfront view just outside. A man of about sixty sat facing the doorway behind a large mahogany desk. He had a typical Russian leader's face—meaty, strong, full-jowled. Very thick black eyebrows contrasted dramatically with a full head of white hair. He had bright blue, very intelligent eyes.

Lina stopped at attention before the desk. "General Chumeiko! Permission to report."

"Relax, Lieutenant Mashikova," Victor Chumeiko said. "No one is watching us."

There was a smile in his eyes. He rose to walk around his desk, a big man, six feet tall and weighing two hundred pounds, wearing a dark blue suit, white shirt, patterned red tie. He gave her a bear hug, smelling of expensive cologne. "I was wondering when you were going to get around to reporting to me in person."

Relieved over his welcome, Lina said, "Respectfully, General, I did not have enough information to justify the risk of meeting."

"Which means you do now. Good." General Chumeiko indicated one of a pair of facing leather wing chairs. "May I offer you a drink, Lieutenant? Vodka? A cup of tea?"

Relaxing a little, Lina sank into the chair. Her face, stiff from riding in the open into the sharp wind, burned in the warm room. She realized that the building, however nondescript its outward appearance, enjoyed the luxury of central heat. It probably also housed very sophisticated electronics and communications systems. "Tea would be welcome, General."

"And why not? Surely it isn't every day that a mere lieutenant in the Army has a general making tea for her, eh? What's your favorite?" the general asked genially. "Irish breakfast is mine—never mind the time of day. I have several other English teas from Fortnum and Mason in London. You've heard of the store?"

"I know the name."

"Let me see . . . English Breakfast, Earl Grey, Darjeeling . . . I don't care for the perfumed teas, or those that taste of lemon or orange."

"Earl Grey," Lina said. She had never heard of it but liked the name.

"Earl Grey it is."

Chumeiko made tea in a huge brown Chinese pot that he placed on top of a large samovar in one corner of the office. "We'll let that steep a moment. Do you know that word, Mashikova? I'm testing your English idiom."

"No, sir, I don't."

"It means to let brew. Strange term, don't you think? English is an idiosyncratic language." He took a matching wingback chair facing hers. "All right, Lieutenant . . . let's hear what you have to tell me."

Lina took a deep breath. This was a moment she had anticipated for more than eighteen months, since Chumeiko had first approached her not long after Yuri's death, seeking to recruit her as an intelligence source under the cover of her legitimate experience as a young journalist. In her grief Lina had resisted, but Chumeiko had shrewdly turned that grief to his advantage. Yuri had been a true patriot, he reminded her. He had served his country honorably as a soldier. He had defied the tanks on the steps of the White House when hard-line dissidents had attempted to bring down the legitimate government of the new Russian republic. The work that Yuri and others like him had begun was unfinished. Russia remained threatened by enemies *within* its borders. There were elements in both the army and the government who wanted to turn back the clock—the same reactionary leaders who had made the criminal Afghanistan adventure possible. Lina was in a unique position to serve her country as Yuri would have wanted.

Victor Chumeiko was both patient and persuasive. It helped that he was not KGB but GRU, the *Glavnoe Razvedy-vatelnoe Upravlenie*—the intelligence arm of the General Staff. Six months after his initial approach Lina completed her training and was commissioned as a lieutenant in the Communications Intelligence Directorate of the GRU.

With the decline of the KGB's power after the democratic reforms, the GRU was now the country's principal defense against internal unrest or foreign intrusion into Russian affairs. It had always functioned autonomously from the KGB, with a budget matching or even exceeding that of the rival service. In addition to sub-directorates for each of Russia's sixteen military districts, there were also four directorates responsible for the four fleets. General Chumeiko was Deputy Director of the Pacific Fleet Directorate, whose security responsibilities included the nuclear submarine base as well as Pacific Fleet headquarters in Vladivostok.

For the past year Lina Mashikova's assignment had been covert intelligence in the Primorskiy province. Until recently she had not understood the importance of her information-gathering activities in this far corner of Russia, but she now knew that General Chumeiko regarded Boris Provalev as a dangerous man, a potential threat to the stability of the democratically elected government.

Speaking slowly and carefully, Lina outlined her observations of Provalev's political activities over the past year, culminating in the initiative that had led to the South Korean logging agreement with Sunsai. She noted that she had found Provalev's political success alarming but not subversive. In the past several months, however, as her written reports to General Chumeiko had indicated, she had developed the conviction that Provalev was embarked upon something of major significance. He had increased his contacts with hard-line, high-level officers in the old Red Army and in the Pacific Fleet. Through informants Lina had also learned of officer and troop reassignments in the Far East, with a growing concentration of armed forces under the command of officers apparently loyal to Provalev and his radical nationalists.

"I am aware of these activities," the general said.

He used the interruption to pour tea for both of them. Lina sipped tentatively. "I'm convinced that Comrade Provalev is planning something very soon," Lina said. "The secretive nature of some of his recent activities, coupled with the known political views of those loyal to him, suggest possibilities of great concern to the Russian republic."

"Go on, Lieutenant. By the way, how do you like Earl Grey?"

"It is delicious."

Chumeiko nodded. "You must have something more specific to bring you here today in person, Mashikova."

"I believe I do. And I believe it has to do with the presence of the South Koreans on Russian soil."

The general frowned, for the first time surprised.

Lina withdrew the photographs from their manila envelope —five of them now, the sixth having been left with Anatoly Bukanin. She explained how the photos had come to be taken by an American scientist working in the Sikhote-Alin Biosphere National Preserve, what they represented and how she had gotten them. "As you can see, General, there are two men in the forest, one of them the poacher who shot the tiger. The incident took place in what is called Sector Five of the preserve, an area which has been designated off limits because it holds the site of the initial logging proposed under the agreement with Sunsai. I think these photos are vitally important—particularly the identity of the two men."

"Do you have the negatives?" Chumeiko asked, studying the pictures.

"No. They were destroyed last night in a bombing and fire at the camera shop where these photographs were developed."

The general looked up sharply at these words. "The initial newscast mentioned an explosion, not a bombing."

"I've seen the police investigator's latest report," Lina said. "The earlier report was in error. Arson investigators have found traces of a plastic explosive in the ruins of the camera shop. I believe the shop was blown up, and the proprietor killed, to destroy any copies of these particular photos. To my knowledge, the copies I have are the only remaining prints."

"These are all of them?"

"The only ones showing the two poachers. There is one other," she amended quickly. "I left it with one of my informants, Anatoly Bukanin."

"Was that wise, Lieutenant? Colonel Bukanin was KGB."

"He is an old friend. He was a friend of Yuri's father. I knew him when I was a young woman, and I don't believe he would betray me."

"You are still a young woman," the general said with an ironic smile, "and you still have a good deal to learn. You are certain that the American who took the photos doesn't have other copies?"

"Quite certain."

Chumeiko nodded and studied the pictures for several moments. "What do you propose, Mashikova?"

"I would like to have these photographs enlarged and enhanced, particularly the faces of the two men. I believe computerized enhancement of the images will enable us to identify the men in the taiga."

"And?"

"Then we'll know why extreme measures have been taken to prevent such identification."

"Have you any theories?"

"I think it has to do with Boris Provalev and the Koreans. The prime minister and Sunsai's chairman arrived in Vladivostok this afternoon, and I understand that their visit is planned for three days, during which time the logging agreement will be signed. It seems possible that whatever Provalev has planned may happen within the next three days."

"There is nothing subversive about cutting down trees," the general said.

"Why would anyone kill a shopkeeper to destroy these photos? Why have I and the American been followed?"

"Why, indeed? Well, I will see to the enhancement of these photographs, Lieutenant. I want the work to be done discreetly. There is no time to send them to Moscow, but there are adequate laboratory facilities at Khabarovsk." The headquarters for the Primorskiy military district were at Khabarovsk, a city on the Amur River about four hundred air miles north-northeast of Vladivostok. "Continue your observations. Report to me every six hours regardless of what you learn. Within the next six hours I should have pictures of your two poachers suitable for framing. I too believe that Boris Provalev is an enemy of the present government of Russia, the government the army has pledged its loyalty to. Do you believe the government could be in serious danger, Lieutenant?"

"Yes, sir, I do."

"So do I. Perhaps more than you know."

Chumeiko's words suggested events going far beyond her own suspicions. "Is that why the *Minsk* has moved out into the harbor, General?"

"It's a reasonable assumption . . . if a crisis occurs, Russia will discover where the loyalty of the Pacific Fleet lies as well as that of the army." His bright blue eyes met hers. "The outcome is, I'm afraid, by no means certain."

As Lina prepared to leave, Chumeiko stopped her at the door. "One other thing, Lieutenant . . . find this man Bukanin. Find out what he has to tell you, if anything. And get back the photograph you left with him."

"Yes, General."

"In six hours, Mashikova."

Lina left the way she had come in, retrieved her motorcycle from the garage and drove directly away from the waterfront.

Ken Langert was elated with his *Global Alert Bulletin.* Chris's photograph of the wounded tiger's agonized leap filled almost the entire front cover, with stunning effect. And inside the bulletin Langert had also used a blowup of part of another photograph in which two of the tiger's young cubs were clearly seen, with all of the appeal of vulnerable young animals.

"Terrific," Chris Harmon said.

"I've already had copies delivered to the Ministry of Environmental Protection and Natural Resources, specifically to the attention of Likhachiev and some of the people we know on the Board for Nature Reserve Management. Other copies are on the night flight to Moscow, so they'll be there by morning. I'm trying to get copies to Boris Provalev as well as all the media, but that may not be so easy with everything that's going on in the city today."

"What else have you got planned?"

"Protest demonstrations outside the Korean embassy and more of the same tonight at the provincial government headquarters building where the Russians are entertaining the visitors. Are you game?"

"Count me in," Chris said.

Where, he wondered, was Lina Mashikova . . . ?

25

THE COLLECTOR WAITED outside his hotel, glanced at his watch. The taxi driver was late, Lemenov noted coolly. He had trained himself in patience and self-discipline. To become nervous, overanxious or angry over delays was to open a crack, however small, of vulnerability.

Through the license number of Mikhail Fyodorov's taxi Sergei Lemenov had been able to identify the driver easily enough. Tracking him down had proved to be more difficult. Fyodorov was an independent driver, working for no company and therefore reporting to no central dispatcher. He could be reached only by leaving a message for him at a telephone answering service. The Collector had gambled. He had left a message saying that he required transportation to the airport from his hotel at three o'clock that afternoon. The gamble was that, even if the taxi driver had other fares he might juggle his schedule to fit in the fairly long and lucrative drive to the airport, where there was also a good chance that he would pick up a passenger or passengers for the return trip into the city.

Lemenov wore black gloves and carried a black greatcoat over his arm. A small brown leather suitcase rested on the sidewalk next to his feet. A traveler without a suitcase aroused curiosity. He felt a nudge of satisfaction when a Lada taxi turned the corner off Aleutskaya Street and approached the portico in front of his hotel. He picked up his suitcase with one hand, raising the other to signal the taxi driver.

"The airport, Comrade?" Fyodorov asked cheerfully as his passenger settled into the back seat.

"Yes, but first I must make a brief stop." He gave an address on Krivitsky Prospect in a warehouse district along the waterfront.

When he had visited the area earlier that day Lemenov had found it nearly deserted. Although some warehouses were still used for storage of naval equipment and supplies there was little activity now. The absence of visible military security suggested that weapons or other high-priority matériel had been moved elsewhere. Many other buildings appeared empty and abandoned. Whatever had been left in them of any value had long ago been looted.

The taxi driver glanced at him curiously in the rearview mirror. "Are you sure of the address?"

Lemenov returned a thin smile. "Quite sure, Comrade . . . Fyodorov." He made a point of appearing to read the driver's name from his identification certificate. "I must pick up some samples from a warehouse."

"You're a salesman then?"

"An entrepreneur. These days one must be many things if one would eat."

"Isn't that the truth," Fyodorov said with a grin.

He was a small wiry man with a large nose and a full gray beard. Not physically formidable but the sort of compact, stringy, energetic man who could be troublesome if not dealt with quickly and decisively. He drove very fast and adroitly, demonstrating quick reflexes by the way he changed lanes often and darted in and out of traffic.

Sensing the driver studying him in his mirror, the Collector gazed out of the side window at the buildings they passed and at a woman with a baby carriage pausing before crossing the street toward a postage-stamp-sized park. The baby was bundled up to his nose in thick clothing, and the woman wore a parka and a wool scarf around her head and neck. In spite of the bright sun the day was still cool, and as soon as the sun set it would be plain cold.

More significant to the Collector's plans had been the latest weather report covering the Primorskiy Kray forest to the north, where a storm descending from northern Siberia was expected to bring freezing temperatures and the possibility of snow.

Very carefully the Collector slipped a coil of braided piano wire from his coat pocket and dropped it to the floor of the taxi. He pulled his suitcase over next to him on the seat and opened it, sifting the contents with one hand for the driver's benefit. When he closed the suitcase he shifted it to the floor, and in the process picked up the piano wire. Making certain that his hands were out of the driver's line of sight, Lemenov played out the length of wire and, in a deft movement that was the result of hundreds of practice repetitions he could do blindfolded, he formed a noose with a slipknot. Close to the knot and attached to one end of the wire was a large brass key, the kind used to wind up older mechanical clocks. Once the noose had been manually tightened, the key's function was to ratchet it tighter with each twist of the key. The device, the Collector would have been pleased to note, was his own creation.

The taxi, having left busier commercial streets behind, worked its way toward the waterfront and the several miles of old brick warehouses that extended along the line of the bay. "Krivitsky Prospect, you said?" Fyodorov asked his passenger.

Coincidentally, their route took them past the cobblestoned street where Lina Mashikova had left General Chumeiko a short time earlier. Sergei Lemenov ostentatiously peered ahead and said, "That's right, it's just a short way. You see that three-story gray building between warehouses? There are offices just around the corner there."

The Lada shot forward along the waterfront, heading for the building the Collector had indicated about a quarter-mile away. Fyodorov careened around the corner in his slapdash style, braked hard and stared at the unpainted facade of an apparently empty building in front of him. "What's this—?"

The loop of wire snaked over his head. For a fraction of a second it caught on the bill of his cap. Sensing disaster even before he realized what was happening, Fyodorov tried to duck free of the descending noose. He was not quick enough. The wire cleared the peak of his cap and slipped around his neck. Taking no chances with the wiry little driver, the Collector jerked the ring tight and in the same motion gave a hard wrench of the brass key.

The wire bit into Fyodorov's throat, cutting off his angry shout. The pain was excruciating. He could not breathe.

"If you struggle any more," the Collector said, "the wire will cut through your neck like a knife. Do you understand?"

The force of the vise around his neck had lifted Fyodorov from his seat. His fingers scrabbled at the wire without effect and came away bloody.

"I know you can't speak," Lemenov told him. "If you understand what I'm saying and you are prepared to cooperate, wave your right hand. Good, that's sensible of you. I only wish to ask you a few questions. You must be very careful to answer me completely and truthfully. If you do, you might not lose your head."

Fyodorov waved his right hand frantically. In response, the Collector turned the brass key a quarter turn to the left, and there was a fractional lessening of the pressure of the wire around the taxi driver's neck, but it remained embedded in his flesh. Fyodorov felt tears streaming down his cheeks into his beard.

"You had a passenger this morning, a young woman, a Russian journalist who had earlier been accompanied by an American. I want to know where you took the woman."

In the rearview mirror Mikhail Fyodorov's eyes begged for the wire to be loosened further. Sergei Lemenov rewarded him with one of his humorless smiles. "I'm going to loosen it slightly. See if you can talk."

The wire's relentless grip eased once more. When Fyodorov tried to speak, only a croaking sound emerged. Cautiously pressing his feet against the floorboards, he pushed up slightly, trying to reduce the pressure of the garrote. Maybe he could still find a way to stay alive . . .

"Another quarter turn, then . . ." the Collector said with a slight frown. He twisted the key. "Do you remember this woman?"

"Y . . . yes," Fyodorov choked out.

"Where did you take her?"

"Kusovsky . . . Park."

"Kusovsky Park? Did she meet anyone there?"

Fyodorov managed to give a slight negative shake of his head. His throat burned, and each attempt to speak was like swallowing a razor blade.

"You're positive there was no one? Where did she go in the park?"

"C . . . cafe."

"She went to a cafe in the park? Did you see anyone else inside? Other than a waiter or counterman?"

The taxi driver's negative response puzzled Lemenov. If the journalist had met no one else, was the cafe itself a drop or message center? But she was a journalist—or was she? Why did she need to employ such arcane maneuvers?

"If you're lying—"

Fyodorov arched upward, hurling himself over the back of his seat toward his tormentor. He was muscular and surprisingly strong, and his surprise move nearly succeeded. The Collector fell away from him. His right hand gave a savage twist of the brass key and Fyodorov's legs shot straight out, involuntarily kicking against the windshield. He arched onto his back, impaled across the back of the taxi's front seat, the wire garrote biting deeply into his neck and choking off all breath. His legs kicked out again, more weakly. His fingers clawed at his throat and his eyes rolled upward, the whites showing.

After a few seconds the Collector released the pressure of the garrote with a full turn of the key. Fyodorov collapsed back into the front seat of the vehicle.

"Do that again and I will cut off your head and stick it on the dashboard," Lemenov informed him. He sounded very convincing. "I'm going to ask you one more time . . . tell me what I want to know and you will have nothing more to worry about. You will never hear from me again. Did you see anyone else in the park? Anyone nearby? *Anyone?*"

Fyodorov tried to speak and could not. Lemenov had to reach in and manually loosen the grip of the wire on the driver's neck sufficiently for him to suck in a ragged breath. "Was that a yes?"

Fyodorov nodded. The tears continued to flow, tears of rage

and shame over what he knew was coming . . . he knew he would tell this murdering bastard anything he wanted to know.

"You saw someone?"

The driver nodded.

"Where?"

"On . . . b . . . bench."

"A man on a bench? Near the cafe?"

Another affirmative nod. The Collector considered the information. If the woman had been meeting the man on the bench she had taken pains not to approach him directly or while the driver was able to observe her. Such precautions made Lemenov even more keenly interested in talking to her.

"You left the woman at the cafe and drove away? You didn't see her approach the man?"

"That's r . . . right."

"Was he old or young?"

"O . . . old. Gray . . ."

An old man, gray-haired. What was going on here? Had the woman simply been meeting her father or an uncle for lunch or tea? No, she had come from St. Petersburg, Lemenov recalled, and lived alone in Vladivostok. Then why the secrecy? Why the old-fashioned tradecraft? Was it possible—?

With a gurgling cry Mikhail Fyodorov threw himself over the back of his seat toward the Collector. Lemenov's reaction was reflexive, the conditioned response of a trained assassin. His right hand twisted the brass key as hard as he could. The garrote cut through flesh and cartilage, severing the driver's jugular. His body spasms twisted him onto his side, and the blood sprayed away from the Collector, painting the rear side window of the taxi with a red mist.

When the spasms ceased, the Collector shoved the lifeless body away from him, glanced down over his coat and pants. Fortunately, he noted, most of the blood had spurted away from him. Except for a few spattered drops on his left sleeve his clothes were clean. He wiped his gloves on the dead man's coat. Then, after peering up and down the empty street, he opened the right side door and stepped out.

Lemenov carefully surveyed the street. The entire area appeared to be abandoned. Checking the front-seat area, he found the ignition key still in place.

Angry now, the Collector dumped the body into the back seat and slid behind the wheel. He drove the taxi a mile before he pulled it into an alley between two empty warehouses, then found a rag and tried to wipe down the red-stained window. When he was unable to completely erase the garish smear he wound the window all the way down out of view and wiped the sill clean. Discovering an old, moth-eaten blanket in the trunk, he threw it over the back seat, covering up the dead body and most of the visible stains. He stepped back to assure himself that there was no other evidence of the recent carnage visible from outside the vehicle to a casual passerby. He knew the abandoned vehicle would not escape the attention of looters for long, but he only needed to buy a little time to escape the area.

Satisfied, his breathing now returned to normal, the Collector walked out of the alley and turned north. A commercial boulevard was less than a quarter-mile away. He slipped on his greatcoat, which had been on the far side of the back seat and so had escaped the blood spatters. Near the boulevard he dropped his bloodstained gloves into separate trash bins.

He caught the first bus into the center of the city. It dropped him off two blocks from his hotel, where Leonid Brunovsky had carried out instructions to leave the Zhiguli in an adjoining parking garage. Only then, when he had returned to his hotel, did the Collector remember for the first time a singular omission.

In his frustration he had neglected to collect his souvenir.

Forty-five minutes later Sergei Lemenov left the cafe at the edge of Kusovsky Park in a better mood. The waiter, who was eager to be bribed, had remembered a pretty young woman from earlier in the day, a true Russian beauty; in fact, he had seen her several times before in his cafe. He also recalled the old gray-haired man on the bench. He was a regular patron and he had met the young woman on other occasions. He lived near the park, the waiter was almost certain. A pensioner, he thought, living alone with his memories. The woman was perhaps his daughter, or a niece?

"Do you by any chance know the man's name?"

"Yes, yes, it is Bukanin. A military man, I think. It's in the way he talks and carries himself, they never lose it. Almost certainly an officer."

"Bukanin? You are certain?"

"Yes, yes, Bukanin. Likes his vodka, that one . . . and why not? What else does he have to live for?"

The Collector felt a jolt of excitement. Colonel Anatoly Bukanin! It could be no other . . .

"Is there a back way out?" he asked the waiter.

"What? Yes, of course, but—"

"Is the cook there? I haven't heard anyone."

"He's gone home. I was about to close up when you came."

"Show me out back," Lemenov said with a smile. He produced a roll of rubles for the waiter's benefit. "I will explain. You've been very helpful and there is one other small thing you can do for me."

The waiter's eyes were on the wad of rubles as he led the way behind the counter and into a crowded galley kitchen. "We don't do much cooking here," the waiter explained. "Just soup and sandwiches. There isn't enough business. If it's a bottle of vodka you'd like, I do happen to have two bottles—"

Which was as far as he got. The Collector held his hand over the man's mouth while the knife thrust did its work. He released the waiter's body only when it had gone completely limp.

It was now dark outside and the park seemed deserted. The Collector turned off all the lights and locked the front door of the cafe behind him when he let himself out.

It was a pity about the waiter, he thought. The man had been very cooperative. However, he would have remembered the inquiries about Bukanin, and he had seen the Collector's face.

26

ANNA ZILYA VALEYEVA licked her full lips with satisfaction. Earlier in the week her lover Boris Provalev had urged her to develop a story on poaching in the protected animal preserves of the Primorskiy for possible use in connection with the story of the thirty-year logging agreement to be signed with the South Koreans. Anna had been skeptical, her producer even more so, but they had prepared a brief segment for the Friday evening telecast. After all, one did not take a suggestion from Boris Provalev lightly.

Thirty minutes before Anna was to go on the air that evening Boris had arrived in the television studios with dramatic photographs of a Siberian tiger being shot by a poacher in one of the preserves. The photographs had turned a potentially dull filler into an attention-compelling feature.

There was more. A demonstration was in progress in front of the South Korean embassy with scores of placard-carrying animal-rights activists and environmentalists protesting both the continuing atrocity of tiger poaching and the new threat to the ancient forests of the Primorskiy. Live coverage of the demonstrations would spice up the telecast, during which Anna would be able to reveal the information, provided to her exclusively by Provalev, that the thirty-year logging contract was *fait accompli,* the signing a formality.

Boris had even added an emotionally charged anecdote to accompany the photographs of the tiger shot in the taiga. The magnificent Siberian had three cubs, visible clearly in two of the photos. A rescue attempt had been proposed by a Russian-American team of scientists working in the Sikhote-Alin preserve. Boris himself was appealing to the South Koreans for some favorable public-relations gesture on their part, encouraging the rescue effort and pledging the most stringent environmental controls in the areas of the Primorskiy Kray forest that were opened to development.

"One minute, Anna," her producer cued her.

She nodded, reflexively licked her lips and began a quick run-through. Lips moist, lipstick in place. Blouse buttoned, collar straight, the new raw silk vest properly adjusted, microphone button in place, script pages in order, cue cards ready. Anna listened to the countdown, watched the nearest monitor and saw the image of the Korean Air jetliner at Vladivostok Airport, passenger door open at the top of the portable steps that had been already positioned. The Korean prime minister stepped into view through the open door, a small man, meticulously groomed . . .

"Good evening, this is Anna Zilya Valeyeva. Tonight's top story, the arrival in Vladivostok of the prime minister of South Korea, Kim Su, the historic first visit of such a South Korean official to Russian soil.

"On hand to greet the visitors was Boris Provalev, chairman of the Primorskiy district council and member of Parliament, Oleg Kholkhov, interior minister of the Russian Republic, as well as other officials . . ."

The coverage of the arrival ceremonies, the brief and familiar diplomatic speeches, the motorcade winding toward the city was routine. Cutting the segment short, Anna's producer switched to live coverage of the conservationist demonstrations at the South Korean embassy, leading to another exclusive revelation Boris had given Anna thirty minutes before the broadcast.

". . . demonstrations from a variety of international animal-rights organizations joined in the peaceful protest march outside of the South Korean embassy after the arrival of the visitors this afternoon. In an exclusive interview with this reporter, Boris Provalev revealed that discussions have been under way for several weeks over a possible visit by the South Koreans this weekend to the Primorskiy Kray forest. According to Comrade Chairman Provalev, such a visit would be made by helicopter flight to Terney, and from there directly to the newly constructed base facility in the Sikhote-Alin Biosphere National Preserve. It would be made to demonstrate the South Koreans' concern for the environmental impact of the proposed logging contract, and the expected minimal impact upon endangered species in the region. It was in this sector of the preserve that the tiger shown earlier on this program was illegally shot by poachers . . ."

As the telecast neared its end Anna's producer gave her a thumbs-up signal and she segued into her conclusion. "This is Anna Zilya Valeyeva with tonight's edition of the six o'clock news. Stay tuned for additional coverage of the historic visit of the South Korean prime minister and his entourage at ten o'clock this evening on 'Vladivistok Tonight' . . ."

"Was it good?" Anna asked breathlessly.

"You were splendid, Anna Zilya," her producer said. "And that angle about the tiger cubs has the phones ringing already. Too bad we didn't have better pictures of the cubs, or videotape of the shooting, but let's not look a gift horse in the mouth, eh?"

"Has Boris called?"

"Not yet," the producer laughed. "But you can be sure he was watching. Perhaps," he added, "the chairman is waiting to tell you in person later."

Anna had known from the beginning that her relationship with the charismatic Provalev could only enhance her career. She had hardly dared to hope that he would actually reward her with exclusive interviews and news revelations. Not that her involvement with Boris had been calculated purely out of self-interest. He was a forceful and highly satisfactory lover. The aura of power and purpose that surrounded him excited her. Now, however, it was clear that what pleased her personally was also a giant step forward professionally.

Tonight's telecast would surely be reviewed by network administrators in Moscow.

The future suddenly looked very bright.

* * *

Anatoly Bukanin, for the hundredth time, stared at the color photograph Lina Mashikova had left with him. His hand trembled slightly as he picked up a jeweler's ten-power magnifying glass and held it over the picture.

The two men in the forest leaped out at him.

Even under the magnifying glass their faces were without distinguishing features. But staring at the images, Bukanin knew that he had seen all that he needed.

He might be mistaken about the shorter of the two figures, but he didn't think so. Bukanin had seen him often, both in person and on television, a background figure but nevertheless familiar. He was Leonid Brunovsky, Boris Provalev's chief aide. Bukanin had always thought Brunovsky had more the appearance of a bodyguard than an administrative assistant, but in Russia the two roles were not inconsistent. They had been common enough during the old glory days of the Soviet Union, Colonel Anatoly Bukanin's own prime years as an officer in the First Chief Directorate of the KGB. The question that came immediately to mind was what was Provalev's aide doing in the taiga with a poacher?

Not just *any* poacher. This particular man.

The second of the men in the woods, a lean, feral figure, was the marksman. An expert shooter, to Bukanin's own knowledge capable of truly astonishing feats of long-range marksmanship. Bukanin did not need to see his features in detail to recognize the KGB assassin whose once top-secret Department V file identified him as Sergei Gregorevich Lemenov. Alias the Collector.

A file, Bukanin suspected, that no longer existed.

He had first met Sergei Lemenov before he acquired his nickname, when Lemenov was a young recruit and a protégé of Yuri Andropov himself. At that time Bukanin was already a captain in the First Chief Directorate. Like Lemenov, Bukanin was a favorite of Andropov's, owing his rise in the secret service to the KGB chairman.

Yuri Andropov was a cultured aristocrat like the Polish nobleman Feliks Edmundovich Dzerzhinsky, selected in December 1917 as the first chairman of the secret Vecheka (almost instantly shortened to Cheka). In all the history of the Cheka, which evolved into the OGPU, the NKVD and ultimately the KGB, three men stood out in stamping the organization with their own mark: Dzerzhinsky, who served ten years until his death and converted the fledgling investigative service into a powerful instrument of terror and oppression for Joseph Stalin; Lavrenti Beria, who in his fifteen-year reign created his own ruthless empire and came within an inch of making himself dictator; and Andropov, who also was chairman of the KGB for fifteen years and actually succeeded in becoming the supreme ruler of the Soviet Union. During those years both Bukanin and Lemenov prospered under the guidance of their benefactor. Bukanin rose to the rank of full colonel in the First Chief Directorate. In that position he was able to follow Lemenov's career, from his successful "wet affairs" assignments abroad to that extraordinary incident in the Ukraine that gave the assassin his alias as the Collector. (That triumph had also provided Yuri Andropov, the art lover, with several priceless medieval paintings and Russian icons for his own collection.)

With Andropov's death in 1984 after a brief two years as the leader of the Soviet Union, Bukanin's career passed its zenith. He was eventually relegated to a desk in the labyrinth of the First Chief Directorate's huge modern headquarters outside the peripheral ring that circled Moscow. Like other agents in the top-secret Department V, Sergei Lemenov simply disappeared.

Now, after the collapse of the Soviet Union and under Russia's runaway inflation, Bukanin barely survived on what his meager pension would buy. But Lemenov, he thought as he stared at the photograph, was still in business.

Assassination never went out of style. Its expert practitioners simply acquired different clients.

Anatoly Bukanin had made a career of analyzing pieces of information and making intelligence out of them. What did the presence of Leonid Brunovsky in the taiga with the Collector mean? What had brought the two men together? From what little Lina Mashikova had revealed, Bukanin surmised that the photograph was extremely important. To whom? To Brunovsky's boss, District Chairman Boris Provalev? What possible purpose could be served by the illegal shooting of a Siberian tiger in the wilderness?

Other bits of intelligence could be linked to the photo. One was the arrival of the South Korean leaders in Vladivostok within days of the poaching incident. Another was the location in the Sikhote-Alin preserve where the tiger had been shot . . . in close proximity to the area where the giant Sun-sai Corporation would soon begin its massive logging operation.

Bukanin saw, or smelled, the murky outlines of a conspiracy, but he could not complete the pattern. He thought of trying to reach Lina but rejected the impulse. Why was *she* so interested? Was it really only a story?

The old man ate little these days, but the rubles Lina had given him had enabled him to buy a cherished bottle of Stolichnaya. As the afternoon waned he sat in his small, bleak apartment without turning on a light, drinking steadily and thinking in the gathering gloom. At one point he dozed, only to awaken suddenly, trembling, with a fragmented memory of a dream. He was running along an endless corridor, pursued by a diminutive, cackling man Bukanin recognized as Nikolai Yeshov, the "bloody dwarf" of the KGB purges in the late 1930s. Terrified, Bukanin fled around a corner, where he was suddenly confronted by another man with a knife. The apparition held a severed human ear toward Bukanin as if it were an offering. "Try it, Comrade Colonel. It's delicious."

Bukanin woke drenched in sweat. *The Collector.*

With an unsteady hand he poured himself another glass of vodka before turning on his television set for the evening news. Frequently he left the set turned on at all hours, both for company and to chase away the nightmares. He slumped on the broken springs of his only upholstered chair and stared at the screen. At first he paid little attention to a brief story about an explosion the night before, now confirmed as a deliberate bombing that police were attributing to mafia extortionists. Then his attention was riveted on the screen. The bombed-out store was a camera shop!

Another link . . . ?

His gaze lingered on Anna Zilya Valeyeva's full-lipped mouth, and he became preoccupied enough that he almost missed the significance of her next words. "Comrade Provalev revealed that discussions have been under way for several weeks over a possible visit by the South Korean visitors to the Primorskiy Kray forest . . ."

Stunned, Bukanin stared at the screen. With another piece of the puzzle falling into place it was not difficult to put the whole together. He didn't *understand* all of it but it was clear that the presence of a photographer in the taiga to record the shooting of the tiger had not been by chance. It was equally certain that Sergei Lemenov had not been there with Boris Provalev's aide on a big-game hunt.

It was coming together . . . Boris Provalev's boundless ambition . . . the Korean logging agreement . . . an incident designed to lure the Koreans into the remote Sikhote-Alin preserve . . . and the presence of one of the former Soviet Union's most skilled assassins. If the conspiracy seemed monstrous, Bukanin's career had made monsters credible.

Poor Lina Mashikova! She thought she could investigate a plot so devious, and deadly, without having her activities come to the attention of someone as experienced, meticulous and ruthless as the Collector.

He glanced again at the photo Lina had given him, and thought about the bombing. *This is what he's after,* Bukanin thought. The pictures of the tiger were meant to be; those of Lemenov and Brunovsky in the forest were a mistake.

Whatever had happened in the Primorskiy that day, and whatever was going to happen, Boris Provalev was behind the plot. And the photograph Bukanin was staring at would give proof of his involvement.

Had Lina been followed? Bukanin felt sweat on his forehead. She had taken precautions—he had insisted on it—but she was really an amateur. Did Sergei Lemenov know about her interest? Did he know she had the photos he must be desperate to destroy?

Bukanin had to contact her, warn her. She had no comprehension of the kind of man she was dealing with.

Bukanin was fortunate to have a telephone in his apartment, a not-so-minor perquisite from his former status as an officer in the KGB. He dialed the number Lina had originally given him. No answer. He dialed a second number, some kind of cutout—he recalled being surprised that she would have thought of such an arrangement—where he could leave a message for her. He waited for the connection to be made, listening to a click followed by a moment of silence. He wondered if someone was there at the other end of the line, waiting, or if there was only a telephone answering machine. He said, "It's Yuri's old friend. Meet me at the alternate site at the designated hour minus five. It is most urgent."

27

AFTER LEAVING GENERAL Chumeiko, Lina Mashikova took a roundabout route on her Suzuki motorcycle back toward the center of the city. She wore goggles against the cold wind and rode with her long leather coat folded up around her thighs. She had not exactly been in dress uniform to visit the general, she thought, but what was the appropriate uniform for an undercover agent in the field reporting to her control?

The designation *undercover agent* always brought her up a little short. She was an investigator, doing much the same kind of things she had done as a reporter, digging up facts and putting them together. It was not even her role to make sense of them. A reporter had an editor to pass out assignments and put together a coherent picture; she had General Chumeiko.

At least that was the way she had looked at her role in the past. Now it felt very different. She was a player in a major game, in a world-class arena, and she had to wonder if she was up to it.

What did the movement of the *Minsk* out into the harbor mean? Was Chumeiko afraid of a coup attempt? Here in Vladivostok? And if that was the case, why only one carrier-cruiser made ready for action?

The outcome is by no means certain. General Chumeiko was unsure of the loyalty of the army. Did that apply to the Pacific Fleet as well? Aside from the ongoing quarrels with other members of the Commonwealth of Independent States over control of the fleet, was there dissension in the fleet command over Russia's future course? Many in the military forces were skeptical of the democratic reforms, some of them outright hostile to change, but had the troubles in Russia pushed the majority into the camp of the hard-liners?

Sometimes a majority wasn't necessary, she reminded herself. A small group of fiercely ambitious partisans could drag masses of the undecided or uninvolved behind them, until it was too late to stop the momentum. It was the history of Russia in the twentieth century.

Lina stopped at the central bus station, where the public telephones worked fairly well—not something to be counted on everywhere. She rang Christopher Harmon at his hotel but was told there was no answer in his room. Might he still be at the Global Wildlife Federation offices? It took five minutes to convince the operator that there was such an organization and to look up the number. The phone was answered almost immediately, and Lina recognized Kenneth Langert's voice.

"This is Lina Mashikova, *Gospodin* Langert. Is Dr. Harmon still there?"

Langert's tone was cool. "Sorry, Ms. Mashikova. Chris left over two hours ago."

"I know he wanted to see your special bulletin. Were you able to receive printed copies?"

"It's on the street. The people you met this morning at our meeting have also been involved in protest demonstrations outside the South Korean embassy all afternoon. That's about to change. The action is moving over to the provincial government administration building now."

"Why is that?"

"I would've thought you'd know that, being a reporter. Boris Provalev is hosting a state reception in honor of the South Koreans. From what we hear, he's also doing some arm-twisting that might do us some good in the Sikhote-Alin preserve. Let's hope so."

"Arm-twisting?"

"Trying to persuade the Koreans to make some kind of conciliatory gesture toward the environment."

Langert didn't like her, Lina thought. Why not? What had she done to make him skeptical or mistrustful? The *photo-*

graphs . . . of course . . . he had acted strangely when she asked for them.

"Do you know where Christopher is now?"

"He should be out there on the street with the others," Langert said, "taking part in the demonstrations. You ought to be there yourself, Ms. Mashikova. Isn't this part of your story?"

Perhaps Langert had been talking to some of the other Russian journalists who were present this morning, Lina thought after hanging up. Asking questions about her. She knew that some of those colleagues whispered about her behind her back, questioning her journalistic credentials, her associations, her lifestyle. She had often wanted to shout at them, *Yuri bought me this coat when he returned from Afghanistan.* He had saved much of his pay, there was no way to spend it in that rocky hell except on drugs, and the expensive coat was both a statement of his love and perhaps a gesture for forgiveness. But if she said all that, to be honest she would also have to add, *I am also paid by the GRU. They bought the Suzuki. My control thought it would be a good way for me to get around the city quickly.*

Well, she had questions for her colleagues. For instance, she wondered about Vasily Gurechev, a political writer with the Vladivostok *Times.* She had been surprised to see him at the wildlife meeting; he didn't fit in. It wasn't his kind of story. Unless . . .

He's close to Boris Provalev, she thought. Some of Gurechev's colleagues were openly contemptuous of the writer, equating him with those hacks who, in the recent past, had served Soviet leaders rather than the people by sacrificing the truth to propaganda, writing politically correct pieces for *Pravda* and *Izvestia.*

Undoubtedly Gurechev was in Boris Provalev's pocket, which meant that Provalev knew everything that had taken place that morning.

She felt very tired. Langert was right, she should cover the demonstrations at the government center. Before the night was over she had to retrieve the photograph from Bukanin, and she also was anxious to see Chris Harmon. But first, after a day riding around on her Suzuki, and two days wearing the same clothes, she badly needed a shower and a change.

She left the bus station and fired up her motorcycle. She would have to hurry . . .

Her apartment felt strange to her, even though she had been away from it only overnight. She turned on her television set in time to catch the evening news with that pouty-mouthed beauty, Anna Zilya Valeyeva. To Lina's surprise, Valeyeva followed up a feature story on the arrival of the South Koreans on Russian soil by showing some of Chris Harmon's photographs of the shooting of the tiger in the taiga, linking this with scenes of the day's street demonstrations by animal activists and environmentalists, the last of these live from the government center. The newscast seemed orchestrated, Lina thought, seeing Provalev's hand with the baton. Valeyeva was another Gurechev, except that the television reporter was not only in Provalev's pocket, she was also in his bed.

As you were in the American's bed, Yelina Vassilyeva, she reminded herself.

She turned up the volume and listened to the rest of the news while she stood under the shower, which was barely lukewarm. Her nakedness, coupled with her wry self-accusation, caused her memory to flash to last night, to Harmon's lean body pressed against hers—he was very fit for a scientist, she thought—and to the awareness that he desired her.

Over the past year she had given herself completely to her work—to her writing, which was essential to maintain her cover, but also to learning the ins and outs of her real assignment in the Far East. There had been no room for emotions. Anyway, Yuri's suicide had left her numb, seemingly incapable of feeling. That had now changed overnight. The numbness was wearing off, like a dentist's painkiller, and she felt herself cut adrift. Emotions were like the hunger most Russians felt for their new freedom to say and do what they wanted without fear. Once you let out such emotions they were no longer under your control. They were demanding, rebellious, impetuous.

She dressed quickly, suddenly anxious. The city outside her apartment windows was already dark.

At her apartment door she stopped. She hadn't checked her answering machine.

There was only one message on her machine, and the urgency in Anatoly Bukanin's voice came through clearly. What had happened? Had he discovered something in the photo she had left with him?

The street demonstrations at the government administration building would have to wait, she thought as she ran out of her apartment building to her motorcycle. Christopher Harmon would have to wait . . .

The alternative rendezvous she had prearranged with Bukanin had never been used before. It was to be employed only if the bench in Kusovsky Park was for some reason compromised. For security purposes the alternative site chosen was much farther from Bukanin's apartment than their customary meeting place in the park. Bukanin's choice of the second site underscored the seriousness of his message.

The designated hour, as it had been for previous meetings, was always midnight plus or minus a chosen number. The time he had selected was seven o'clock. She was already late.

She raced through the darkness of the city streets toward Vladivostok University, where for a brief period following his forced retirement Anatoly Bukanin had given lectures on Russia's relationship with the Western powers. Specifically, Bukanin was to wait for her near the traffic circle on Universitetsky Prospect. She was to motor slowly around the circle twice, giving him time to make certain that she had not been followed before he showed himself. Lina had scouted the area and guessed that he would wait in the shadows of the meeting hall that faced the circle, one of those oversized Communist-era buildings more suited to political meetings than academic pursuits. He would be behind one of the columns at the top of the steps, she thought, or in the deep shadows at the side of the building.

She slowed as she neared the traffic circle, from which paths and streets radiated outward past the bulky university buildings. The popping of the Suzuki's motor seemed incredibly loud.

She circled slowly. There was no other traffic, and she passed from one pool of overhead streetlights to another, marveling that not a single lamp was broken, trying not to stare toward the meeting hall. No sign of Bukanin. She made a second circuit, and a third. Anatoly would not fail to keep this rendezvous, not from the sound of his voice on her machine. There had been more than anxiety shaping his words; there had been blatant fear.

She stopped, cut her motor. On impulse wheeled the bike out of the nearest pool of light into relative darkness beyond the edge of the traffic circle.

Silence. The university appeared empty at this hour on a Friday night. Lights in some of the buildings, but that probably meant *provodniks* carrying out routine cleaning and maintenance.

The stillness lengthened.

If he sensed trouble, suspected that she was being followed, or was agitated about what he was getting into because of her, Bukanin would be cautious indeed. Okay, Anatoly Isaevich, you've had your look, there's no one behind me, come on out.

In the distance, far across the university grounds, a door opened, spilling a yellow rectangle of light into the darkness. A figure moved in the doorway, went back inside, and the door closed. Not the old KGB agent. Where was he?

After another five minutes Lina chained her motorcycle to a post and walked the perimeter of the traffic circle. She climbed the steps of the meeting hall, heart beating faster as she watched the shadows, anticipating a change in one of the shapes.

There was no one at the top of the steps or hiding behind one of the thick concrete columns that supported the roof overhang. No one at either side of the building. No one.

She watched a car approach the traffic circle, slow as the driver spotted her motorcycle. The chain was clearly visible, and after a slight hesitation the car moved on. One of those small German cars, she noted, a Rabbit, not a black Zhiguli sedan.

By then it was twenty minutes past the hour. Fussy about his tradecraft, Bukanin would never be this late unless something serious had delayed him.

When Bukanin—acting more out of friendship than need— had agreed to help her out occasionally with information, rumor, gossip or advice, she had put down his insistence on elaborate precautions to the paranoia of a lifetime Cold Warrior and a survivor for thirty years in the ruthless infighting of the KGB and the Communist Party. One of the rules he had established from the start was that they would meet on neutral sites, never at his apartment or hers, where they could be linked by a neighbor, a janitor or anyone else seeing them together.

"What would be the harm?" she had asked him. "We are old friends from Moscow and St. Petersburg."

"My dear Yelinita, it is never wise to create paths for an investigator to follow."

"Who is going to be investigating us, Anatoly Isaevich?"

"You never know. This is still Russia—don't try to predict the future."

When Lina liberated her Suzuki and drove away from the university, she knew it was time to forget caution. Engine winding up to a scream, she headed straight for Bukanin's apartment.

28

"WHAT HAVE YOU heard from Comrade Lemenov?" Boris Provalev was saying.

"Nothing. He was looking for . . ." Leonid Brunovsky broke off, glancing around the spacious reception room, which seemed much grander at first glance than it was on closer inspection. It had the sheer size so admired by leaders who saw themselves as giants, like Stalin and Hitler, but it lacked the true opulence found in the most modest czarist palace. Take away the gold-threaded draperies, the brocaded chairs, the china and the crystal, and you had a warehouse, Brunovsky thought. He said, ". . . the taxi driver."

Provalev looked at him. "Is he crazy? I've heard the latest news, a man found dead in his taxi. Was it—?"

"The same man."

"The police—"

"—suspect mafia gangsters. A bullet hole was found in the back of the taxi and there was a report of a shooting last night at one of the mafia-run black markets."

Provalev sipped from a slender crystal flute that contained vodka, not champagne. Earlier he had toasted the Korean dignitaries with French champagne, which he despised. Across the wide room that decrepit old *apparatchik,* Oleg Kholkhov, the current interior minister, was talking to the South Korean prime minister, Kim Su. Sunsai's chairman, Chang Pyon, stood nearby flanked by his bodyguards.

"How is it going?" Brunovsky asked.

"Kim Su is resisting the idea of visiting the preserve. I doubt the man has ever set foot where there wasn't a carpet or at least a sidewalk."

"What about the other man?"

"He says nothing. He also misses nothing."

"You did not request any action by the militia to disperse the demonstrators outside."

"Of course not." Provalev smiled. "They are my secret weapon." He paused a moment. "I'm having a private meeting with Kim Su and Chang Pyon shortly. That little dandy Kim is a politician, he can be manipulated even if he is reluctant. The other one, Chang . . . he holds the answer."

"To your whole plan."

"To the future of Russia," Provalev said intently. He studied the men across the room for a moment, then added, "If all goes well, the Collector must leave tonight for the preserve. Make the necessary arrangements."

"He seems determined to cover all his tracks—"

"He does not set the agenda," Provalev said. "Find him for me."

When the knock came on his apartment door Anatoly Bukanin was not even surprised. He was expecting it.

He had thought of running, but a sense of fatalism had taken over his will. Besides, he was too damn old and tired to run. He sat in his worn chair with its broken springs and stared at the door, making no move to answer the knock. His bottle of vodka lay on its side on the floor beside him, empty. Russian cars should carry one of those bumper stickers seen on American cars, he thought: Never leave before the bottle is empty. Thank you, Yelina Vassilyeva. Not only for the vodka, but for making me feel alive again, if only for a little while.

The knock was louder, hard enough for the door to vibrate. "Comrade Bukanin! Open the door!"

"*Ktoh etah?*" he called back. But he knew who it was.

"An old friend, Comrade."

"All my old friends are dead."

"This is foolish. I only wish to speak to you."

"I have no wish to speak to you."

There was a brief silence. Then, to Bukanin's surprise, he heard the scraping of a key in the lock. Tumblers clicked and the knob turned. As the door opened, Bukanin bit down on the capsule he had been holding in his mouth. He smiled at the irony. He had kept the capsule as a macabre souvenir of the old days, it was never something he intended to use. He doubted that he would have had the courage to use it back then if he had ever fallen into the hands of an enemy. Life had been too precious. In his heart he knew that he would have cooperated with the enemy, if spilling his guts was the price of survival.

Now . . . this was different.

He recognized the lean, sharp features of the man in the doorway. Sergei Lemenov's thin, bloodless lips formed a cold smile. His eyes were dead, Bukanin thought, like a snake's.

"I have been expecting you, Comrade Lemenov."

"The landlord gave me a key to your apartment, Anatoly Isaevich. I managed to convince him that you were not well and that, as a friend, I wanted to check on you."

"You were quite correct, Lemenov . . . I am not well."

Bukanin felt the pain seize his stomach. So soon, he thought. Behind the agony was a flicker of satisfaction as consternation erased that bloodless smile from the Collector's face.

Bukanin tried to smile in triumph, but his facial muscles were frozen. The knife of pain struck again, doubling him over. He toppled from his chair. In his mind he called out, *It's not your knife, Lemenov, it is my own, damn you.*

Lemenov's hands dragged him up from the floor, flung him into his chair. Shouted words seemed to come from a long way off. "You damn fool . . ."

The Collector's fingers pried at his mouth, forced the locked jaws open, clawed inside.

The pain was consuming him. After a while he felt himself drifting away from the pain, like a blackened ash rising. No pain at all now, the angry shout pursuing him, futile to call him back.

Outside the government complex near the Central Square the wind had picked up, adding to the bitter cold. Chris Harmon

was almost grateful for the need to keep moving back and
forth with the crowd of demonstrators.

Unlike most of the marchers, he carried no sign or placard.
He had never been much of a joiner or demonstrator, even in
his animal-rights activism, preferring to let his work speak
for him. But tonight he knew he belonged on the line, lending
his physical presence to the protests. Inside the administration building Boris Provalev and the South Koreans were pre-
sumably hammering out the final terms of the logging agreement for the Sikhote-Alin preserve, an agreement Chris saw
as a criminal act.

Rival television crews had sought him out earlier, having
learned that he was an American biologist who had been
working in the preserve. Cameras focused on him, microphones were thrust toward him, provocative questions. The
new Russian journalism—aggressive, demanding, competi-
tive—was already beginning to resemble its Western counterpart, the good and the bad of it, the openness and the appetite
for the sensational.

"Why are you here, Dr. Harmon?"

"I came at the invitation of the Russian government, as
part of a joint tiger research project in the Primorskiy Kray
forest."

"Why is an American attempting to interfere in a Russian
problem on Russian soil?"

"Most of the people you see here are Russians. I'm not in-
terfering with them, I'm joining them in their legitimate protest."

"Do you expect to be arrested?"

"No, of course not."

"Do you think the rights of wild animals prevail over human needs?"

"I believe we need to learn to live together—humans with
humans, nations with nations, and all of us with the other
species who share the planet with us. It's not an either-or
question."

Apparently his responses were too bland for effective television bites and the reporters quickly lost interest in him and
moved on.

Do you expect to be arrested? The question had made Chris pause. It underscored the dramatic changes in Russian society. A few short years ago simply participating in a protest march outside of a Russian government complex would have brought him to the immediate attention of the Fifth Chief Directorate of the KGB, whose sole function was to crush internal dissent. Arrest and detention would not have been surprising. The Russian people might be having trouble making democracy and the free-market economy work overnight but they were making progress. Chris doubted if the country would ever be the same again. Some things, having been tasted again after a long drought, would never be given up. The freedom to sell goods in an open market, the freedom to exchange ideas, opinions, insults in an open forum, the freedom to protest without fear of repression.

Letting himself flow with the crowd marching before the massive government buildings, watched without apparent concern by uniformed militia stationed around the square and blocking the entrances to the complex, Chris kept searching the faces of the marchers and new arrivals. Where was Lina?

Instead he saw Ken Langert emerging from a taxi, looking around, taking in the scene. Langert carried a stack of leaflets. His bulletin had already received wide distribution. The leaflets, Chris guessed, were another salvo.

Langert passed out leaflets to some of the organizers of the demonstration and, spotting Chris, he hurried toward him. "Supplemental bulletin," he said, handing one of the leaflets to Chris. "Does the same thing as the other but at a lot less cost for street handouts."

"It looks good," Chris said. "The first bulletin had a terrific impact on the environmental community here."

"On the already converted," Langert agreed. "But we're also getting international media attention. The BBC is picking up the story, the Associated Press and the Los Angeles *Times*. It has to have an impact on the Russian bureaucracy."

Langert glanced around as they walked along among the sign-carriers, many of them still chanting slogans. There were scores of Russians among the demonstrators, most of them young people. Chris listened to snatches of conversation swirling around them. Not all of it had to do with the logging controversy. ". . . a third of my week's pay to buy a half-liter of vodka. How can we survive?" . . . "In two years a loaf of bread has gone up 1000 percent." . . . "My wife's cousin, his farm is bursting with produce, everything he can grow—they eat like princes. But he can't sell what he grows at a fair price. The mafia won't let him." . . . "The mafia are eating up Russia and what do our leaders do?" . . . "The country is not going anywhere." . . . "That's not true, my friend, it is going to hell . . ."

Russia was a cauldron of heated opinions, complaints, angry questioning, Chris thought. But had it been much different when a young America lurched toward democracy and an uncertain future?

"Have you seen your girl friend?" Langert asked him.

"She's not my girl friend."

"You could've fooled me. She called earlier at the office, asking for you."

"When was that?"

"Couple hours ago . . . must have been around four. She's not here?"

"I haven't seen her."

Chris read the question in Langert's eyes. Lina Mashikova had been one of the first journalists on the tiger story and she had taken that group of Chris's photographs with her this morning. Why wasn't she following up? Admittedly the demonstrations were mostly about logging in the Primorskiy, but the danger to the Siberian tiger and other species was a significant part of the story.

Taking Chris by the arm, Langert pulled him away from the marchers. "Have you heard about your taxi driver?"

Puzzled, Chris shook his head.

"I just heard it on the news. Wasn't his name Mikhail Fyodorov?"

"That's right . . . He drove us over to your office this morning."

"And your friend left the meeting with him. He's dead, Chris."

Chris stared at him.

"Murdered. He was found in his taxi down near the waterfront. Police suspect a mafia killing. That's what they said about that camera shop being blown up with the owner inside. God knows, gangsters are bad enough in Russia today, but they're also a convenient scapegoat." After a pause Langert added, "That's two people close to you who've been murdered in the last twenty-four hours, Chris. I'd be very careful if I were you."

"Why should I be at risk?" Chris glanced down at the latest leaflet Langert had printed. The wounded tiger seemed to leap off the page. "Not over a poaching charge. That's a slap on the wrist if you're caught, it's not worth killing for."

"There has to be more to it than that. The question is . . . what?"

Langert didn't have to voice the other questions that came to both of their minds. What does your girl friend know about it . . . and where is she now?

29

THE LANDLORD HAD small suspicious eyes in a peasant's weathered face. "Comrade Bukanin is at home. If he doesn't answer your knock it can only mean that he doesn't wish to be disturbed."

"How can you be so sure? I'm concerned about him, do you have a key to his apartment?"

"How many keys do you think I keep for each apartment? His other visitor took the only one. I want it back."

"He had another visitor?" Lina Mashikova felt cold. The building, especially the unheated hallway where she stood outside the landlord's apartment, seemed to have a permanently built-in chill, but it wasn't that that touched her. "When?"

"I'm not his keeper. I don't keep records of his callers. Not long ago, within the hour."

Lina could smell her own fear. "You must have another key. If something is wrong, you will be held responsible. You say Comrade Bukanin is in his apartment but he doesn't answer. If you wish, I can call the police. Perhaps they can break the door down."

"The police! What do they have to do with anything? Okay, okay, there is a key for maintenance. No need to involve the police. Comrade Bukanin is probably passed out from too much vodka, it would not be the first time."

He disappeared briefly into his apartment, returning with a large ring of keys. He detached one, held it for a moment while his suspicious eyes studied her, a woman much too young and pretty for old Colonel Bukanin. He handed her the key. "I must have it back, is that clear?"

"Very clear."

The rickety elevator creaked noisily upward, and Lina's anxiety rose with it. At the sixth floor she got out and hurried along the drab corridor. The walls were thin enough for her to hear voices as she passed several apartments. Any commotion in Anatoly Bukanin's apartment would have been clearly audible.

At Bukanin's door she paused, heart racing, fitted the key into the lock, turned it quickly, pushed the door open.

The smells overwhelmed her fear. Stale cigarette smoke was pervasive, but the smell of death was stronger. Lina turned away from the spectacle of Anatoly Bukanin propped in his chair, the side of his head and his shirt and the arm of the chair drenched in blood. It was a moment before she could bring herself to look at him again. Then she realized that the oddly out-of-balance shape of his head also accounted for the blood. His left ear was missing.

General Chumeiko was not immediately available. Lina left the phone number of Bukanin's apartment along with the message that she had to speak to the general as soon as possible.

Within five minutes he called back and she described the scene in Bukanin's apartment.

"How was he killed? With a garrote?"

"A knife. There is some mutilation, his left ear was cut off but . . . his lips and tongue are black. I believe he may have taken poison. That means—"

"It means he must have been prepared for his visitor. He must have seen something in the photograph that we didn't see. He knew the man's identity."

And was frightened to death, Lina thought.

"How long has he been dead?" the general asked sharply.

"Less than an hour, I think. I'm not an expert in such matters, but the body is still warm. And the building landlord confirms that he had a visitor within the hour—a thin, well-dressed man. An aristocrat, the landlord thought."

"What about the photograph you gave Bukanin?"

"It's gone. At least I've been unable to find it . . . The police will have to be called."

"I will take care of it. You leave. Tell the landlord under no circumstances to open the apartment until authorities arrive."

"He's afraid of the police," Lina said.

"He will be even more afraid of me if he opens that apartment for anyone else." Chumeiko paused. "The situation has become volatile and dangerous, Lieutenant Mashikova. I think it would be best—"

"I'm not quitting now, General."

"It isn't a question of quitting—"

"I've been in this from the beginning, you recruited me yourself. I'm responsible for Bukanin being killed. I also know more of what is going on than anyone else you could assign."

"It's true you know this American scientist, Harmon. That's important. I believe his life may be in danger . . . along with your own, Lieutenant."

"Why should it be? The poachers now have the photograph—"

"I believe the man who caused Colonel Bukanin to take his life is a professional assassin," Chumeiko said. "He may suspect you have other photos. He's eliminating any risk of identification. Along that line there is something else you should know . . . it concerns a certain taxi driver. You have accompanied the American in a taxi driven by Mikhail Fyodorov, is that correct?"

"Yes . . ." She didn't ask how Chumeiko knew. It was hardly surprising that he might have had other agents monitoring her.

"Fyodorov's body was found in his taxi late this afternoon in the waterfront district. Not far from our own meeting place. He was murdered."

Lina could not trust herself to speak. She had trouble breathing, her legs felt weak. She put a hand on the edge of Bukanin's scarred desk to steady herself. Bukanin dead, and now Fyodorov.

"Was he . . . was there any mutilation?"

"No. He was garroted."

"Is that why you asked how Bukanin died?"

"Yes."

"Have you received the computer-enhanced photographs?"

"Unfortunately there has been a delay," the general said acidly, frustration in his voice. "A malfunction with the computer at military district headquarters in Khabarovsk. It's being corrected."

"Is there any question of . . ." Lina stumbled, aware she was on sensitive ground. "A question of loyalty, General?"

"No, there is only a question of a computer-program failure, which is hardly revolutionary. I will have the enhanced photographs by morning. Copies will be flown here in two separate Su-17 all-weather reconnaissance aircraft. There is snow and very cold temperatures over the northern half of the province tonight, but a high-pressure system behind the front will bring clear skies by morning." He grunted. "We all watch too damn much television. We begin to sound like meteorologists."

"What are my instructions?"

The general's silence seemed to stretch on interminably. Finally he said, "Warn the American. We don't want an international incident."

Chumeiko's reasoning seemed cold-blooded in its pragmatism but Lina was pleased . . . the general was giving her what she wanted, the chance to see Chris Harmon again, and he was keeping her in the game.

"Tell this man Harmon as little as possible. You must maintain your own cover, at least for the present. I'll have further orders after reviewing the photographs of the two men whose identities seem to be so significant. By morning we may also have another relevant piece of information."

"What, General?"

"Whether Boris Provalev has succeeded in persuading the South Korean principals to visit the Sikhote-Alin preserve."

It was beginning to come together, Lina realized—the shooting incident in the taiga, Christopher Harmon's photographs, Boris Provalev's behind-the-scenes political manipulations, and now two deaths—three, if the camera-shop owner was included—all linked.

". . . by seven o'clock tomorrow morning," General Chumeiko was saying. She had missed his first words.

"I will wait in my apartment to hear from you," she said.

After a barely perceptible hesitation the general said, "I believe it would be inadvisable for you to return to your apartment, Lieutenant."

"The killer—"

"Is a very thorough man. He has followed a trail from Fyodorov to Colonel Bukanin. We can anticipate he will not stop there."

"I'll make other plans, General."

"I'm sure your American friend will not mind," the general said dryly. "Wherever you are, you will call me promptly at seven o'clock."

"Yes, General—seven."

She had to see for herself. She had to know.

Lina Mashikova left her Suzuki motorcycle a half-mile from her apartment building in the parking lot beside a small busy neighborhood restaurant. The popping of the motorcycle's engine was audible over a considerable distance, especially at night, and she was taking no chance that it might be heard.

She covered the distance quickly on foot. The temperature had dropped swiftly with the coming of darkness and the cold was invigorating. Fear was also a stimulant.

Knowing the area intimately, she was able to approach her building along back streets and through alleys. She had no trouble entering an apartment building across the way from hers and a short distance up the street. She took the stairs two at a time to the third floor and walked along an unpainted corridor with a threadbare carpet that might have been in her own building. At the far end the corridor faced a fire escape. She paused at the window overlooking a rusty wrought-iron platform, a narrow side street and the street on which her apartment fronted. She tried to ease the window open. No use—it was painted shut. It was only good luck there had been no fire here in many years, Lina thought. However, the window offered a clear view along the street in front of her apartment building and of the side street directly below her. The latter was a good place to park unobtrusively, she noted, with a view of her building's entrance.

She searched for a black Zhiguli sedan. All of the cars seemed to look much alike from above—black or dark gray sedans. She was not expert enough at differentiating silhouettes to identify different makes from this vantage point. Yuri, who was crazy about cars, would have identified every model at a glance . . .

For several minutes she watched, standing motionless at the side of the window. She searched for the flare of a match, the movement of a shadow behind glass, the cracking of a window. Nothing.

He wouldn't show himself so readily. He's a professional.

There had been two men initially in the Zhiguli, later only one had tried to follow her. The two men captured in Harmon's photographs? That seemed almost certain. The bulldog and the Saluki. The bulldog had tried to follow her that morning. The Saluki was more dangerous, she thought. The face of an aristocrat, but Dimitri Zhdanov had died horribly in a fire, Mikhail Fyodorov had been garroted, Anatoly Bukanin had been so terrified he had taken his own life rather than confront the man whose face he must have recognized. *Who was he?*

Poor Fyodorov. What harm had he done? Why had he been sought out and murdered? One could comprehend the camera-shop owner being killed over the photographs, the assassin was being efficient. The same was true of Colonel Bukanin. But why Fyodorov? Because of her?

She had managed to sort out the parked cars a little better by now, and was fairly certain there was no Zhiguli sedan among them. You parked a half-mile away, why wouldn't he? she thought.

He could be waiting for her right now in her apartment. It faced the front of the building, three stories up from where she watched, but she could pick it out easily enough. One, two, three, four windows over from the west end of the building—there. Out of habit she had drawn the draperies over the front window before leaving. She always did.

The line of light, pencil-thin and visible for only the briefest instant, might have been her imagination, but it was like an ice pick stabbing her. She couldn't breathe, she had to grip the window frame. Her breath clouded the cold glass.

The curtains had been parted for someone to look out, and when they fell back one fold had failed to close completely, leaving a small triangular opening for the gleam of light to show through. A flashlight, Lina thought, flicked on for an instant. She hadn't imagined it. Fear hadn't created that stab of light, but it had produced the heightened awareness that enabled her to see it.

Staring across the dark street, eyes straining, she saw the curtain move, the fold straightening out, covering the small black triangle. Almost as if he sensed that I was watching, Lina thought.

She slipped quickly, quietly down the stairs, letting herself out into the small yard at the back of the building—out of sight from her apartment window.

Hurrying through the cold darkness toward the restaurant where she had left her motorcycle, she had one thought: *Find Christopher Harmon, he doesn't realize the danger.*

30

IT WAS LIKE a mutually agreeable seduction, Boris Provalev thought. The most important concession was the first one, however small. The most important word was the first *yes* or even *perhaps*. Everything else followed, a ritual of move and countermove, step and sidestep, in which each partner knew how the dance would end.

The formal reception had begun with toasts of champagne and vodka. Tables bowed under enormous bowls and platters of plump shrimp, cold Australian lobster, black caviar from the Caspian Sea, smoked salmon from the Bering Sea, Georgian cheeses, hot and savory sausages. Between toasts and courses there were flattering speeches—all designed to make the visiting South Koreans feel pampered, courted, favored.

By ten o'clock that evening, when the principals withdrew from the large banquet hall to a small adjoining conference room, both of the South Korean principals had a high coloring from the rich feast of food, drink and flattery. Prime Minister Kim Su was a fastidious man who sipped rather than swallowed, tasted rather than gulped; all the same, his eyes were brighter than usual and his face red. He was a fraction of a second slow in focusing on Provalev's words. His translator, a young Korean woman, had to repeat them.

"We are in agreement then, Mr. Prime Minister . . . this is an historic moment for our two countries."

The signing, a formality, its terms long since agreed upon, had been delayed until now. Provalev signed the thirty-year logging agreement with a flourish, held the pen out toward the prime minister. Kim Su hesitated, glanced aside toward

Chang Pyon, nodded. He stepped forward, leaned over the table and signed his name. Above it, Provalev's signature was a bold sprawl of his pen; Kim's was a neat, indecipherable squiggle of lines.

The signatures of Oleg Kholkhov, the interior minister, for the Russian government and Chang Pyon for Sunsai Corporation, which would carry out the actual timber-cutting operation, followed.

Provalev smiled, summoned a waiter to pour more glasses of vodka. Just so that old fool Kholkhov doesn't fall on his face, he thought as he held up his glass. "To a new partnership in peace!"

Kim Su waited, nodded, murmured something that his translator quickly rendered as, "A most appropriate salutation, Chairman. Might I add, peace and prosperity."

From the shadows of an empty kiosk just around the corner from the entrance to the Hotel Vladivostok, Lina Mashikova whispered his name like a hiss.

Chris Harmon paused on the steps, as if thinking that he might have imagined the sound.

"Christopher!"

He turned toward her, eyes searching the darkness. She watched to see how his face would change when he saw her, the reaction his eyes would mirror. His expression pleased her as he hurried down the steps and over to her. "Lina, where have you been? I've been worried, a lot has been happening—"

She pulled him behind the kiosk. "I have much to tell you." *And much that I cannot tell.*

"What are you doing here?"

"I would have waited for you in the parking lot but some of the young gangsters hanging out there thought I had something else in mind."

"You could make a fortune." Chris's tone quickly sobered. "You've heard about Fyodorov?"

"Yes . . . it is terrible."

"It's that, all right." The delight he had shown when he first saw her had changed to a questioning scrutiny. "It's also kind of scary. Do you want to go inside? We can talk safely in my room—"

"Not safely, Christopher."

"There's no one there—"

"You should not go to your room. Listen to me . . . it may be very dangerous."

"You can't be serious. Why?"

She looked behind her along the street, then past his shoulder toward the entry to the hotel. She felt exposed. "Not here."

"Then why not my room?"

"You've already been robbed there. Why should you think it is any safer now?"

What he read in her eyes, even more than her words, convinced him. "Okay, okay, I'm all yours. Where do we go from here?"

Chang Pyon threw his head back, downing his vodka like a Russian. He was a harder nut in every way, Boris Provalev thought. As expected. Tonight Chang had matched his Russian host drink for drink, and Provalev, like many of his countrymen, had a prodigious capacity for vodka. Now he spoke to both of his guests but his words were mostly meant for Chang.

"We must move quickly to influence world opinion. These demonstrations"—he waved toward the front of the building where the chants of marchers could still be dimly heard—"are troublesome, but I believe we can turn them to our advantage."

"They are like students in my country," the Korean prime minister said through his interpreter. "They make noise but are of no real importance."

"Unfortunately these are not just students. And they are not only Russians. These people represent wildlife agencies and conservation groups from around the world. Russians welcome our agreement, but these other groups have great influence in the United States, Great Britain and parts of

Western Europe." Provalev carefully avoided mentioning Japan, South Korea's chief economic rival and an equal-opportunity offender in the eyes of the world's environmental activists.

"Their voices will grow hoarse, especially when they find that no one is listening."

"The trouble is, too many people *are* listening," Provalev said. "And these people have one very powerful weapon."

Kim Su's eyes, which had been wandering, tried to focus on Provalev.

"A boycott," the Russian said. "Such people have vocal supporters in the countries that make up the best markets for Sunsai products . . . especially America."

"People quickly forget," Kim said angrily. "South Korea will not be threatened or coerced—"

"Nor will Russia be diverted from its true course," Provalev agreed. "But a wise man does not try to push an elephant out of his way when he can lead it with a handful of peanuts."

Kim frowned, making a visible effort to concentrate. "And what peanuts do you propose to offer them?"

"We offer only what we would willingly do from our own concern for the great Russian taiga, one of my country's richest resources. And, Prime Minister, what I am certain that you and Comrade Chang would also wish: a long-term plan for an environmentally friendly, sustainable timber harvest in the Sikhote-Alin preserve, one that produces the maximum economic benefit for our two countries while minimizing the environmental impact and the threat to endangered species in the region. In other words, we tell them that Sunsai is not coming to the Primorskiy forest to rape it but to milk it, not to destroy but to harvest and replenish. These marchers are idealistic, náive," he went on as he saw the flicker of interest in Chang Pyon's eyes. "They chant slogans but we deal in facts. They see a forest fantasy, we see a treasure to be expended wisely. Don't you agree, Comrade Prime Minister?"

Kim looked toward Chang before nodding without enthusiasm. "Yes, yes, we are no villains . . ." the young Korean woman translated for him.

"What specifically are you suggesting?" said Chang Pyon.

He startled Provalev by addressing him bluntly in Russian. His accent was execrable but his Russian was obviously fluent.

Recovering quickly, Provalev said, "You have seen the photograph of the tiger wounded by illegal poachers?"

"We have seen it. How does it concern us?"

"The incident was a catalyst for these demonstrations. The photograph is receiving considerable attention worldwide. This shooting occurred near the perimeter of Sector Five of the preserve, which has been declared off-limits to all unauthorized persons pending our agreement. It seems that the wounded tiger may still be alive, and that she is a female with cubs. A proposal has been made by biologists working in the preserve—one of them an American—to rescue the tiger and her cubs. Until now that effort has been forbidden by my government. However, it might be that in your generosity you would see fit to urge that such a rescue mission be carried out promptly."

The two South Korean leaders exchanged glances. Chang said, "How far is this location from our initial logging site?"

"More than five miles, I am told."

"I see no reason not to offer the elephant this peanut," Chang said, stone-faced.

Boris Provalev smiled.

The mating dance continued.

"Why here, if you don't mind my asking?" Chris Harmon said.

"Because I am hungry."

They were in a small restaurant less than a mile from the Vladivostok Hotel. They had reached it, however, by a roundabout route covering at least three miles. Chris on the back of Lina Mashikova's Suzuki motorcycle, his arms around her slim waist, feeling the pull and shape of her taut stomach muscles each time the bike leaned around a corner.

"You're sure it's safe here?"

"No one followed us, I am sure of that." After a pause she added, "Do not make fun of me, Christopher."

She ordered cabbage soup, black bread and a half-liter of vodka. When the waiter had left the bottle and two glasses Chris said, "What happened to *kvas?*"

"Tonight I need vodka." Her tone became flat. "You do not believe me."

"Take it easy. I don't know what to think. You take off without a word, you take those photographs. I don't know where you've been or what you've been doing. Then you show up and . . . I don't know why you're here or why you think someone might be hanging around in my hotel room."

"Aren't you *listening* to me? Aren't you even listening to yourself? Fyodorov is dead—garroted. Why do you think he was murdered? Because of me—us! And before him there was Dimitri Zhdanov. And after him—" She broke off, looking quickly around the restaurant.

"I'm sorry, Lina, I'm not making fun of you or doubting you, it's just that, where I come from, it's hard to think of your room in the city's best hotel as not being fairly safe."

"You had better change the way you're thinking. You are not where you came from."

"I've spent the afternoon and evening with a lot of other people in peaceful protests about the situation in the preserve and this South Korean agreement. No one threatened us. The militia was there—"

"Your friends are puppets. They are being used . . . *you* are being used, Christopher—even your photographs!"

Chris sat back. In spite of Lina's outburst no one in the restaurant seemed to be paying any attention to them. Lovers' quarrels weren't unusual in any country, he thought. He realized that Lina had deliberately chosen a table in a back corner, lit only by candlelight with no one sitting nearby.

He watched her down her vodka, pour another drink. "I think you'd better tell me what you know," he said.

"I do not see the necessity of making such a trip at this time," the Korean prime minister said stiffly.

"You are here, Comrade Prime Minister. The time is right

to take the initiative, defuse these protests and score a public relations triumph."

"You should not have gone public with this proposal without our prior approval."

"I made this proposal openly weeks ago," Provalev answered. "The decision has always been yours, of course . . . although it was my understanding that Comrade Chang, whose people have already been at work in the preserve, has expressed interest in visiting the site where the preliminary base camp has been set up." He glanced at Chang. "Your geologists and engineers have made extensive studies of the area."

Chang nodded, giving nothing away.

"You are wise in the ways of politics, Comrade Prime Minister," Provalev said, again addressing Kim Su. "It is no different in Russia, in America, in all countries where the people are free to voice their passions. Making a gesture of concern for the environment of the Sikhote-Alin preserve is a small thing that can pay large dividends in good will. This is not capitulation, this is simply good politics."

"In my day we wouldn't have stood for such nonsense!" the interior minister of Russia declared suddenly in his quavery voice. "They would have been shot—"

You're an old fool, Provalev thought. But he smiled and said, "A wise sailor adjusts to a changing wind, he defies it at his own peril."

"What would such a visit to the preserve involve?" asked Chang Pyon.

Provalev did not smile, gave no indication of the excitement that ran through him. Now was the most sensitive moment, the suitor whispering, stroking gently, no need to rush.

"I could make arrangements tonight. Depending on the weather, we could fly to Terney in the morning and by military helicopter to the logging camp early in the afternoon. We could return to Vladivostok before nightfall."

"And if the weather is bad?"

"The forecast is favorable. However, the timetable is yours . . . we are completely at your disposal."

*   *   *

The cabbage soup was hot, thick and delicious, the black bread, as usual, to die for. Bad metaphor, Chris thought.

"How did you know Fyodorov was garroted?" he asked. He liked watching her eat. She even ate her soup with grace.

"It is my business to learn such things."

"What did you mean when you said, 'And after him—'?"

"The man—*men*—in those pictures do not wish to be identified. Zhdanov's shop was bombed—the police report now says that an explosive was used—because of the photographs you left with him. I took those pictures of the men this morning, and someone tried to follow me. Fyodorov threw them off. I think he may later have been tortured to make him say where he drove me. I gave one of the photographs to an old friend. He was once a colonel in the KGB. I wanted to know if he recognized either of the two men in the taiga who shot your tiger. Now . . . my old friend is dead."

"Good God . . ." It took Chris a while to absorb it all. Then he blurted out, "KGB?"

"A long time ago, many years . . . but he knows many people. Knew," she said quietly.

Chris saw her biting her lip, her fists clenched at the edge of the table. He reached out to take one of her hands. At first she resisted, then her tight fist loosened, her hand opened out and her fingers entwined with his.

"I found him in his apartment. Afterward I went to my own apartment but I was careful, I looked from across the street and . . . someone was there. I saw a flashlight, just for an instant." She looked up at him. "*Now* do you understand why I did not think your room was safe?"

"Yes," Chris said, still holding her hand.

They finished their meal in silence. Chris was surprised how filling the soup and bread had been, how good the meal had tasted on this cold night. Over strong hot tea he noted that their half-liter of vodka was empty. He was surprised that he didn't feel it. That comes when you try to stand up, he thought.

"After last night I would have said there were no secrets between us. That's not true, is it?"

"There are always secrets."

After another pause Chris said, "Where can we go?"

Boris Provalev reached Brunovsky on the portable phone he was now carrying. "Have you heard from the Collector?"

"No, but I believe I know where he is."

"We've done it. Get Lemenov—he leaves for the Primorskiy tonight!"

"I'm not sure . . . he is determined to find this woman, the journalist—"

"Remind him how much he is being paid, and what for," Provalev said tightly. "And tell him that you will take care of the woman."

"It will be my pleasure."

"What is this place?" Chris whispered. They were in an attic bedroom in an old house high on one of the hills overlooking the city and the sweep of the bay. The two elderly people he had met briefly downstairs had gone to bed, also whispering to each other. The room was lit only by the light coming in the narrow window that faced the bay and a single candle in a holder on the small dresser.

"They are friends. No one knows about them . . . we are safe here for tonight."

"And tomorrow?"

"You say you will return to the preserve no matter what. I will also do what I must do."

"But you can stay the night with me." He made it a statement, not a question, his hands reaching under her sweater to lift it. She raised her arms, helping him remove the sweater. She wore no bra. Her breasts were small and firm, the nipples pointing slightly upward. He traced their hard outlines with the edges of his thumbs.

He watched the color rise in her neck, to her cheeks. He

had forgotten how appealing—and how rare—a blush could be. Her eyes were bright with something other than tears.

"I will stay with you," she whispered. He kissed the hollow of her neck, lowered his head to find a breast that rose to meet his lips as she arched her back. "Promise me one thing, Christopher . . ."

"Name it."

"If there are any explosions in the night, you will wake me."

Chris paused, flicked her nipple with the tip of his tongue. "If there are any explosions tonight, Yelinita, I promise you will know all about them."

31

THE SNOW WAS dry and powdery, the air very cold as temperatures dropped well below freezing. Two hours after midnight the snow stopped. The storm with its thick cloud cover still hovered over much of the taiga but it was pushing eastward toward the sea. Behind it to the west, the sky over the Sikhote-Alin range was clear, bright with stars and a crescent moon. The snow glittered in the pale light, lying in feathery arms on the branches of fir and pine and birch trees, sifting downward as the wind stirred the branches.

The taiga was very still, sounds muffled by the mantle of fresh snow.

Before first light the tiger eased out of the shelter of her den. She snarled at one of the cubs that tried to follow her. The youngster, still sleepy, crept back into the hollow of the den, seeking the warmth of the other cubs.

The Siberian padded quietly in a complete circle around the den, her paws leaving broad prints in the snow. The trail identified her: in each sequence three fully defined footprints and a fourth print either missing or visible only as a brushing of the surface as she favored her left front leg.

Her shoulder was hot, inflamed by infection, and the pain had increased. It was making her short-tempered. Yet she moved easily, powerfully on her three legs.

She was hungry, but it was not hunger that drove her from her den. She was restless, as if sensing that something was about to happen.

First light began to seep through the forest as the Siberian went down to the river to drink. She took her time, surveying the grassy slope in front of her and the woods beyond. Limping, she climbed back toward the tree line. The morning sunlight was visible only as a thin red line against the horizon to the east, framed by the wall of the forest below and by the lid of storm clouds above.

A distant growling.

She felt the thrust of anger, hatred. The sound was familiar. It was drawing closer. It reminded her of the growling of the machine in which the two-legged hunters came to the taiga, but it was also different, louder and deeper. And it came from above.

Five minutes later she saw it crawling across the sky, much louder now. It flew like a huge, ungainly bird, passing almost overhead where the tiger crouched in the tall grass, and passing on in the direction of the rising sun.

She listened until the sound diminished to a hum. The bird flew lower, disappeared from view, and the deep silence returned to the snowbound forest.

Hungry, curious, the Siberian started through the taiga to the east, where the growl of the airborne hunter had died away.

PART THREE

THE HUNT

32

At 5:36 A.M., at thirty-second intervals, two Su–17 all-weather aircraft hurtled down the runway at the military district air base in Khabarovsk, climbed steeply through a layer of clouds and burst into the clear, cold skies above the dissipating storm front. The two aircraft leveled out at sixteen thousand feet and went to afterburners as they raced south.

At 6:31 A.M. the first of the Su–17 reconnaissance planes touched down at the naval air station southwest of Vladivostok. Two couriers waited on the airstrip, motorcycle engines idling. The riders wore thick jackets, knitted hoods and gloves, and their breath vaporized in the freezing cold. As soon as the wheels of the first aircraft touched the macadam, a motorcyclist raced out to meet it. The plane taxied clear of the runway and braked. The motorcyclist retrieved a pouch thrown down by the pilot and immediately raced off. The routine was repeated as the second Su–17 landed.

Twenty-one minutes later the first of the pouches landed on the desk of General Victor Chumeiko, who was waiting for it in his office, a mug of Twinings English Breakfast tea at his elbow. Behind him, Colonel Gennady Beretnikoff stepped forward to peer down at the photographs Chumeiko dumped out of the pouch and spread across the surface of his desk. A Deputy Director of the Anti-Terrorist Subdirectorate of the GRU, Beretnikoff had an intimate knowledge of the *destvitelni otdel,* the Operations Directorate of the old Soviet KGB, and of its agents.

The two men stared in silence. The general's finger stabbed one of the photos. "Do you know him, Colonel?"

"Leonid Andreyevich Brunovsky. He is Boris Provalev's chief aide."

"That ties the chairman directly into the plot. And the other man? The marksman?"

"His name is Sergei Gregorevich Lemenov. He was once attached to Department V of the Committee for State Security. More recently he has acquired a reputation as a highly paid assassin. He is on Interpol's 'A' list of most wanted criminal agents." The colonel paused a moment. "His predilection for collecting body parts has made him notorious in some circles. In the KGB his code name was the Collector. It appears that he still enjoys that reputation."

"You are certain? There are no photographs of the Collector in our files or those of Interpol."

"I am certain, General. I met him myself more than a decade ago . . . at Chairman Yuri Andropov's funeral."

"I see." Our first piece of luck, Chumeiko thought. Was it an omen for the coming crisis? "Where is Lemenov now?"

"We have been unable to intercept him . . . but we believe he has already left Vladivostok for the Primorskiy forest."

"By commercial flight? We could—"

"By military helicopter," Beretnikoff said crisply.

General Chumeiko stared at him. "Then it's begun. Provalev is making his move."

"It would appear so, General."

Lina Mashikova's call was put through to General Victor Chumeiko at 7:03 A.M. "I trust you found a secure location for the night, Lieutenant?" he asked.

"Yes, General."

"Where is the American?"

"Harmon has just left for the airport. He learned that the Ministry of Environmental Protection has had a sudden change of heart about his attempt to rescue the wounded tiger and her cubs in the taiga."

"Ah, yes . . . Provalev's work."

"Provalev? I don't understand—"

"An announcement was made late last night. As part of the

accord between the Russian government and the South Koreans, approval was given for this environmentally friendly
gesture on the part of the tree choppers. I suspect the chairman simply wanted this American and his problem temporarily out of the way."

"Shall I continue to—"

"Report to my office at once, Lieutenant. An insurrection
has begun." After a slight pause the general added, "There
has also been another murder."

"Who . . . who has been killed?"

"A waiter in a cafe next to Kusovsky Park. His body was
mutilated in a similar manner to Colonel Bukanin's. It is a
. . . trademark of the assassin."

"Have you identified him?"

"Yes, Lieutenant. Thanks to your photographs, the identities of both men are now known."

"Who—?"

"Report at once."

The line was disconnected.

Chris Harmon's flight was uneventful, but considerably more
comfortable than his last trip from Plastun to Vladivostok in
the *Spirit of St. Louis*. This time he flew in a relatively modern, Russian-manufactured Antonov AN–28, a twin-prop aircraft that carried fifteen passengers in a well-appointed main
cabin in addition to the pilot and a passenger in the front
cockpit. The seating was five rows deep in a two-plus-one con-
figuration. Boarding early, Chris was able to get one of the
single seats by a window. He paid little attention to the other
passengers—there were seven in addition to a VIP sitting
forward with the pilot. Chris spent most of the short flight
staring out the window at the forested hills and reliving the
night he had spent in an attic room with Lina Mashikova.

Especially the last moments.

"I think I'm falling in love with you, Yelina Vassilyeva," he
had whispered, propped on an elbow and staring down at her
soft mouth, slightly puffy as if bruised from their lovemaking.
Her blue eyes studied him.

Louis Charbonneau

"Shhh." She put a finger to his lips.

"Why? Not talking about it won't change—"

"This night was beautiful. Isn't that enough?"

"No. I don't want it to end here. Tomorrow—"

"Tomorrow you will have unfinished business, not only here but in America. And I will have . . . what I have to do."

"None of that changes anything."

"You only want to pretend these things are not important. It's nice to pretend for a night—it's wonderful—but it is foolish to think the night will not end."

"Maybe if you told me a little more about this *duty* of yours . . . I know you're not just a reporter . . ."

"We have so little time." Lina kissed his lips, his chin, his neck, his chest. He lay back as her hand strayed over his flat stomach, exploring further. "And I believe you are well rested now. There, you see . . ."

"Yelinita . . ."

"So much talk, and so little time."

Her kisses reached his navel, fluttering across his skin as soft as butterflies. Chris groaned, reaching for her. . . .

She had dropped him off at a taxi stand after explaining that she could not drive him to the airport.

"I have things at the hotel—"

"Leave them, Christopher. Please—don't go there. I will see that your things are held for you. It's safer if you leave at once."

He had watched the Suzuki buzz away, ducking through traffic, Lina's long coat bunched around her waist, the bike fishtailing a little as she went around the corner too fast. Then she was gone and the clear cold morning seemed suddenly empty.

The AN–28 descended over a white world, achingly bright and clean in the brilliant sunshine. Chris saw a yellow bus and a few other vehicles standing near the cluster of frame buildings and hangars at the small airfield in Plastun.

He had telephoned Alex Grovkin in Terney as soon as he

received word that clearance had been given by the Ministry of Environmental Protection for a rescue team to enter Sector Five of the preserve and was relieved to see Alex waiting for him at the arrival gate. And he was both surprised and delighted to recognize the tall figure of Gregory Krasikov standing beside Grovkin. The Russian biologist, rangy and rawboned with broad shoulders and a full blond beard, would have appeared at home on the Great Plains. Just a few days ago he had been abruptly transferred to another preserve by Vladimir Yavlinsky. What was he doing here now?

"I was in Terney to pick up some of my supplies," Krasikov explained after effusive greetings. The biologist spoke fluent English. "Alexander Semyonovich told me what has happened with the ministry. The Board for Nature Preserve Management has concurred in the minister's decision, of course. I am able to join your rescue mission." He grinned. "Comrade Yavlinsky is not happy."

"I kid you not!" Grovkin exclaimed, trying out one of his American idioms. "Comrade Yavlinsky is more than unhappy. He try not to help us—he say my Jeep being used somewhere, he cannot tell me where."

"How did you get here?" Chris asked as they emerged from the low building that served as a terminal, passing from a blast of overheated air into icy cold.

"You have your bag?" Grovkin said. "Where is it?"

"I left it behind."

"At hotel? You were in such big hurry?"

"You could say that. It's a long story, Alex . . . I'll tell you on the way. Are we taking the bus?"

Grovkin grinned. "We do better than bus. Comrade Krasikov arrange it."

"What—?" Chris stopped cold, staring at the vehicle to which Grovkin had led them. "Good God—what's this? Isn't it . . . what you call a Black Maria?"

"Is same! You know it?"

"I've heard of them . . . and I read what Solzhenitsyn wrote about Black Marias in *The Gulag Archipelago*. How they used to rumble through the streets at night carrying their secret cargo of prisoners to the railroad stations and the trains waiting to take them to the Gulag . . . the fear they used to inspire. The name comes from . . . ravens, right?"

"That is correct."

Chris stared from the vehicle to Krasikov and back. "How did you get it?"

A smile emerged from the blond beard. "I bought it on the black market and had it stored here in Terney. Everything is for sale these days, and the price on these was rock bottom. Nobody wanted them. I thought it could be a useful utility vehicle. It rides as if it has iron wheels but you can't break it down. For a Russian vehicle," Krasikov added with an ironic smile, "it is very reliable."

"Better than Russian truck," Alex Grovkin agreed.

The Black Maria was painted a dirty faded gray rather than black. Sometimes labeled the Hearse from Hell, it resembled an early 1930s vintage American armored car or minivan. The shell was armored with solid windowless side panels and a narrow one-piece door set into the back. The front and side windows in the cab were bulletproof.

Chris opened the door at the rear to peer into the interior. There was a narrow bench of wooden slats along one side and, opposite, three animal cages. Cardboard boxes held medical supplies. Otherwise the shell was empty.

"You've fitted it with cages already!"

"We work very fast," Grovkin said. "As soon as we learn we can go after tiger cubs."

"We didn't want to give the ministry a chance to change its mind again," said Krasikov, "or to give Comrade Yavlinsky's poaching pals time to make trouble for us."

"Poachers are angry over tiger pictures," Alex said with grim satisfaction.

"I guess we'd better get going, then," Chris said. "Should I ride in back?"

"There is no room in front for three," Alex apologized.

Krasikov laughed. "We can trade off, Chris—you don't want to try riding on that bench all the way to the preserve. The suspension in one of these things . . ."

* * *

Leonid Brunovsky, who had also been startled by the unexpected sight of the infamous Black Maria, watched it pull away from the terminal. He closed his greatcoat around his throat, the collar up. The air was freezing cold and a sharp wind stirred up miniature funnels of snow that blew in his face. Brunovsky picked up his single suitcase and carried it over to the waiting bus for Terney. So, he thought, the woman did not come with him.

Brunovsky had been on the same flight as the American scientist. Even though he did not believe the American would recognize him he had made arrangements to ride in the extra seat in the cockpit beside the pilot. For Boris Provalev's aide such privileges were not even questioned.

The overnight change in plans had upset Brunovsky. He had been looking forward to tracking down and interrogating the female Russian journalist who had eluded his attempts to follow her. After another clandestine midnight meeting with Sergei Lemenov, however, Provalev had told him to forget her. She would be taken care of later. The South Koreans had finally agreed to his urging to visit the Sikhote-Alin preserve, Provalev confirmed. He ordered Brunovsky to follow the Collector to the taiga.

Sergei Lemenov would be flown there by military helicopter so that he would have time to be in place before the arrival of the visitors in Sector Five. Brunovsky was to travel to Terney via Plastun on the first available commercial flight, reclaim the Range Rover that had been garaged in Terney and drive it into the preserve. On a map covering the southeast quadrant of the preserve, including Sector Five, Lemenov had marked the coordinates showing the location where Brunovsky was to wait for him. It was not far from the area where the tiger had been shot.

"You will leave the area together," Provalev said. "If for any reason you are stopped—which is not likely—you will be able to confirm that Comrade Lemenov was with you all the time."

The bus left the airport, bouncing along the uneven gravel road. The road climbed through a mountain pass. Fresh snow mantled the drooping branches of the trees on either side and lay inches thick on the ground as the bus gained altitude. The crown of the road was relatively clear, however, and the bus had no difficulty. Did the driver have chains? Brunovsky wondered. What if we're stranded in the mountains? It would be harder going in the preserve, he thought, especially if the temperature climbed a little and the bright sun melted the snow and softened the ground.

He stared through the dust-coated side window of the bus at the passing wall of trees, their autumn colors tempered by the fresh fall of snow. Too many sudden changes in plan, he thought. Even though he had known the general thrust of Boris Provalev's intentions and guessed most of the rest, understanding his patron's ambition, only in the last forty-eight hours had Brunovsky been briefed on the full details of Provalev's planned coup and the role the Collector was to play in it. He had assumed that Lemenov would make his own way out of the preserve after completing his assignment. There had been no talk earlier of Brunovsky returning to the preserve to help Lemenov escape.

All along Brunovsky had pictured himself at the center of the storm, standing at Boris Provalev's side.

Now . . . it would all happen without him.

That was bad enough. What disturbed Brunovsky even more was the prospect of being once again alone in the wilderness with the Collector.

33

LINA MASHIKOVA STUDIED the computer-enhanced enlargements of the photographs that revealed the two poachers in the taiga. She marveled at their clarity of detail.

"His name is Sergei Gregorevich Lemenov," General Victor Chumeiko said. "He was an agent of Department V of the First Chief Directorate of the KGB."

"I know about Department V—"

"Then I don't have to tell you that he is a skilled assassin."

"For the KGB? But I thought—"

"Not for the KGB, no. Not any longer. More than five years ago he disappeared from their files, all records erased. There was no place under the new *perestroika* for such a man." The general's tone turned harsh. "Lemenov is an assassin for hire. He is known for his practice of mutilating many of his victims, usually severing an ear or a finger and taking it with him. That's how he got his KGB code name, the Collector. It has stuck with him."

"What was his real purpose in the taiga? And why is he here in Vladivostok now?"

Chumeiko smiled grimly. "Good questions. There has been no public announcement, but the visiting South Korean dignitaries are to fly by helicopter this morning to Sector Five of the Sikhote-Alin Biosphere National Preserve. Chairman Provalev is to accompany them. Does that answer your questions, Lieutenant?"

"The Collector will be there . . ."

"Precisely. He went there before to create an incident for the attention of the South Koreans. Now he is waiting for them to come to him. Lemenov flew from Vladivostok during the night in a military helicopter. The aircraft evaded radar scrutiny from Khabarovsk but we were able to track it otherwise."

Lina didn't ask how. "But Provalev is the one who engineered the agreement with the South Koreans. Why would he do anything to sabotage that accord?"

Chumeiko shook his head. "The agreement is a *fraud*. A setup to gain his ends. I'm convinced that what he has planned is the assassination of the South Korean leaders, an act which would almost *certainly* trigger armed conflict between our two countries. Then North Korea would inevitably be drawn into such a conflict, perhaps China . . . others."

"Why? This is crazy—"

"Crazy, yes, but with a design. It is meant to create the chaotic conditions under which Provalev and those who support him can seize power in Far East Russia. With our nation as a whole in turmoil, who is to say where such a design will end?"

"Surely he can't believe the people would choose to go back—"

"He is a fanatic," Chumeiko said. "All such men are true believers in what they want to believe. There are men like Provalev elsewhere in Russia and in the former Soviet republics. There are hard-liners in the Red Army who would celebrate his success. I'm absolutely certain that Provalev believes these so-called patriots will ignite like-minded uprisings all across the Rodina . . . and *he* will ride this wave to power."

"It's all about power," Lina whispered.

"It is *always* about power."

After a pause Lina said, "Is Provalev correct in his assessment? If the assassin succeeds . . ."

"We will have the answer in the next few hours, Lieutenant. Provalev is not waiting to learn if his assassin carries out his assignment. He has gambled. Tanks of the Nineteenth Guards Tank Division are at this moment moving toward the city."

"That's *treason,*" Lina said.

"There are many kinds of treason. Betrayal is only one. Our carelessness in guarding the Rodina is also a form of betrayal. Cowardice or inaction in the face of such betrayal is also treason."

"Then you will try to stop him."

"Of course. I must also tell you that if we are able to stop this insurrection, your nation will be grateful for what you've done."

"I have done very little, General." Lina hesitated. For the first time her thoughts moved beyond the disaster that Chumeiko had sketched. Her personal feelings were not important but she could not deny them. "Christopher Harmon is also on his way to the preserve . . ."

Chumeiko flipped a hand dismissively. "That is not our priority."

"But surely the assassin *is* a high priority. Can such a man be allowed to go free? You spoke about the loyalty of the *spetznaz* units. Even a small team of such soldiers would be able to track the Collector down in the preserve before he can disappear again. I respectively request permission to accompany such a team."

Chumeiko sighed. "Plans have already been made. I can't spare additional troops to accompany you, Lieutenant. We will try to intercept the South Koreans and prevent disaster at this end, not in the taiga. After that we must deal with the military insurrection that has already begun."

"Then, with the general's approval, I will go alone."

"No," Chumeiko said flatly. "Your work is done. The rest is for soldiers."

"What about the militia in Terney? Aren't they loyal? I could accompany them into the preserve to search for the assassin. We *can't* let him escape—"

"The militia . . ." The general shook his head but the suggestion caught his attention. Damned if he wanted Sergei Lemenov to walk away from his treachery and this conspiracy. He was too dangerous, and if he escaped, others would seek him out in the future. Still . . . "It's too great a risk," he said.

"Can't we trust Russian soldiers to act like true Russians?"

Lina asked with feeling. "I will take that risk. Let me go to militia headquarters in Terney and see what will happen. We can also try to keep the American safe and avoid an international incident."

Chumeiko stared at her, weighing the consequences of granting Mashikova's request. If her mission went badly, the burden of his responsibility would be intolerable. But if she succeeded . . .

It was a time for risks—for him no less than for Boris Provalev, he finally decided, and said, "I have already planned for a squad of hunters to go by helicopter to the logging camp in the forest. But that would leave the assassin's escape route open to the west. I can perhaps spare one additional helicopter . . ."

The Mi–24 Hind helicopter bristled with rockets and guns. It was designed to carry up to eight troops in addition to the flight crew of two. Lina Mashikova was alone in the cabin. "At least you will travel faster with a light load," General Chumeiko said before she left. "You'll also be stretching the limit of the Hind's range without refueling. Good luck."

"Thank you, General—"

"Thank me when you return, Lieutenant."

When you return . . . The phrase triggered a memory of her last moments with Chris Harmon that morning . . . *Will I see you again? . . . I don't know. . . . Will you be here in Vladivostok when I return? . . . I'll give you my phone number* . . .

Now she was following him into the taiga. So those painful moments of parting had not been the last, she would see him again. When she thought about him it was like having the breath squeezed out of her. In a pleasurable way . . .

The Mi–24 took off from the naval air station and swung east over the bay. Clearing the harbor, it turned north, following the rugged coastline, where steep wooded hills spilled down to a deep blue sea. The chopper flew so low that Lina could see the foam where whitecaps crested and rolled.

Had Sergei Lemenov flown this way in the darkness before

dawn? If so, he was already in his blind, waiting. Unless the Koreans could be interdicted short of their destination in Sector Five, there would be no way to stop the international crisis that Boris Provalev had set in motion.

At that moment the Collector was gazing down at the group of prefabricated huts and a long metal-roofed shed that made up the base camp occupied by Sunsai's advance engineers located at the eastern edge of the Sikhote-Alin preserve, less than two miles from the coastline and the Sea of Japan. No one had appeared in the camp in the early hours of morning but a plume of smoke rose above one of the huts from a metal chimney. No more than three or four men, Provalev had assured him, all Koreans. No soldiers.

An area of a little over five acres had been cleared to make room for the camp. A dirt road threaded off through the forested hills to the south. At one end of the clearing even the tree stumps had been hauled away to create a flat, clear field. The helicopter landing pad, Lemenov thought.

His vantage point on a bluff at the edge of the forest overlooking the camp was elevated about two hundred feet above the clearing and no more than three hundred yards from the landing pad.

Lemenov picked out a clump of grass for a tighter reading with his laser range finder. The bright morning sun made the reading difficult and he had to find a small patch of shadow to focus on. Suddenly the door to one of the huts opened and a man emerged. He was short, wore black pants and a bulky black anorak with a hood that concealed his face. He plodded through the layer of powder snow toward a metal privy. Lemenov tracked him with the range finder. Two hundred and ninety-eight yards to the privy door.

He looked back to the helicopter pad. Its center, the approximate area where the helicopters would set down, was 304 yards away—912 feet. A clear shot, nothing between him and the targets.

The Korean stepped back out of the privy. Lemenov heard the metal door bang shut. Sounds carried clearly in the stillness and the dry, cold air. The man stood for a moment, gazing up at the forest. He seemed to be looking right at Lemenov, who did not move. Motion drew the eye's attention. The Korean's gaze passed on. He had seen nothing.

Kill him now? Him and his companions? No, it was too risky. Nothing was to be gained.

Two of the men coming in the helicopters from Vladivostok were his designated targets—the South Korean prime minister and the chairman of Sunsai. He had four bullets in the magazine of his custom sniper's rifle. At this distance he felt he couldn't miss. Two bullets would be enough to take care of his principal targets. Their bodyguards were of no consequence. Before anyone in the camp had time to react, he would be gone.

It was almost too easy, he thought.

And he was always suspicious of anything that seemed too easy. It was why he had survived for so long.

The Siberian rested after her late night and early morning prowl through the taiga. The alien sound that had first alerted her had long since disappeared. Now she felt a brief shift in the prevailing wind, which had been blowing away from her toward the distant sea. The swirling draft, which lasted for only a few seconds, carried a tantalizing scent.

It brought her to her feet again, face lifted into the wind.

It was the smell of her enemy.

34

SULLEN STARES FOLLOWED the noisy progress of the Black Maria along Terney's main street. Chris Harmon, Alex Grovkin and Gregory Krasikov all sensed the anger and hostility.

"Are they staring at us or the Black Maria?" Chris wondered.

"The Raven interests them," Grovkin said, "but what we do makes them angry."

News of the official approval for their rescue attempt had quickly gone through the town. Clusters of men stood on corners or outside the bars and restaurants. "Not much question most of them are either poachers themselves or have friends or relatives who are," Chris said. "We won't win any popularity contests here."

"It's their work, their livelihood," Krasikov said. He was riding now with Chris in the back of the vehicle. A heavy metal grille separated them from the cab, which let them carry on a conversation with Grovkin up front at the wheel. "We threaten them."

"How did they learn what's going on? So quickly, I mean. We just got here."

"Yavlinsky make sure they know," Grovkin said.

During a brief confrontation in his office shortly after Chris and his colleagues arrived from Plastun the preserve's director had made no effort to hide his hostility. With specific orders having come down from his superiors that morning, he hadn't dared oppose them openly, but he had done as little as possible to cooperate. No other guards were available to accompany the rescue team; all were, he said, away on assignment. Grovkin's Jeep was still unavailable. There was a half-hour's delay before tranquilizer ammunition and rifles were found. Fortunately Grovkin and Krasikov had already commandeered the three cages in the back of the Black Maria along with ropes and nets, antibiotics and other medical supplies, and ten pounds of frozen meat to feed the cubs if necessary.

"Don't come back!" a man shouted at them.

Someone else threw a rock that banged off the armored wall of the van. More angry shouts.

"What are they saying?" Chris asked, peering ahead through the grille.

Grovkin allowed a smile. "Yankee, go home!"

They were at the edge of the town when the steady beat of a helicopter's rotor blades became audible above the rasp of the Black Maria's motor. Grovkin slowed, squinting into the bright sky. Moments later a black shape swooped into view—a Hind Mi–24 helicopter that came to a hovering position over a clearing south of the preserve director's headquarters.

"What is it?" Chris and his Russian colleague said from the back of the van, where they could only see forward through the narrow grille.

"Red Army chopper," Grovkin said.

"What's it doing here?"

Grovkin shrugged, but his foot became heavier on the accelerator, sending the van bouncing along the road north toward the Sikhote-Alin preserve. "As long as they don't shoot at us, we not care, eh?" he said uneasily.

Studying the drab, cheerless town of Terney from the air as the helicopter approached it, Lina Mashikova was startled by the sight of what appeared to be a Black Maria driving away from the outskirts, raising a cloud of powder snow behind it. She hadn't seen one of *those* notorious vehicles since leaving Moscow, where many of them had been converted into delivery vans for bread or meat or even, incongruously, flowers. The brief glimpse in this remote setting still evoked a subliminal fear, like a loud knock on one's door in the middle of the night.

She dismissed the thought as her helicopter slowly descended. Snow covered the roofs of cottages and shacks and lay thick on the flat-roofed frame buildings along the main street. During the last hundred feet of its descent the chopper churned up a small snowstorm, and Lina stepped out into a thick white cloud that billowed away from the helicopter. Ducking under the whirling blades until she was clear, she waved to the pilot and turned away, shielding her face and eyes as, by prearrangement, the Mi–24 immediately lifted off.

No one knew for certain what Lieutenant Mashikova's reception would be in Terney. Elements of the Red Army had apparently spent the last twenty-four hours choosing sides. The helicopter ascended to a height of three hundred feet and hovered there. It would wait for her signal—or the lack of it.

Lina walked out of the cloud of powder snow and found herself at the edge of the town—little more than a village, she thought. She took in the modest cottages and neglected buildings fronting the single main street. She suspected everything appeared a lot cleaner and fresher with its snow cover glittering in the morning sunshine than it would have looked twenty-four hours ago. Some chickens were searching in the snow for food, pecking randomly, and a fat pig plodded slowly across the street.

Some men in front of a restaurant half a block away watched her curiously—but apparently not curious enough to wander over. The helo has intimidated them, she thought.

She started toward the men, intending to ask directions. Crossing a rutted side road, she glanced to her right and immediately spotted the insignia of the Red Army militia headquarters. Two men had come out of the building in response to the arrival of the Mi–24. One of them, she saw, wore a captain's bars.

Her heart beating rapidly as she neared the moment of truth, Lina briskly approached the militia captain, stopped a few feet away and gave him a crisp salute. He was young for a captain, she saw, about her own age, with sharp, intelligent brown eyes, a blue haze of beard and a lean body. In the city he would be coveted by a thousand women, she thought. He must hate being isolated here at the rim of the Russian world . . .

"Lieutenant Mashikova reporting." She fished General Chumeiko's dispatch from her breast pocket, rebuttoned the pocket and handed the communiqué to the young officer. "My orders, Captain, are to request whatever assistance you are able to give me."

The officer read the report quickly, glancing up halfway through and again at the end. His face remained expressionless. "You had better come inside, Comrade Lieutenant."

From the driver's seat of the rusty red Range Rover parked down the side road within sight of both militia headquarters and the administrative offices of the Bureau for Nature Preserve Management, Leonid Brunovsky stared hard at the Russian journalist until she followed the militia officer up two wooden steps and disappeared into the long frame building.

Brunovsky's first thought was that he could hardly believe his good luck. He had been dreaming about this woman with her long slender legs and golden hair, fantasizing the moment when he would have her alone. Boris Provalev had even offered him a free hand with her before ordering him to Terney.

But what was she doing in Terney? Was she following the American scientist Harmon? If so, what was she doing at militia headquarters? And wearing, now that he took note of it, a soldier's winter greatcoat?

The questions were bothersome. So was that helicopter hovering overhead with its guns and missiles visible. Under other circumstances Brunovsky's first impulse would have been to notify Chairman Provalev right away. But circumstances had changed.

Provalev's orders had allowed no argument. Immediately after his arrival in Terney, Brunovsky was ordered to drive the Range Rover into the taiga, park it as close as possible to the designated coordinates Lemenov had given him and wait for the Collector to appear. He and the Range Rover were Lemenov's way out of the preserve before any investigation could be organized. "Without me," Brunovsky muttered to himself, "Sergei Gregorevich would be on foot in the wilderness."

No one else has seen his face. That realization had come to Brunovsky during the long, boring ride over the mountains from Plastun to Terney. He didn't know why he hadn't given more thought to it earlier. Even the chairman himself had been kept from seeing Lemenov's face. In their rare private meetings the assassin had been adamant about preserving his anonymity.

But why should the Collector have worried about Boris Provalev seeing him, when Brunovsky had eaten and bunked with him, traveled with him into the taiga, even shared with him the ultimate act of murder? When Brunovsky could draw his face from memory?

A tickle of fear trailed along Brunovsky's spine. It was like a tickle in the throat—he couldn't get rid of it.

Matter of fact, the dangers inherent in a conspiracy leading to a military insurrection, a clear act of treason against the elected government of his country, did not frighten Brunovsky the way another meeting with the Collector in the wilderness did.

I'm the only one left, he thought. No one else would recognize him on the street.

He stared at the militia headquarters building. What was the journalist doing inside that building? Did her presence here mean some kind of threat to Provalev's coup? Should he carry out his orders to drive straight into the preserve for his rendezvous with Lemenov? Or should he take the initiative and wait to see what the journalist was up to?

He shook his head. Forget her. The woman, the American and his colleagues were all irrelevant. The events now set in motion, in Vladivostok and in the taiga, could not be stopped.

He turned on the motor, switched the heater back on high, engaged the clutch. The Rover eased onto the dirt road and drove slowly past the militia building. The building's door stayed closed. Brunovsky came to the main street and turned left. Moments later the last poor shacks on the outskirts of the town were behind him. Ahead were bare snow-covered fields reaching out toward foothills and the green wall of the taiga.

Looking back, he saw the shape of the heavily armed Mi–24 Hind hovering over the edge of the town, the mutter of its rotors fading behind him.

On this day, he told himself grandly, the course of Russian history was being changed. He had believed himself to be part of that national destiny. Now, brooding as he drove, he thought of Andrei Petrikov standing at Boris Provalev's elbow in his place when the great announcement was made— when the chairman reached out to take hold of the reins of power. He would be four hundred miles away, completely cut off. So who was irrelevant now? Brunovsky asked himself.

Who was dispensable now?

Lina waited in an open area next to a railing at the front of the room. There were three desks, a few chairs and file cabinets, a wooden bench against the front wall under the window. The all-purpose building held offices, storage rooms and a small barracks for the squad of militia stationed here. Through a half-windowed wall she could see Captain Pavel Antonovich Rykov talking animatedly on the phone. The dispatch from General Chumeiko lay on his desk.

Suddenly she saw the expression on Rykov's face undergo a series of changes: shock, disbelief, a flush of anger . . . He got to his feet, setting the phone in its cradle. He pulled himself upright. By this time the anger had overridden his other emotions—his face was red, and through the window his eyes found Lina.

"Sergeant," he shouted. "Bring Lieutenant Mashikova in here—*now.*"

35

A VIP HELICOPTER pad on top of the northeast terminal building at Vladivostok Airport was painted with the concentric circles of a large target. Two huge Red Army Mi–10 helicopters stood on the pad in the bright morning sun. Up on the roof the cold wind blew sharply, tugging at the black greatcoats of the civilians gathered there, not disturbing the bulkier coats of the high-ranking military officers but knifing through the less cumbersome coats worn by soldiers from the ranks who stood guard.

Boris Provalev, wearing a black coat with a black ermine collar and a matching fur hat, stood out from the group, more by his dominating personality than his size. He bowed the first of the visiting South Koreans, Kim Su, into the lead helicopter. Chang Pyon followed, then Kim's translator, a group of Korean bodyguards, a Korean geologist who had carried out surveys of Sector Five and three Russian soldiers, one a major.

Provalev waited until the door of the first Mi–10 closed before he joined the group waiting to board the second helo. One of them was Major-General Pyotr Yaklov, the commander of the Nineteenth Guards Tank Division. Another, one of the first to board, was young Andrei Petrikov, an aide who, observers noted, was playing a more prominent role in the chairman's inner circle, raising questions about the absence of Provalev's longtime assistant, Leonid Brunovsky.

As the first helicopter lifted off and rose away from the rooftop there was confusion around the second chopper, it appeared to be delayed. Military and other personnel milled around before the door closed and the big overhead rotors whined into action. Several figures ducked away, retreating toward the stairwell at one end of the pad. The Mi–10 climbed into the sky and immediately swung east after its companion aircraft. As if on signal, both helicopters flew out over the bay and the crowded harbor that some called the graveyard of the Pacific Fleet.

Except that one huge carrier-cruiser, the *Minsk,* both chopper pilots noted, had put out to sea.

At that same moment units of a tank battalion of the Nineteenth Guards Tank Division entered the outskirts of the city. A tank battalion normally numbered thirty or more but in this deployment there were only a dozen on the move—eight T–64 main battle tanks and four T–55 medium tanks, supported by twelve armored personnel carriers. At a major intersection on the main highway the tank force separated into four columns. Each group included two T–64s, one T–55 and four APCs. One headed toward the airport, a second diverted toward the telephone exchange building, a third proceeded to the civic center and the last column took aim at the scaffolding visible around the rising spire of St. Innocent's Cathedral directly across the street from the state television studios.

Normal traffic flowed past the military vehicles. Some people stared at the big tanks rumbling by and moving more swiftly than one might have expected. Others hardly gave them a glance. There was an odd sense of dislocation about the scene, as if it were part of a fantasy. No one could take it quite seriously. There was no reason for panic. Life went on— one was late for work, had a toothache, admired the calves of the secretary on the sidewalk in front of him, worried about his or her daughter who spent half the night listening to incomprehensible Western music. The tanks were an anomaly, some sort of military exercise, perhaps, the days when one shuddered with fear at the thunder of their steel treads were over.

The column of vehicles assigned to take control of the area surrounding the television studios was the first to reach its goal. One of the T–64s took its position in front of the steps leading up to the front entrance. Its 125–mm main gun pointed outward away from the building. So did the machine gun on top of the central turret, which the crew inside the tank could fire by remote control. The two remaining tanks stationed themselves at either end of the street in front of the building. The APCs diverted to the side streets. Armed soldiers spilled out of two of the carriers and marched toward the steps leading to the main entrance. Others ran toward auxiliary doors leading to and from the block-long facility on the east and west sides.

Neither the tank crews nor the armed soldiers did anything to interfere with street traffic, pedestrians or those who were entering or leaving the studios.

They appeared to be waiting, for something . . .

General Chumeiko was briefed by radio on the movement of the Guards tank units into the city. Colonel Beretnikoff was already in the field, monitoring events from an ACRV–2, a fast-moving armored command and reconnaissance vehicle equipped to function as a roving command post and in radio communication with Chumeiko's headquarters.

"How many tanks?" Chumeiko demanded.

"So far we count only a dozen entering the city," Beretnikoff reported. "Three others have been seen near the outskirts, possibly ready to deploy toward the navy administration buildings."

"Only fifteen," the general said with tight-lipped satisfaction. "Half a battalion. Where are the others?"

"We don't know, General."

Could it be that they had refused to join the treacherous action? It was the sign Chumeiko had been hoping for. "How many APCs?"

"Also a dozen. We estimate no more than five hundred soldiers deployed in the streets, not counting the tank crews."

"Provalev is trying to pull it off on a bluff. The army is holding back. Who is in command in the field?"

"Major-General Yaklov."

"Yaklov! One of the Old Guard." Chumeiko paused, summoning up General Yaklov's beefy red face, his chest full of medals. Chumeiko's blue eyes were like deep ice. "We will soon learn which one of us has misjudged the Russian soldier. We will see if the army will fire on its own. Have Provalev and the South Koreans taken off?"

"Two helicopters," Beretnikoff said. "Ten to twelve persons in each one."

Chumeiko turned to an aide. "Contact CINCPAC." The commander-in-chief of the Pacific Fleet, Admiral Dmitri Sholykin, was on board the *Minsk*. "Request Operation Intercept be carried out as planned. Bring them down."

Fifteen minutes before General Chumeiko's order signaled the start of hostilities, Chris Harmon and his colleagues had crossed the southern border of the Sikhote-Alin Biosphere National Preserve. A sea of green only a few short weeks ago, the taiga had changed dramatically. Stands of birch trees stood bare, their peeling trunks as white as the snow that now covered the ground. Alder groves shivered in the cold wind, bursts of orange and yellow and red. The denser evergreen forests were mantled in white shrouds.

Chris thought about the wounded tiger. If the lithium battery powering the transistor in her collar was still good he should be able to pick up her signal once he was close enough. Tracking her otherwise would be a matter of luck. In the thicker parts of the taiga the forest floor was relatively clear of snow, which lay only on the upper branches, and a tiger's passage through the palette of new growth and moss and ferns often left no trace. Only in clearings and open spaces would the snow make tracking the tiger and her cubs easier.

"Maybe we're in luck with this snow," he said to Gregory Krasikov, loud enough for Alex Grovkin to hear him.

"Maybe not so lucky," Grovkin said.

He stared off to his left. They were approaching a perimeter road that circled inside the preserve. To the east lay Sector Five. Grovkin had slowed for the intersection. As he turned right onto the perimeter road two off-road vehicles burst out of the cover of some trees fifty kilometers to the west and came toward them.

Grovkin accelerated. Even though they could not see out, the sudden burst of speed and escalation of the van's rattles and shakes alerted Chris and Krasikov in the back of the van that something was happening . . . "What is it, Alex?" Chris called out.

Before Grovkin could answer, Chris heard the roar of racing engines. He peered forward through the open grille past the driver's shoulder. A black Toyota 4–Runner pulled past the Black Maria, sending up a spray of white powder that smeared the windshield. Grovkin flipped on the windshield wipers. "Poachers," he yelled.

As the windshield cleared, Chris saw an open window on the passenger side of the Toyota. A rapid-fire weapon projected through the opening. He caught glimpses of a half-dozen angry shouting men inside the vehicle. And in the big rearview mirror on Grovkin's door a white Ford Bronco appeared, slewing close to the Black Maria's rear bumper.

Suddenly the Toyota cut across the front of the van. Grovkin had no option but to jerk the wheel hard to the right. The tail of the Raven swung outward in a skid on the snow-slick road. With a grinding crunch of metal the spinning rear of the van hit the Toyota. Grovkin wrestled with the steering wheel, but the heavy and cumbersome armored vehicle skidded out of control and lurched off the road into a shallow ditch and Chris and Krasikov were thrown onto the floor in back. The front wheels slammed into the rise on the far side of the ditch, bounced into the air and came down in a snow-drift. The engine belched and died.

The Ford Bronco had stopped safely behind the Black Maria, the Toyota 4–Runner twenty yards ahead. In the momentary confusion as the van spun off the road and jolted to a stop, spilling him once again into a side wall and jamming his shoulder, Chris hadn't time to question what was happening. He was stunned by a second violent shock: the chatter of automatic rifle fire, and the entire van was engulfed in an unholy din.

The windshield of the Black Maria—supposedly bulletproof like the side windows but brittle and weakened with age—disintegrated as Grovkin dove across the seat. Bits and chunks of glass stung his cheeks. His only thought was that the pellets stinging his face like insect bites were rounded rather than stiletto-sharp slivers of glass. Bullets hammered the armored shell of the Black Maria.

Gregory Krasikov had struck his head against a corner of one of the steel cages when he was bounced around the interior of the van. Dazed, he felt blood trickle from his temple into his blond beard. Chris reached for the rifle he had brought to fire tranquilizer bullets. It was a conventional Kalashnikov rifle and he had regular ammunition for it in one of the supply boxes. Alex, if he wasn't hurt too badly, had his vintage World War II Simonov carbine in a cradle above his head in the cab.

Fumbling for a loaded magazine to arm the Kalashnikov, Chris listened to the staccato bursts of the attacking poachers' rapid-fire assault weapons. The Black Maria saved our lives, he thought . . . but for how long?

A mile behind the Black Maria, Brunovsky heard the gunfire, pulled over to the side of the road, opened the door and stepped out of the Range Rover.

Another rattle of gunfire. The surrounding wilderness had gone still. Brunovsky knew he was not imagining things . . . what he heard was automatic-weapon fire. The American scientist didn't carry an assault rifle, neither did any of the preserve guards . . .

All of this morning's anxieties crowded about him. He thought of Sergei Lemenov waiting for him at their designated rendezvous. Of the mystery of the Black Maria driving into the taiga. Of the alien hammer of gunfire. Of the female Russian journalist swooping down on Terney in a Red Army helicopter.

The firing had ceased for a moment. Now there was another short burst. It covered a different sound, like the beat of a chopper's rotors, but then the muttering died away.

The forest was still, waiting and listening like Brunovsky. *You're the only one who has seen his face.*

Brunovsky's fear was palpable, stuck in his gullet. His

mouth was dry, it was hard swallowing. *Boris Maximovich Provalev has betrayed you . . .*

After another moment Brunovsky climbed back into the Range Rover, turned the wheel and made a U-turn. He drove for a mile back in the direction of Terney. There he pulled over to the side of the road again and opened up the maps of the taiga that Provalev had provided for him. The roads shown as thin red lines wriggling through the Primorskiy, through the mountains and the endless forest, would be dirt tracks, steep and twisting, little more than a pair of ruts, questionable even without snow on the ground. But if he went back to Terney his movements could easily be tracked later.

He stared toward the first range of mountains to the west. The Range Rover was a rugged, durable vehicle built for use in the most difficult terrain. On Brunovsky's map one of the red wriggles led over the mountains and connected with another red line that made its way to a town called Ariadnoye. From Ariadnoye a wriggle of another color, blue, went west to Lazo. The blue line represented a railroad. And at Lazo it connected with Rossiya, the Trans-Siberian Express that eventually went five thousand miles across Siberia to Moscow.

Whatever happened in the Primorskiy and in Vladivostok on this day, no one would be looking for him on the train to Moscow. Not so soon.

Brunovsky had made his decision. He had no intention of meeting the Collector alone in the forest.

36

As PART OF its normal armament the *Minsk,* one of three Kiev-class carrier-cruisers in the Pacific Fleet, carried twelve fixed-wing VTOL Yak–38 Forgers and from eighteen to twenty-one Hormone helicopters. Four Yak–38 aircraft took off in their screaming vertical leaps within three minutes of the receipt of General Chumeiko's message on the bridge of the cruiser. Two Hormone helicopters lifted off in the next minute.

The six aircraft flew north along the coastline at an altitude of four thousand feet. Twenty minutes after takeoff two bright green blips appeared on the radar screen of the leading Forger. Thirty seconds later the Mi–10 helicopters carrying the South Korean visitors and their Russian escorts were visually sighted.

The Forgers separated, one of them coming up on each side of the two Mi–10s. The Hormones, meanwhile, having approached within a mile of the other aircraft, went into stalking mode, maintaining their position. The Forgers were armed with both guns and air-to-air missiles, the AAMs mounted in pods under the wings. The Hormones were even more heavily armed with both heat-seeking missiles and Gatling guns.

The pilot of the lead Forger contacted the Mi–10s by radio.

"What's the meaning of this?" one of the helicopter pilots sputtered.

The Forger answered, "You will turn about and return to the harbor at once. We will escort you."

"To hell with you . . . this is an official Russian government mission—"

The Forger fired one of its guns across the nose of the leading Mi–10.

The huge troop-carrying helicopters being used to transport the two parties of dignitaries were also heavily armed but they were much slower and less maneuverable than the Yak–38s. Over the open sea there was no place for them to duck and hide. Moreover, the lead chopper was carrying the prime minister of South Korea, the chairman of one of its major corporations and others from that country, for all of whom the pilot felt responsible. Important Russian officials and militia were in the second Mi–10. And neither the helicopter pilots nor their crews had any knowledge of the political upheaval that had broken out and overtaken them.

Glancing past the Forgers that were herding him, the pilot of the leading Mi–10 saw the pair of Hormones following them at a distance. *"Mudnya!"* he muttered. Six against two.

Shepherded by the Forgers, the Mi–10 helicopters with their bewildered passengers turned back. Less than thirty minutes later they were nudged by their escorts toward the flight deck of the *Minsk,* which was in the outer harbor off Vladivostok, its crew at battle stations.

"You will put down on the flight deck," the lead Forger commanded.

"This isn't a Navy helicopter," one Mi–10 pilot protested. "I can't land there—"

"You can and you will. One way or another."

By this time both of the helicopter pilots were at least convinced that something very serious was under way. The moment when they might have resisted had come and passed in the first stage of confrontation with the Forgers. Now they really had no choice but to obey, and they began their descent toward the deck of the *Minsk.*

"What the hell is going on?" the helicopter pilot demanded as he jumped down onto the flight deck. "That son of a bitch—"

He broke off. CINCPAC was standing at the far side of the deck flanked by other high-ranking naval officers and one man wearing the uniform of an Army major. The South Koreans, bewildered, were spilling out of the two Mi–10s onto the deck.

Admiral Dmitri Sholykin walked forward toward the knot of South Koreans, who had drawn into a tight circle, as though for some sort of mutual protection. "Welcome aboard, Your Excellency," Sholykin addressed Kim Su directly. "The Russian government wishes me to express its regret over this interruption in your journey into the taiga, but a matter of security for Your Excellency and his party has made this precaution necessary. If you will come with me I have some refreshments waiting for us and I will answer all of your questions."

At that moment the admiral noticed a commotion near the second Mi–10. The major hurried across the open deck toward CINCPAC. "I must contact General Chumeiko at once, Admiral."

"What is it, Major?"

"It's Chairman Provalev—he was supposed to be aboard the second helicopter. He's not there!"

Three of the poachers who ambushed the Black Maria were armed with AK–47 automatic rifles. Firing on semi-automatic, the three men pumped more than a hundred rounds in the first minute against the van, its walls becoming pitted and cratered.

The two bulletproof side windows in the cabin began to blacken, twist and sag. Crouching below the window line, Alex Grovkin waited between bursts, reared up and fired single shots in the direction of the poachers.

The attackers, Chris thought, had fired their weapons mindlessly, without aiming. Apparently they hadn't expected real opposition or they would have rushed the van in the first minutes of the attack. Instead, one of Grovkin's first shots had hit a poacher, who was now sitting with his back against the front wheel of the Toyota, holding his hands over his stomach, which was drenched in blood. His blood had a sobering effect on his friends.

Time to sober them a little more, Chris thought, and poked

his rifle through the grille, sighting through the front of the cab where the windscreen had been. "Stay down when I'm shooting," he yelled to Grovkin. "I'll shoot over you . . ."

"Say when, my friend."

"*Now.*"

Just when the attackers were convinced the driver was finished, Chris's surprise fire came from the invisible interior of the Black Maria, and when Chris ceased firing Grovkin bobbed up again for a snapshot with his Simonov, one of the shots nicking a second poacher alongside his ear.

The attackers' firing slowed down now as the poachers belatedly realized that their target's armored walls stood up well to the hail of bullets. They also understood that their only risk lay at the front of the van since the shell behind the cab was completely enclosed, and it occurred to one of them that he could approach the back of the target vehicle with impunity.

An emergency gas can was found in the Bronco, three-quarters full. The enterprising poacher soaked a rag in the gasoline and stuffed it into the open top of the can, then crept toward the Black Maria.

For a moment all the shooting stopped. After the clamor of the last few minutes, the three men inside the van held their breath. Chris's ears were clogged, and from his position in back he couldn't see the grins or hear the jeering calls from the poachers. Very soon now, the attackers were taunting, it was going to get very hot inside the Hearse from Hell.

As soon as he was briefed by telephone on the situation in Vladivostok, Captain Rykov had not hesitated. "General Chumeiko has ordered me to assist you in every way possible, Lieutenant," he told Lina. "What can I do?"

After a quick explanation Rykov and three militiamen joined her in the Hind helicopter, which landed on her signal to pick them up. Lina then explained in more detail en route. When the Hind's pilot spotted the Black Maria and the poachers in their off-road vehicles, the tactical situation dramatically changed.

"They're under attack!" Lina called out.

"The American scientist is in the Black Maria?" Rykov asked.

"Along with some Russians . . . I don't know who the attackers are . . ."

"Mafia gangsters," the captain said quickly. "They think the preserves are their private hunting grounds—" He broke off, shouted at the pilot, "Can you take us down there?"

The forest had been cut back ten feet on each side of the two roadways, so at the intersection there was plenty of room for the Mi–24 to set down safely in the middle of the crossroads.

The pilot yelled back he could land, and did the captain want to let the attackers blow up the Black Maria?

"No . . ." from Lina, who had just seen the poacher with the makeshift bomb running in a crouch toward the rear of the van.

The Mi–24 swooped down on the poachers. Caught up in their anticipation of the fiery explosion about to consume the Black Maria, their hearing blocked by their own gunfire, they weren't aware of the helicopter until it was almost on top of them. The man with the improvised Molotov cocktail was caught in the open.

He looked up just as a single burst from the Gatling gun on its mount at the rear of the Hind stitched a path of bullets across the road, visible in little erupting craters of snow. Two of the bullets penetrated the gas can, others plucked at the arms, chest and shoulder of the poacher, who was dead even before the ball of fire engulfed him.

Inside the Black Maria, Chris and the two Russians were rocked with the force of the explosion. The van's rear wheels lifted into the air and slammed back down. Stunned, the men inside waited for their world to disintegrate around them.

It was close, too close, but rising up on the front seat at the beat of the helicopter's rotor blades, Alex Grovkin yelled out, "Sons of bitches, do you hear that, my friends? Is Army! Look at those bastard poachers run . . ."

* * *

His hearing still muffled after the din inside the Black Maria, Chris Harmon stumbled out of the van through the back door. The Hind helicopter had just touched down in the middle of the crossroads. Alex Grovkin staggered up to him, bleeding from facial and arm wounds that appeared to be superficial. He pounded Chris on the back. "You are okay, my friend? Gregory Ilych okay?"

"I think he has a concussion," Chris said. "He's going to need medical attention . . ."

Chris stared now at a man's arm lying in the ditch beside the road, surrounded by a spray of red stains in the snow.

"That explosion . . ."

"He try to blow up our Black Maria," Grovkin said with satisfaction. "To blow *us* up. Instead he blow himself up."

Not without help, Chris thought numbly as the door of the Hind opened and soldiers jumped out, ducking low as they ran under the rotor blades toward Chris and Alex. Both soldiers were officers, Chris noted with surprise, the one in the front a slender, boyish figure. When that officer looked up . . . was it unreal?

"Christopher . . ."

Lina Mashikova was coming toward him, swallowed up in the winter greatcoat of an army officer.

Not unreal, Chris thought, embracing her, hearing her mumble "Thank God, thank God" against his chest.

Boris Provalev was about to go on the air, his image and words to be seen or heard over radio and television all across Russia. Anna Zilya Valeyeva licked her upper lip nervously as she waited for her cue. She looked radiant, like a woman coming from a satisfying rendezvous with her lover. This was better, the most exciting moment of her life. To have the honor of introducing her lover to all the Russian people at this signal moment in the history of the nation, to be at his side . . .

Troops outside the studios at this moment—on the steps

out front, in the corridors of the building, controlling the studios—and all under Boris Maximovich's direction and command.

She could see her own excitement mirrored in Provalev's face, which was flushed, his eyes unnaturally bright. He was nervous—fidgeting, pacing back and forth, rereading his speech, making changes and changing them back, glancing at the clock.

He was called to the telephone, listened briefly, gave an order, turned from the phone toward her, slammed a fist into the meat of his palm, a smile breaking out. It was his triumphant moment.

He hurried over to her. The assistant producer of her regular news program—the producer had been summarily hustled away by soldiers when he protested the takeover of the television studios—was running back and forth in the control room. Provalev slid onto a seat behind the news desk at Anna's side. He appeared larger, more imposing on-screen when sitting down.

Provalev nodded. "Now, Anna Zilya—now."

The red light came on for the camera directly facing her. She licked her lips and said, "This is Anna Zilya Valeyeva interrupting our regular programming with an important news bulletin. Attention, all Russian citizens. Today, responding to a tragic accident in the Sikhote-Alin Biosphere National Preserve in which the prime minister of South Korea and others in his party were killed, Boris Provalev, Chairman of the Primorskiy Provincial Council, has ordered Russian troops into the city of Vladivostok to maintain order and to anticipate possible reprisals threatened by the South Korean government. Here now is Chairman Provalev . . ."

For a dramatic moment Provalev stared into the camera. Then: "Comrade citizens. Today the Motherland faces the gravest crisis since the supposed end of the Cold War threat from the Western powers. In truth, such an imaginary thaw has always been more wish than reality. The Russian people have always desired peace. We continue to work for peace. But an overt threat has been made against the Republic of Russia by one of the satellites of those Western powers—the

Republic of South Korea. It is in answer to this threat that I have called upon the Red Army to join me and my fellow citizens in taking immediate action to secure our borders against attack.

"In addition I have called for the suspension of all communications outside our borders and for the temporary dissolution of the People's Parliament. These may seem harsh measures, but the threat we face must be met with courage and determination. The Russian people will not accept the insults by foreigners who came to destroy our forests and natural resources, even our magnificent Siberian tiger. And now accuse *us*. A helicopter taking these foreigners into the taiga crashed this morning. It is not yet known if there are any survivors, but Russia stands accused of an aggressive and dishonorable attack against visitors that we welcomed to our country.

"I reject these accusations and defy those who make them. Russia will continue to embrace peaceful relations with our friends throughout the world—but we only seek peace with honor. Peace with dignity. Let our friends *and* enemies know once again the greatness of Russia, compromised and forgotten by weak, incompetent leaders. We arm ourselves with truth—and with the sword . . ."

"The bastard's jumped the gun!" General Chumeiko said savagely, watching Provalev on television from his headquarters command center. "He should have waited until his assassin did his work. Now the truth will destroy him!" Chumeiko jabbed the two-way speaker button that activated radio communication with Colonel Beretnikoff in the roving command vehicle. "Our units are in place, Comrade Colonel?"

"Yes, Comrade General. We await only your arrival to join us." The troops in question, a thousand strong, were elite, specially trained soldiers attached to the 220th Guards Air Assault Regiment, including a *spetznaz* unit of thirty-six specialists in such varied skills as riot control, sabotage and assassination.

"I'm leaving now. Remember—they are not to fire unless

fired upon. We will not be the first to shed the blood of Russian soldiers on our own soil."

"Our soldiers know their orders, Comrade General."

"As always, everything depends on them." Chumeiko paused a second before adding, "I want Comrade Chairman Provalev taken alive, no matter what." His attention returned to the television screen. "He doesn't know it yet, but he's finished."

37

For Sergei Lemenov the long morning, begun in darkness when he flew out of Vladivostok, had seemed to drag on forever. By now all four men in the logging camp had appeared, gone to the privy, returned to the heated cabin for breakfast. One of them came out later and made a brief tour of the camp. Just getting some exercise, Lemenov thought with amusement. The Koreans obviously saw no need for a sentry here. The man went back inside. Smoke curled upward from the single chimney stack to smudge the clear blue sky.

The Collector's eyes ached from squinting into the morning sun and from snow glare. The helicopters should approach the camp from the east, flying inland from the coastline. Well, where were they?

It was more than an hour beyond the scheduled time of their arrival in the taiga. He dismissed the possibility that something had gone wrong. Every arrangement had been made. All that had remained in doubt was the stubbornness of the South Koreans, and they had finally relented. Chang Pyon had made the decision. He was the real power there, Lemenov thought.

He stood, stretched, walked around his ledge, keeping back from the rim out of the line of sight from the shacks below. The loggers were oblivious of danger, expecting nothing. There was a short-wave radio in the shack, a loose coil antenna trailing out the window to the roof. The soon-to-be-arriving dignitaries could be warned off if he were accidentally detected . . .

Where were they?

Lemenov glanced around at the thick forest behind him, vaguely uneasy, as if—unlike those men in the camp—his more finely tuned instinct for danger had caused some antennae of his own to quiver. What could threaten him now? Sector Five had been effectively cleared of dangerous animals. The area had also been closed to humans, even the preserve's own guards. He turned back toward the camp.

A faint, distant rumbling like far-off thunder alerted him. The choppers were coming.

He peered through binoculars across the snow-clad sweep of the ancient forests toward the horizon. A black dot appeared, low in the sky. Then another. The rumble became more audible, taking on the characteristic flap of approaching helicopters.

The Collector quickly returned to his station. He took his most comfortable shooting position, lying prone on his stomach, legs spread to anchor him, the long, heavy-barreled rifle in this instance resting on a fallen log. Working the bolt action, chambering a bullet, he caught the faint smell of oil. He flexed his cold fingers to ease their stiffness.

He watched the helicopters grow, filling his sights as he aimed at them, not yet to shoot but to track them in.

About a mile to the north, for she had lost her enemy's trail in the deep forest and overshot his position, the Siberian tiger heard the growl of the big birds she associated with the enemy. She had been retracing her steps, abandoning the pursuit and returning to her den. The morning was growing old, and her hunting passion warred with another equally powerful instinct, a mother's protective concern for her cubs. They would be wide awake now, hungry, prowling about restlessly. They had been left alone too long.

Emerging cautiously from a dense growth of spruce, she saw the helicopters. She flattened herself in the undergrowth at the edge of the woods, invisible with her natural camouflage. One of the helicopters, circling beyond the camp, passed near her without hesitating. Then it dropped out of sight, settling below the line of a ridge.

The tiger waited, watching and listening, wanting to return to her den but pulled also by curiosity . . . and hate.

Five miles west as the crow flies, the tiger's cubs were up and out of the den. They had been romping for more than an hour in the fresh snow, which was new and strange to them, so light and cold. They chased and snapped at clumps of the white powder only to have it dissolve in their mouths.

Tiring finally of the game, one of the cubs, the more aggressive male, led the way out of thick woods toward the thinner trees and brush above the river. When they came to a grassy slope at the bottom of which the stream danced over rocks in the sunlight, they gamboled down the incline, skidding and slipping in the snow. At the river they drank greedily.

The male looked up, alerted by some small movement. Thirty yards away a small deer stood rigid. A fawn, she had been startled by the sudden appearance of the tiger cubs. Fear held her motionless, as if that way she might not be seen.

The tiger's reaction was instinctive. Watching the deer, he settled flat on his belly, tail lashing slowly, gathering his weight onto his hind legs. One of the fawn's huge ears twitched. As if that were a signal, the tiger cub charged.

It was a brief, furious chase. In the first seconds of his charge the cub closed the gap on his prey with the speed of jaws clashing. But the brown lightning bolt hurtling toward her broke the deer's paralysis. Her first bound carried her fifteen feet, then she skittered across the snow, bouncing. The tiger threw himself after her, his paws slashing at air. He tried to turn as quickly as the fawn, lost his footing and tumbled head over heels in the snow.

The cub clambered to his feet, licked snow from his nose, and growled.

His prey was gone.

He would learn.

*   *   *

Lina Mashikova rode in the back of the Black Maria with Chris Harmon.

The two Russians were in the cab up front. Alex Grovkin had received a number of small cuts and abrasions from flying glass but was not seriously hurt and was still able to drive. Gregory Krasikov shared the front seat with him. Though admitting to feeling dizzy and somewhat disoriented, Krasikov had insisted on riding along. He could stay with the Black Maria, he pointed out. He could help with the tiger cubs if they were found alive and caught. He could monitor the radio receiver used to track tigers in the preserve that had been tagged. The radio was now tuned to the frequency assigned to the tiger named Risa.

Captain Rykov and the small squad of militia had set off in pursuit of the fleeing poachers. Lieutenant Mashikova had pointed out that the chance of encountering the would-be assassin in the vastness of the taiga was remote. The poachers, on the other hand, were an immediately accessible target. It was one thing for a gang of poachers to shoot a bear or a tiger; it was quite another to attack a group of scientists and a preserve guard with intent to kill. Even Yavlinsky would be unable to ignore such a criminal assault. Besides, as Chris Harmon noted, a noisy helicopter could prove counterproductive in the search for the tiger and her cubs. It would merely drive them to cover.

Alone with Chris in the back of the van, Lina had outlined Chairman Boris Provalev's attempted coup, designed to be triggered by an assassin's actions in the taiga.

"You're saying this assassin is the marksman in my photos? And he's back in Sector Five now?"

"We believe so."

"I still don't see why he staged that tiger shoot for Alex and me. At the time I thought maybe he was clearing the area because of the proposed logging, but it never made sense he would do that in front of witnesses."

"It was done to provoke the South Korean leaders into visiting the taiga. Your photographs caused much excitement.

And concern. The Koreans couldn't ignore it, this was territory they would be logging. And Comrade Provalev made certain they would give in to this pressure, this worry. And then he would kill them . . ."

"So he and his people were using me . . ."

"Yes."

The Black Maria jolted over dips and ruts in the frozen road, body-slamming the riders in back. Chris grinned at Lina, who had bounced nearly a foot off the bench seat. "Sorry about the ride."

She smiled back. "It is not important."

He watched the color rise into her cheeks. She looked away. "Okay . . . back to business. Provalev wanted to lure the South Koreans into the taiga, where they were vulnerable, with a skilled sniper set up to take them out. But what in God's name did he really hope to gain?"

After a pause Lina said, "All of Russia. We believe he's attempting to seize power, beginning here in Far East Russia. The attack he planned was meant to create conflict with South Korea. There would be chaos even worse than there has been in my country. The people are already confused, unhappy with our government leaders, afraid of the future. Provalev wants to be seen as some sort of savior to make Russians proud again . . . even if it means war. Especially if it does, I think."

"Is there any chance . . . ?"

"Well, the assassination has failed, the South Korean leaders are safe. We intercepted them."

"Will that stop Provalev?"

"I don't know. He's a very ambitious man, also clever and ruthless. It's possible that he has gone too far to stop, even though his excuse for an uprising has been taken away."

"So you don't know what's happening in Vladivostok . . ."

"No."

While Chris and Lina had been talking the Black Maria had turned off the perimeter service road and started into the hills, following the rudimentary fire trail that led toward Mount Cherchi. Even if Chris had not noticed the turn, the tooth-loosening ride made it obvious. He and Lina had to hang on to keep from being thrown around the shell. One of the animal cages, shaken loose by the pounding, slid across the floor and banged into the back wall.

After a while Chris said, "Your general must think an awful lot of you to send you into the taiga after the assassin alone."

"That wasn't the intention." The color deepened in Lina's cheeks. "I was . . . I wanted to be certain that you were safe . . . you and your friends, I mean. Others are flying to the Koreans' logging camp to hunt for the assassin. Captain Rykov and his militia would have continued with us but it seemed best for them to pursue those poachers who tried to kill you. It's not likely we'll meet the assassin, but if we should . . ." She indicated the Kalashnikov rifle on the floor beneath the bench. "I am a soldier, too, Chris. That's what I couldn't tell you before."

"Fine, you're a soldier . . . but we're talking about a professional killer—an assassin . . ."

Lina peered forward through the metal grille toward what little she could see of the surrounding forested hills. A strong cold wind blew in through the unprotected front of the cab. "I am not so foolish as to hunt this man alone," she said, her voice so low Chris had trouble hearing her.

But they were coming closer to Sergei Lemenov. The murderer of Anatoly Bukanin and Mikhail Fyodorov, of Dimitri Zhdanov and others was out there, angry, frustrated. Such a man would be hard to capture, she thought. If General Chumeiko's soldiers—*spetznaz* fighters like her Yuri—did not surprise and take him. Lemenov would be running hard.

Running toward her.

Not expecting another hunter to be waiting.

In Vladivostok crowds had grown throughout the morning. They surrounded the government buildings at the civic center and filled Central Square, held back only by the presence of tanks and soldiers guarding access to the official buildings. At the State television studios, which Boris Provalev had turned into his command and communications center, the surrounding streets had filled up. In the park directly across the way, where the new cathedral was rising, excited citizens climbed the walls of the unfinished structure, straddling the flying buttresses and hanging out of open windows to gain a better view.

Wild rumors and unanswered questions fed the general excitement. Terror in the taiga . . . tanks in our streets . . . The South Koreans, well-armed by the Americans, were threatening war. The entire Red Army was mobilizing. Parliament was in emergency session. The president was in seclusion.

With his televised speech, Boris Provalev had acted to address the rumors and to channel public apprehension into patriotic fervor. His appearance also delivered another message: in the Far East, at least, someone was in charge. Here was a man who didn't merely wring his hands or run for cover.

But as the morning lengthened and the crowds grew, their mood began to change. At first, there had been curiosity, confusion, excitement over what was happening. But tanks and soldiers delivered a blunt message of their own. Some of the citizens' faces became sullen, angry. A few of them shouted at the soldiers surrounding the big T–64 battle tank directly in front of the steps of the broadcast studios, its cannon pointed outward.

When Major-General Pyotr Yaklov came through the front door and spoke to the tank commander, someone shouted, "What are you going to do—blow up the cathedral?"

"Yeltsin is a buffoon," another called out, "but we don't need your tanks!"

The young soldiers on the steps exchanged glances, tightened their grips on their Kalashnikov rifles, looked toward General Yaklov and their other officers.

There was a sudden stillness, followed by a rising roar as Chairman Provalev emerged from the main entrance at the top of the steps. He was bareheaded, his curly gray hair shining in the sun. He was wearing his black greatcoat with its ermine collar. As the crowds in front of the building and in the park across the way and along the adjacent streets watched, Provalev moved forward, nearly strutted. Television camera crews scrambled for position. Provalev—the crowd's clamor growing louder with each movement—clambered up on top of the big T–64.

The symbolism was clear to everyone. Yeltsin on a tank in front of the White House in Moscow defying rebellious troops. In the drama of the moment few seemed to notice that Provalev had turned matters upside down—that he was not challenging an illegal coup but leading one.

And he had chosen his forum with great skill. In Russia, as in the West, this was the television age. What was important was not so much what actually happened as the *perception* of what happened. And perception could be manipulated.

The scene had been carefully stage-managed. In addition to television cameras, a system of loudspeakers had been set up in advance outside the building to amplify the chairman's voice. Once on top of the tank, he stood erect and threw up both arms in a classic pose of victory.

The crowd roared.

In Moscow the president gaped at the television screen in the conference room of the White House to which he had hastily summoned his leading ministers.

"What's the son of a bitch up to?" His voice was hoarse from a combination of a cold and speechmaking before an unruly Parliament.

"He's trying to take over," the foreign minister said, pointing out the obvious.

"Is it true about the Koreans? Have you heard from their government?"

"I'm meeting with the ambassador within the hour. No one knows what's happening. If it's true about their prime minister . . ."

"If it's true, how in hell did it happen? For that matter, *what* happened?"

"We don't know yet . . ."

Both men stared at the television screen, dominated by Boris Provalev's powerful image. "Look at those people! He really plays them." The president felt a chill. "Can he be stopped?"

"The Army is moving against him."

"Then what about those tanks? What is that he's standing on?"

No one answered him.

38

THE TIGER HAD caught the scent of her enemy once more. This time the human smell was upwind of her, being carried toward her by the prevailing breeze.

She came upon the strange tracks in the snow. They covered her own footsteps from earlier that morning. Here was a tree where she had marked the border of her territory.

The new tracks led deep into the forest . . . into the territory she claimed as her own.

Sergei Lemenov was running now.

He had known something was wrong the moment the first helicopter landed in the clearing below him. When the door opened, soldiers, not Koreans, spilled out. They shouted at the Koreans who had come out to greet them and who seemed bewildered as they were bullied back into their cabins. The soldiers fanned out swiftly, securing the perimeter of the camp.

Where were the targets?

Furious, Lemenov watched as the second helicopter landed and the scene was repeated—armed soldiers jumping to the ground, ducking under the rotor blades and fanning out across the camp. The first group was already moving out, extending the perimeter.

No South Koreans, no civilians at all . . .

Lemenov didn't wait. He faded away from the ridge into the cover of the forest. The soldiers would find his position soon enough if they carried out a thorough search, and their swift, decisive deployment after landing left little doubt that they *knew* he was there. How was that possible? Had Provalev compromised him? If not him, who . . . ?

He checked his compass—it was easy to lose one's way in the taiga. He bottled his rage, using it as fuel as he ran. Half the money he was to be paid had been deposited in advance into his Swiss bank account before he accepted the assignment; the other half was due on completion, which he had considered a formality. Now Provalev would not pay. What had happened in Vladivostok? What could have gone wrong in those last hours—even after the helicopters carrying the South Koreans to him departed? He had had radio confirmation of liftoff . . .

Dressed in black, from his knit wool cap to his anorak to his boots, he moved like a shadow through the forest. He carried only his rifle, which was as natural to him as another arm. Within the old-growth taiga the snow cover was light and often nonexistent on the forest floor, so Lemenov's progress was swift. After some minutes he came across his own trail, marked here and there where the snow had reached the ground. Once he heard a helicopter overhead. He paused under an old spruce that screened him from view. The aircraft made a scythelike sweep to the south and soon left him far behind.

He had no concern about being spotted himself, but what if Brunovsky and the Range Rover were poorly hidden or even in the open? Brunovsky wouldn't be expecting a search by air—

The chopper returned. This time its path carried it eastward, the flapping of its blades diminishing to a faint buzz. Returning to the logging camp? The Collector felt his tension ease. He hadn't been aware he was holding his breath.

He started moving again, stepping up his pace.

Stopped dead.

He stared at the tracks in the snow—tracks that crossed those he had made himself that morning while it was still dark in the woods.

Huge footprints, their size and shape unmistakable. The tracks of a Siberian tiger. And not just *any* tiger, Lemenov realized as he studied the giant footprints. The chill crawled down his spine. A tiger on three legs!

He peered around him. How long ago? In the freezing cold the snow on the ground was relatively undisturbed, any tracks as fresh as when first made. No way to tell when the tiger had passed this way. But one thing was certain: the beast had changed course after coming upon Lemenov's trail. At some point this morning, without Lemenov's knowledge, the tiger had been stalking him.

Although the snow had largely obliterated the firebreak, along with the tire marks Grovkin had cut only a few days ago with his Jeep, the Black Maria was penetrating deeper and higher into the wilderness than Chris Harmon and his colleagues had dared hope. Twice Grovkin had to bail out of depressions, rocking back and forth to break the wheels free of snowdrifts, but somehow they kept climbing.

Now they were in sight of the distant blue peak at Cherchi Point when the trail disappeared completely. They had reached an elevation of thirty-five hundred feet, and in the open or in the thin growths where the van had to go the snowdrifts were deeper. The surrounding forest of spruce and pine looked familiar to Chris; so did the stream cutting through a canyon to their left, flashing silver and white in the midday sun. He called to mind the photographs he had taken. No more than a short hike up the slope to that ridge . . .

The straining of the Black Maria's engine, along with the banging and crashing of its undercarriage and the rattling of the cages inside the shell, had pretty much discouraged any conversation during the climb. Now, as if exhausted, the van's engine coughed, stuttered and died. Grovkin slammed the heel of his palm against the steering wheel. "Don't give up now," he pleaded.

"I think this is far enough, Alex."

"We walk from here?"

They all clambered out. Chris felt the cutting edge of the wind. He listened to it sighing through the tops of the trees, the only sound in all that wilderness. If there were any animals in the woods nearby the snuffling and roaring of the Black Maria had silenced them.

Grovkin glanced toward Lina Mashikova, noting the rifle she carried. "Is okay for you to walk from here?" he asked.

"I am not a ballet dancer, Alexander Semyonovich. I can walk."

Grovkin grinned back at her. "What if this marksman is waiting? Can you also shoot well?"

"Better than you drive."

"Hah! Women always know better how to drive."

Beyond the dancing river a grove of aspen shook like painted tambourines, and the gusting wind stirred up flurries of white powder along the banks of the river. The scene was stunningly beautiful, the fresh snow giving it a quality of soft, untouched purity.

Gregory Krasikov had been fiddling with the radio, fine-tuning and listening for even a faint whisper of a beep from the collar Risa carried around her neck. "Nothing," he said.

"She can't be far," Chris said. "We know this is her territory." He looked at his companions. "We'll spread out and go north. That way we'll keep the river in sight on our left. It's not likely she's moved her den in the last few days. She won't go far from water, so she has to be north of where we are." To Lina he said, "Alex and I both have tranquilizer bullets. If you see her first, let us handle it."

"If she hurt bad, she not go far anyway," Grovkin said with true Russian gloom.

"What about you, Alex?" Chris asked. "You're sure you're okay?"

"Sure, sure, I bleed a little, that's all. Is nothing. Besides, if your soldier friend is hunting a man, you will need me to help you find tiger, yes?"

"Let's hope the assassin is long gone."

Lina said nothing to that.

Chris turned to Krasikov, who was pale, "If you see or hear anything—anything at all—use the horn." In the stillness of the taiga, under its smothering cushion of snow, an automobile horn would be audible for miles. "Okay, let's get started—"

A faint beep interrupted Chris. He stared at Krasikov.

"It's Risa!" the Russian said. "The signal is weak. If she's on high ground she could be as much as two miles north-northeast. No more than that, probably less."

"Keep listening," Chris told him. "When you think she might be getting close, give us two taps on the horn—not enough to scare her off."

As Chris set off with Alex and Lina across a snow-covered clearing toward the shadowed forest, Krasikov called after them. "Another signal, she is coming your way!"

Minutes earlier the tiger had had her first glimpse of her enemy. The figure was far off, visible for only an instant, moving with the speed and sureness of a forest animal and disappearing quickly into the taiga. But the glimpse was enough. She knew where her enemy was. She had its scent and the occasional tracks in the snow to guide her. She knew that her prey was within striking distance.

The tiger quickened her pace. Her fatigue and pain were forgotten. The fever in her blood blended into the fire of her hatred. She was also goaded by another concern—her enemy was drawing closer to her den and her three hungry cubs.

Limping on three legs, the Siberian moved through the forest.

For a brief period the tumult Boris Provalev had ignited when he climbed on top of the T–64 tank drowned out all other sounds, even the rumble of other military vehicles approaching over cobblestone streets. Observers on the outskirts of the crowd were the first to see a column of armored personnel carriers lumbering toward them in the direction of the cathedral.

The thunder of the APCs finally began to drown out the general clamor. People stopped to listen. The first of the carriers reached the far side of the park, crowds running before them to get out of the way. The column split, half of the vehicles circling the park to approach the television broadcast studios from the west. The other half turned sharply across the short street in front of the cathedral. People gave way, clearing the street.

Troops spilled out of the APCs even before they came to a full stop. These were not young earnest soldiers like those who had arrived earlier along with the tanks to take over the civic center and the telephone exchange and the TV studios. Some of the people recognized the distinctive soldier patches —*spetznaz*. And elite units of the 220th Guards Air Assault Regiment. Theirs were older, tough, seasoned faces; these were not boys but men who formed ranks with precision and self-assurance.

Within minutes of the first sighting of the new arrivals, the lines were drawn. Russian soldiers faced Russian soldiers across a narrow strip of no-man's-land no wider than a street. The people who moments earlier had been cheering or jeering Chairman Provalev now mingled with the newly arrived soldiers, many calling out encouragement. The soldiers kept their eyes on their counterparts on the steps of the building and deployed along its front and sides.

Silence now. The young soldiers on the steps unsure, wondering what was happening, the older soldiers waiting.

Worried that his initiative might be slipping away, Provalev seized command of the silence. "Don't be afraid, comrades. These reactionaries cannot silence the voice of the hungry Russian people . . ." His voice boomed out from the loudspeakers over the heads of the crowds and the ranks of soldiers. "Red Army soldiers, join hands with us. We are taking control of the new Russia in your name. We no longer bend to foreigners who threaten to destroy us. Have we forgotten the great and proud Russia of our youth? Of our Patriotic War? Today it is the Americans' lackeys, the South Koreans, who accuse and threaten us. Who will it be tomorrow? I say, let *others* tremble when the Russian bear growls . . ."

Scattered shouts and cheers, but the earlier enthusiasm had been lost. The moment clearly hung in the balance.

At the far side of the park a commotion caught the crowd's attention. Someone tried to push through the congestion. As people gave way the first newcomer was an old white-haired man. Directly behind him came General Victor Chumeiko, Hero of the Soviet Union. He was in full dress uniform, his stone face and his broad chest with its rows of ribbons and medals familiar to all those close enough to see him. Behind Chumeiko came a cordon of *spetznaz* soldiers, tightly ranked to encircle another small group of men who seemed to be in civilian clothes.

The old man, emaciated and frail, was seventy-two-year-old Oleg Kholkhov, the interior minister. He spoke in a quavery voice. Without a microphone and loudspeakers he could be heard by only a few—but among those were the young troops on the steps of the building. "Russian soldiers, put down your weapons. Do you want to make war on your own people? Do you turn your guns on your brothers and sisters, your mothers and fathers?"

"The Koreans say we killed their leaders!" one of the soldiers shot back. "Their prime minister is dead. You heard what the chairman said."

"Yes," Kholkhov answered, "we all heard the chairman's *lies.*"

"Don't listen to him," Provalev called out. "We, the *people* of Russia, have already won victory. Vladivostok is ours. All across the Motherland the people are rising up in protest . . ."

Kholkhov turned toward General Chumeiko. At a nod from the general the circle of *spetznaz* soldiers moved forward, escorting the civilians concealed behind their tight formation. Abruptly that circle parted. Two slightly built men stepped into view. One, dapper in a light gray suit under a camel's-hair coat, was the prime minister of South Korea. Beside him stood Chang Pyon, the stolid chairman of Sunsai.

Excitement rolled across the crowd. One of the television cameras on the steps used its telephoto lens to move in for a close-up while retaining a split-screen view of Provalev astride the tank. Ironically for Chairman Provalev, through his own connivance and the magic of television, the split images were viewed simultaneously in Moscow and Kiev, in St. Petersburg and Sverdlovsk and Novosibirsk and Khabarovsk. Their impact was indelible. Provalev, stunned, listened to the dapper prime minister say in fluent Russian that surprised everyone, "As you can see, you have been misled. Thanks to your Army"—a nod toward General Chumeiko—"Chang Pyon and myself are very much alive."

Rioting broke out in the streets as one reckless citizen rushed the steps, climbed halfway onto the T–64 battle tank, grabbed Boris Provalev by the ankle and hauled him from his perch. The soldiers on the steps fell back. The angry crowd closed around Provalev.

At General Chumeiko's command a dozen riot-trained *spetznaz* soldiers ran forward, bulled their way through the mass of people and surrounded Provalev, who lay curled on the ground with his arms around his head.

The merciless eye of a television camera recorded the end of the coup.

39

LEMENOV CHECKED THE coordinates on his map. Cherchi Point was behind him and to the west. The perimeter service road was a faintly discernible rent in the fabric of the forest to the south. There was no mistake, *he* was in the right place. Brunovsky wasn't there.

This was not supposed to happen to the Collector. People were afraid of him—including those who hired him. Perhaps especially those who hired him. His actions were meticulously planned. Using Brunovsky to provide his escape route out of the taiga had been ordained from the start . . . Brunovsky was the only one capable of identifying him. Therefore Brunovsky would have to be eliminated. It was the only way the Collector would ever feel totally safe once Provalev came to power. He knew how such men's minds worked. Provalev would see him as a continuing threat, and as long as Brunovsky was alive, Provalev would always be able to use him to reach out and find the Collector. In a Russia ruled by such a man, only an invisible man would be safe.

Brunovsky knew and had betrayed him. That conviction now sprang full-blown into Lemenov's mind. He stared out across the sweep of forest that receded from him in giant steps. He had, of course, sensed Brunovsky's fear of him, but he had put it down to the familiar reaction he provoked. He had underestimated Brunovsky. He had, for once, ignored his own intuition.

There was no point in looking further, hoping that the Range Rover had broken down or Brunovsky had been delayed. *He was not coming.*

Lemenov glanced over his shoulder into the deep woods he

had vacated a moment before. He thought of those huge tiger tracks in the snow. His shoulders shifted uneasily. The soldiers flown to the logging camp who should have picked up his sign by now did not worry him. The tiger did. She should have been dead. That she was still alive suggested the intervention of something perverse that he had no control over. And such thoughts made Lemenov—who believed in nothing but himself—profoundly uneasy.

He started down a gradual slope through a stand of birch trees. His course was due south—the shortest route to the service road. Brunovsky might have run off but sooner or later there would be others along that road—guards or poachers.

He came to another ridge, a natural lookout. Off to his right, perhaps half a mile away, the river was visible over the tops of the next wall of evergreen forest. In a moment he would be within that dense green sanctuary, invisible from the air, his scent smothered . . .

Something picked at his eye like a speck of dust. He forced himself to survey the landscape. He brought out his binoculars and focused with care as he moved the glasses slowly across the horizon line from south to west, hunting for that elusive speck. *There.*

His body went rigid. He struggled to control his breathing. It was not a snow mirage. It was a *vehicle,* a strange sort of vehicle to be here in the middle of the taiga, some kind of van that actually resembled a Black Maria. One man leaned against the open door of the cab. A tall man, bearded. Lemenov didn't recognize him.

There would be others. With his binoculars the Collector studied the terrain near the van. It had stopped at the foot of a relatively open slope that climbed upward to another virgin forest. The snow glare made it impossible to see anything . . .

A layer of cumulus clouds drifted between Lemenov and the sun high overhead. Their long shadow chased over the broad expanse of the taiga, over trees and canyons and snow meadows. And in the moment when the shade covered the Black Maria and the rise to the north of it, through his binoculars Sergei Lemenov was able to see footsteps in the snow. Three sets of tracks, diverging as they angled toward the woods, creating a design in the snow like a huge three-tined pitchfork, suggesting one of those giant mysterious patterns visible only from the air that believers cited to prove that aliens had once visited the earth.

But these were not extraterrestrials, just three ordinary men heading into the woods, leaving one man behind with their vehicle. The Collector did not care what chance circumstance had brought them to the taiga at this moment. Their vehicle was his way out.

Lemenov smiled. Four men. His rifle's magazine carried four bullets. He would not even need to reload.

He quickly left his high point, following an animal trail and plunging into the forest. Invisible once more, silent and lethal, a hunter closing in for the kill.

Alex Grovkin was the first to spot tiger tracks in the snow. He had taken the left flank when he separated from Chris Harmon and Lina Mashikova. Chris was in the center, Lina off to the right, each distanced from the next by about fifty yards. Close enough to stay within sight of each other when trees and terrain permitted, or to hear another's shout. Grovkin was nearest the river, and it was here, above the bank, that he saw the distinctive prints of tiger cubs in the snow.

Chris heard the shout and looked off to his right, where Lina had disappeared into the forest. He hesitated but couldn't resist the lure of Grovkin's discovery and headed for the sound of his voice.

As close as he was to the Russian, the forest was thick enough to screen both Grovkin and the river from his view. This was old growth—trees rising a hundred feet and more into the air, cutting off the sun. Chris blundered through the trees and undergrowth, slowed by the lack of a clear trail. Hearing Alex call out again, he regretted that he hadn't called to Lina so she would know where he was.

A growl stopped him in his tracks. He swung around, eyes probing the undergrowth. A tiger cub thrashed out of some brush not thirty feet away. It stared at him for a moment, growling and pawing the ground. Then its brief show of defiance ended in a quick retreat.

Relieved, Chris called to Grovkin, "I've found one of them, Alex! In the woods . . ."

"I hear you, keep talking, I'll come to you—"

A rifle shot racketed across the frozen wilderness, its crack almost lost in the piercing blare of the Raven's horn. That raucous peal went on and on, as if the horn button were jammed. Then it stopped abruptly, and the sudden stillness vibrating with menace more nerve-racking than the horn itself.

Gregory Krasikov had seen the man in black emerge from the woods some four hundred yards to his right and a little north. For a moment he was too startled to react. Then he remembered what he had heard of the conversation between Chris Harmon and the lieutenant—he'd been woozy from the blow to his head so he had missed much of it—about an assassin in the taiga.

He lunged for the cab. Because of his concussion his movements were less quick, less coordinated than normally. His foot slipped and he caught hold of the door handle to keep from falling. His finger stabbed the horn button at the same instant the bullet smashed into the side of his head. A detritus of bone and blood splattered the door frame and the back of the front seat. Dead before he hit the seat, Krasikov's hand was jammed against the horn.

It kept on bleating, as if he were clinging to life on a thin thread of sound.

Lemenov pivoted smoothly as the tall bearded man fell into the cab of the Black Maria. The blare of the horn was only an annoyance.

He had already picked out his second target, a bulky man in a preserve guard's yellow anorak and fur hat. The man's shout had caught his attention. The guard clambered up a short slope from the river and stumbled in the snow at the moment Lemenov's finger brushed the hair trigger of his rifle.

The man disappeared from sight. Lemenov cursed. Had the guard's stumble made him miss? Then he saw the figure in the yellow anorak rolling down the slope, tumbling sideways until he bumped to a stop against a nest of rocks on the river-bank. The body lay face down, unmoving.

The Collector relaxed, turned and ran back into the dark shadows of the forest.

Chris Harmon had nearly reached the open when a second rifle shot sent him sprawling to the ground, half-buried in the undergrowth. He lay there for a few seconds—only long enough to realize that the shot had not been meant for him. He pushed to his hands and knees and, crouching at the edge of the forest, looked down the slope toward the river. *Alex.* His friend lay motionless beside the river.

God, he was the one who had forced the issue of a rescue mission, bulldozed Russian authorities into letting him go back to the taiga, dragged Alex and Gregory Krasikov with him. Now both men were down, shot . . .

No, stop it. His friends believed in their work as strongly as he did. Blaming himself was cheap, it demeaned what they, like himself, had chosen to do. There was plenty of blame to go around—the ambition of a ruthless demagogue, the twisted psyche of a professional killer, the greed and indifference that permitted the wanton destruction of habitat.

Chris had no doubt the same expert marksman who had shot the Siberian tiger had targeted Gregory Krasikov and Alex Grovkin. Sound was deceptive in the wilderness, but the shots had seemed to come from somewhere east of his position. The only apparent vantage point from which the killer had a clear view of both Krasikov beside the Black Maria and Grovkin near the river was a bluff hundreds of yards off. No way, Chris decided, that *he* could hope to hit anything at that distance. The sniper was free to pick them off one by one, Krasikov and Alex and—

Lina. She had taken the right flank as they entered the

forest. She was closest to the point from which the shots had come. Why hadn't she answered Grovkin's yell? Had the assassin got to her first? A professional killer would be as skilled with a knife as with a rifle, at home in the woods, trained in infiltration . . .

Chris started running through the woods toward the assassin's last position, unaware that the Collector had already hurried off to meet him.

The shots had slowed the Siberian tiger. She associated them immediately with her enemy, and also with pain. For a brief time she lay hidden, deep in the forest, watching and listening.

Her shoulder burned, the fever in her blood had weakened her. As a hunter she had infinite patience, but her den was near, as well as her enemy, and she could not remain where she was for long.

She heard a rustling not far away. Stealthy movement along the forest floor.

She began to edge forward, belly dragging on the ground.

Smelled it then. The smell of her enemy.

Close by.

The trees thinned out and she saw a flicker of movement. A shadow separating from a tall tree trunk, crossing a few steps, melting behind another tree.

A little more light penetrated the gloom of the old forest, thinned out by some ancient catastrophe. The additional light and thinner growth made Chris feel even more vulnerable. These woods were not immune to the daily life-and-death struggle of nature in the wild, but man had brought a new and different kind of killing, not for need of food or survival. For the marksman, and the demagogue who pulled his strings, the tiger was simply a tool to be used, as unimportant as the forest itself. Chris and his friends were minor impediments to be brushed aside.

How many had already died at this assassin's hands? The

owner of the camera shop, Fyodorov, Grovkin, Krasikov. And Lina?

Then Chris spotted her no more than fifty yards away, only a glimpse of her black fur hat and a trace of boot showing. He started to call out, instantly checked himself, realizing he would be giving them both away.

He began to work closer to her, searching the forest on all sides. He could provide a covering fire for her, an extra pair of eyes if the killer was stalking her.

Could they reach the Black Maria? No way. Too much open ground. One way or another, the issue would have to be settled here in the taiga.

Chris's breath caught. Another shape materialized in the undergrowth—first a massive head with its beautiful markings, then the long, powerful body of a tiger.

No question it was the wounded tiger. She dragged a front leg as she crept forward. No question either that her gaze was fixed on Lina. She settled low to the ground in that awesomely familiar gathering of all her strength and fury—*about to charge.*

Chris fumbled in his pocket for one of the tranquilizer shells. The rifle was a bolt action and the tranquilizer bullets had to be loaded individually. His fingers felt clumsy and stiff from cold. He dropped the cartridge, pawed for it in a patch of snow. Found the shell, wiped it clean, dropped it into the chamber and eased the bolt into place. In his ears the tiny click as the bolt locked was like a small explosion.

In spite of the cold he was sweating. He wiped the sweat from his eyes, raised the rifle and peered through the sights.

The tiger charged.

Chris had no time to think. He dropped the sights onto the tiger's flank with a reflexive skill he didn't know he had. He felt rather than heard the shot, felt the kick hard against his shoulder.

The figure hidden in the woods spun toward Chris at the sound of the shot, then froze with shock at sight of the shape hurtling toward him.

Him. Not Lina, but the marksman!

Halfway across the thirty yards separating her from the

enemy, the tiger bucked from the impact of the bullet that struck her right side, an impact that triggered a second charge, driving a plunger forward to inject the powerful drug into blood and tissue.

Her momentum kept the beast going. Then, it seemed to Chris almost in slow motion, her right front leg buckled. With the other front leg already useless, she pitched forward, tumbling out of control.

The power of her charge nearly carried her all the way. Scrambling, her prey managed to elude the raking claws that missed flesh and bone and ripped the cloth of his pant leg. Then, with a loud cough, the tiger collapsed at her enemy's feet.

Sergei Lemenov stared through the thin screen of trees at the man who had saved his life. His thin lips stretched into a grin. What he then saw was not a savior but a fool—the American scientist, helpless, trying to jam a magazine into his rifle.

Lemenov lifted his own weapon. "You lose," he said in Russian.

The shot seemed oddly thin in the vast expanse of the taiga. Too small a sound for the massive blow that struck him between the shoulder blades and knocked him forward. His legs began to fold just as the second blow hammered his spine and he dropped to his knees, his rifle slipping from his hands.

The pain, when it came, struck like another blow—the pain he had seen so often in others' eyes.

The Collector managed to twist his head around and saw the soldier facing him through the spruce trees and over a field of snow. The fourth one, he thought. He had been so sure of the first three he had allowed the fourth to get behind him.

It had the face of an angel. He tried to laugh at the irony, but the blood filled his throat and mouth. He knew better, anyway. No angelic chorus waited to sing the Collector to his rest.

EPILOGUE

═══

A WEEK AFTER the collapse of the coup attempted by Boris Provalev, Chris Harmon caught a charter flight out of Plastun. It was late afternoon by the time the plane took off, delayed by an overnight storm that dumped nearly a foot of snow over the Primorskiy. He thought he would be fortunate to reach Vladivostok before dark.

From the aircraft he looked down at the endless panorama of snowbound forest, and felt a sense of loss over leaving a place he had come to love.

He leaned back wearily, resting his head against the seat. A week since it all came together there in the taiga. The whirl of events over those seven days was a blur. The moment of holding Lina in his arms after she had killed the assassin. The raw grief over Gregory Krasikov was at least somewhat balanced against the relief when they found Alex Grovkin alive, more angry than hurt. The assassin's bullet had creased his back and gouged a piece out of his right buttock. A rock on which he had struck his head, temporarily knocking him unconscious, had probably saved his life.

Then the Army helicopters dropping out of the sky, soldiers taking charge, flying Alex out of the wilderness to a hospital in one of the helicopters, the bodies of Krasikov and the dead assassin in the next. Lina reluctantly accompanying them, her face against the window looking down at Chris as the last chopper lifted away.

That night Chris had stayed alone in the forest with the wounded tiger after injecting her with a massive dose of antibiotics. He had removed bone chips from her shoulder but otherwise he believed she would heal herself once the infection was brought under control. The meat transported in the Black Maria, injected with vitamins and minerals, had been left where the cubs would find it, and Chris heard them fighting over it during the night.

At noon the following day the arrival of additional help, a Russian biologist and a veterinarian, precipitated a sometimes acrimonious debate through the afternoon. The biologist, a man Chris had worked with before, argued that the tiger's survival was so problematical that her cubs should be taken back to Terney and raised there. Eventually they could either be returned to the wild or a home might be found for them in one of the North American zoos where they would become part of the captive breeding program that would ensure the survival of the species. The veterinarian felt equally strongly that there were enough tigers in zoos, that the mother had a good chance to survive and that cubs raised by humans were a danger to themselves and others if returned to the wild, where they tended to hang around human settlements, attacking livestock or people. When Chris sided with the veterinarian, it was two to one.

For the next twenty-four hours the team monitored Risa's progress. A fresh battery was inserted in her collar before she was given an antidote for the sedatives. She was in an ugly temper when she began to come out of her drug-induced sleep, and her new caretakers quickly distanced themselves from her. By the time she was able to walk on wobbly legs, one of the female cubs had found her and its noisy greetings lured the others out of hiding. Radio surveillance over the next week established that the tiger was active, which was the best anyone could hope for.

Behind him now, Chris thought, looking out at the darkness gathering over the taiga. Even the attempted coup, which had ended in the arrest of Boris Provalev and a Red Army general, was last week's news in Russia, which seemed to lurch from crisis to crisis.

All over except for one thing.

Chris searched in his coat pocket for the slip of paper on which Lina Mashikova had written her phone number. Beneath it, just before she left the taiga, she had scribbled a few lines from memory. "The poem is Anna Akhmatova's," Lina wrote, "but she speaks for me."

> *And two footpaths crossing in the forest,*
> *And in the distant field a distant light—*
> *I see it all. I remember it all.*
> *I keep it lovingly, gently in my heart.*